Published in 2024 by IngramSpark.

ISBN: 979-8-9891034-1-6

Also in the Orlell Chronicles

Book 1 - Guardians of Gayrile

Book 2 - The Jewel of Power

Book 3 - The Quest for Drisilas

Book 4 - The Shard and the Shadow

Book 5 - The Curse of the Compass

Book 6 - The Prophecy of Three

Book 7 - The Song of the Stars

THE ORLELL CHRONICLES

Book 6

The Prophecy of Three

Alice G. Bjornstedt

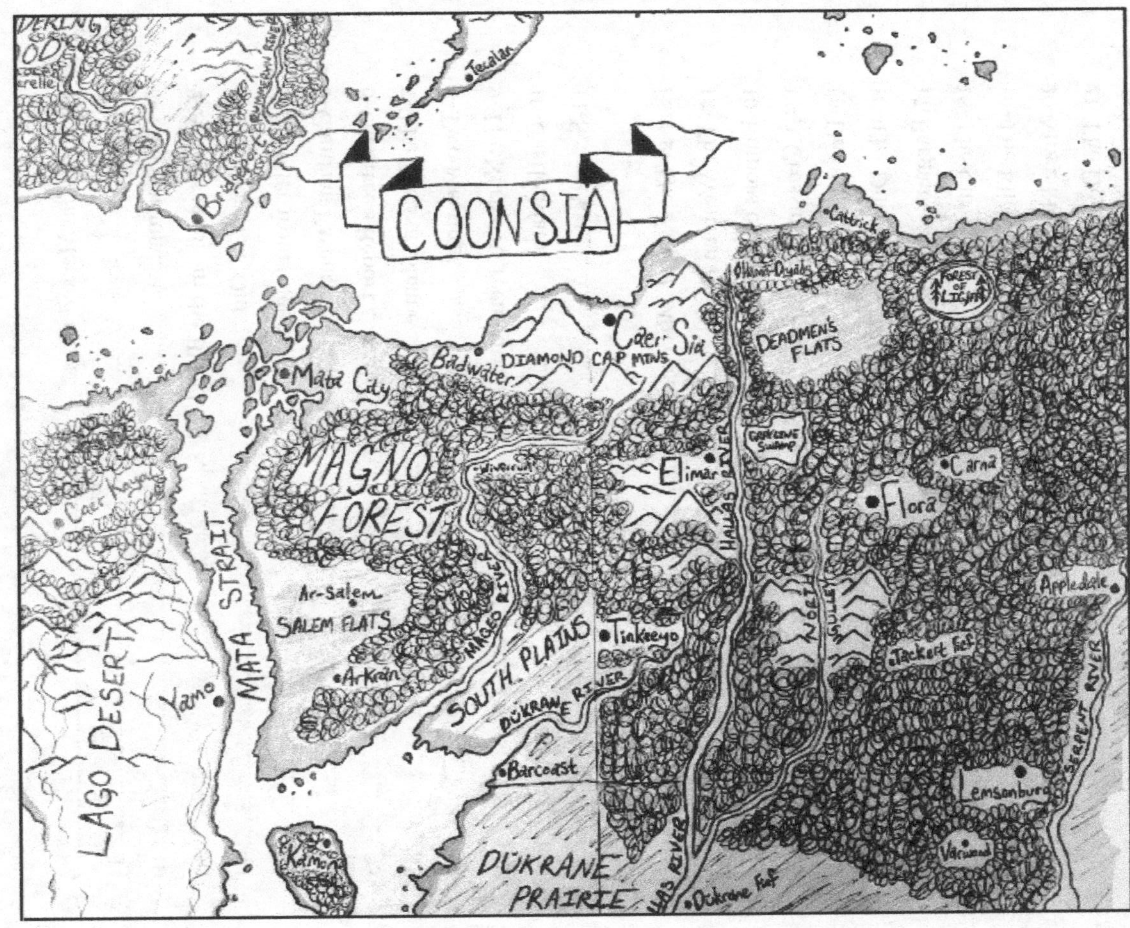

COONSIA
Tecalan
Bra
Cattrick
DIAMOND CAP MTNS
Caer Sia
Othani-Dyads
DEADMEN'S FLATS
FOREST OF LICYM
Badwater
Matu City
GRAVEYNE SWAMP
MAGNO FOREST
Riverwut
Elimar
HALLAS RIVER
Carna
Caer Koog
Flora
MATA STRAIT
Ar-Salem
SALEM FLATS
MAGEO RIVER
Appledale
SOUTH PLAINS
Tinkeeyo
Arkain
Jackert Fief
LAGO DESERT
Varno
DUKRANE RIVER
Barcoast
SERPENT RIVER
Lemsonburg
ILLAS RIVER
Kalmo
DUKRANE PRAIRIE
Dukrane Fief
Valewood

Table of Contents

for Levi, who encourages me onward,

Amanda, whose excitement for this story means the world,

and for Lannie, who is here for the Coopers.

PART 1

The Marked Ones

Prologue
Months prior

A lonely crescent moon shone upon the desolate wasteland of the Salem Flats, a pale crease in the starless sky. Expectant silence filled the winter evening, heavy with anticipation.

The moonlight reflected upon the climbing rise of broken stone to the north, which formed a short range of craggy hills. Here stood the castle, built centuries before. For many years, these ruins had overlooked the empty expanse of land, spires scraping the sky, crumbling walls outlined by the moonlight.

Yet now, the castle had been rebuilt. The crumbling stone had been replaced by gleaming black beams stronger than steel, the spires cased in silver ice, the walls shaped and strengthened by unnatural forces. Black banners hung from the towers, trailing in the wind like smoke.

The darkness of Castle Salem contrasted with the ghostly gray of the surrounding land, yet darker still were the beings that had made their dwelling here and raised the crumbling walls. It was they who had given a new purpose to a palace once named for peace; now, its name had become a mockery of itself.

On the highest balcony of the castle, the Ace-Lord looked out over the shadowed Flats. Clouds drifted across the sky, periodically allowing brighter beams of moonlight to break through.

The Ace-Lord turned his withered face to the sky and smiled

in silent challenge. The moon was no threat to him, though his smaller, weaker servants might shy from the glaring light. He had no such qualms. Let the light come. Let it shine on the darkness of his deeds, illuminate them in glorious splendor, and shrink away in retreat again at the slightest shadow. Light was too fickle to pose any real threat to his coming empire.

"My lord."

The quiet voice interrupted his musings. There was a muted clinking of armor as the Ace entered the room and knelt.

"I sense you come with a question, my Deputy," the Ace-Lord said without turning.

"Yes, my lord," the Deputy replied. The voice was cool and smooth as ever, but the Ace-Lord detected the cautious note of curiosity in it. His servants usually avoided asking questions or inquiring about his plan, but now, clearly, the Deputy's patience had run out.

Then again, he had good reason to be intrigued. For months, the Ace-Lord and his remaining ten servants had thrived off the growing fear of the mortals, growing stronger and bolder. Gathering forces across Orlell, constructing this fortress, growing their power—it had been for a purpose, as they all knew. With the war halted for now, the fear and uncertainty could sit and fester in the minds of the mortals.

Since the Shards had been joined, however, the mortals' growing fear had been halted, replaced by a dangerous amount of defiance. The Prophecy of Three had awakened hope in the mortals again, hope that threatened to persevere.

The Ace-Lord exhaled slowly, his breath crystallizing white ice on the balcony rail. "Speak," he breathed, his voice low.

The Deputy remained kneeling as he replied. "The mortals plan to strike back, as I am certain you have sensed. The words of their accursed Prophecy give them strength." He glanced up, studying the cloaked form of his master, waiting for a response. When there was none, he went on. "Our operation in the Magno Forest is not yet complete. Without the strength the Twelfth would provide, we are at a disadvantage."

At twelve in number, the Aces had their greatest strength. The Ace-Lord had been the first, imbuing eleven mortals with his power, forging them into his servants, and leading them as a brethren of twelve long ago. But now, their ranks numbered only eleven. The twelfth—the Ace-Messenger—had been killed months ago. Hatred chilled his veins at the reminder, but he made no reply.

"We have sensed that something is coming," the Deputy said. "I do not doubt your plans, my lord, but we know that we must act swiftly. We eagerly await your orders."

His words fell into silence. At last, the Ace-Lord turned to him. Shadows gathered in the folds of his cloak, sweeping about his frame like fog. His purple-red eyes glinted from the depths of his hood, and he nodded thoughtfully.

"Walk with me. I will answer your questions."

Together, they walked from the room, down the winding stairs and along the dark corridors.

"The mortals desire a war," the Ace-Lord said. "Should they fight, they will undoubtedly bring about their own demise. Nevertheless, I do not wish for all to perish. That is why I have waited until now. We must act wisely if my plans are to succeed. We are, I trust you know, bound by the same rules as the mortals."

"By the Prophecy?" the Deputy asked, disdain evident in his tone.

"Precisely. It is a fact you must accept, my Deputy," the Ace-Lord said. "Our actions must be within the lines of the Prophecy. Its words offer the mortals hope, but they will yet secure our victory. The Prophecy's words will become my words. The hope of the mortals will turn to fear. And, in the end, the only strength they glean will be what I give them."

The Deputy hesitated, allowing the silence to stretch as they walked. Finally, he said, "Then what shall be done regarding the Twelfth?"

"My plans are not dependent on the number of those who follow—rather, the dedication of they who serve me," the Ace-Lord informed him. His voice, though still low, held a displeasure that chilled the air around them. "The role of the Twelfth and the fate of the Wielders will both be attended to. Yet you forget it was I, and I alone, who brought about the Dividing War." For a moment, his ruined form flickered away, replaced by the shining illusion of the silver-armored lord he had been while mortal. His eyes flashed as he looked at the Deputy. "My servants were committed then. I trust your dedication will not waver, not even in the face of the mortals' stubborn hope."

The Deputy nodded swiftly, shivering involuntarily at the cold. "Never, my lord. You have my eternal loyalty and servitude."

"Indeed," the Ace-Lord breathed. He rested a hand on the banister of the stairwell as they walked down the steps, sending ice spreading down the black stones.

"The cold," the Ace-Lord mused softly, watching the pale ice. "Strange how the mortal's view of it can change, is it not? How one can fear it, despise it, and yet when the heat and flames of war are fanned, one will welcome the cold of death with open arms."

A wide archway framed the wall of the ground floor before them, large enough for carriages to enter side by side. Likely, it had been used centuries ago as a back entrance. Now, it would become something more.

The Ace-Lord stretched out his hands to the archway. Ice crept up the frame, casing the black steel in white frost, then stretched across the distance like a massive spiderweb. Gradually, the ice filled in the gaps, until the archway glittered in a mirror of white.

The Ace-Lord pulled out a small satchel from the depths of his robe. Once, it had borne the emblem of a Crime Ring to the south. Now, it contained only a handful of fine black ash. Only a few days had passed since the Ringmembers had completed their task in destroying the compass, and so brought the Jewel's power back to its rightful Wielder.

"The mortals fear us now," the Ace-Lord continued. "Their fear may give us strength, but strength is nothing compared to willing minds."

"My lord?" The Deputy sounded slightly confused.

The Ace-Lord drew a pinch of ash from the satchel and flung it against the icy mirror. As the black particles made contact, the ice seemed to pulsate, vibrating like a giant drum, then became clear as glass, like a window looking into the night. At last, the glassy surface vanished, replaced by blackness that swirled and twisted like a curtain of pure shadows.

"The hope and trust of the mortals is necessary, if we are to overcome the Prophecy," the Ace-Lord said. "Hope and trust, my Deputy, in my coming kingdom, which secures the selfish desire for safety in every mortal heart. Without their willingness, we have no chance of completing this conquest. The mortals would fight to the death, and I would be ruler of an empty and lifeless Orlell."

"Is that… not desirable?" the Deputy asked.

The Ace-Lord smiled humorlessly. "I can assure you, I have grown quite weary of ruling the dead. What I require are willing subjects, submissive to my kingdom." He raised his hands again, and the frames of the archway were strengthened by a second layer of ice. The void gaped before them, a doorway only the ash of the Jewel's magic could open.

"There are many pressing matters I must attend to," the Ace-Lord said. "The wraith must be reawakened. The vessel must be chosen and bound. In the meantime, the operation in the Magno forest is now your responsibility. I trust you will complete it?"

The Deputy bowed. "It would be my pleasure, my lord," he said, his voice barely hiding his excitement. "Wiverrun will be conquered, and we will be prepared by your return."

"Good." The Ace-Lord stepped toward the doorway. "I will arrive when that time has come. In the meanwhile, I will send the Messenger."

The Deputy's face showed his surprise. "The... I... my lord," he stammered finally. "Is the time upon us?"

"It has begun," the Ace-Lord replied. "What you have said is true. The hope of the mortals is a danger I cannot risk—a chance, however slim, that they will persevere. If the Wielders will not serve willingly, then they must be corrupted so thoroughly that even the Prophecy will not save them. A new Messenger must be sent, and so fulfill the role of the Twelfth. With the power I grant him, he will tear the mortals apart from within. Hope will hardly stand against such a thing as he."

The Deputy nodded, trying to hide his disbelief and excitement. At long last, the accursed words of the Prophecy's second stage would come to pass. The Messenger would be sent. "I shall await your orders, my lord," he said, bowing his head.

The Ace-Lord stepped inside the doorway. The blackness swirled around him as he turned and glanced back at the Deputy. "Indeed you will," he replied, and with one last skull-like smile, he vanished into the archway.

In his place came something else.

A creature of darkness, prowling out of the doorway to the void. Claws and teeth glinted in the pale moonlight. Black and silver striped fur rippled along a muscular feline frame, but not fully concealing the scars left by futile struggles of previous prey.

And its eyes, redder than blood, were filled only with the desire to kill.

The creature stood in the shadows. A low growl came from its chest as it spoke. "I have been roused. I have come. What is my task?"

The Ace-Deputy studied the beast, nodding slightly to himself. His master always had a plan. He had begun, at last, to understand the reasoning behind this latest one.

"Welcome back to the land of the living, Redeyes," he greeted the beast calmly. "Now, come. We have much to discuss."

1

The Waiting

Rain showered the spires of Castle Sia, dripping in rhythm against the window. The monotonous tapping sound of the spring rain, the murmur of voices elsewhere in the castle's halls, and the distant hum of activity in the capital city made it harder for Asescia Ki to focus on her reading.

She straightened in the cozy library chair, shaking off the drowsiness, and adjusted the book on her lap. Yesterday had been a long day, packed with the many studies required of the heiress to the throne. First, her daily lessons in history, foreign languages, mathematics, and geography. Then came her protocol and debate lessons, overseen by her mother Ajaha, who was one of the head couriers of Caer Sia.

After that, she'd observed her uncle's meeting with a delegation of Elven lords. In addition to the growing threat of the Aces, Jan was currently engaged in a debate with the Elimar Council. Allie didn't understand everything the situation entailed. But she'd learned enough in her eighteen years to know that the Elves of Elimar were hesitant to join the Liznees against the Aces. Clearly, they hoped their people could stay out of the growing conflict, and avoid risking lives.

That was unlikely, Allie knew. The time had long passed for neutrality. The Ace-Lord wanted Orlell, and he would strive to take it whether or not the Elves resisted.

The thought brought darkness creeping into her mind and returned distant sounds from her memories. Memories of a day when the Aces had attacked Caer Sia—not yet a year ago now, though the fear was as fresh as ever. She remembered orcs and Jenna prowling the streets, remembered the broken city walls, remembered the white ice that glittered over the lifeless chests of far too many fallen.

"You're up early."

She jumped as the voice jarred her out of the dark thoughts. The book slipped from her hands—she caught it before it hit the floor, but the pages fell closed over the place she'd been reading. She threw a playful glare at the speaker. "I thought you were meeting with my father."

Rygal walked into the library. The young warrior had come from the isle of Gayrile a few days ago, bringing news and updates for Allie's father Dandio, who led Caer Sia's military. Rygal's visits had become routine over the last three or four years, and now he was a familiar face around the castle.

He leaned against the nearest bookshelf and straightened his jerkin collar, which was of a finer make than his usual trail clothes. Joining Dandio's war council must call for more professional attire—not that Dandio himself would enforce that rule. But then again, Allie thought, Rygal had only recently been promoted to second-in-command of the Guardians of Gayrile, so he must be trying to make a good impression.

"The meeting's in an hour or so," Rygal said. "We're waiting for the generals to arrive."

"Jan won't like to postpone it," Allie commented with a wry grin.

"He doesn't mind. I think he wanted to discuss a few things with your father, anyway." Rygal gave up adjusting his collar and ran a hand through his dark hair. "What are you reading?"

Allie held up the book with a grimace. "History lessons. My tutors still want me working on my studies, war or no."

"Thought you didn't mind studies," Rygal said.

"I don't, not normally," Allie said, flipping through the pages and trying to find the place she'd left off. "But I feel like we have more important things to worry about now than old readings."

She had voiced this question to Iriam, her advisor and tutor, last night, during her astronomy lesson. The Neutral had only smiled slightly and shook his head. "What is important and what is needed are two different things," he had told her, his voice low and calm. "One is dependent on circumstance, and the other aids growth."

Allie had dismissed this as another of Iriam's cryptic statements. She enjoyed the Neutral's company; he was practically a grandfather to her. But there were times where she wished he was more… direct.

Rygal sat down on the floor, his back against the bookshelf, and took a book from behind him. "You don't have anything here about Essence channeling, do you?"

Allie looked at him with a slight frown. "No, I don't think so. Liznees don't have to learn about channeling our Essence, you know. That's Garilian magic." She paused. "Why?"

Rygal shook his head quickly. "Never mind. Just something I'm working on with Iriam."

Allie dismissed her curiosity—there were other things she wanted to know. She scanned the rest of the history chapter, then closed the book and turned her attention back to Rygal. "So, what's the news? Any updates on the Aces? What are you discussing in the meeting?"

Rygal glanced around the shadowed library, making sure there were no listening ears, before speaking quietly. "Jan is fairly certain the Aces are in the west, near the Flatlands. But no one knows for sure—that's just based on a few reports from the Hyenins."

The Hyenin people dwelt in West Coonsia, in the vast expanse of the Lago Desert. Their lands neighbored the flatlands, on the opposite side of the Strait. Any news from that part of the world would likely come from them.

"Did General Arrex bring that report?" Allie asked. General Arrex was a Hyenin and acted as an ambassador between Caer Sia and his people's kingdom of Yamo.

"He did," Rygal said, still skimming the book he held.

Allie slid out of the chair to sit cross-legged on the floor before him, leaning forward expectantly. "And?"

Rygal grinned slightly. "And, it's still just a guess. The Hyenins have sent a few scouts to the area so far. While they've found traces, no one's seen the Aces yet."

Allie let out an irritated breath. "Then what's Dad planning?"

"Your father wants to gather more information about what's going on in the Flats," Rygal said. "We need a more definite plan before we can send armies of warriors marching in."

Something connected in Allie's mind. "That explains why Jan wants to meet with the rangers," she said thoughtfully. Rygal glanced a question at her, and she elaborated. "Yesterday, Jan said he's summoned some rangers from the west. He'll be meeting with them over the next few days—I didn't understand why he wanted to see so many at once, but it makes sense if we're trying to gather news about what's happening over there."

Rygal nodded thoughtfully. "Most likely. Does that mean Aryion and Mel will be here too?" he added hopefully.

"No," Allie said with a sigh. "They're still in Appledale, I think."

She hadn't seen Mel or his mentor Aryion in three months. The two rangers had brought their report of their mission in Esile City mid-winter, which was the last time Allie had seen them. She knew they'd completed one or two short missions near the Elimar region before returning to Appledale to stay with Mel's family. Likely, Mel wanted to spend time with them before the next stage of the Prophecy called him back into action.

From what she knew, Mel had read the Prophecy of Three when he'd last been in Caer Sia. Allie had seen him just before he left and asked about it, but he'd said very little. He had seemed quieter than normal, thoughtful and serious. Allie let it lie, but she couldn't help wondering about it.

Rygal looked disappointed, but shrugged. "Well, they'll be back soon. As soon as we know our next move, we'll need them here."

"As soon as we know," Allie echoed wearily. "In the meantime, I'm getting tired of waiting around."

There was a short silence. Then Rygal looked at her with a crooked grin. "Want to spar?"

Allie smiled. "Beats history lessons. Let me go get my sword."

She jogged out of the library and through the bright halls of Castle Sia. The servants and court attendants were up and about with the activity of morning, making the halls rather crowded. Allie slipped around them, answering their greetings with a good morning.

She had left her training sword in the dining room—she had come directly from dueling lessons to supper last night and hadn't had time to put it away. It was still there, leaning against the wall. The sturdy wood sword was roughly the same weight and balance as her real blade, making it ideal for practice. She snatched it up and headed back down the hall for the main doors.

Rain pattered down on her, forming puddles on the cobblestones. Allie splashed her way to the covered area in the corner of the courtyard. Rain drummed on the roof, but underneath was sheltered and fairly dry.

Rygal was already there, holding his training sword at the ready. He had discarded his formal jerkin, and his shirt and breeches were already splattered in mud. "Square up," he said as Allie arrived.

Allie caught her breath and adjusted her stance, weight on her back foot, eyes locked on Rygal's. Swordplay was one subject of her studies that she truly enjoyed. Dandio usually taught her, but in the months following his capture and rescue from the Aces, Rygal had stepped in while he recovered.

They circled, swords at the ready. Rygal held his practice sword loosely, that crooked smile on his face, practically daring her to make the first move. Her patience ran out, and she lunged. Rygal parried the blow, which she had expected—she allowed the momentum of the missed strike to carry her to the right, then pivoted and stabbed sideways. Rygal blocked her sword with an upwards cut and slashed down at her knees; she vaulted over the blade and sprang away.

They circled again. "You look tense, princess," Rygal commented.

"Don't call me that," Allie said, lunging at him again. She swung three blows in rapid succession. Rygal blocked the first two, then dropped under her last strike. Her blow glanced harmlessly over his shoulder, and she felt his sword tap warningly across her stomach.

"And that would have gotten you killed," he said, as Allie stepped back with a frown. "You had your blade up too high."

"I have done this before, you know," Allie couldn't resist informing him.

"Overconfidence," Rygal said, shaking his head. "The quickest killer on the battlefield."

Allie let out a breath. He was right, as usual. She could argue, but

Rygal did have more experience than she did. As Iriam often pointed out, it was better to learn than to argue.

She settled in her stance, forcing herself to slow down and think, identifying the best way of attack. Rygal had his sword at the ready, but he tended to have a weak point… there! The slightest drop of his right shoulder. He was expecting her to slash from above again.

She allowed herself to circle for another moment, then lunged, bringing her sword across in a wide slash. At the last second, she reversed her grip and brought the blade up, hilt against Rygal's cheek so that the blade brushed over his chest.

"Better," Rygal said, stepping back. "Good use of your advantages."

Allie was at least a head shorter than he was, so he would outmatch her in brute strength. However, his height could be a disadvantage to him—he had more vitals to cover, and a quick blow like she'd just done would be difficult for him to counter in time.

"Most everyone you fight will be taller and stronger than you," her father had warned her once. "That's something to be aware of. But there are ways to use it against them."

They clashed again, training swords clacking in rhythm with the dripping rain. Rygal landed a blow against Allie's unprotected leg— not hard enough to hurt, but hard enough to get the point across.

"Watch your left side," he said as Allie stepped back. "You tend to leave it exposed."

Allie nodded, catching her breath before charging again. This time, she dropped low to avoid Rygal's sword, then straightened and stabbed upward, her full strength behind the blow. The flat of the sword pressed against Rygal's chest and pushed him back into the wall with Allie's momentum.

They stood there for a moment, out of breath. Rygal nodded, satisfied. "Good. That was good. If you paired that with a dagger, it'd be even more effective."

"I'm not very good with a dagger," Allie admitted with a grin.

"Neither am I. Maybe you could ask one of the generals for pointers," Rygal said. He set his stance again, both of them breathing hard. Rygal was smiling. He looked genuinely happy, which made Allie realize how long it had been since she'd seen him like this. Ever since returning from the quest for the Shards, he had been quieter, graver, his usual joking and lighthearted manner extinguished.

She knew he had lost someone on the quest, though he'd never talked about it. It wasn't surprising to see how that affected him. She sensed he still wasn't ready to talk about it, and she didn't want to press him.

A new voice spoke from behind them, slightly amused. "The generals may be preoccupied for most of the day, Asescia."

They both turned. Ajaha stood just outside the covered area, wearing a cloak to shield her from the rain.

Rygal snapped his fingers, alarmed. "The meeting. What time is it?"

"Twenty minutes until," Ajaha reassured him. "But I assume you will want to dry off before it begins."

Rygal looked relieved and nodded. "Right. Well, I'll see you tonight before I leave, Allie."

Allie frowned. "You're leaving? I thought you weren't going back to Gayrile for another few days."

"I'm not. I'm going with Iriam to Mata City, to speak with Lord Roan and the Coopers," Rygal said. He pulled on his jerkin and headed back inside the castle.

Allie turned to her mother. "I finished my history," she said quickly. "At least, I finished the chapter—I can do the rest tonight."

Ajaha nodded. "Good work. But that is not why I'm here. Your uncle is meeting with one of the western rangers today, and he asked you to join him."

Allie looked up hopefully. Though observing Jan's meetings was included in her studies, they were usually quite dull. News from the west would be anything but that. "Really? When?"

"A little before noon," Ajaha told her.

Allie felt a surge of hope. News from the west. A meeting with a ranger. This would make the day far more interesting. "All right," she said, sliding her training sword into her belt and following her mother back toward the castle doors. "What's Dad's meeting about?"

"Asescia, you know I am sworn to secrecy as a courier of Sia," Ajaha said, but a hint of a smile played on her face. "I can tell you," she said, lowering her voice, "that the Aces' position in the Flats has been confirmed."

Allie stopped in her tracks, startled to hear this. "Confirmed?" she repeated. "Then—are we sending soldiers to attack?"

"Not yet," Ajaha answered. "Your father and uncle will determine what is to be done, with the advice of Iriam. We have yet to learn the strength of their army or if the Ace-Lord is there, as well as the exact details of their location."

The guards swung open the heavy doors, admitting them into Castle Sia. Ajaha walked, poised and elegant as ever. Allie followed, louder and slogging mud. "So, what now?" she asked eagerly. She knew the couriers and reconnaissance teams would have to work hard to find out any information about the Ace-Lord's actions.

It would be tedious, careful work. But they would do it. Her mother's cunning strategies and the skilled spies of the Red Dawn would learn the truth.

"Now?" Ajaha asked with a slight smile. "Now, we wait."

Allie's heart sank. She had expected as much, but it was disappointing to her impatient mind. She'd hoped for something a little more exciting, a straightforward battle plan that she could be involved in. She longed for adventure, for a chance to prove herself, an opportunity to learn the sort of things Rygal knew so well.

She hoped for something else, too, hard as she tried to ignore it. But the desire was awakened every time she saw the blood stains in the courtyard, the cracks in the streets of Sia, the burns in the library that had not yet been painted over. The Aces had left lasting scars on the city and people of Caer Sia, scars on her father and her family.

Deep down, she wanted revenge.

2

News from the Blackbird

Allie followed her mother through the bustling corridors of Castle Sia to the council hall. A large group waited within the spacious round room; their voices were audible from outside.

Ajaha was whisked away almost immediately by about twenty couriers and attendants all asking questions at once. Her slender frame was nearly invisible in the crowd, but Allie could hear her calm, measured voice answering their hurried words. She saw Rygal across the room; he caught her eye and winked.

Most of the people gathered were military officers. Allie recognized the majority of them, greeting them with a smile. Having grown up as the daughter of the Red Dawn's commander, these generals had been present for most of her life. They were her father's chosen warriors, many of them his close friends.

Her father's voice spoke nearer to her, talking briskly over the noisy crowd. "Quiet down, quiet down, we'll begin in a moment. Take a seat, gentlemen. Has Admiral Dessian arrived?"

Dandio emerged through a throng of couriers and Red Dawn officers, still speaking. "General Leopold, we'll postpone the examination of the recruits today—yes, I *know* they won't like it, but we *do* have a kingdom to defend. I'm sure they'll understand."

He noticed his daughter, and a smile broke over his scarred face as he stepped toward her, waving off the rapid questions of the crowd behind him. "Morning, Allie," he greeted her with a hug. "Finished your sparring practice, I assume?" He wiped a spot of mud from her cheek.

Allie nodded. "Morning—yes, and I wanted to ask about learning to fight with a dagger too."

"Ah, well, perhaps I can teach you some later today." Dandio's gaze flicked across the room, and he frowned. "Rygal looks too well for wear. Don't tell me he beat you."

"He definitely didn't. He's just happy Mum interrupted the match before I beat him worse," Allie said with a grin.

Dandio smiled. "Now that is more like it. Have you talked to Jan this morning?"

"No, I came inside to find him. I heard he has a ranger coming to meet with him today," Allie said. "Do you know who?"

Dandio shrugged slightly. He'd never cared for the political side of his position as commander, preferring the straight-forward, to-the-point solutions of a battlefield. Since Jan's responsibilities were considerably more formal—and less exciting—Dandio tended to pay little attention to his brother's schedules. Then again, he had enough things to do himself.

"I am not sure which ranger," he replied. "You'll have to ask Jan."

"All right." Allie lowered her voice before asking her next question.

"Do you have a plan of attack against the Aces yet?"

A half-smile flickered over her father's face. "We are working on it. I'll have to tell you more later. Now, go find your uncle."

He turned back to the soldiers, moving slowly and carefully. Allie watched his movements with a pang of sorrow in her heart. Her father had recovered greatly since his rescue, but his imprisonment at the hands of the Aces had taken a heavy toll on his body. He moved slower, as though five weeks had aged him twenty years.

He was making progress. But remembering how strong he had been before, how he used to fight, how fast he could run, made it painful to note the changes now.

Allie shook the heavy thoughts from her mind and headed up a flight of stairs to her room to change out of her damp clothes. She brushed through her long brown hair, then headed into the washroom to remove any lingering spots of mud.

She heard the hall clock chime the half hour. If she was going to talk to Jan before the ranger arrived, she'd have to hurry.

She headed downstairs again, moving through the halls to the throne room. This space served as a larger, more formal meeting room than the council hall, where matters were brought to the king for discussion and issues of justice were handled. Two guards were posted outside; they greeted her, then opened the tall bronze doors.

The throne room was a long rectangular shape, with windows along the right wall. The rain had finally stopped, and sunlight streamed inside, filling the room with light.

The High King stood at the far end of the room with a group of advisors, looking through a stack of papers. He turned at the sound of the doors opening. "Good morning, Allie. Where have you been?"

"I was working on my history lessons," Allie told him. "Did you know your great-grandfather had an alliance with the Wildkids?"

"I did know that," Jan said with a nod. His green eyes twinkled with a hidden smile. "How was sparring?"

Allie raised her eyebrows. "Sparring in the rain? Who'd do that?"

"You would. So would Rygal, who I assume joined you," Jan said, no longer bothering to conceal his smile. "Who won this round?"

"We had to pause it," Allie said, then added, "but I was winning."

"Well, good work," Jan congratulated her.

Allie took her seat next to the throne and accepted the breakfast the servants brought her, waiting for the king to finish speaking with his advisors. Jan had eaten hours ago, she guessed—he liked getting an early start.

She sipped her tea and looked at her uncle again. "Which ranger are you seeing today?"

Jan found the schedule in the pile of papers and handed the rest to his secretary to sort through. "Let me see… ah, yes. Kenneth Baro, better known by the ranger name Meadowlark."

The name was vaguely familiar. Allie connected it to the face of a white-haired, grizzled ranger who had brought a report to Jan a few years back. "Do you think he'll have any important news?" she asked, careful not to reveal her curiosity. She felt a little guilty for her desire for action. Battle with the Aces was not something to wish for. All the same, these months of waiting were grating on her patience.

"I am not sure," Jan said. "He is from the Wiverrun area, farther northeast than where we believe the Aces are currently. However, if the goblins of the Magno Forest have joined the Ace-Lord, the rangers would know about it."

Allie let out a breath, a little disappointed. Wiverrun was much farther northeast than the Aces' presumed location. Rygal would probably hear more about the Aces in his meeting with Dandio and the generals.

Then again, knowing who was allied with the Ace-Lord was just as important as knowing where the Aces were, she reminded herself.

"When's Glentree bringing his report?" she asked. Glentree was Dandio's deputy and second-in-command of the Red Dawn army. He had been away for the last week on a mission south to Tinkeeyo.

"Tomorrow," Jan said. "Then I may send him east to speak to the Elimar Council."

Allie glanced at him. "Have the Elves been persuaded to join us yet?"

Jan shook his head, his silver-skinned face grim. "Not yet. Your father asked to ride there tonight and save Glentree the trouble. I haven't decided whether he needs to go or not."

Allie took another sip of tea to hide her smile. The fact that Dandio's presence was being considered told her the situation was dire indeed. Dandio's tactics of persuasion tended to be a little… rougher than Jan's. If he went to Elimar, the Council would hear a few words. On the plus side, he might actually convince the Elves to help.

Allie finished her tea, mentally running through the list of formalities her mother and Jan had taught her for formal meetings. Jan would do most of the talking, of course, so there wasn't much to remember. Don't show anger or frustration. Remember proper grammar. Don't shout. Don't interrupt, and don't speak unless asked.

She sat up straighter, keeping her head up and shoulders back. Slouching was a habit she was still trying to break. One of the advisors took a seat on Jan's other side. The other advisors and court attendants took their seats around the room, waiting.

Jan sat calmly on the throne, his golden crown catching a beam of sunlight, waiting. The clock chimed.

They did not have long to wait. The bronze doors opened, admitting a travel-stained man dressed in black. His cloak, slightly tattered and mud-streaked, billowed behind him as he walked towards the throne.

There was an almost imperceptible murmur of interest from the waiting court attendants. Allie glanced quickly at Jan—her uncle's face was still calm and welcoming, but his brow had furrowed slightly in surprise. He, along with the attendants, had noticed the same thing she had. This was not Kenneth Baro.

This man was young, probably around Rygal's age. His hair was reddish-blond, as was the stubble around his chin and lips. Yet it was the scars that caught Allie's eye—three diagonal scars creasing his young face, barely avoiding his hazel eyes.

He reached the throne and bowed slightly. "Good morning, your Highness. I hope my mentor's message found you well?"

Jan shook his head slightly. "I did not receive a message from him. You are his apprentice?"

"I was, sire. I've since completed my training and taken a position under the Duke of Wiverrun," the young man corrected. "My name is Darion Blackbird. My former mentor is recovering from a bout of sickness, but when I left him the doctors were optimistic that he will recover."

"Ah. Well, welcome to Caer Sia, Master Blackbird," Jan said. "And I wish your mentor a swift recovery. What is your report?"

Darion nodded, looking relieved. His eyes swept briefly over the room before he launched into his report. "Wiverrun Fief is well enough, considering the times. It was a bad season for yellow fever last fall—almost everyone in town was sick. But the plague is all but gone now. We've recently encountered a… different problem." He paused. "Have you received word from the duke?"

"Our most recent report from him was six months ago," Jan said. "It was a routine report, regarding the business and internal matters of Wiverrun." He studied Darion carefully. "Has anything happened since then?"

Darion let out a breath. "Aces, sire. Around three months ago, a messenger came from Ar-Salem to offer an alliance."

Allie looked at Ĵan sharply. Ĵan leaned forward, his face serious. "What was the duke's reply?"

"He refused and ordered the messenger out of Wiverrun Fief," Darion said. "But now we fear there may be some retaliation from the Aces. It's not a small thing to tell the Ace-Lord no."

"Indeed," Ĵan said, looking thoughtful.

Allie was eager to voice her questions, but she forced herself to remain silent. Darion paused, waiting for Ĵan to say more. When he didn't, the young ranger continued. "The duke is requesting a garrison of Red Dawn warriors to join our forces in Wiverrun. The fief has enough soldiers to keep guard, but we'd hardly stand a chance against the brutes the Aces have hired."

"Have you any news on who has sided with the Aces?" Ĵan asked.

"We've only heard rumors, sire," Darion said. "Wiverrun is al-lied with a few tribes of native orcs, and they let us know which of their fellow tribes have joined the Aces. From the sound of it, around half the orc clans have banded with the Ace-Lord, and headed west toward the Flatlands. There's also been word of other creatures joining the Aces. Strange creatures." He shuddered and moved on. "In better news, however, the orcs told us that the Jenna have cut all ties with the Aces and have gone back to Sikhazi."

Ĵan raised his eyebrows. "That is good. Our informants had only speculated this before."

Darion nodded. "The Aikala Jenna lost their chieftain in the Kamon battle, as you know. Without a leader, his tribe might have stayed with the Aces. Except another Jenna took command—Shâkra, son of the former chieftain Irshkhân—and led the retreat east."

That was not surprising, Allie thought. She knew the Jenna had suffered heavy casualties in the Kamon battle, due to their chieftain's refusal of the Ace-Lord's enchantment. The enchantment destroyed all of one's memories, but it also made them invulnerable in battle. Irshkhan's insistence to keep control of his warriors had led to his own demise, and that of many of his people. It seemed now, without their chieftain to order them to their deaths, his warriors had left the service of the Aces.

"I am glad to hear that," Ĵan said. "The Jenna will be one less foe to deal with. Have you heard anything further from the Aces? I am surprised Wiverrun has not seen any kind of retaliation thus far in refusing the Ace-Lord."

"No, sire," Darion said. "All seems well currently. But we would greatly appreciate support."

"And support we will give," Ĵan told him. "I'll speak to Dandio about sending a company there."

"Thank you, sire," Darion said, relief spreading over his scarred face.

Jan smiled slightly. "Is there any other news of interest from the Magno Forest?"

"Aside from the Jenna leaving, not particularly," Darion said, then paused. Allie had the sense that he was trying to decide whether or not to share the next piece of news. But the hesitation was pushed away as he looked at Jan and continued, his voice low and careful. "There is one other thing, sire. We have reason to believe that Redeyes is back."

Cold silence met the words, as though the room were encased in ice. The scribes, who had been recording the discussion, stopped in unison, looking in confusion at the young ranger. The advisors had reacted, too, yet Allie noticed the oldest among them were looking not at Darion, but at Jan.

She glanced uncertainly at her uncle, wondering what was going on. Some faint memory stirred in the back of her mind at the name, but she couldn't place where she'd heard it before.

Jan raised his eyes to meet Darion's inquiring gaze. His voice was still level, but the words sounded strained. "It is another rumor, nothing more. We can know that this tale, at least, is false. And I'd ask you not to speak that name within Sia's walls again, Master Blackbird. If that is all…you are dismissed."

Darion bowed shortly. "My apologies, sire." He nodded to them, then turned to go. The silence stretched on, broken only by the thud of the heavy doors falling closed as the ranger left the throne room.

Allie looked at Jan, trying to read an answer—any answer—in his face. His face was measured and calm, his expression unreadable. But there was something in his green eyes that she had rarely seen before, something that chilled her to the bone.

Fear.

3

ᔐ ᔐ ᔐ ᔐ ᔐ ᔐ ᔐ ᔐ

The Words of Old

The sound of the closing doors echoed in the throne room, fading into the silence. Slowly, the court attendants began speaking quietly, breaking the awkward silence with their uncertain murmurs.

Allie looked at Jan again. "Did I…?" she began.

Jan seemed to snap back to the present. "What? Oh—yes, you did quite well."

Allie raised her eyebrows. Typically, after she'd observed a meeting like this, Jan would give her detailed feedback about how she'd acted or discuss the meeting with her so she could ask questions. "Who's—" she started.

"You have other lessons to attend to today, Asescia. I will see you at supper," Jan said shortly. He stood and moved to talk with the scribes.

Allie stared after him, concerned now. Her uncle was a busy man, but he *never* brushed her off so briskly. That, and the use of her full name, told her something was troubling him. His brisk words did not hurt as badly as the fact that he was clearly hiding something from her.

She watched as Jan talked with the head scribe and heard him

41

order one of the servants to fetch Dandio immediately. Dandio's meeting with the generals wouldn't be finished for some time. If Jan needed to talk to Dandio about sending soldiers to Wiverrun, surely that could wait until the end of the war council. There must be something else he wanted to talk about, she thought. Still, what could possibly prompt Jan to interrupt the council? Interrupting official meetings went against every protocol Allie had been taught.

Jan left the room through the side door. Allie sat for a few more minutes, thinking. The growing sense that she had missed something important rang through her mind. She was nearly certain that it had something to do with that name—Redeyes.

She tried to think of who the name could apply to. The Aces all had purple-red eyes, of course—most of the Netrocrian species did. Yet she'd never heard any of the Aces referred to specifically by such a name. Besides, the way Jan had reacted had made it seem almost personal.

Questions crowding her thoughts, she stood and headed out the side door, then stopped in the hall, staring.

Jan was pacing, one hand pressed to his brow, the other resting on Drisilas' hilt, muttering under his breath. Urgency and worry were written in every line of his stance. Allie had never seen him look so powerless, and it pulled her up short.

"Jan?"

At her voice, Jan turned swiftly to face her, forcing a smile on his face. The concern was locked away in an instant. "Asescia. What is it?"

"That's what I was going to ask," Allie said slowly, glancing back at the throne room. "Is something wrong?"

"No," Ĵan told her, too quickly—Allie raised her eyebrows, and he shook his head wearily. "It's not for you to worry about, Asescia. I am only wondering about something."

"Is it about Redeyes?" she asked slowly, hoping to pry answers out of him. The name tasted strange on her tongue, as though she spoke of a creature from a fairy tale, or of a mythical beast whose power lay only between the pages of a book. Not of a name that bestowed such fear and uncertainty as Ĵan displayed.

Ĵan shook his head again. "I told you, it's nothing to concern yourself over."

Footsteps echoed on the tile behind them, halting Allie's further questions. Dandio approached, a confused frown on his face as he studied his brother.

"You wanted to see me? Now?" he asked slowly. His gaze flicked to Allie, and a spark of humor twinkled in his eyes. "I hope it's not about Asescia. Did she throw something at an overbearing duke?"

"Not Allie," Ĵan said, ignoring the joke, while Allie heaved a sigh. "I believe—"

"A baron, then?" Dandio asked, smiling wider. "I've certainly raised her right."

Ĵan pointed an accusing finger at his brother's chest, though a small smile had begun to crack the shell of worry on his tired face.

"Stop. Your daughter is a better court attendant than you will ever be, and I hope you never forget it."

"Well, I hope she grows out of it," Dandio replied immediately, watching his brother's face until Jan finally smiled back. Once he had relaxed, Dandio grew serious. "What is it?"

"We received a report," Jan said. "I have a developing theory about the Aces, and specifically, their allies."

"A report from the Meadowlark?"

"Yes and no. He was unable to be here. His former apprentice brought the report in his place, a certain Darion Blackbird."

Dandio frowned. "That's odd. You never received word about this new ranger?"

"No," Jan said, "though if it was a sudden sickness, it's to be expected. The important thing is the report itself. There is a rumor that Redeyes has returned."

Dandio stared at him for a long moment, shaking his head slowly. "Redeyes… Jan, you know that is impossible. Rumors are often exaggerated and unreliable. The Aces have started several such tales themselves, to spread fear. Misinformation can be a valuable tool for them in these dark times."

"True," Jan said, "but if the theory we discussed this morning is correct, we must examine everything in a different light."

Allie looked between the two men, feeling left out. "Who, or what, is this Redeyes anyway?" she asked slowly. "If it's nothing to worry about, why are you two worrying about it?"

"This is different, Allie," Jan said, shaking his head. "Please, go to your protocol lesson."

"I don't have protocol today, Jan," Allie said, feeling a fresh wave of concern for him. First interrupting Dandio's meeting, then pacing in uncertainty, then forgetting schedules—all of it was very unlike her uncle, and only showed how rattled Jan was. "I just want to know what's going on," she said. "I've helped you before—I helped fight the Darkness and expose Drona's treachery. I fought orcs and Jenna when they invaded Sia. Why can't I help with this matter about Redeyes too?"

"Because Redeyes is dead," Jan said flatly. There was a short, tense silence. Jan let out a breath. "This matter—it is one I must attend to." *Alone*, was the unsaid implication. "We can discuss this later. Now go."

He turned away with Dandio, walking down the hall. Allie could hear their low voices as the conversation continued without her. With a frustrated sigh, she turned and headed in the other direction, trying to make sense of the tangled information. Redeyes, whoever he was, was dead and gone. But if that were true, why would Jan concern himself over this rumor at all?

None of it made sense. More troubling to her, none of it lined up with Jan's character, which she knew to be so calm and capable.

She climbed the stairs to the east wing of the castle. It would be nearly impossible to sit and focus on further lessons today. Iriam would be displeased; the wise Neutral was very strict about her teachings.

Iriam. An idea came to her. If Jan would not tell her about Redeyes, there was a very good chance that Iriam would. As well as being one of Jan's oldest advisors, he also oversaw her lessons in the Words of Old, having her memorize and write out sections or verses. Writing out long passages was often painfully tedious, and Allie found the long pieces of history less exciting than other areas of her studies. But now she hurried faster. Maybe she could learn something else today, too—something that related to the here and now.

The east side of the castle was quieter than the bustle of the lower corridors. She climbed two flights of stairs and entered the quiet study.

"You are late, Heiress," came the Neutral's low voice from within.

"Yes—sorry, Iriam," Allie apologized, closing the door behind her. "I was talking with Jan."

Iriam's purple-red eyes held a light of quiet humor. "Well, I cannot begrudge the king for spending time with his niece. Sit down, child."

Allie sat at her desk, her eyes straying to the tall bookshelves behind Iriam. Huge, weathered tomes and scrolls, many cracked with age, filled the dark wooden shelves, lit by the daylight that the rain-splattered windows allowed inside. An oil lantern burned on her desk, casting a cheery golden light over her waiting parchment.

"Which of the Old Stories are we doing today?" Allie asked, trying to act natural and give her attention to the lesson.

"Is there a particular one you would like to study?" Iriam returned, a half-smile on his dark face. Allie wondered if he could guess the true motive behind her question. He almost seemed to be able to read her thoughts.

But she kept her expression nonchalant. "Not really. I was just curious."

Iriam nodded thoughtfully, though she could tell he didn't believe her. "Curiosity is not a bad virtue," he said, half to himself. "It depends entirely on the subject that motivates it."

"Is anything really bad to learn, though?" Allie asked. "You always say that knowledge is important."

"Important, yes, but not always good," Iriam said. "The Words of Old, for example, are full of good knowledge, every word important and pure. But there are other subjects of study better left to the shadows."

His eyes remained fixed on her as he said this, and Allie guessed he knew, in part, what she had been hoping to ask about. From his implication, he believed that the subject of Redeyes was one that should be left for another day. But she refused to let the matter go so easily. "Iriam, what do you know about—"

She was interrupted as the door opened, and a servant looked inside. "Excuse me, Master Icecloak, but you have been summoned by the king. He wishes your advice and counsel."

Allie tried to hide her frustration. It was to be expected, she thought, that Jan would want Iriam's advice on the mysterious report.

Iriam nodded. "Very well. I shall be there momentarily." He selected a scroll from the shelves and moved to Allie. "I hope you will forgive my absence, Asescia. Your lesson will be a brief one today, I think. There are other matters to attend to."

Allie looked at him, interested. "With the war, you mean?"

"Perhaps. I think this should answer your questions in part." He set the scroll on her desk. "Copy it for memorization. I shall return when I can."

With that, he left the room, black robes billowing behind him.

Allie returned her attention to the scroll. The ancient parchment was worn after years of study. Gently, she opened it to reveal the title.

The Prophecy of Three.

Her heart leapt. She had read the cryptic words once before, but only once. Now, in light of all that had happened, the marching rhythm of the Prophecy captured her attention, bound its mystery to her mind, and drove out all other thoughts.

And so she read the Prophecy whose words would dictate so much.

When the Aces have arisen,
The brightest place will darken.
When a New Blood stands unbidden
Mortal guard what was united,
Then the world shall yet survive.

The time is coming soon, coming soon, coming soon;
Your futile battle sealed your doom.

The signs have all been scarred,
By the Messenger of lost Stars

While the Mortal be unwilling,
A spell has made the binding
When the Shadow has arrived.

Light shall ever fade, ever fade, ever fade
Beware the Twelfth who stands unnamed.

When sun and stars are darkened,
To the call you must still hearken,
When willing warrior be gone at dawn,
Ace-Lord, Mortal, together one
Lest the Shadow ever thrive.

The time has come, time has come, time has come
The heart betrays what must be done.

When nameless New Blood knows their call,
If Mortal's heart remains unmarred,
When Lord of Death brings life to all,
The spell that bound leaves deeper scars
Than the Shadow that awakened.

Spells and Stones, mortal roles, hold your hope
Lest the Ace-Lord take your bones.

4

A Letter from Caer Sia
Appledale, Daffodalion

Mel allowed the door to quietly close behind him and slipped outside. The sun had sunk below the horizon, the sky faded to deep blue, and it was growing chilly as night fell. A faint murmur of voices came from inside the house as he walked into the field behind the yard, breathing in the evening air, clutching his bow and quiver of arrows.

Normally, he loved these quieter moments of archery practice. This evening, he found it hard to focus on anything besides the Prophecy's words, which drummed a rhythm in his mind, like a clock counting down the time.

When the Aces have arisen,

The brightest place will darken.

When a New Blood stands unbidden

Mortal guard what was united,

Then the world shall yet survive.

Pushing the thoughts away, he set his stance and drew the arrow back, trying to focus on his target practice for now. Yet the Prophecy's words remained in the back of his mind. Mel hadn't realized he'd memorized it. He'd read it through two or three times in Caer Sia months ago, skimming the cryptic words to see if he had missed anything, then discussed it with Iriam. It seemed to have been branded in his mind.

He'd relaxed the bowstring while thinking, and now drew the arrow back again, then sent it zipping toward the target his father had set up for him a few days before. It struck the base of the painted circle.

Mel and his mentor Aryion had returned to Appledale two weeks ago, bringing the report of the Prophecy and stories from their mission. Mel's first mission had brought them south to Esile City, where they had worked with the Wildkids and a crew of pirates to defeat the outlaw Terrax.

It had been a long journey, and their mission had been hindered as they'd uncovered a conspiracy involving the corrupt Esile Council. But in the end, Terrax had finally been brought to justice, the corruption in the Council stopped, and the Crime Ring in Esile toppled at last. The two rangers had returned to Caer Sia and brought their report to the High King.

Iriam had met with them there, with the words Mel had long awaited. Words that confirmed the second stage of the Prophecy had begun.

What had prompted it, no one was quite sure yet. They had been preparing for war ever since the Shards had been joined. Regardless of what started it, the waiting was over.

He selected another arrow and drew it back.

Strange how his urgent curiosity to read the Prophecy at first had since developed into a sort of dread. He realized he'd half hoped the Prophecy would pass by unnoticed, now that his task in it was completed. The mission to Esile City had made him realize how much he enjoyed the simplicity of ranger life, of long days of travel and training, and evenings around a campfire. The second stage of the Prophecy represented a change in life, one he'd been putting off with the hope that it would not come for another few months, years even.

Nevertheless, the time would arrive with or without his encouragement. An inevitable ending was coming, and the events foretold in the Prophecy would soon occur.

He let another arrow fly. It sank into the target, a little above the place he'd been aiming, but more accurate than his first shot.

His mind returned to the Prophecy, working to decipher its clues.

When the Aces have arisen, The brightest place will darken. Mel assumed this referred to the Forest of Light, which had been completely destroyed by the Aces. That was months ago now. Whether or not the Forest would be revived if the Aces were beaten was still to be seen.

When a New Blood stands unbidden, Mortal guard what was united, Then the world shall yet survive. These lines referred to Mel himself, or at least, the role he'd filled when he had joined the Shards. The New Blood. The Cantrian mortal who guarded the Blue

Stone. There was an inkling of hope in the stanza's last line—that once he'd rose to the role and joined the Shards, the world would live on.

That hope seemed to diminish by the next stanza, two lines that sent chills down his spine.

The time is coming soon, coming soon, coming soon
Your futile battle sealed your doom.

At the Council of Flora several months ago, the Star Queen Cahadras had explained that the Ace-Lord had been behind every battle and struggle in Coonsia in the last decade or so. The Ace-Lord had orchestrated the rise and defeat of Kado and Safacon, had led them to the breaking of the Jewel, had guided the mortals to destroy the Darkness. He had been behind it all: granting power, controlling minds, pulling strings, playing every side of this deadly game he had so carefully crafted.

In recent months, Mel had begun to worry that breaking the compass—a cursed pirate artifact he and Aryion had discovered on their last mission—had also aided the Ace-Lord's cause. Perhaps the compass' destruction was what had started the second stage.

However hard he tried to decipher it, the meaning of the second stanza still confused him. War was futile, because it would only further the Ace-Lord's cause. Yet at the same time, war was inevitable. He couldn't make sense of the lines, nor see any way around their bleak message, which contradicted everything Iriam had ever told him about the hope of the Prophecy. Victory seemed impossible.

Then again, Mel thought as he drew back and released another arrow, he'd seen many impossible events in the last year or so. You didn't necessarily have to completely understand something to believe in it.

The third stanza was the one he'd studied the most, as the events of the next stage were laid out.

The signs have all been scarred,
By the Messenger of lost Stars
While the Mortal be unwilling,
A spell has made the binding
When the Shadow has arrived.

According to Iriam, each stage of the Prophecy involved different people and the roles they must fill. The New Blood had been mentioned in the first stage, and Mel had fulfilled those actions. The second stage mentioned two people—the Messenger and the Mortal.

Upon his first read-through, Mel had thought that the mortal mentioned here was just a different title for the New Blood. After all, the wording was quite similar to the lines in stanza one—*Mortal guard what was united.* But that wasn't quite right. For one, this mortal was described as *unwilling*, which was far different from the unbidden choice of the New Blood in stanza one. *While the Mortal be unwilling, A spell has made the binding.*

Secondly, Iriam assumed that since the role of the New Blood was filled by a being of the Cantrian species, the Mortal would be a different Essence type—either a fire-channeling Fyrocrian like the Liznees, or a dark and icy Netrocrian such as the Aces. Iriam had admitted that this theory was largely speculation, and he was not sure which Essence type it would be. But in the same way that the three Star-Stones required a Wielder of each Essence type, it was possible the Prophecy had a similar rule.

There were hardly any other clues about the Mortal. Who were they? Would they be on the Aces' side, or the Liznees? And what about the "binding spell"?

He moved on from the Mortal and turned his thoughts to the Messenger. *The signs have all been scarred, By the Messenger of lost Stars.*

Those lines were as cryptic as the previous ones. All the same, they recalled an echoing voice speaking over the compass' destruction, of a familiar rippling laugh that rang from the shadows:

"The signs have been scarred. The Messenger has come. The Twelfth will rise."

The Ace-Lord's words when the compass had been broken confirmed Iriam's assumption that the Messenger would be a servant of the Aces. The line about "lost Stars" added certainty to this—after all, the Ace-Lord had once served the High Light before the Dividing War.

As best he could understand, the second stage would require a servant of the Aces and an unwilling Mortal. What they would each do was yet to be discovered.

The back door creaked open and closed behind him, and there was a soft rustling in the grass. "Hey, Misty," Mel said without turning.

"How'd you know it was me?" came his little sister's quizzical voice.

Mel looked over as she approached, bundled up in her coat, wispy blond hair trailing down her back. "You're not as quiet as Aryion, but you're not as loud as Dad," he answered, grinning.

She smiled, her blue eyes glancing in the direction of the last arrow. "It's getting dark out. Can you even see the targets?"

"It's not too dark yet," Mel replied. "Besides, I need practice. Bryn told me that's what helps your aim the most."

Bryn, a reformed bounty hunter and Aryion's twin sister, had given Mel a short lesson in archery during their mission in Esile City. Between his journey to Caer Sia, the short missions along the border, the time spent with his family, and the Prophecy's cryptic words, Mel had had little time to practice.

Misty looked at his bow. "Can you show me how to shoot?"

Mel nodded, and she beamed and moved to stand beside him. "Hold the bow here," Mel instructed, guiding her small hands. "The arrow nocks here—just use two or three fingers. Put the target on your left—like this."

He took her shoulders and turned her around until she stood at the correct angle. Misty pulled back the arrow, straining slightly under the draw weight, then let the shot fly with a small grunt. The arrow glanced off the top of the target and shot away into the woods behind the house.

"Have fun finding that," Mel said with a grin.

Misty looked at him, irritated. "I couldn't hold it back any longer. I think I aimed up at the last second."

"Yeah, that's easy to do," Mel said. "You'll build up your strength with practice—that's what I'm doing now." He took the bow back from her, unstringing it with a strap of leather.

Misty looked uneasily at the shadowed woods. "Do I still have to find it?"

"We can do it in the morning," Mel reassured her. "You're right. It's getting dark."

He and Aryion had been in Appledale for two weeks now. After completing their mission to Esile City and arresting Terrax, they had done a few short missions to Elimar, reporting to Elven Councilors and tending to 'local business,' as Aryion called it. This included meeting with the respective officials of each city sector, helping the occasional farmer protect his property from a large predator, and working with the captain-of-guard to recruit and train new cadets.

After that, they'd returned to Appledale, and life had quieted down. The sudden inactivity had driven Mel wild with restless energy at first, but now he was starting to relax and enjoy it. The slow days allowed ranger training with Aryion and time to spend with his family. Misty was home on spring break before her school term began again in Lemsonburg, and Mel's mother was clearly delighted to have everyone at home. The rest was also a welcome distraction from the dark things to come.

He and Misty put the archery gear in the shed, then walked inside. The warmth of the fire and the lingering smell of his mother's cooking embraced him as he entered. Conversation came from the parlor; his father's energetic voice, offset by Aryion's quieter, amused tone.

Mel walked into the firelit room. His father Joseph and Aryion were talking at the round table near the hall. His mother sat on the sofa across from the back door, crocheting and listening to the conversation with a smile. The scene was so simple and happy that Mel immediately put his questions about the coming struggle aside. Everyone was so cheerful and relaxed. It wouldn't do to bring up the Prophecy now.

Aryion glanced over as he entered, a smile glimmering in his dark eyes as he saw his apprentice. "Finish your practice?"

"It's getting too dark to see," Mel said. "I'll do more tomorrow."

"Fair enough. No point in losing arrows," Aryion noted.

"Misty's losing them for me," Mel couldn't resist teasing.

"Still a better shot than yours was," Misty retaliated.

Both men laughed. Mel threw Misty a playful glare, but it was so rare anyone made Aryion laugh that he let the jibe pass.

Misty settled next to their mother Elonie on the sofa with a book that probably weighed more than she did. Mel sat at the table, only half listening to the conversation next to him. His father was talking about gardening. The time had come for new seeds to be sown, now that the frost was gone for good. Maybe the Smallbuttons would purchase sheep this year, Joseph mused, to which Elonie argued that sheep would eat the lawn.

Mel sat and enjoyed his family's company. The question of tomorrow seemed irrelevant and distant. Suddenly, he wanted nothing more than for the war to be over, for the fear of the Aces to be gone, and for every day to be as simple and peaceful as this.

Surprisingly, it was his father who brought it up. As the conversation left sheep behind, Joseph glanced at Aryion and Mel. "So… what does spring bring for the war against the Aces?"

The lighthearted manner was gone in an instant. Misty closed her book, looking up with a sort of nervous interest. The mood became serious.

Aryion stroked his beard in thought. "I can't say for sure. Iriam seemed quite certain that the events of the Prophecy will begin to play out soon, but it has been months since we last spoke with him."

"Perhaps the Aces will give up, with the Shards joined," Elonie suggested slowly. "Perhaps they'll retreat like they did last time."

"Maybe," Mel said, but he knew that was wishful thinking. The Ace-Lord had plotted this conquest for centuries. He wouldn't give up now.

Misty moved to sit at the table next to him, her brow furrowed. "What about the other Star-Stones? You said the Ace-Lord wants to get them all."

Mel nodded. "He already has one Stone—sort of. The Jewel of

Power's magic just went back to the Dark Realm when it was broken, since it was corrupted. He'll need to get the Blue Stone too." He rested a hand on his pocket, feeling the reassuring weight of the little Star-Stone inside. He'd nearly lost the Stone to Terrax on the last mission, and he had promised himself he wouldn't let that mistake happen again.

"And Isilas," Misty pointed out.

"And Isilas," Aryion agreed.

"Wonder how he plans to gain that one," Joseph murmured. "He can't touch the Stones, even if he was able to draw the sword." He winked at Mel. Their attempt to draw and wield Drisilas when Mel had accidently received it for his birthday was a sort of inside joke between them now. How very long ago that felt, before Mel had ever heard of Star-Stones or Prophecies or Aces.

"Knowing the Ace-Lord, he's got a plan to get it," Mel said. "The sooner we find out what that is, the better."

Someone knocked on the door, quieting the conversation.

Out of reflex, Mel's hand flew to his pocket while his other went to his knife hilt. The dark topic of the Ace-Lord's schemes had him on edge. The horrible fear that the Aces would find them somehow and come for his family surged to his thoughts before reason calmed him.

His mother noticed his reaction and raised her eyebrows. "Calm down, Mel. It's probably one of the neighbors."

Joseph hoisted his stocky frame from his chair and moved to answer the door. Mel remained in his seat, forcing his heartbeat to settle.

"It's all right," Aryion told him quietly. "I saw them walk up the road through the window. It looks like a courier."

At his mentor's calm words, the fear was replaced by curiosity. A courier, he wondered. What was a courier doing here? His family received news from the mail carriers, nothing more official than that. Couriers only brought the most urgent and important news, usually between kingdoms.

He could partially glimpse his father around the short curving hall that separated the front door from the parlor. He heard the click as the door opened, then Joseph's friendly, "Good evening, can I help you?"

A second voice replied, carrying the elegant and proper Caer Sian accent. "I beg your pardon, Mister Smallbutton. Is the ranger called Hummingbird here?"

Aryion stood and moved down the hall, shadowed by Mel. Misty jumped up and followed them. Standing on the front porch was a man dressed in the crisp uniform of a courier. He bowed shortly as he saw them and held out an envelope. "Hello, rangers. Forgive the late hour. This message is for you."

Aryion took it, studying the seal on the back. Mel recognized the Liznee emblem instantly. This was an official message. He waited breathlessly as Aryion undid the seal and opened the letter, holding it so Mel and Misty could read too.

To the Hummingbird and Mel Smallbutton,

I had hoped to delay this letter, but something has occurred that I must ask your help with. Caer Sia is well, we have heard very little in the way of Aces. But the fief of Wiverrun has sent a call for aid. It seems the Aces are attempting to force them into subjugation.

The Red Dawn will be sent, but it will take us days to mobilize. That is why I ask you two to go ahead of us and see what is happening. We will meet you there.

Many thanks,

Jan Ki

"Wiverrun?" Misty wondered quietly. She had reached the end of the letter well before Mel—but then, she'd always been faster at reading.

Mel's heart had plummeted in fear at the letter's initial appearance; it was all too similar to the message he'd received from Rygal right before the quest for the Shards. That letter had been nothing but bad news. This message wasn't exactly good news, but at least this was something they could help with.

And it gave them a heading.

"Wiverrun is a small village in the Magno Forest," Aryion mused. "It's miles northeast of the Flats, and where we presume the Aces are. I wonder why the Ace-Lord wishes to claim it."

Mel looked over at his parents, who were waiting in the hall. The worry on their faces was masked as they gave him encouraging smiles. "Back to the action, then?" his father asked with a chuckle that sounded forced.

"This will be a short mission," Mel said with a glance at Aryion.

"Wiverrun isn't far from Caer Sia. We're just going to make sure the town is safe."

Aryion nodded. "I assume the Red Dawn will handle it if there is to be fighting," he said to Mel's parents. "We'll send word once we reach the fief, and maintain contact during the mission."

"It'll be quick," Mel reiterated. He could tell neither of his parents were happy about it. That was the hardest part about these moments at home. It was good to reconnect and enjoy everyone's company, but inevitably Mel would be called away into potential danger again. This pattern of life was something they were all still getting used to. "We'll be careful," he added.

"I know you will," Elonie said, squeezing his shoulder, but she said nothing more, her face tight with worry. Mel wished he could reassure her, but the truth was that every one of her fears was well-founded. This coming war would be more dangerous than anything they had faced before, and he could say nothing to change that.

The courier still stood on the porch, waiting uncertainly. "Would you like to send a return message to the king, rangers?" he asked finally.

Aryion turned to him and nodded. "Yes. Tell the High King we'll meet the Red Dawn in Wiverrun."

5

Cantrian Essence

Night was falling, and the cabin floor of the ship was damp and uncomfortable, but the solitude and the light from the lantern was all Rygal needed at the moment.

They had left Caer Sia's harbor a few hours ago, sailing for Mata City. Iriam, after meeting with Jan, had decided to accompany them. Rygal was not yet sure what awaited them in the Cooper city, but he'd think about that later. For now, he sat, back against the wall, one leg extended before him, the soft creaks and sounds of the ship accompanying the rustle of the withered pages.

Rygal was studying magic.

The book was one of several tomes he had found that dreary summer day upon returning to Gayrile after the quest for the Shards, returning to a lonely house that had once been lit with quiet cheer. A thin layer of dust had covered the floor, but the home had been as clean and tidy as if its owner was still alive to tend to it. Then again, Norrin had always been more organized than his adopted son.

Thinking of Norrin brought a familiar empty ache to his chest. He returned his attention to the page.

Though a Cantrian's Essence is not elemental, one can channel energy through a concentrated source, such as a staff. To accomplish this, one's thoughts must be in tune with one's intent. Channeling this energy requires a mastering of one's emotions and a quieted mind.

Along the left-hand margin was Norrin's handwriting, the ink slightly smudged. He'd probably been writing quickly. These were old notes, memories from long ago, when Norrin had trained young warriors to become Guardians of Gayrile. The ancient tomes were covered with his handwriting. He'd drawn an arrow to the last sentence, attaching his note to it:

"Quiet of mind is gained through focus upon the High Light, the source of all life on Orlell. Beware of an absent focus—dark is an opportunist."

Rygal added this to the steadily growing pile of notes. In eight months' time, he had learned more from these books and Norrin's knowledge than most would learn in years. It was progress, but not progress enough. *"Dark is an opportunist,"* he wrote, then flipped the parchment over to write on the back.

Iriam had said something similar—albeit less poetic—earlier that evening, when he had joined them for the trip to Mata City. Rygal wished he'd written it down. He was sure it had been important. Facts and readings did not tend to stick in his mind as easily as they did in Allie's, though the young heiress was skeptical of the importance of such studies. Essence channeling came easy to

Allie—if he'd talked to her about it, she probably would have said something along the lines of 'just let it happen,' and not to overthink it.

Well, that was easy for her to say—she was a Fyrocrian, after all, and the fiery Essence in her veins came as easily as breathing.

For the Cantrians, though, their Essence was not elemental. Thus, channeling it was more of a process, something they must learn to summon, drawing on the High Light for their power. Focus was the most important part of it, and it was equally important to be aware of where your focus was oriented. After all, as Iriam had told him before, the Jewel of Power had been used to draw magic from the Dark Realm, not the Land Immortal. If one was not careful, the same thing could happen if you opened your mind to the wrong kind of source.

There were a few battle stances drawn on the bottom of the page. The wizard in the drawing held his staff at different angles, demonstrating different attacks and defenses as yellow fire spread along the staff.

Norrin had been able to do the same thing, Rygal remembered. His fire had been brighter than the flames in the drawing, bright pinwheels of swirling, crackling sparks.

It was this skill that set the Guardians of Gayrile apart, the way they could channel their Essence into physical form, no matter the wizard's species or Essence type. The Guardians had fought with that power in the battle against Safacon, forming an army of men and women illuminated by their multicolored fire.

That had been four years ago, and in that time, the Guardians had been allowed to grow and thrive again in Gayrile. Their unique form of magic had been taught to their apprentices for the first time in nearly twenty years, without Safacon to keep them in exile.

Rygal wished, more than anything, that he had learned more from Norrin while he'd had the chance. But his mind had been on other things during that short time of peace—sword play and battles, the quest for Drisilas, reporting to Caer Sia. Military only, never seeing the bigger picture, never thinking to seek the truth behind the steadily growing darkness.

By the time he'd realized the truth, it was too late. The shadow had come. Norrin was gone forever, and any teachings he could have imparted upon Rygal were gone with him.

The most common form of Cantrian magic is channeled through a staff. Staffs can be made of any sturdy, lightweight wood preferred by the user. Hazelwood is recommended for its durability and weight.

The lantern was burning low, sinking the cabin into shadows. The sea was relatively calm tonight, though it had been pouring rain when they'd left Sia's harbor. Rygal had retired to the cabin once they were at sea, deciding to study as much as he could. Now, he heard only the lapping waves and billowing sails, which meant that the rain had stopped at last.

And that, he decided, meant he could practice.

He slipped a bookmark into the heavy volume, stacked the pages of messy but plentiful notes beside the books, and left the cabin, walking through the berth deck to reach the stairs. Several sailors filled the berth, moving supplies or taking a brief rest. Rygal smiled a greeting to them and jogged up the steps to the main deck.

Iriam stood speaking to the helmsman. The Neutral's gaze turned to Rygal as he appeared on deck, weaving his way toward the tiller. The helmsman noticed him too, and a smile spread over his broad, weathered face as Rygal approached.

"Ah, back at it again, sir?" he asked, a hopeful light in his cheery eyes as he glanced between Rygal's face and the sword and shield in his hands.

"Now that the rain's stopped," Rygal replied. "I hope it's not a distraction."

When they'd first left Sia's harbor a few hours ago, Rygal had completed a short training session with Iriam before the rain had prohibited further practice. He'd gathered a small audience of sailors while doing so.

"Not at all, not at all," the helmsman assured him quickly. He had spent most of his life serving in Caer Sia's navy, which meant he had seen many strange things. But the training of a Guardian of Gayrile was not something he'd ever witnessed, and he didn't want to miss it.

Iriam looked at Rygal too, unbothered by the frigid wind whipping around his tall frame. Then again, he was a Netrocrian, and his veins were filled with icy Essence. "I take it you have completed your reading?" he asked.

"Just the section on channeling sources," Rygal answered. "Do you think it'd be better to learn with a staff?"

He had wondered this for some time, ever since he'd first begun studying magic after the quest for the Shards. That was at least eight or nine months ago, but he still hesitated to claim a staff as his method for using magic. It felt disrespectful to Norrin's memory in a way, like a cheap copy of the man who had been so skilled.

If Iriam shared his reasoning, he didn't show it. He only shook his head slightly. "No, a staff is not necessarily needed. I think it best to stay with the weapon you know and are comfortable with. You have trained with a sword. That will be one familiar tool in an area that is unfamiliar." He stepped down to the deck they had used as a practice space earlier.

Rygal frowned, still feeling unsure. "The book said it's better to use a staff."

"That is because a wooden staff is a natural thing. Purer, less hardened, not yet wrought through fire. It is easier to connect with the Essence of such a weapon." Iriam paused. "In that way, your sword is more akin to your own nature."

Rygal spun his sword experimentally in his hand. The familiar weight and feel of the blade helped settle his uncertain thoughts. He'd received this sword from the Direns in Gayrile during the quest for the Jewel—the steel was some of the finest in the north. "I read a few of Norrin's notes," he said. "He said the weapon you use doesn't matter as much as where your focus is."

"And he was right, as usual," Iriam said, his tone softening. "The sword will do. If you choose to equip both hands with a weapon, in lieu of your shield, then you might try a secondary blade."

Rygal looked down at his shield, a new piece of equipment to him. The Liznee rune and crest was emblazoned on its gleaming silver front. Coupled with the Garilian sword, the two moved in his hands as though an extension of his own body. All the same, there'd been nothing in the book about someone using a shield.

"The book said—" he started doubtfully.

"I can well imagine what the book said," Iriam cut him off, though there was a glimmer of amusement in his eyes. "Its words are important, Rygal. But knowledge is nothing without experience and action." He shook his head in mock dismay. "Between yourself and the young heiress of Caer Sia, my students appear to be either ends of a spectrum—one who knows only the rules and words of magic, and the other who pays them no attention whatsoever and chooses to rely on her emotions."

"Allie's still a better student than I am," Rygal said, and for some reason he felt himself blush.

"Of that I have no doubt. Now, enough words. Show me what you have learned."

Rygal set his stance, took a breath, and cleared the thoughts away. The words in the ancient book echoed in his mind, Norrin's voice speaking through what he had read. "*Forget your fear. Center your mind on the*

Light. Sense the Essence and breath within you, and allow it to flow."

The whistling wind, the lapping waves, and the creaks of the ship faded away. He was acutely aware of his own heartbeat, as though he could sense the very blood rushing through his veins. He exhaled slowly, felt the slight quickening of his pulse, and sensed a strange peace settling over him like calming wings.

His eyes snapped open, and with a short whoosh, a small flash of sparks spread down the blade of his sword like a shooting star, vanishing just as quickly.

There was a murmur of interest from two impressed sailors, who had stopped to watch. The helmsman gave them an order and they returned to their tasks. Rygal let out a pent-up breath, shoulders sagging forward.

"Your focus is anchored," Iriam said. "Your mind is in the right place. The technique will come later."

Rygal studied the blade of his sword. The steel was unblemished by the short rush of heat and light. The Diren steel was ideal for Essence channeling, as if it had been made for him to learn this. All the same, he couldn't help feeling disappointed.

"Not even hot enough to warm the blade," he said bitterly.

"Not yet," Iriam told him. "That will come in time. Sometimes it is easier in the… heat of the moment." Halfway through the sentence, he raised his hands and flung a bolt of deep blue ice in Rygal's direction. Rygal raised his shield—the bolt struck it with a resounding clang, and he stumbled back, trying not to slip on the wet deck.

"A shield will be little use against the Aces," Iriam warned him. "Focus. If you can accomplish it in a moment of quiet, you can do it in battle as well."

"Harder to focus when there's a bolt of ice flying at your face," Rygal couldn't resist retorting.

"That is not something you will have much control over," Iriam said. "Accept the fact. The only thing you can control is your response."

Rygal nodded, took another breath, and looked up to see Iriam raising his hands again. As he caught the blast on his shield, sparks shot around the rim, shattering the bolt and spraying the deck with deep blue fragments of ice.

"That is better," Iriam said, sounding pleased. "Think of the years of training you spent learning to use your sword. This is no different. Be patient. Allow yourself time to learn and refine the skill."

Rygal nodded again. Patience, he thought wryly, had never been his strong suit. While he'd made progress in the last eight months, he still needed to work on the skills he'd studied.

"Now," Iriam said, "set your stance again. Let us continue."

6

∽ ∽ ∽ ∽ ∽ ∽ ∽ ∽ ∽ ∽

Glentree's Report

Allie had a harder time than usual focusing on her politics lesson the following morning. Firstly, there was the fact that Dandio had been sent to speak to the Elimar Council that afternoon, which meant he'd probably return with news tomorrow. Then there were the lingering thoughts surrounding Jan and his strange behavior yesterday after Redeyes had been brought up. He'd summoned Darion Blackbird for a follow-up meeting about Wiverrun the previous afternoon, a meeting that Allie was disappointed to miss.

Of course, she had been reading the Prophecy yesterday while that meeting had happened.

The Prophecy. There lay the third source of confusing thoughts.

She'd read through the Prophecy of Three yesterday, wrote it down, and memorized it. It was odd that she hadn't done so before, she thought. The Prophecy held the hope of the mortals, as Iriam had told her. Why not have everyone read it, and help them all learn what to do against the Aces?

She had a guess now, after reading it herself. *The time is coming soon, coming soon, coming soon; Your futile battle sealed your doom.*

The Prophecy held hope, yes. But it wasn't a hope that would come through peaceful talks, practical reasoning, or, alternatively, a bloody war. Only fulfilling the tasks written in the Prophecy's cryptic words would defeat the Ace-Lord; any other action would aid their enemies' cause.

Why?

She wasn't sure. Either way, she now understood that very few people read the Prophecy because, simply, they didn't understand it. It was easy to say that the Prophecy contained hope, but that was hard to believe when the words themselves seemed to hold nothing but death and gloom.

Dully, she continued writing. Her hand moved of its own volition, her mind barely thinking about the words she read.

She wanted to talk to Iriam. He was probably the only one who could answer her questions. But the Neutral had gone west with Rygal last night after meeting with Jan.

At last, she finished her notes on politics and flipped through her notebook to look over the Prophecy of Three again. The third stanza offered her a few insights into what the second stage would look like:

The signs have all been scarred,
By the Messenger of Lost Stars.
While the Mortal be unwilling,
A spell has made the binding,
When the Shadow has arrived.

Well, the Shadow was here, all right. The question was if the other players mentioned had arrived as well. There was the Messenger—who or whatever they could be. And what was the line about the unwilling Mortal, bound by some sort of spell? She wondered if it might refer to the Aces' soldiers, most of whom were enchanted and mindless. But that couldn't be right. Those soldiers weren't unwilling. From what Mel had told her, you had to be willing for the Ace-Lord to enchant you. Besides, the soldiers weren't exactly mortal anymore, either. Bound by the enchantment, they were invulnerable as long as the Ace-Lord had need of them.

She snapped her notebook shut, leaned back in her chair, and let out an irritated sigh, feeling restless and unhelpful. Her father, Iriam, and Rygal were all three away on missions. Her mother was organizing a reconnaisance trip to the Flats.

Jan, meanwhile, was receiving reports from different lords and dukes. For his part, after meeting with Dandio, he had seemed remarkably normal again. Any sign of the fear from the day before was gone, or else very well hidden. Allie assumed the latter, but she doubted she'd get any more information out of her uncle.

Then again, there was nothing stopping her from asking him questions, even if he wouldn't answer them. She decided to go talk with him while he was between meetings this morning. At the very least, he might give her a task to do. Anything was preferable to waiting uselessly in the library.

She strode down the halls toward the throne room. The two

guards stood in their places by the bronze doors. A third person stood there, too, hands clasped behind his back. Darion Blackbird, a lean shadow in his dark cloak.

Allie slowed her pace, startled to see the ranger again. After finishing his report with Jan yesterday, he should have returned to Wiverrun.

Darion noticed her approach and gave her a slight smile. "Morning, princess."

"Morning. What are you still doing here?" Allie asked.

"Waiting to speak with the king," Darion replied, unconcerned by her blunt tone.

"I thought you had a follow-up yesterday," Allie said, puzzled. "Wouldn't you have answered his questions then?" Usually, if Jan had more questions outside of the report timeframe, he would request a follow-up meeting shortly after the first. Allie knew Jan had already met with Darion yesterday afternoon.

"I did," Darion said, the slightest hesitation in his voice as he spoke. "We decided… that is, he wanted an additional meeting as well."

There it was again—an unexplainable change in schedule that made no sense. Jan clearly wanted to know more about the rumor regarding Redeyes, but it was strange that he'd wanted two additional meetings to discuss that. There seemed little else for Jan to ask about. "Did he have more questions about your report?" she asked, trying to read Darion's expression.

The ranger shook his head slightly. His scarred face was as impassive as ever. "More answers than questions. He wanted to reassure me that the rumor was false, so that it doesn't spread. Our meeting was cut short yesterday so the king could meet with Iriam."

"I think he's confused by the news you brought," Allie said, feeling somehow defensive of her uncle. "He wanted to talk to a few people about Redeyes."

The barest trace of a frown crossed Darion's face. "I take it you… haven't heard about Redeyes before?" he asked slowly.

Allie shook her head. "No. Should I have? Who is Redeyes?" she demanded immediately.

"Never mind," Darion said swiftly. "I just wondered." He paused, looking for a change in subject. "It, ah, sounds like the Red Dawn will travel to Wiverrun in the next few days. With luck, they'll arrive within a week."

"That's good to hear," Allie said, though her mind was racing with questions. "You haven't seen any Aces in Wiverrun yet?"

"No. I don't know if they'll attack at all. It depends if the Ace-Lord wants the town or not," Darion said.

"And if he does?" Allie ventured.

"If he wants it, he'll have it," Darion said grimly. "His desires are as good as law, you know." He let out a breath, face suddenly drawn. For the first time, Allie realized how heavily his mission weighed upon him. Here he was, a newly appointed ranger, only a few years older than she was, taking the responsibility of his mentor to carry the concerns of his fief before the High King. She had viewed him as yet another source of stressful rumors, but he was trying to help his village.

"The Red Dawn will help," she said, offering some reassurance. "As soon as my father returns from Elimar, I'm sure he'll mobilize a company and send them to Wiverrun. That should discourage any attacks from the Aces."

"I hope so," Darion said, but his eyes were distant. Finally he shook his head, seeming to put the subject aside. "So, why are you here?"

"I honestly just need a job," Allie said ruefully. "My days are mostly studies and lessons, but I think there are more important things to do right now."

Darion shrugged. "Every job's important," he pointed out.

"I suppose so," Allie said with a slight grin. "Still, studies won't defeat the Aces."

He nodded, but said nothing more. They stood for a few moments in silence. Allie strained her ears to try to hear the conversation behind the bronze doors, but the words were too faint to make out.

A sudden crash of closing doors made her jump, and she and Darion turned sharply. Frantic voices came from the courtyard, growing louder as they drew closer. She heard hurried footsteps, heavy footfalls, a few snatches of words—

"Get him to the hospital wing immediately, he needs medical attention—"

"Hold on there, sir, you'll be all right—"

A third voice, familiar to Allie but almost unrecognizable between ragged gasps for breath, cut in. "No. Take me to the king. Urgent… news…"

A tall, burly figure stumbled up the wide stairs leading from the gates, supported by two soldiers. The guards jogged to aid them. Allie's heart lurched.

Blood streaked the big man's features and dripped from his leather armor. His face was pale and drawn with pain, but she recognized him instantly. "Glentree?" she began, running to meet him.

The giant warrior looked up wearily at her voice and managed a weak smile. "Aye, lass, glad you're safe. I rode 'ere quick, but I wasn't sure… he's got strange powers, or so the legends say." He coughed, fighting to keep his feet.

One of the soldiers supporting him looked uncertain. "Sir, you need to go to the hospital wing. You've lost a lot of blood."

"No," Glentree rasped. "No hospital, not till I see the king—let me in—"

Darion, who had followed Allie to see what was happening, turned back as the guards opened the heavy bronze doors. The small group stumbled inside.

Jan was sitting on the throne, speaking with a finely dressed lord. The lord looked over in irritation at the sound of the interruption, but when he saw what was happening he quickly stepped aside.

Jan had looked up with a startled frown, but concern filled his eyes as he registered Glentree's wounds. "What happened?" he demanded, hurrying forward to meet them.

"We don't know, sire," one of the soldiers stammered. "He arrived on horseback a few moments ago."

"Yer highness," Glentree greeted Jan, saluting weakly, then, his strength spent, sank to his knees.

Jan knelt beside his friend, looking into his face urgently. "You can tell your report after you've rested. These wounds are serious even for someone of your strength."

"No," Glentree repeated, looking up painfully. "Not till I've told my piece. It's bad, sire—very bad news." He broke off, coughing. Allie rushed to the table at the side of the room and snatched a few tea towels, then moved to Glentree. The leather armor had been shredded, a deep wound scoring over Glentree's shoulder blade and back. She pressed the cloths against the wound, trying to staunch the bleeding. The thin cloth soaked through almost immediately, and the gash came into focus.

Three diagonal slices, etched deep into the muscle of the giant's back.

Glentree grunted in pain. Jan motioned for the servants to bring water and cloths, and they hurried to obey.

Darion spoke slowly, deep concern on his face. "How… how did you say this happened?"

Glentree looked at Jan. "It's Redeyes, sire—Redeyes himself—I've seen him, in the wood, prowling the Magno Forest as he did in the old days. He's *back*."

The word hissed through the hall like steel on stone. Allie looked at the faces around her, reading different levels of concern there. The guards and soldiers looked uneasy, gripping their weapons. Darion's face was drawn, his jaw tense. But Jan's seemed a deeper sort of fear, a fear that showed very little on his features. Only his green eyes betrayed the dread that sent chills down Allie's spine.

Glentree let out a ragged breath. "Terrible thing, he is. He's huge—near the size of a pony—all covered in scars. But his eyes—them's the worst part of it. Empty pits of red fire."

"Did he speak to you?" Darion asked.

Glentree glanced at him, confused by the unfamiliar voice, but continued painfully. "Aye… he said he was on his way. Said he'd come to fulfill the Prophecy—the second stage—he'd come to mark the way, to mar the—" He coughed again, so hard he nearly fell to the ground.

Jan took his shoulders. "What else was there, Glentree? What else did he say?"

"The Ace-Lord," Glentree rasped, his eyes going in and out of focus as he fought to stay conscious. "He's the reason behind it all—he's the one what brought him back—and he's going to bring something else, something worse—to follow Redeyes' commands—"

"He's going to bring what?" Jan persisted, his voice tense.

Glentree fell forward onto his hands and knees, trembling with the effort, yet he looked up and forced the words out. "The wraith, sire. He's going to bring… going to bring the Darkness back."

And with that final effort, he collapsed into Jan's arms.

7

§ § § § § § § § §

The Scars of Shame

Jan's meetings were canceled for the remainder of the day.

The dukes and lords were dismissed. A brief word about what had transpired, and they returned to their fiefs and villages without complaint. The generals were summoned to the castle. With Dandio in Elimar and Glentree out of action, General Arrex was placed in charge of the war council. Couriers swept in and out of Caer Sia all afternoon and late into the night. Ajaha's team was overloaded spreading news across the kingdom.

Allie's many questions had to wait as the flurry of activity in the castle continued into the evening. She lingered outside the council hall, watching as crowds of generals, couriers, and advisors went in and out in turns, speaking with the High King. Her uncle's voice reached her occasionally, measured yet urgent as he answered questions and issued orders.

Finally, as the hours of the day crept into evening and evening into night, she left the corridor and returned to her bedroom, frustrated and fearful. The night passed in restless sleep. The noisy activity in the rest of the castle continued without her. By morning, the couriers were still at work, the councils were still meeting, and she was no closer to learning any answers to her concerns.

Without much else to do and feeling useless, she headed to the hospital wing to check on Glentree. Here, at least, it was quieter. She sat on the bench outside Glentree's room, listening to the faint noise of activity filling the rest of the castle. Morning had brought no ease to her uncertainty, only replaced her curiosity with dread.

She tried to fight it with little success. Her chest and throat felt tight with anxiety. People moved past her in a swirl of sound and motion. Finally, a doctor came out of the room and gave her a short report. Glentree was still resting, but the deep gashes had been tended to and the wound would heal in time. "Other men have died from half the amount of blood lost," the doctor told her, shaking his head. "But he will live."

Allie thanked him. This news should have filled her with joy, but it only furthered her growing fears. Yes, she was greatly relieved Glentree would survive. But the very fact that something had *nearly killed him* drove that relief away. Glentree the Giant, as the young recruits called him, was unstoppable, untouchable in combat. She had seen him hew his way through walls of opponents, unaffected by injuries. Yet this Redeyes had defeated him with a single blow, and would have likely killed him if he hadn't fled to Sia in time.

At least the incident had partly answered her question about Redeyes. A creature out of legend, long thought dead.

Now, the Ace-Lord had some way to bring his fallen servants back into the mortal world. How he could do this, there was no telling, but Allie knew all would be lost if they didn't learn the truth of it soon and stop him. If the Ace-Lord could bring Redeyes back, what was stopping him from doing the same with the Darkness? Memories of the horrific shadowy wraith, of the deadly fog that consumed its foes, filled her mind again. It was the Ace-Lord who had ordered its demise, lest it affect his plot concerning the New Blood. And, she realized, it would be the Ace-Lord who ordered the Darkness—or another wraith like it—into the battle now.

Glentree's weak voice from yesterday afternoon filled her thoughts again. *"He's going to bring the Darkness back."*

A gentle hand on her shoulder brought her back to reality. "How is he?" It was Jan.

"They said he'll be all right," Allie answered softly. "The doctors said they patched him up. He's resting now."

Jan sat beside her on the bench. Allie waited in silence, unsure where to start in her questioning, listening to the muted conversations of the doctors and the distant swirl of activity elsewhere in the castle.

"I am meeting with General Arrex in an hour," Jan said after a long pause. "We are discussing the fate of Wiverrun. I would appreciate your attendance."

"Really?" Allie asked, glad to be included. She studied her uncle's face for a moment, trying to read beyond his calm expression. The fear in his eyes remained like faint embers. "Do we have a plan?"

"The safety of Wiverrun Fief must be secured before we turn our focus to Glentree's report," Jan said. "That news will need more details before we can act. Your mother is already coordinating the investigations to the Flats. I have sent word to Tinkeeyo as well—they might have more information about the happenings in the Magno Forest." He paused. "In the meantime, a company will be sent to Wiverrun."

"All right," Allie said. It was slightly reassuring, knowing there was a plan to act on. It was better than waiting in uncertainty. But the shock of Glentree's appearance and the news he had brought had discouraged some of her curiosity. She felt almost afraid to know the answers to her questions.

Jan watched her carefully. "Is there anything else you would like to know?" he asked softly.

"Who is Redeyes?" Allie asked. She spoke just above a whisper, yet the name seemed to echo in the hospital wing.

Jan's gaze was distant, and he remained silent for a long moment. When he spoke, his voice was quiet. "Redeyes is a servant of the Aces. A creature of darkness, but not a wraith. His appearance can vary, depending on his powers and strength. Most often, he wears the guise of a large black tiger."

"And… he was presumed dead?" Allie guessed, piecing together the fragments of information she'd gathered.

"Not 'presumed.' Killed, by your father's hand," Jan said.

"But…that's not possible," Allie said, not sure what else to say. "Are you sure…"

"I was there. I saw," Ĵan answered. He seemed about to say more, but remained quiet.

Allie nodded slowly, knowing better than to disbelieve the truth. "What does he do for the Ace-Lord, then?" Knowing the Ace-Lord and his meticulous schemes, every servant had a unique task and purpose in his plan. The Ace-Lord had neither favorites nor sentimentality, only useful servants. Thus, Redeyes must have a specific purpose.

Ĵan thought for a moment. "I assume for two reasons," he said at length. "I spoke to Iriam just after Darion brought his report. We have begun to wonder if Redeyes will fulfill the role of the Twelfth Ace. He was mortal, and a Cantrian as well. While his resurrected state would render him less powerful than the other Aces, he would still bring the Aces to their strongest number."

The news startled her. "You think the Ace-Lord would turn him into the Twelfth?" She knew the other Aces had been men once, transformed by Kahlifis, the rebel Netrocrian lord who now claimed the name Ace-Lord. The Ace-Lord had once offered to make Mel the Twelfth, which would gain him both the New Blood and the Blue Stone. But Mel had refused to join him.

"He might," Ĵan said. "It's only a theory at this point, but I would not be surprised if it is part of Redeyes' purpose."

"What's the other part of that purpose, then?" Allie asked. "You said there were two reasons."

Ĵan let out a breath. "Yes. Before he was defeated, Redeyes was the Ace-Lord's executioner."

"So the Ace-Lord wants him to kill," Allie said slowly. That seemed odd. The Aces were more than capable of killing on their own.

But Jan shook his head. "Not just kill. Redeyes is here to cause total destruction, to break the spirits of the mortals, though not alone." He paused. "You remember that the Darkness had no mind of its own—that it was simply a force, a power commanded by the Ace-Lord?"

Allie remembered. She recalled every detail of that terrible day almost two years ago, when the Darkness had come to Sia—the white frost glittering on the grass, the lifeless skulls of the outlaws, the swirling black inferno of the wraith. She nodded, concealing a shudder of fear.

Jan went on. "Redeyes used to act as the handler for the Darkness. His claws laid scars upon individuals whose actions demanded recourse— Blood Oath-breakers, magic-benders—in those days, nothing was equal to the shame and finality that those scars brought. These were no simple wounds—they were Marks, healing unnaturally fast, utterly permanent until atoned for."

His voice was suddenly distant, as though looking back on days filled with fear. "There is no forgiveness for those accused by Death itself. No atoning besides death. Beyond the sign of the scars, the Marks form a traceable curse. Following the scars, the Darkness would destroy entire cities along with the Marked one."

He paused. "After Redeyes was killed, we assumed the Darkness would remain powerless, a force without a master. We were wrong, of course—the Darkness' true master was the Ace-Lord, who took command of it when the time was right for him to do so."

He shook his head wearily. "The Darkness is destroyed, but we can assume that it was only one of many such wraiths. If the Ace-Lord can bring Redeyes out of the realm of death, he must have some way to access the Dark Realm and bring another wraith into the mortal world."

The implication had begun to dawn on Allie, but it took an effort to say. "So… the Ace-Lord's brought Redeyes back so he can command another wraith… and send it to kill…?"

She trailed off, already knowing the truth.

"Everyone," Ĵan said quietly. "With Redeyes leading the way, whatever wraith the Ace-Lord calls forth will destroy everything."

Silence fell for a moment. The activity in the hospital wing had slowed, and the only sound came from the soft patter of falling rain.

Allie thought of Redeyes, prowling the dark wilds, preparing to resume his role as the Ace-Lord's executioner. She thought of the gashes on Glentree's back. Three diagonal scratches—not the curse-bearing Marks Ĵan had described. No, these scratches were just a warning—a reminder of what Redeyes was capable of. A sign of the Ace-Lord's power and accusation.

Like a flash of lightning, the words from the third stanza of the Prophecy entered her mind: *The signs have all been scarred; By the Messenger of Lost Stars.*

"Redeyes is the Messenger in the Prophecy," she realized aloud. "He's the one the Ace-Lord sent."

"So we can now assume," Jan said.

Allie looked at him in disbelief. "Did you know this? Did you know Redeyes was coming back?"

Jan sighed. "I had a guess. I thought it too far-fetched. After all... Redeyes was dead."

"*Was*," Allie muttered.

"The Messenger would have come either way," Jan said gently. "Either Redeyes, or something worse. We know the Ace-Lord must work within the Prophecy, and he will seek to raise up his own players to fill its roles. I did not know Redeyes had returned until Darion brought his report, and even then, I admit I doubted it."

Allie nodded, but her mind had paused at the mention of Darion. Thinking of the young ranger, the wary light in his hazel eyes while he'd brought the news, the scars that creased his face...

Three diagonal scars.

"Darion," she breathed, unable to believe it. "Darion didn't just hear a rumor Redeyes was back... he's *seen* him... he's been *Marked* by him..."

She looked at Jan, seeking his face for any sign of the same realization and disbelief. But he only gave a very slight nod. "Yes. He has."

He said nothing more. Allie stared at him, unable to understand how he was so calm. "He lied," she stammered at last. "Darion said the news was just a rumor—we might have sent a company of warriors into the Magno Forest on false pretenses! How does that not concern you?"

"It did. I have addressed it," Jan told her. Yet there was another note in his measured voice. *Don't pursue this, Allie. Let me handle this.*

"You knew he was scarred by Redeyes, then," Allie said. She was so shaken she could hardly form words. "Why? What else is Darion hiding?"

Jan met her eyes. "Darion has hidden nothing. Everything I need to know, I have learned from him now. The truth of this matter is a dark one, Asescia—and it must remain secret for now. I will tell you everything, one day. But not now."

His words held little reassurance, only adding to the turmoil in Allie's mind. Darion's hesitation to speak the truth, and the fact that he himself was scarred by Redeyes, marked him as suspicious. Yet Jan seemed unconcerned. Whatever he and Darion had discussed in their second meeting without her had rid him of his earlier uncertainty. He was steady again, calm and acting forward with a plan he would not share.

Not even with her.

"What do we do now, then?" she asked, forcing the troubling thoughts aside.

"For now," Jan said, with the trace of a smile, "I must prepare for another meeting. I intend to accompany General Arrex's force west as well, to meet with the duke of Wiverrun and better assess what is happening."

Allie looked at him, surprised. "You're going to Wiverrun too?"

"I believe it wise," Jan said, standing. "I have not spoken with the duke for some time. Beyond that, I think the matter of the Aces and their strategy is worse than we have been led to believe by the duke—of that, Darion is certain. I fear strange things are astir at Wiverrun."

8

Two Meetings

If Jan shared Allie's distrust of Darion Blackbird, he did not show it. They left the hospital wing, and Jan walked briskly down the hall back toward the throne rooom, leaving Allie waiting uncertainly at the base of the stairs. Conflicting thoughts churned in her mind.

Darion had been scarred by Redeyes. When, and for what purpose, she had no clue. *I should have noticed that sooner*, she berated herself. Jan had recognized it early on—that must have been why he'd requested so many follow-ups. What information had he learned from Darion? What was his plan?

Too many secrets. Too many questions, with hardly any answers. She walked slowly down the halls toward the distant murmur of conversation near the council hall. Her decision to trust Jan fought with a nagging desire to learn the truth, and today, her need for answers won. She would find Darion, demand answers, learn what he really knew; she would—

"How's General Glentree?" came Darion's concerned voice behind her.

She turned sharply. He had approached without her noticing, the buzz of conversations within the meeting hall concealing his every sound. Then again, he was a ranger, and had been trained to move silently.

"They said he'll recover," Allie answered, rattled by his sudden appearance. Her eyes were drawn immediately to his scars. While they matched Glentree's wounds in shape, these looked quite different—darker, stretched over the skin, like a burn from a brand.

Darion noticed her scrutinizing gaze and frowned slightly. "Is there something else?"

"Your scars," Allie said. "You got them from Redeyes, didn't you."

That had an effect, she could see it in his eyes. His guise of nonchalance faltered a moment. He glanced quickly around the corridor, then spoke quietly. "Where did you hear that?"

"I didn't hear it anywhere. I know you brought news about Redeyes, I saw Glentree's wounds, and I guessed the rest," Allie said.

"Did the king tell you… never mind," Darion broke off, shaking his head slightly. "Yes. The scars came from Redeyes."

"Then you knew," Allie pressed. "You knew he was back. Why didn't we hear of this before?"

Darion started to speak, but she cut him off. "And why didn't you just tell us the truth when you first brought the report? You said it was 'just a rumor,' but you've clearly seen him yourself."

She stopped, fighting to control herself and force her frustration and suspicion away. *Don't become emotional,* her mother had taught her. It was something she was still working on, as her impatience often got the better of her. When gathering information from a source, you needed to be calm and respectful.

That, of course, was easier when it was a trusted source. At the moment, every part of her mind screamed distrust at the ranger before her.

Darion ran a hand through his messy red hair, seeming to decide how to reply. At last he looked at her, lowering his voice. "Yes, I've seen him. Felt his claws. He's real, princess. I thought—I knew no one would believe me if I stated the news outright. You saw how the king reacted, even at the mere mention of the name." He smiled bitterly. "I can't blame him for that. Hardly anyone can trust or be trusted in these times. Thankfully Deputy Glentree brought more substantial evidence."

"*Substantial evidence?*" Allie repeated dryly. "You had a first-hand report."

A general walked down the hall to enter the council room, causing Allie and Darion to pause the conversation. Once he was gone, Darion turned to her again. He spoke haltingly, as though unsure of his every word. Almost as if he were trying to decide how much to tell her. "I do. I don't—I didn't come here to bring news about Redeyes. My task was—"

He trailed off as a group of court attendants brushed past them, then he continued in an even quieter tone. "I should have brought the news as soon as it happened. There were reasons keeping me from doing so—but that's what the king wanted to discuss in the follow-up."

"He wanted to know how you got the Marks," Allie guessed slowly.

"How… and why." One hand brushed the scar below his right eye, as though trying to wipe it away. "The king has a plan. That's all I can say for now. Any other answers, you'll have to get from him."

"I haven't had much luck with that," Allie said irritably, still not sure what to make of the young ranger. "If Jan has a plan, that's reassurance enough. But you knew more and chose to keep it hidden, so you'll have to start telling the whole facts of the matter before I'll trust you."

"That, princess, is why I'm here," Darion told her with a slight smile.

A small group had already gathered inside the council room as Allie followed Darion inside. Jan had arrived, too, seated at the head of the table. Allie sat a few chairs down from Jan. Her earlier anger had faded, and her emotions felt under control again.

Darion, though she hated to admit it, was right. Even if he'd told them straight out that Redeyes had returned, she doubted Jan would have believed him.

Would I? Probably not.

She glanced across the table at Darion, who waited expectantly, eyes on the High King. Jan seemed to believe him now, and he trusted him with whatever plan they'd discussed. He had also, it seemed, recognized Darion's scars the day he'd arrived. Odd that he hadn't said anything about it to her. Almost as strange as the fact that, the more Allie thought about it, Jan had shown no surprise to the news of Redeyes' return. He had been fearful, yes, but not surprised. He'd acted quickly and come up with a plan.

Almost as if he'd been expecting it…

She tried to focus on the meeting. One of the generals was speaking. "Have we received word of the Aces' position, sire?"

"No, not yet," Jan said. "Lady Ajaha and the couriers will embark on their reconnaissance mission soon. Light willing, we'll receive their report upon our return from Wiverrun." He studied those assembled. "Our mission is twofold—we must secure the safety of Wiverrun Fief, and gather any news about the Aces' movements in the area. General Arrex will lead the mission, on which I ask him to speak."

General Arrex nodded from his place beside Jan, golden eyes serious. From the shoulders up, his features were foxlike, ears and fur the same sandy gray as the wolves in the desert where his people hailed from. His voice was low, with the slight rasp of an accent. "We will leave the day after tomorrow, as soon as our force is assembled, and take the southwest road through the mountains. The snow has thawed by now, but the way will be treacherous. The ranger Darion Blackbird will accompany us, as he knows those paths well."

Darion nodded to him but said nothing. Allie had assumed he would return to Wiverrun with the garrison. She wondered if he would tell General Arrex about his past dealings with Redeyes— whatever those dealings were.

"I hope to reach Wiverrun within four days," Jan said. "After my meetings with the duke and once the garrison is secured, I will return to Sia."

"My men will prepare to leave," Arrex said. "There is an old ruin near the northwestern side of town, and I believe we might use it as our barracks while we are stationed in Wiverrun."

Darion looked up, his face uneasy. "I wouldn't recommend that, General. That ruin…"

"You believe the stories, ranger?" one of the older generals asked mockingly. "Believe it to be haunted?"

"No," Darion said levelly, "but you never know what the Ace-Lord's up to with old ruins."

Jan looked at him. "Do you believe the Aces have settled there?"

"I'm not sure. I do think, if the Ace-Lord wants the town, his servants are likely to be nearby, keeping watch on any activity," Darion said. "The ruin seems a bit too convenient a location in my mind. The Aces may have settled there to strike the town."

"It pays to be cautious," Arrex conceded. "We will scout the ruin thoroughly before establishing a base there."

"Why Wiverrun?" a younger soldier inquired. "What's the Ace-Lord want with such a small village?"

"He wants soldiers," Darion told him. "Gullible, fearful people are ideal for his enchantment. From what I know, he's already seized a few small farms in the Magno Forest." His face was grim and sad.

Allie looked at him, another question on the tip of her tongue. General Arrex asked it for her. "Then do you believe the Ace-Lord can forcefully inflict the enchantment upon his soldiers? I thought it was only for the willing."

Jan turned to Darion. "When the Aces sent notice to the duke of Wiverrun, what was the nature of the message? Did it sound like the people must be willing?"

"Yes, and no," Darion said slowly. "The messenger was a familiar face—a young man who used to live near Wiverrun. He was enchanted, you could tell by a glance. He said the enchantment would protect the people, that it would protect our families. He warned that if we refused it, the Ace-Lord would destroy us all along with the town."

He paused. "I'm trying to learn what I can about the Ace-Lord's enchantment. Whatever spell binds the soldiers to his will, there must be some way to break it. I do know, at least, that the people need to be partially willing to take the enchantment. But most of the time, the threats of losing their homes and families are enough to drive them to willingness."

There was a thoughtful pause. Allie wondered about the enchanted soldiers, bound in servitude to the Ace-Lord. The spell inflicted upon them had emptied them of all humanity—their memories, their lives, all was cleared away by the spell.

Yet if the people had chosen the enchantment, perhaps they could choose to escape it, too.

"That is interesting," Jan said in reply to Darion. "If the western fiefs blindly believe the Ace-Lord's lies, he could enchant as many of them as he needed, while they believe his false promises."

"Remember how Kado tricked the Hazes during the rule of Safacon, sire," Darion pointed out. "The Hazes were ordinary people, snared by the spell, just like the enchanted soldiers are trapped by the Ace-Lord. What if there's a way to free them and break the enchantment?"

"There may be," Jan said, though he looked uncertain. Kado's spell with the Hazes some twelve years ago had been a faulty one, and the Hazes had been freed once the weakness was discovered. Allie doubted the Ace-Lord's plan would be so easily dismantled.

She also didn't like the implication that the enchanted soldiers were still… well, human. It didn't align with the vengeful thoughts she often felt. She'd come to think of those soldiers as nothing more than crooked, heartless men who had joined with the Aces of their own twisted volition.

But what if Darion was right? What if some of them were just misinformed, lied to, tricked? What if their actions were no longer their own? What if, deep down, they still had some humanity?

"Perhaps we can investigate the enchantment during our time in Wiverrun, sire," General Arrex suggested. "Those people saw first-hand how one of their own was enchanted by the Ace-Lord. Others may have more details."

"Perhaps," Jan agreed. "It would be worth investigating further. If we could turn the Ace-Lord's forces against him, we could end the war without further bloodshed." He frowned thoughtfully. "I will have to assign a courier to lead that mission—meeting with the duke and establishing the garrison will leave little time to learn about the enchantment."

Allie looked at him as an idea came to her. "What if *I* led that part of the mission?" she asked slowly. "While you meet with the duke, I can try to learn about the Ace-Lord's spell and his plans for Wiverrun."

Jan turned to her. "You'd like to come to Wiverrun with us, you mean?"

"We can accomplish two tasks at once," Allie said, pressing her advantage. "I can speak with some of the townsfolk and see what they know. You said the Aces have approached the town recently," she said, turning to Darion.

The young ranger nodded, looking a little confused. "Well, yes, but I don't know how much the townsfolk would know."

"If the Ace-Lord's servants have been sent to try and sway the townspeople to his side, that would be key information to know," Allie said, turning back to Jan. "We might learn the Ace-Lord's tactics. And, if we find out that the Aces are threatening or bribing, then we'd learn the enchantment has to be voluntary."

She tried to hide her growing excitement at the idea. It had been over a year since she'd last helped with an investigation like this. The matter with Pellion Drona didn't count in her eyes, because she'd discovered his treachery completely by accident. She had survived the Aces' occupation of Caer Sia only from the shadows, waiting and hiding.

But if Jan agreed, she might help gain vital information that could even end the war.

"I expect the couriers are planning such a mission," Jan said, still looking unsure.

"They'll be in the south, near the desert—not in the Magno Forest. If we're in Wiverrun, it may be good to investigate there," Allie pointed out. She could tell no one much liked the idea of having the heiress of Caer Sia joining a potentially dangerous mission—Jan least of all.

"The townsfolk might be inclined to trust her over the official team," Darion conceded, glancing at Allie. "The western fiefs are notoriously close-lipped around strangers, sire. They'd be hesitant to tell a Caer Sian courier anything. But they might talk with the princess."

Allie threw him a grateful smile, surprised by the support. She turned to Jan again, studying her uncle's face. "The soldiers will be there to protect me. I won't do anything risky. If I uncover something dangerous, I'll be sure to involve you and General Arrex."

Jan thought for a long moment, then finally nodded. "Very well. I can see you're set on it. Work with Darion and see what you two discover in Wiverrun. And I have your word that you won't take unnecessary risks."

Allie decided not to point out that such risks were hardly something she could control, or that some risks were necessary for the mission's success. She only nodded, hoping her calm expression hid her overflowing excitement. Jan had agreed.

9

The Narivo Agreement

General Arrex decided that a force of one hundred soldiers would make up the company headed to Wiverrun, with the bulk of that number set to stay with the local garrison. After a few more questions were answered and logistics agreed upon, the council was adjourned, and the council room cleared out.

Determination and hope had replaced the restless uncertainty that had plagued Allie for months. Now, she would do something worthwhile. Not only would her mission lend aid to Wiverrun, she'd have the chance to prove to herself that she was capable of such a quest.

She lingered in the room to talk to her uncle, who was speaking to General Arrex. It was good to see Jan in control of the situation. His manners were calm and confident, befitting the High King of Caer Sia.

Once General Arrex had left, Allie moved to Jan. "So, we leave in two days?"

"Yes, if all goes according to plan." Jan studied her for a moment. Allie waited for him to warn her about the dangers of the mission or tell her not to worry, but all he said was, "You seem eager to go."

"I am. I mean—I know it's dangerous. But I'm glad we finally have a plan to act on," Allie said.

"Fair enough," Jan said with a slight smile. "And what of your own plan? What do you intend for this investigation of yours?"

Allie hesitated. Truth be told, her desire to go stemmed from ridding herself of the pent-up energy and anger that had been simmering inside her since Caer Sia had been attacked. It was not a quest for vengeance, she told herself firmly—she had better motivation than that. "Well, I thought I might talk with some of the townsfolk, and maybe the town guard too."

"That would be a good place to start," Jan said. "Darion is probably right about the people trusting you more easily than they would a courier." A thoughtful look entered his eyes, as if he was trying to decide how much to tell her. But all he said was, "I trust you will stay with the soldiers. General Arrex and his men will protect you better than I can."

"I'll be careful," Allie said. "We won't be fighting, will we?"

"Ideally," Jan said, but a faint smile touched his features. "Have you talked with Darion about your investigation?"

"I talked to him before the meeting," Allie said slowly. She was sure Jan wouldn't approve of the blunt questions she'd flung at Darion. "I was just… curious about the Marks, but he told me to ask you." She studied her uncle's face hopefully, wondering if he would elaborate. "He said that you have a plan."

"Ah. Did he ask you to join the investigation to Wiverrun?" Jan's face gave nothing away.

"No, I only thought of that during the meeting," Allie told him. She was glad he hadn't scolded her for asking Darion about the scars—not that Darion himself had told her anything of consequence. Part of her wanted to press for more details from Jan, but she decided against it. If she was going to Wiverrun, she would learn about his plan soon enough.

"Well, Darion is keen to learn about the enchantment," Jan said. "He is hopeful there is a way to break the Ace-Lord's hold on his soldiers. Since he has been investigating it longer, he might know more about it."

"Darion seems to know a lot of things," Allie said irritably. "I'm not fully convinced he's trustworthy—I don't like that he knew about Redeyes and didn't tell us right off. It… it reminds me of Drona."

The name tasted bitter in her mouth. She still felt a familiar anger remembering the treachorous former steward, and his conniving plan against Caer Sia.

"Darion is not Drona," Jan said. "I can judge that much of his character. He is impulsive, quick to act, reckless at times… like someone else I know," he added gently. "But he has also told me his story in full. I will explain everything soon, but for now, it must remain hidden, if our mission is to be successful."

Allie sighed and nodded, knowing he was right. "So, what else was Darion here for?" she asked. "He said he had a different task in coming to Caer Sia."

A frazzled-looking servant interrupted them before Ĵan could answer. "Excuse me, sire, but General Dandio has returned from Elimar."

Muffled voices came from down the hall, growing closer.

"Good," Ĵan said, satisfied. "I will meet with him once he has rested."

"Yes, well, he's decided to meet now," the servant said tiredly, glancing over his shoulder. The voices grew louder. Allie recognized her father's voice, the tone of which told her the news would be anything but agreeable.

Ajaha's voice was audible too, measured and patient, her words becoming legible as she approached. "It is wrong, yes, but it *is* legal, you know. There is still something we can do about it."

The servant stepped out of the way. Dandio entered, breathless, still wearing his full armor. Ajaha came after him, clad in the elegant uniform of a courier. The contrast between them was accentuated by the calm in Ajaha's manner and the obvious fire in Dandio's movements.

"Sorry to interrupt," Dandio said to Ĵan. "They said your meeting was over."

"It is, and it is of no matter," Ĵan told him. "Welcome back. How was your journey?"

"Journey was fine, though I'd have liked to have gone under different circumstances," Dandio said shortly. "It seems all darkness has broken loose while I was gone—is Glentree all right?"

"Glentree is recovering, and the doctors have tended him well," Jan answered. He looked at Ajaha. "I trust you told him of the situation here?"

"Partly," Ajaha replied. "I have further reports for you once Dandio has shared his news. My teams are prepared for the investigation."

"Investigation where?" Allie asked, looking at her mother.

"I'll tell you in a moment," Ajaha said, looking at Dandio, who had launched into his report as soon as Jan had reassured him Glentree was doing better.

"Yes, well, I'm glad he's improving, because I'll need his assistance in dealing with those Council buffoons later. Would you like to know what they told me—what their excuses were for staying out of the conflict?"

He paused for breath. "They said they will avoid the fight as long as they can. They said they don't *need* to become involved in a 'Caer Sian war'—now, I told them the war would affect us all, but they refused to listen—cowardly, Light-blasted mud—"

"Language, dear," Ajaha said mildly.

"Excuse me, love," Dandio apologized, then turned back to Jan. "At any rate—the Elimar Council cites the Narivo Agreement as reason to refuse giving aid. I fear the only thing that will convince them to join us would be an Ace attack on their city."

"The Narivo Agreement?" Allie repeated.

"Yes, it was a pact made between Caer Sia and Elimar before the

Dividing War," Dandio said. "Narivo was a Liznee—a diplomat. He helped form an alliance between Sia and the Elves of Elimar."

"I know what it is," Allie said. "How does it give them a reason not to help us, though?"

"The Agreement was written so that the Elven nation could remain independent of Sia's leadership," Jan told her. "At a time when nearly every kingdom was battling to reign supreme, the Liznees and Elves chose to ally as equals. It meant neither nation would hold power over the other."

"But Elimar is still a Coonsian city," Allie said, confused. "Don't you technically rule over them?"

"I do," Jan said slowly, "but according to the agreement, the Elves of Elimar have the right to make their own decisions in the event of war. We can't order them into battle. They must agree it is in the best interest of their people."

Allie looked at her father. "But I thought you have command over all the armies of Coonsia in times like this."

"Every army except Elimar's," Dandio said dryly. "They must make the choice to fight themselves. We can't recruit them into the war otherwise."

Allie frowned. She understood the importance of allowing Elimar the freedom to send their soldiers into battle, but now was not the time to argue over aiding their allies. "The Aces won't care whether Elimar is allied with us or not, though," she said. "If the Ace-Lord wants Coonsia, he'll attack Elimar eventually."

"True," Jan said, looking at Dandio. "I trust you made them aware of that?"

"Oh, as well as I could," Dandio said wearily. "They seem convinced that Elimar will remain protected by Sia's forces whether or not they send men to fight. They firmly believe the knights of the Red Dawn will defeat the Aces." He smiled wryly. "If they were not so drastically mistaken, I'd be flattered."

"The Red Dawn will need aid," Jan said. "Elimar must make an effort to defend itself. We can't protect every city in the north without help."

"And we won't have to," Ajaha said, tucking her notebook under one arm. "These agreements always have a loophole, as my dear husband calls them. The Narivo Agreement has such an exception, which states that in a time of national crisis, Elimar must investigate the matter themselves. If we present a detailed report that shows the true gravity of the Ace-Lord's schemes, we might persuade Elimar to protect themselves against him."

"And your team will cover that investigation?" Dandio asked. A little of the fire had gone out of him. He looked calmer.

"I am sure we can manage," Ajaha said, turning to Jan. "I am sending couriers and spies to the south, near Yamo. It is directly across the Mata Strait from where we assume the Aces to be. My couriers will also meet with the lord of Arkran—his warriors have kept a watchful eye on the Flats since we learned of the Ace-Lord's whereabouts there. After our investigation is finished, we will join the Elimar Council in Mata City so they can learn what we have found."

"And if the Council refuses to act even after your report?" Ĵan asked.

"Then that is breaking the Narivo Agreement, which is grounds for treason," Ajaha said calmly. "They will not go back on their word. The reports will call for action, and they will be forced to investigate. Once they do, they will find that the Ace-Lord is not a threat to be taken lightly. I highly doubt they will refuse to fight."

Ĵan and Dandio nodded thoughtfully. Allie hid a smile, impressed. "I thought we couldn't force them to do anything," she said to her mother.

"We aren't," Ajaha said. "We are only strongly suggesting—and once they find the truth of the Aces, they will know that they must join us in protecting the north."

Allie knew she was right. It was a tedious way to get Elimar's army to act, but she was sure it would work. Once Elimar understood the danger of the Ace-Lord's power, they would see the need for action.

"Well, I am thankful for your advice," Ĵan said. "Will you accompany your team south?"

"No, I will go to Badwater first, and speak with my contacts there. Then I intend to join Iriam's group in Mata City," Ajaha said. "The Coopers may have information about the activities near the Mata Strait. The Aces' soldiers may be ferrying forces south."

"The Coopers would know—they know the Strait better than

anyone," Dandio agreed thoughtfully. He turned to Jan. "You are leaving as well?"

"Not as far west as Mata City, but yes," Jan said. "I am accompanying General Arrex's men to Wiverrun." He threw Allie a smile. "And your daughter has a mission of her own."

Dandio arched an eyebrow at Allie. "Indeed?"

Allie nodded, eager to share her plan. "Yes—I'm going to investigate the Ace-Lord's enchantment. Darion Blackbird thinks the spell binding the Ace-Lord's soldiers can be broken. If we can figure that out, we might be able to free the enchanted soldiers and end the war."

Dandio looked impressed. "Well, that *would* be something. But if the Ace-Lord's soldiers have chosen their own fate, you would have to change their minds before breaking the spell."

"I know," Allie said, a little discouraged by that thought. "That's why we're hoping the soldiers didn't choose their fates—not directly, at least. Maybe they were tricked, like the Hazes were."

"Maybe," Dandio said thoughtfully. He turned back to Jan. "What do you need of me while you're gone?"

"You need not handle any logistics," Jan told him. "General Leopold will manage business here while I am gone. You may turn your full attention to preparing the Red Dawn."

"Good," Dandio said, satisfied. "I've already written up a few battle plans. The Guardians have agreed to set a blockade along our northern shores, and Admiral Dessian is coordinating our naval forces. Our strategy should be fully outlined by the time you return."

"I look forward to seeing it. Try not to wear yourself out," Jan said, only half joking.

It was good to see Jan's usual quiet humor had returned. He had been so grave and worried the last few days that Allie had begun to worry too. Now, with the plan decided and a journey awaiting her, she felt far more confident. Her mother's team would investigate in the south, and her father and the Red Dawn would protect Caer Sia and the north.

As for Allie herself, the intrigue of her coming mission helped distract her from the very real danger that lurked on the edges of her mind.

10

Castle Mata

The sun shone through a dreary cover of clouds as the ship
entered Mata City's harbor.

After his training session with Iriam, Rygal had returned to his
cabin and continued reading from the massive tome. He wasn't
exactly sure how late he'd stayed up. He'd fallen asleep sometime during
the night, still holding the quill, and found that he'd smudged
ink on his shirt sleeve. He had awoken to the cheery call of the
lookout—"Mata City to starboard, Cap'n!"—and hastened to get
ready.

Fifty members of the Guardians of Gayrile were to meet in Mata
City this afternoon. Rygal peered through the round window of the
cabin and watched as the ship swept inland. Massive rock outcrops
stretched toward them from shore, like a host of rugged watchmen.
The rocks were treacherous to the inexperienced seaman, forming
a natural barrier between the Cooper city and any unsuspecting
enemies. To their allies, however, the way was known, and ships
could be guided into the harbor with relative ease.

They passed the rock outcrops, entering one of the many canals
that crisscrossed the city. The Cooper people were an aquatic,

otter-like species, skilled in all manners of sea-faring, having lived and died by the sea since the world was made. They had mapped the treacherous rocks, carved out the canals so their ships could pass easily through the Strait, and made a kingdom on the rugged coast. Nowadays, Mata City was one of the principle ports in the northwest, situated between Caer Sia to the east, the isles of Gayrile and Kilee in the north, the settlements of West Coonsia, and the isle of Kamon directly south down the Strait.

A blistering cold breeze whipped Rygal's face as he stepped on deck, and he smiled idly at the thought of Kamon. A few day's sail south, and the weather would be warm and tropical. He'd travelled to Kamon during the quest for the Shards, and well remembered the soft sand and plentiful jungle trees.

"I hope your energetic expression means you have completed your reading," came Iriam's deep voice. Rygal turned to see the Neutral approaching, a hidden light of humor in his red eyes.

"I finished the chapters about fire forms," he answered with a nod, then admitted, "I'm not really sure I understand them, though."

Fire forms were the Guardians' equivalent to different spells and patterns they could use in combat. Certain words must be spoken while the staff—or sword—was positioned in just the right place. The slightest miscalculation could result in a different spell entirely.

Rygal had written down nearly half of the forms the book mentioned before falling asleep—there were still forms to study. He had made a list of all the uses of each spell. He'd also found, to his surprise, that some of the words were familiar to him. *Ventara* produced a vivid wall of flames. *Raeortar* caused an invisible shield to form before the wielder. *Revrandar* could intercept opposing spells and redirect their power.

"Did Safacon study Guardian magic?" he asked, as the memory came to him. "I recognized some of those spells. They could be used by the Objects of Power."

He had seen some of those spells used by Morel, one of his companions on the quest for the Jewel. He knew she had learned and studied what the Brownaes called Jewel-lore.

"Safacon was a pupil under Norrin before he was seduced by the Dark Realm," Iriam answered. "The Jewel's main power once came from the Land Immortal, as you may recall. As a Star-Stone, it held significant power over the Ring or the Knife. The Objects could be used as channels, just like a wizard's staff." His face was suddenly grave. "It was that combination of magic—the Jewel's twisted power, and the knowledge of Guardian fire-forms—that made Safacon such a threat."

Rygal well remembered those powers. There were other spells, unpleasant curses, that he had recognized in the book too. *Escrariae* could melt a man's skin like wax. *Relarg* caused the victim to be crushed by invisible stones. *Devrando* killed the person in an instant.

Norrin had written in the margins of these pages, too. "*Use only as a last resort,*" had been his thoughts on the killing curse, and "*Do not use unless necessary,*" near the other two.

Rygal didn't think he would need to remember the rest of the curses—most of them seemed either too complicated or too drastic to ever inflict on an opponent. But he mentally stashed away *Devrando.* He'd seen Deathcap, the maniacal owner of the Knife of Destruction, use that spell twice, with chilling success. It was a terrible curse, but it might be the Cantrian equivalent to the Aces' power of Essence destruction, which snuffed out life like a candle.

Iriam was studying him, as though he could read his thoughts. "The curses are less effective against the Aces," he said at length. "To take the Guardians' magic and use it in such a harmful way is corrupted magic, just as Kahlifis corrupted the Jewel by causing it to draw power from the Dark Realm. I think it wise to use the power as the High Light intended."

Rygal nodded shortly, knowing Iriam was right. After all, the Ace-Lord's ultimate strength would come from eroding the morality and hope of the mortals. He also knew, in a deeper part of him, that Norrin would disapprove of using such curses, even against the Aces.

"I'll focus on the other spells for now, then," he said, turning his attention back to the half-moon harbor before them. "Looks like we're coming up on the pier."

They had left the sea behind them, moving into the wide pathway of the Mata Strait. The rocky coast appeared the same on both sides of the Strait, but to the left was the island of West Coonsia, smaller and more rugged than its Mainland twin. While the main hub of Mata City was located on the Mainland, the city stretched across both sides of the Strait, like a stitch joining the country as one.

The curving harbor arched away on both sides of the ship. To their right, the rocky cliffs rose high above the sea. There perched Castle Mata, a simple yet well-built stone fortress overlooking the harbor. Rocky jetties and piers extended out into the harbor—Rygal could see a few Coopers seated on the jetties, fishing poles and nets in their furry hands, unperturbed by the chilly wind. Other ships and skiffs of varying design were tied at the dock. It was good to see that, despite the unrest and trouble in the world, business still continued up and down the Mata Strait as it had for centuries.

The sailors lowered the sails, allowing the ship to come to a gradual stop at one of the piers. Five Cooper dockhands bounded to meet them, helping the human sailors. Despite their small size, the Coopers worked quickly and efficiently, and the gangplank was soon lowered. The dockhands called greetings, padding back on their four webbed paws, thick fur protecting them from the cold sea air.

"Good morning," Iriam replied with a rare smile as he stepped down the gangplank. "Thank you for your assistance. Would you please inform Lord Roan that we have arrived?"

"That'll be my job," came a familiar voice.

Rygal turned, grinning. A male Cooper with dark brown fur was padding towards them with a smile almost too large for his otter-like face. "Jarus! It's good to see you."

"You too," Jarus replied. "Hello, Iriam. I hope your trip here went smoothly."

"It was quite enjoyable," Iriam replied. "I trust your family is well?"

Jarus nodded rapidly. "Yes, we're all doing fine. Maya is excited to see you," he added to Rygal. "She's begun designing a different type of skiff—she says it's based off of the ones that the men in Gayrile use to weather the Eastern Currents. I told her she'd better talk to you about that."

"I'm looking forward to hearing about it," Rygal replied. The dark conversations about curses had been cast aside by this reunion with the Cooper. "What's this about you reporting to Lord Roan?" he asked, studying Jarus carefully. Jarus seemed the same as ever, his dark brown fur clean and groomed, his blue eyes twinkling with cheer. But over his shoulders he wore a neatly designed sheath for his knife, and a small gold chain around his neck.

Jarus gave a small shrug as he led them down the pier. "Oh, well— news for you. I've been promoted to chief diplomat in Garilian matters in Lord Roan's court."

"You have?" Rygal said incredulously. "That's wonderful, Jarus. I knew you'd been working as a scribe in the castle, but that's quite a promotion."

"Yes," Jarus said, sounding slightly embarrassed. "I haven't really— that is, I didn't study to be a diplomat—still don't really know what the job entails, unless Lord Roan orders me somewhere specific. I think since—since I know people in Gayrile, like Lord Casper of the Direns, and the Brownaes—but I definitely didn't expect it, though."

"I am glad Lord Roan appointed you to that position," Iriam said, sounding satisfied. "He was wise to take my recommendation."

Jarus rounded on the Neutral; since Iriam was about four times his height, the effect was rather comical. "*You* recommended me? Light above, why?"

"I thought you the best selection for the job," Iriam said. "Your qualities recommend you very well. You are unassuming, quick to think the best of others, and naturally friendly and honest. After being away from your family on the quest for the Shards, it seemed the proper course of thanks."

"Well, thanks," Jarus said, a little awkwardly.

Rygal threw him a grin. "Iriam's right. You're the perfect pick for the job."

Jarus smiled again, clearly grateful despite himself. "Well—anyway, I've had that position for about seven months now, so it still feels new. Still having to get used to longer hours, different tasks, those sort of things."

"How's little Ella?" Rygal asked.

"Just turned a year old and she'll already talk your ear off," Jarus chuckled. "Sometimes I envy you humans—your children don't start talking till they're two or three at least. She's got about as many words as her mother does when she's on a tangent. Don't tell Maya I said that," he added hastily.

Rygal shook his head and laughed softly.

Jarus led the way down the stone walkways flanking the many canals in Mata City. As a port town, Mata City's canals allowed ships to sail directly through the town. Coopers perched on flat rafts, paddled skiffs, or swam through the canals. A few humans and Liznees were here too, and Rygal caught snatches of conversation in varying languages as they walked through the city center.

"Lord Roan met with Lammar just yesterday," Jarus said. "I think he wants to know how the Guardians are faring up north. You haven't seen any Aces in that area?"

"Not yet," Rygal said. "Lammar's had us on the lookout, though. Most people might not recognize the Aces' servants if they saw them."

"Lammar's taken over leadership of the Guardians?" Jarus asked.

"Temporarily," Rygal answered. "He doesn't want full command. Just directing us until someone steps up to the job." Normally, someone would be prepared to take command when the previous leader stepped down. Norrin never had the chance to select his successor.

He moved away from that topic. "Lammar was here yesterday, you said?"

"Yes, he'll be back in a few days. He took a quick trip back to Gayrile, said he wanted to meet with the Direns."

Lammar had mentioned this plan to Rygal a few weeks ago before Rygal had gone to Caer Sia. With everything that had happened since, he had forgotten about it.

They left the canals behind as the road sloped upward to Castle Mata. To the right, the cliffs fell away, revealing the thundering coast below.

Four burly Cooper guards stood at the castle entrance, but stepped aside as they recognized Jarus. Though built by the Coopers, the stone corridors and halls had been designed with taller species in mind. Iriam, the tallest of their party, did not even have to stoop as they entered the castle. Inside, a silver and blue banner with a golden fish in the center, the emblem of Mata City, hung from the high ceiling. A short hallway spanned the distance between the entrance and the meeting hall.

Waiting outside the hall was another Cooper, his dark fur only just beginning to show signs of gray. He wore a slender circlet of gold on his head, and smiled as they entered. "Good morning, and welcome to Mata City," he said with a slight bow.

"We thank you, Lord Roan," Iriam said, returning the bow. "Jarus tells me all is well here."

"Indeed it is. We are blessed with peace for the time being," Roan answered. "Please, come sit." He led the way inside the council room. A round table filled most of the room, with some short chairs set around it. A large window on the back wall offered a prime view of the sea, and the fire burning in the hearth filled the room with warmth and light.

"Jarus says you met with Lammar a few days ago," Rygal said once they were seated. "Did he explain our plan to blockade the northern end of the Strait?"

"He did," Roan said with a nod. "I believe it best, however unfortunate. Lady Ajaha Ki has sent a report to me as well, informing us that the Aces may be in the Salem Flats."

"So we believe," Iriam said. "And if it is true, their allies may be able to travel freely up and down the Strait. While we have heard the Ace-army does not have a large sailing force, we also know that the Ace-Lord will capitalize on any opportunity, and we must be prepared."

Roan nodded in grim agreement. "Well, the blockade will impede the Aces' progress to the north. But what of the smaller settlements in the south? What of Kamon?"

"It would be wise to send warriors to guard the south end of the Strait," Iriam answered. "We owe Kamon much after their faithful protection of the Shard, and the sacrifices they have made. Perhaps you might station three or four ships near the mouth of the Kamo Bay."

"We'd have to watch out for pirates," Jarus pointed out. "That's not far from Esile Bay, and a lot of pirate ships tend to sail through there."

"So they do. You might be surprised, though," Roan told him. "The last few traders who have sailed south have reported a shockingly low number of pirate vessels and minimal crime ring activity. The Dricaster Crime Ring of Esile City has reportedly vanished, though I can't imagine what could have led to such a thing."

"Nor I," Iriam said, but Rygal noticed a twinkle in his eye and assumed that Iriam knew, in part, what had led to the Crime Ring's end. "Thank you for your aid. Whether or not the Aces are in the Salem Flats, I believe we shall learn soon."

Rygal knew the couriers of Caer Sia would be working quickly to learn more about the Aces and their forces. He'd heard that Jan had received word about the Aces causing trouble in the Magno Forest, and would soon investigate it.

It was odd, he thought, that the Salem Flats and Wiverrun had both reported Ace-activity; they were miles and miles apart. Where was the Ace-Lord, and what was his plan?

The answer to those questions must be answered soon, he knew. Once they knew more about their enemies' movements, they'd gain an advantage in the coming war. But the question remained if they could learn that crucial information before the Aces made their next move.

11

Scars Past

It was late into Mel's turn at watch when he heard Aryion's voice, muffled with sleep, whisper the words of the Blood Oath.

Aryion had never told him certain details of the Oath. He had explained the solemn, unbreakable vow it represented, and told Mel how he'd sworn it to avenge his father. He'd expressed his regret of taking the vow, as well as the dark choices he had made while trying to fulfill it.

Since his Blood Oath had been fulfilled with the death of the orc chieftain Hagshrub, Aryion had changed. He was no longer the grim, world-weary ranger he'd been when Mel had met him. His mood was lighter; the weight of the Oath having lifted from his shoulders. And since resolving matters with his sister Bryn during their time in Esile, Aryion seemed truly free.

Mel was grateful for that. Nonetheless, he knew the past burden of the Blood Oath still lingered on his mentor's mind. The details had to be pieced together slowly, carefully, like a broken sculpture. To swear a Blood Oath of vengeance, as Aryion had, meant it would not be forgotten easily. Mel had been reminded of this last night, as he sat on watch next to the fire, listening to the distant wild sounds of the night birds. Across the camp, Aryion slept soundly, murmuring things Mel could only just catch. One phrase repeated itself more than once.

Warrior here this Oath I swear.

The Blood Oath might be gone, but it had dug its teeth into his mentor's life so long, it had almost become a part of him.

When Aryion had woken and relieved Mel of watch, Mel's thoughts lingered on the Oath as he tried to sleep. He dozed in and out of rest for the remainder of the night.

Aryion's voice called him out of half-sleep. "Up, Mel. We need to get moving."

Mel sat up and stretched, squinting in the pale light of early morning. The rising sun illuminated the budding trees surrounding the glade, and a thin coat of frost dusted the ground. He'd slept in his woolen jacket and vest, but the chilly air seemed to penetrate even his warm clothing.

"Cold," he commented groggily.

"Still early spring," Aryion pointed out with a slight smile. "I'm going to check the traps."

Mel nodded and edged closer to the fire while Aryion faded into the woods. Once he'd warmed up, he set the kettle to heat over the fire. If there was time to check the traps, he thought, there was time for a hot drink.

Out of habit, he checked their supplies. Plenty of food and clean water. They had stocked up before leaving Appledale three days ago, and could probably make it to Wiverrun with the supplies they had. Still, it was always worth getting fresh meat, which was preferable to dried trail meals.

Misty had sent him with a small tin of his favorite tea. The pleasant aroma cheered him up and dispelled the lingering thoughts of the Blood Oath.

By the time the water had boiled, Aryion had returned, carrying the traps in one hand and a field dressed grouse in the other. "Smells delightful," he commented. "Misty's gift, I assume?"

"Yep," Mel said, carefully pouring the tea into the mugs.

"Well, we have fresh meat to go with it," Aryion said. "Pass me the seasonings, will you."

Mel slid him the small pack containing the cooking supplies. At first, the newness of having to hunt their own food had felt utterly foreign. Now, months into ranger training, he was used to it. After all, this was the life of a ranger—long days of tracking and traveling, followed by evenings around a fire. Different, yes. Easy, no. But he wouldn't trade it for anything.

Aryion sliced the meat, seasoned it, and laid it in strips on the small cook rack over the fire. Mel handed him his tea, and they sat there in silence for a few moments.

"You were talking in your sleep last night, about the Blood Oath," Mel said at length. He was hesitant to bring it up, but he knew it was better to voice his thoughts than to let them fester.

Aryion glanced at him with a slight frown. "Was I?"

"Just a few words that I could catch," Mel said, trying to remain lighthearted. "You said a few things more than once. Have you been thinking about it a lot?" He could understand feeling remorse over the past—he still struggled with that himself.

"I suppose." Aryion took a sip of his tea and let out a breath. "It is fulfilled now. I suppose… it has been a part of my life for so long, my thoughts are slower to be rid of it." He glanced at his apprentice. "My actions to reach that point were wrong, as I have told you. But the Oath itself is not inherently evil."

The Oath, Mel knew, was a solemn promise sworn by a warrior only under the most serious of circumstances. He'd always assumed that promise must be grim and dark, and had never thought one could swear it for a good cause.

"I've never heard of that," he said, then admitted, "but I haven't met many people who've sworn Blood Oaths. Just you."

"And I am a poor example," Aryion said with the hint of a smile. He turned the meat over to cook on the other side, then leaned back. "If taken wisely, the Blood Oath can persuade you to do right. Swear it for the wrong reasons, or allow it to consume you, and you'll only harm yourself and others. Swearing the Oath for vengeance… that brings the person to a very dark place of mind."

He had grown quieter, staring into the fire. Mel felt bad for bringing it up, but he still had a question. "What do you say, in the Blood Oath?" he asked slowly. "Is it like… like a spell?"

Aryion shook his head. "The words are no more magic than any ordinary promise. It's your reason for swearing the Oath that holds true power, your frame of mind. The Oath itself…" He thought for a moment, recalling the words, then recited:

"Warrior here this Oath I swear,

May no dark night or mortal fear

May nothing cause this Oath to break,

This promise sworn, this Oath I make.

"And then you must seal it with your blood," he finished, holding out his hand to show the thin pale scar on his palm. It had faded slightly after nearly sixteen years, but remained a reminder of what had happened in the long past.

This was the most Mel had ever heard him talk about the actual swearing of the Oath. The truth was grim, but he felt better with his questions answered.

"Now," Aryion said briskly, seeming to set aside the memories, "eat, and let's talk travel plans." He divided up the meat between the two of them. It was a little tough and chewy, but the savory spices paired well with the sweet tea. Mel ate as Aryion unfolded the map.

"We're here," his mentor said, tapping an area in the dense woods east of the border. "South of Flora. Wiverrun is about forty miles northwest."

"Where will we cross into Coonsia?" Mel asked, a little warily. For some reason, crossing the border always involved some problem or other. On his first quest, they'd traveled through Deadmen's Flats in the far north to enter Coonsia, and had been attacked by a serpentine. Later, on the quest for the Shards, the companions had taken a shortcut over the Hallas River... where they had also been attacked by serpentines.

"The good news is," Aryion said, clearly guessing Mel's line of thought, "it's too cold for serpentines right now."

Mel grinned. "Good. But doesn't that mean the mountain passes will be blocked by snow?"

"They probably are, but we don't actually have to go through the mountains to reach Wiverrun," Aryion said. "We go around them. Skirt the foothills and head due northwest as if we're going to Badwater, but we won't go that far north."

Mel looked at the map. "So, we'll basically take the same road as we did on the quest for the Shards, then cut north?"

"In a nutshell, yes. I suppose Rygal's shortcut will be of some use again." Aryion turned a hard look to his apprentice—he'd been nothing but skeptical of Rygal's shortcuts during the quest for the Shards. "Don't tell Rygal I said that."

"I'll try to remember," Mel said lightly, looking at the map. "We're kind of far north to take that road, though. Does that mean we have to go south first?"

"Only to avoid the mountains," Aryion said. "We'll angle towards Tackert Fief, and cut west near the North Gulley cave area."

North Gulley.

Caves.

Darkness, seeping from the shadows.

Mel's whole body had suddenly tensed at the very thought of the caves, as though preparing to flee, and he shook his head. "No. We can't go there. We shouldn't go there. Not with the Stone."

He sensed Aryion looking at him with a puzzled frown, but Mel already felt the fearful memories filling him, like cold claws on his chest. It had been over a year—and yet he still felt the fear, saw the frantic flight through the caves as though it had just happened. He remembered running in the dark, striking his knees against the jagged rocks, fleeing for the distant light at the end of the passage. Remembered the trail giving way under his feet, the wraith of death lurking in the shadows for him.

"*Run, and don't look back,*" Llyrion had ordered, and Mel remembered the flare of blue light that protected him from meeting the same fate as his friend.

Aryion's hand on his shoulder steadied his reeling mind. "You're safe," he said quietly. "You're safe and you're right. We won't go that way. It's too far into Dwarve territory, and some of those tribes have allied with the Ace-Lord."

"I'm sorry," Mel mumbled, his face burning with shame. "I shouldn't have…"

"Don't apologize." His mentor's low, calm voice finally caused the swirl of painful memories to fade from his mind. It was past. Nothing he could do would change what had happened.

He took a shaking breath and looked up. "We… we can still go that way, if it's faster. Since we wouldn't actually go into North Gulley."

"No, we would not. But I would like to know what you prefer to do," Aryion said. "The Stone is yours to guard."

Mel slipped a hand into his pocket, fingers closing on the smooth Star-Stone within, and took another breath. "That way is faster. We need to get to Wiverrun."

"Very well." Aryion folded the map and gave him a slight smile. "Dark conversations for a bright morning, aren't they. Blood Oaths and caves."

"Yeah," Mel agreed, managing a weak laugh. The subjects were weighty ones, easier if left unsaid. But there was no forgetting, and so it was better to talk about it. His father always said it was smarter to learn from the past than to try to forget it.

And Mel *had* learned since then. Llyrion had died and Mel had been unable to do anything to help. From then on, he'd been determined that such a thing would never happen again. He was training of a ranger to protect his family, to protect Aryion, to protect the Stone, to protect anyone else that needed him.

They packed up camp and began to walk. The sun had risen, thawing the frost. Birdsong filled the woods.

They traveled for several hours, moving steadily southwest. Aryion had been teaching him Elvish, and had Mel recite what he'd learned as they walked. Finally, when the land sloped down toward the rocky hills circling the North Gulley, they cut due west. The

Diamond Cap Mountains were just visible above the foothills and towering trees.

Aryion called a halt a little past midday, and they ate lunch.

Mel's thoughts had moved away from Elvish verbs, and he had a different question. "Aryion, where do you suppose the Wildkids went?"

In an unexpected encounter, he and Aryion had met with a Wildkid reconnaissance team during their journey to Esile City. The group had been led by Mel's friend Dusty, the daughter of one of the Wildkid chieftains. It was Dusty's intent to rally her people against the Aces and renew the old alliances with the Mainland kingdoms. This was easier said than done—there were decades of hurt and mistrust between the Wildkids and Mainlanders.

Dusty's group had come to gather more information about the Ace-Lord and his forces, which might persuade the Wildkid Clans to join the fight. The last Mel knew of her, she and her group were travelling west from the coast, heading toward Coonsia—if Coonsia was their destination, which he wasn't sure about.

Aryion thought for a moment. "They mentioned meeting allies near central Coonsia," he said. "The Wildkid Clans have remained allies with many of the Diné—the native people of the Mainland. But they might have been delayed on the road."

"Delayed" could mean anything from bad weather to being attacked, Mel thought. There was just no way to know for sure. He was fairly convinced the Wildkids could survive anything, but he couldn't help worrying.

"Maybe the Liznees will send a group to find them," he wondered. He and Aryion had suggested this to King Ĵan and Dandio when they'd given their report after their mission. But Mel doubted this would happen. Even if the Liznees tried to go find the Wildkids, there was no guarantee the Wildkids would let themselves be found. No one knew where they were heading.

He knew they'd have to trust Dusty. She would join them eventually, so hopefully they'd see her soon.

They began walking again, continuing west. Mel was used to long days on the trail, but his legs were aching by the time evening fell, and they stopped and set up camp.

The woods had changed, the oaks and birch intermingled with the towering evergreens that made up the Magno Forest. They must be nearing the border.

"No trouble yet," Mel commented, relieved. His earlier observation that something always went wrong while crossing the border had been proven false. They had seen no serpetines, nor any other signs of danger. The journey had been a smooth one so far.

"Nothing yet at all," Aryion mused. "Have you noticed?"

Mel looked at him with a slight frown. "What do you mean?"

Aryion nodded at the road. "We've only just split from the main road to go north. That road is the main thoroughfare from Flora into Coonsia. It seemed a bit quiet today. Besides that, this has to be the quietest I've ever seen the Magno Forest," he added, gesturing around them.

Mel frowned. He hadn't noticed this, but now that Aryion pointed it out, they hadn't passed a single traveler today. Aside from the occasional bird, they'd seen next to no wildlife, either.

The Magno Forest was silent, drained of activity, as though the living things had fled before a coming storm.

PART 2

The Fate of Wiverrun

12

The Western Roads

"Company, halt!"

At General Arrex's order, the Red Dawn soldiers reined in their horses and came to a halt on the hilltop. The animals snorted and nickered, their breath making clouds in the chilly evening air.

Allie swung down from the saddle, patted her horse, and tried to stretch her aching legs. Despite the long ride and the growing cold as evening fell, she was thoroughly enjoying the journey. Anything, she thought, was preferable to the months of anxious boredom she'd endured recently.

It had taken a day to assemble and prepare the company. One hundred riders had left Caer Sia this morning. Allie had wished her parents goodbye, then joined Jan, General Arrex, and the rest of the soldiers in the courtyard to begin the journey southwest.

Since leaving Sia behind, they'd stopped only twice for brief rests. General Arrex led them at a brisk pace, alternating between walking and jogging the horses up the winding mountain roads. Now, the soldiers came to a halt on a flat-topped hill shadowed by redwood trees.

"Have a drink," Jan said behind her. He held out a flask.

Allie took it and drank gratefully; her throat was parched. "Thanks," she said, then added, "Are we camping here tonight?"

"That is a question for General Arrex," Jan said with a slight smile. "But I would expect so. We have made good time. The route ahead will be slower and more tedious."

"Why?" Allie asked.

Jan nodded to the left, where the land sloped gradually up. Through the trees, Allie could see an endless rising and falling of wooded hills. The road snaked up each slope in a series of switchbacks before descending the opposite side.

"The road becomes treacherous in this part of the Magno Forest," Jan told her. "All those ups and downs over the hills will be very taxing on the horses. We will have to go carefully."

Allie stared at the immense forest, awed by the vastness of the land. From their position, the woods seemed to stretch on forever, an endless carpet of green. Far ahead, she could just make out the dip in the land that marked the Mageo River. The village of Wiverrun, she knew, lay in that valley. "How long do you think it'll take us?" she asked.

"Two days, perhaps more with a group of this size," Jan said.

Allie nodded. Laden with supplies as they were, the progress over the foothills would be slow. "You came through this way from Kamon during the quest for the Shards, right?" she asked. "How long did it take then?"

"Not long, but it was not this exact route," Jan said. "And remember, we were carried most of the way by Fireclaw, king of the kragons."

"Maybe we could do that," Allie suggested with a grin.

"Maybe," Jan said, shaking his head. "Though finding such a kragon could be difficult."

They set up camp and built a few fires. Allie and Jan joined General Arrex and Darion Blackbird at a campfire. The Hyenin general and the ranger were deep in conversation.

"How far from the edge of town is it?" Arrex was asking as Allie sat down.

"Five miles, maybe," Darion said. He had etched a map in the frosty ground beside the fire. "You have the city here, on the other side of the hills across from it."

"Across from what?" Allie asked.

Darion glanced up. "The ruins I mentioned at the meeting. An ancient monastery, the locals think."

"We may be able to use it as our barracks, sire," Arrex said to Jan. A thoughtful light filled his golden eyes. "It's near enough to the village for us to work with the town guard, but we'd have more room to house the men."

"You might," Darion said slowly, "but like I said before, you may want to scout the area first. Someone or something may live there now."

Jan was frowning slightly. "Where did you say this ruin is?"

"On the outskirts of the town," Darion said. "The villagers avoid it—they believe it to be cursed."

"They have good reason to believe that," Jan said slowly. "The ruin has been there for centuries—I am surprised it is still standing."

"Do you know anything about that area, sire?" General Arrex asked.

"A little," Jan said. "It was a castle, Darion, not a monastery. But its construction is unlike any other in Coonsia." He paused. "I thought it was deconstructed by the inhabitants of the Magno long ago."

Darion shook his head. "It's been plundered, but it still stands."

"Whose castle?" Allie asked. "Weren't these lands once ruled by the Elves?"

"It did not belong to the Elves," Jan said. "This area was known as Caer Droco." He paused again before finishing. "It was the domain of Kahlifis."

There was a brief, stunned silence, broken only by the crackle of the fire.

"I… I thought the Aces ruled from the Salem Flats the last time they were here," Allie said finally. From the little she knew of the first Ace-rise, the Ace-Lord had taken control of a farming village and turned the eleven inhabitants into the Aces. That had been over thirty years ago, during the reign of her grandfather King Galaruel.

"They did, but Kahlifis' kingdom was here long before he claimed the title Ace-Lord," Jan said. "Before the Dividing War, Kahlifis ruled from Caer Droco, in the heart of the Magno Forest. After he was defeated, the area was all but forgotten. Then the Aces reappeared, striking from Ar-Salem."

"Why didn't they retake their old castle?" Allie wondered.

"I believe they would have," Jan said. "But there was something else in the ruin of Castle Droco at that point—the wraith that served the Ace-Lord's purposes."

Allie had forgotten the Darkness had been in Orlell at that time. The first Ace-rise had been followed shortly thereafter by the Darkness' attacks. "Was… was Redeyes in Castle Droco then, too?" she asked. "You said Redeyes used to command the Darkness."

"He was," Jan said. "It was he that ordered the Darkness into Caer Sia—though he was not there during the attack." He moved past the painful topic, turning to General Arrex. "If the castle ruins are truly uninhabited, then your men would do well to settle there. It is a prime position."

"*If* it's uninhabited," Darion echoed uneasily. "It's too ideal a position. I would be surprised if the Aces haven't noticed that."

"Do you believe they've taken the ruin?" Arrex asked him.

"I don't know," Darion said. "There's… something there, I'm sure of it. It might be a servant of the Aces, or something else. I don't believe all the local superstitions, sire, but I do think the Aces have a plan for the ruin."

Jan studied him a moment, then turned to Arrex. "Scout it well. I agree with Darion—while the Darkness is gone, there are other creatures in the Magno Forest that may now inhabit the ruins. We also need to be on the watch for Redeyes."

Though his expression remained calm, Allie noticed the lines of worry etched into his tired face. He seemed to become grimmer at the mention of Redeyes.

Her gaze travelled across the fire to Darion. The yellow light played over his face, reflecting in his hazel eyes, accentuating the burn-like scars. She thought back to what he'd told her in Caer Sia— he had met Redeyes at some point, been Marked by him. When and why, she had no idea. Part of her still felt suspicious—another part wanted of her to trust him, if only to learn more of Redeyes.

General Arrex stood. "We will investigate the ruin either way. If the Aces intend to gain Wiverrun, they may attempt to retake Caer Droco." His foxlike face was thoughtful. "I will scour the maps."

"I want to look over our route as well," Jan said, standing to join him. "It would be wise of us to learn more of the land."

The two of them walked over to a group of captains who were pouring over a map by another fire. Allie watched them go, wondering about the Ace-Lord's schemes, about the plan Jan kept hidden, about the scars. Darion remained seated. There was a short, awkward silence.

"So… do you have any ideas for investigating the enchantment?" Darion asked eventually, glancing up at her.

"A few," Allie said slowly. "I don't have a solid plan. I've never really done anything like this before," she admitted.

"Well, that makes two of us," Darion said with a wry smile. The expression did not reach his eyes—they remained serious and sad.

"When did… this happen?" she asked after a pause, bringing her hand at a diagonal across her face to mimic the scars.

Darion stared into the fire. "About two months ago."

Allie raised her eyebrows. "That's not long ago. How did they heal so quickly?"

"The Marks aren't normal wounds," Darion said slowly. "They stop bleeding very quickly, like they've been cauterized." He gave a slight shrug. "Redeyes can't have his targets bleeding to death before the curse takes effect, after all. They need to be an example, a sign of the curse."

Jan had said something similar when he'd told her about Redeyes, Allie remembered. The Marks represented the curse, the Ace-Lord's promise of an eventual reckoning. With the Darkness gone, the Aces would either have to summon another wraith, or fulfill the curse themselves.

"So...Redeyes Marked you to curse Wiverrun?" she asked slowly. It was strange referring to the scars as Marks. Reducing a living person to nothing more than a symbol, a representation of the destruction to come. How cruel to place that burden on someone. She continued. "Why wouldn't the Aces just destroy the town themselves?"

Darion thought for a moment. "I'm the ranger of Wiverrun. I suppose they wanted to show that no one, not even a ranger, was invulnerable to their power."

Allie nodded slowly. That made sense. Causing panic among the people made it all the easier for the Ace-Lord to force them into his service. His power would grow with their fear.

"Why didn't you send word to Caer Sia sooner?" she asked. "We could have helped."

"The duke deemed it unnecessary," Darion said. "I think he feared that no one in Caer Sia would believe the truth. After all, Redeyes was believed dead."

"That hardly seems his decision to make," Allie said, shaking her head.

He smiled again, that faint, almost sardonic smile that covered any other emotions on his face. "The duke did what he thought was best. Once he was persuaded that the Aces were a threat, I was sent to Sia."

Allie frowned. This account did not align with what she had assumed of the duke. Up till now she had thought of him as a courageous leader, sending a plea for help for his village. To know he had willingly concealed the Marks and Redeyes concerned her.

"Jan won't like that," she said, half to herself. "*I* don't like it, either. I feel a lot of information has been left out."

"We'll get to the bottom of it," Darion said. He cleared his throat, seeming to move past it. "So—what do you know of the enchantment so far?"

Allie nodded, grateful for the change in topic. "Yes. I don't know much. Jan's told me some—they interrogated a goblin captive after the Kamon battle, who had served one of the Jenna chieftains. The goblin told them a bit about the enchantment then. I know it erases memories." She paused, a little uncertain on the subject. "I've only seen the enchanted soldiers up close a few times. They look normal, except…"

"The eyes?" Darion finished for her, and when she nodded, he shook his head. "Blue and empty. The enchanted soldiers are still people, as far as I can tell, but they're completely controlled by the Ace-Lord's power. They're empty vessels for his plan now."

Allie could understand that. From the little she'd seen, the enchanted soldiers had hardly any free will. They fought as a mechanical force, controlled by the Aces.

"I wonder if they have any conscious thought of their own anymore," she mused. "Do you think you can still break the enchantment if they can't think for themselves?"

"Maybe not by words," Darion said, "but there has to be a way. The Liznees thought the same thing about the Hazes, you know— and yet your father learned how to turn them back."

Allie hoped he was right. Yes, the Liznees had managed to turn the Hazes back to mortal men. From what she'd heard, once the Hazes had been reminded of their past lives, they had managed to break free of Kado's mind-numbing control. But that had been a fluke, a twist of fate thanks to Kado's faulty spell. She doubted they'd so easily break the Ace-Lord's enchantment.

. . . . . .

The morning dawned gray and cloudy. Allie woke shivering, packed up her bedroll, and hurried to warm up by the fire. Her body ached from yesterday's long ride. The stiffness in her muscles and the bitter chill of morning dampened her excitement for the mission.

General Arrex wanted them on the road as soon as possible. Allie had time to eat a biscuit and take a few sips of coffee before the camp was packed up, and she was back in the saddle, climbing the first of the rising hills. The sun rose behind them, warming her back, and easing her sore muscles.

She turned in the saddle to look back at Darion, who rode just behind her. "You've been learning about the enchantment for a while now, right? What have you learned so far?"

"Not enough," Darion said grimly. "The Aces keep their secrets close." He thought for a moment. "I'm fairly certain the enchantment is a choice. Whether or not the people understood what they were choosing, that's what I'm trying to figure out. I've seen enough of the enchantment to convince me the Ace-Lord needs willing servants, and he'll do what he can to gain them."

"How many other villages have the Aces taken?" Allie asked.

"Four, five maybe. There are a few small farms in the Magno Forest, not far from Wiverrun," Darion said. "We've only heard rumors."

The trail slanted sharply downhill, and Allie's horse whinnied uneasily as they began the steep descent. General Arrex called from up ahead. "We may injure our mounts on these roads. Better to walk them until the road is easier."

The company dismounted. Allie's stiff legs protested, but the walking eased the cramps in her muscles after a bit. Darion walked behind her, leading his horse. He moved easily, clearly used to walking the steep roads. "You look comfortable," Allie remarked to him.

He shrugged slightly. "I was trained here. Walking these mountain trails helps condition your body for long days of travel."

Allie skidded and had to catch herself against the rock face on her left. "I can understand that," she said.

"We should be grateful there's no snow up here," Darion said. "These trails become very slippery with winter."

"Bet they make for perfect sledding though," Allie said with a grin. "When it snows in Caer Sia, we go up into the hills to sled or race dog teams."

"Yes, we do that in Wiverrun too," Darion said, smiling. "They used to train the dogs up here in the winter—these sharp trails are perfect for it. We'd come up here as kids to watch."

"We?"

"My brother and I—he's five years older." A little of the light had faded from his eyes, and his expression was solemn again.

"I always wanted a sibling," Allie said, keeping the subject light. "It was a little… lonely, growing up. Outside of school friends, I was alone a lot."

"I doubt you're alone much now," Darion pointed out.

"No," Allie agreed with a smile. The friends she'd made in the last few years—Rygal, Mel, Misty, Dusty—they felt like part of her family now. It had been a long time since she'd felt lonely.

They talked of other things as they rode. Allie found there was little Darion had not done—he and his mentor had travelled across most of Coonsia, walked the rolling dunes of the Lago Desert, and sailed to the empire of Kilee in the far north. The Meadowlark had trained him in both archery and knife work.

Allie listened eagerly as he told her of his travels, and in turn told him about her own adventures in Caer Sia. Darion was clearly impressed as she told him about the battle against the Darkness two years ago. She felt a renewed sense of satisfaction that she could be involved in the fight again.

At last, the party reached the ravine at the base of the hill. Towering trees cast deep shadows around them, their trunks as wide as a carriage. Some of the trees had been hollowed out so that the path wound through them. The company was embraced by the forest, and the pleasant smell of evergreen filled the air. The clouds had faded away, and midmorning sunshine illuminated the branches.

A brook flowed through the tree-filled ravine, and they stopped to allow the horses a quick drink. The next hill rose before them, and Allie already felt tired looking at the steep trail.

"Just a few more climbs," Darion said.

"Glad to hear that," Allie said dryly.

The horses finished their drink, and Allie had just swung back into the saddle to begin moving again, when a sudden wind rippled through the ravine, shaking the boughs of the towering trees. The horses startled, snorting and shuffling back with nervous whinnies.

"Archers, form up," General Arrex ordered sharply, and the warriors grouped together, with a ring of archers taking positions before them.

Allie steadied her horse, glancing swiftly around the glade for any sign of danger. Nothing moved in the shadowed trees. Yet she sensed, more than saw, a presence that had entered the ravine, as though the trees were suddenly watching them with unfriendly eyes.

Uneasily, she drew her sword. Beside her, Darion had nocked an arrow to his bowstring, his hazel eyes scanning the woods.

"Hold," came Jan's steady voice. He stepped forward, one hand on Drisilas' hilt, the other held up in caution.

"What is it?" Arrex asked, his voice edged in uncertainty.

"They say there's ghosts in these parts of the Magno, sire," one of the soldiers commented fearfully.

"Wait," Jan said simply. With a sign from Arrex, the archers lowered their bows, waiting as the wind swirled around them.

A slender figure seemed to rise out of the ground before Jan in a cloud of swirling leaves. A woman, her skin translucent green like the water of a river, her hair as delicate and green as new ferns as it floated around her face. She hung suspended by the breeze, deep blue eyes filled with an ancient and wild light.

"Son of Sia," she breathed, her voice like the wind whispering through the firs. The horses shied uneasily, and the archers raised their bows again.

"Wait," Jan repeated, standing between the figure and the soldiers. His hand remained on Drisilas' hilt, but he did not draw it as he took a step forward. "I am here. Speak, lady of the dryads."

The woman let out a shivering breath. The wind shifted around her translucent frame. "I come on behalf of my brethren. If ever your people cared for our sake, we beg you help us now. It is naught but sunrise that dryad blood has been spilled."

Allie gripped her sword tighter, a different fear filling her. Jan's voice was calm, but heavy with concern. "What are you saying? Who has dared threaten the dryads of the Magno?"

Anger and grief flashed in the dryad's strange eyes. "Kahlifis, the Lord of the Realm Beyond," she replied. "His Messenger came in the night, as in the days of old, and demanded our surrender. We refused, and so the Messenger destroyed five of our court. Their trees stand dead and silent." She bowed her head, and the wind tore the branches of the trees around them in a tempest of her grief.

Jan looked stunned. "The Ace-Lord," he murmured, half to himself. "Why would he dare strike the ancient trees?"

"He knows of our powers, sire," the dryad answered. "He fears us, we who see all and speak of none. He fears the alliances of the old days, when my people aided the mortals in their fight against him."

Allie exchanged a quick glance with Darion and saw from his face that he was as confused as she was by this new information. She knew the dryads had dwelt in the Magno Forest since the beginning of time, but she had never heard of an alliance between them and the mortals.

"Return to your people," Ĵan said finally. "Caer Sia will investigate this. For now, I urge you and your people to travel east, to our allies among the hama-dryads." He paused. "There is one thing more I must ask. It has been many years since the alliance you speak of, but you know we will need your aid to defeat the Aces. The trees must be our eyes and ears. You must seek the Druids."

"It shall be as you ask, sire," the dryad agreed.

"Our thanks and prayers go with you," Ĵan said. "May the Light guard your steps."

"And yours," the dryad returned. The leaves swirled around her as she bent in an elegant bow, then vanished before them in a final gust of wind. Allie could hear the breeze of her invisible passage as she swept away deeper into the Magno Forest.

General Arrex broke the stunned silence. "I did not know the dryads still inhabited these lands," he said. "It is good to know. But what alliance did you and the lady speak of?"

Ĵan was silent for a moment. "My father told Dandio and me stories when we were boys," he said. "Stories of how the dryads allied with the mortals during the Dividing War, seeing every action of Kahlifis and sending messages among the allies. I fear the time has come again for them to help us."

He turned and swung back into the saddle. "For the dryads to flee their lands tells me the situation is dire indeed. We need to get to Wiverrun as soon as we can. Once there, I'll send a message back to Sia letting them know what's happened."

"Sire," one of the captains ventured uneasily, "does this mean Redeyes is already in these lands?"

"Possibly," was all Ĵan said.

Allie sheathed her sword as they started up the winding road, and jogged her horse forward to Ĵan. "Who are the Druids, Ĵan?"

A slight smile crossed her uncle's face. "Well, that's something you shall have to ask Iriam. Nonetheless, if the dryads are to join us, the Druids must reveal themselves as well."

Allie was left wondering as they continued the perilous ride uphill. They saw no more of the dryads. But occasionally, a stray breeze blew past them headed east, and if Allie looked just right, she could have sworn she saw piercing wild eyes.

13

Rumors of the Shadow

Mel's uneasiness grew as he and Aryion journeyed deeper into the Magno Forest. Despite the well-worn roads and occasional traveler they passed headed one way or another, the strange silence continued as they continued southwest. Aryion's observation was right, the forest seemed devoid of activity. It was fortunate they'd set the animal traps before crossing the border—since entering Coonsia, they had seen no game at all, aside from a few skittish birds that flew up in a chorus of squawks as they passed.

Mel could tell the ominous quiet had begun to grate on Aryion's nerves too. His mentor urged them on faster, stopping only when it grew too dark to see, then continued as soon as dawn had arrived. The relatively easy roads of west Daffodalion soon sloped into treacherous draws and gulleys, rising up and over the foothills.

As the third night fell in the Magno Forest, a thin layer of frost dusted the ground, a soft wind blew to the east, and the quiet seemed as impenetrable as the darkness. They stopped at a spring to refill the water flasks. Aryion, his jaw set in a tight, worried line, set to work lighting a fire in silence while Mel refilled the flasks.

"What's going on here?" Mel asked at last, no longer able to stand the tense silence.

Aryion let out a breath, his dark eyes scanning the shadowed woods. "I can't tell," he said, his frustration and unease evident in his tone. "There are no tracks, no signs, no indication of a mass migration. The animals are simply gone, as if they've vanished into thin air."

Mel laid out his bedroll, racking his mind for an explanation. He could think of nothing that explained the lifeless state of the forest. "Do you think… do you think it's because of the Aces?" he asked.

"Maybe," Aryion said. "If the Aces were near, the animals probably would have fled… but if that were so, we would have seen their tracks. We've found no sign of anything at all."

Mel nodded, searching for another theory that explained the vacant woods as he unpacked the rest of the gear. Each thought became darker. Finding no explanation, he huddled by the fire. The massive trees had offered a pleasant shade in the day, but in the growing darkness they felt ominous, towering guardians of a forest that no longer felt safe.

"I'll take first watch," he offered, partly because he could tell Aryion needed the rest, and partly because the nervousness made it impossible to feel tired.

Aryion agreed with a short nod. Mel sat with his back to the fire, staring into the dark woods, holding his dagger in one hand and the Blue Stone in the other. The pure blue light comforted some of his fears, and reminded him of the promise of the Prophecy. The High

Light was watching over them, even here.

And yet…

The time is coming soon, coming soon, coming soon,

Your futile battle sealed your doom.

He hunched down, trying to steady his breathing and listen for any sounds of life in the woods. There were none. The only noise came from the crackling fire and the quiet breathing of the two rangers. The Magno Forest absorbed their sounds and gave none in reply.

Aryion relieved him of watch in a few hours—his mentor had the uncanny ability of waking up exactly when he needed to—and Mel tried to go to sleep. But the doubt and unease lingered in his thoughts. Why couldn't they—for once—get a straight answer from the High Light of what to do? Why couldn't they get a detailed plan, instead of a cryptic Prophecy that seemed to spell out their end?

His nervousness turned to frustration. The quest for the Shards had made the High Light's presense and promises seem so real. The victory against the Aces, his own involvement in the Prophecy, and Cahadras' reassurances had reinforced his faith that all would end well. Yet here, alone in the desolate wilderness, he felt forgotten. It seemed the Prophecy had moved on and left the New Blood to fend for himself alone.

Maybe I am forgotten, a nagging voice suggested from the corners of his mind. He knew it was a lie. But the fact that the New Blood's role had ended, as written in the Prophecy, brought him no comfort.

To him, it was another grim reminder that there was no longer a promise guaranteeing his own survival.

· · · · · ·

Dawn brought no ease to his troubled thoughts, but at least the morning light calmed his nerves. They packed up and began to walk again, crossing the Hallas River. Here the dwindling path intersected with the road heading northwest, leading up and over the rolling forested hills. Aryion found tracks he did not recognize, but they seemed animal, which reassured Mel that there was still some life in the Magno Forest.

Mel's thoughts turned to Wiverrun, and what they might find there. Jan's letter had given very few details. He'd only said that the Aces wanted to claim the town.

"Why?" he wondered to Aryion as they walked. "Wiverrun's a small village, isn't it? They won't have many warriors. What do they have that the Ace-Lord wants?"

"I'm not sure," Aryion admitted. "I doubt he wants the land itself, unless he has a need for marble."

"Marble?" Mel repeated, puzzled.

Aryion nodded. "Wiverrun's largest resource is the marble in the hills. The town was founded on it. They export it to the larger cities in the north."

From what Mel had seen of the Ace-Lord, he knew he had planned out every step of this conquest. But Mel doubted the Aces would try to seize a quarry, not without an ulterior motive.

They continued on, hiking up a series of switchbacks. Despite the chill in the air, Mel was soaked in sweat by the time Aryion called a halt in a shallow draw. A creek flowed through the ravine, and the towering redwood trees filled the valley with pleasant shade.

"Catch your breath," his mentor said. "We'll continue in a moment."

Mel sat by the creek, breathing deeply as he watched the water stream by. To his right, the next hill loomed before them as though to taunt him. His heart sank a little.

Aryion's call startled him. "Mel—come quickly."

Mel drew his dagger and ran through the ferns to reach him. Aryion stood on the road, hands on hips, studying the ground. "What is it?" Mel asked, relaxing as he saw there was no immediate danger.

Aryion nodded to the ground. Recent tracks marked the path—horse hooves and footsteps, many of them. "What do you make of that?"

Mel frowned. "A mounted force… a lot of them."

"Looks like it," Aryion said thoughtfully. "I noticed it when we came up the last hill, but I had not realized how fresh these tracks are."

Mel had worried at first that it could be Aces, but that seemed unlikely. The Aces had no horses, and from what he'd heard, none of their forces did, either.

He walked down the trail a little ways. The tracks, he could see, had come from the northeast, and they seemed to be headed for Wiverrun.

"Elves from Elimar, maybe?" he suggested at length. "But this is a big group."

"A very big group," Aryion agreed, stroking his beard as he studied the ground. "I'd assume an entire company. Who they are and where they're from, we can only guess, but they appear to be headed toward Wiverrun."

Mel looked at the tracks for a long moment, hesitating to suggest his idea. "Aryion," he began finally.

His mentor glanced at him. "Yes?"

Mel nodded to the trail. "A group this size won't be travelling very fast on these roads. Do you suppose we could catch up to them and figure out who they are?"

A slow smile appeared on Aryion's face. "We might," he replied.

14

A Crossing of Paths

Noonday sun shone down on the Red Dawn company as they rode west.

There had been no sign of the dryads since yesterday's interaction. Allie hoped they had taken Jan's advice and headed east to join the hama-dryads. That area, at least, would be safer for now. She also wondered about the alliance Jan had mentioned, and if the dryads would join the mortals against the Ace-Lord. Such a thing had not happened since the Dividing War, centuries ago now. The dryads had not been present during the first Ace-rise, or at least, not involved in the fight itself. But the Ace-Lord had evidently attacked the dryads regardless, and that might sway them to join the Liznees.

She guided her horse closer to Jan's as they crested another hill and started down the steep slope. "Jan, do you think the dryads will join us? If the Aces attacked them, it might be enough to convince them to join the war."

"It might," Jan said slowly. "The dryads have not interfered in the affairs of mortals since the Dividing War. I believe the only species they interact with at all nowadays is the Stars."

"The Stars?" Darion repeated, interested. He rode a little behind

Allie. "Do you think the Stars will fight with us, then?"

"Maybe. It's difficult to predict what the Stars will do," Ĵan said with a slight smile. "They must do as the Prophecy has said, and I doubt they can interfere otherwise. Still, they will help if the High Light commands them to do so."

"Well, let's hope that happens," Darion said wearily. "We could use their help."

"Yes. But we must continue to act without them," Ĵan said. "Wars have been won without them in the past. The Prophecy assures us of our victory with or without the Stars."

Hopefully, Allie added mentally, but kept the thought to herself. She didn't want to voice her doubts now. The Prophecy's confusing words hardly reassured her of victory. They remained an ominous, cryptic warning she could not decipher.

"How does the Prophecy say we'll defeat the Aces?" Darion asked her as Ĵan moved forward again.

"To be honest, I'm not sure," Allie said. "Iriam had me memorize it for my studies, but I still don't understand it." She recited the Prophecy as they walked.

Darion frowned thoughtfully as she finished. "Not what I pictured," he said. "At least, I expected more of a plan. *Do this and you'll win,* that sort of thing."

"Me too," Allie said with a sigh. "Iriam said the words will reveal themselves in time, but I don't understand them. Besides, if the second stage is here now, shouldn't we know what to do?"

"You'd think so," Darion agreed. He thought for a moment. "That third stanza is about the second stage, right?"

"Third and fourth, from what I can tell," Allie said. The Prophecy followed a fairly basic layout. The first and second stanza contained the events of the first stage—most of their words had been fulfilled when Mel joined the Shards last summer. The third and fourth stanzas were the second stage, and those events were happening now or soon. The fifth and sixth showed the end of the war—the third and final stage, events that must happen for victory.

The seventh stanza, she had assumed, was a review of everything that had been prophesied, as though reiterating that every event was interconnected. As for the eighth… well, that just seemed like another ominous warning:

Spells and Stones, mortal roles, hold your hope,

Lest the Ace-Lord take your bones.

Not very comforting.

The land had begun to change as they continued west. The hills, though still numerous, were less steep here. The valley they entered was filled with lumpy gray rocks and scraggly bushes standing out from the tall redwoods. Allie knew the Magno Forest would begin to thin out the farther west they went, where the towering redwood trees would fade away before the rocky shores of the Mata Strait. Allie strained her eyes to glimpse it, but could see nothing over the rolling hills.

"There's one area of the Prophecy that might help us now," she said to Darion, returning her attention to the conversation. "That part about the unwilling mortal, bound by a spell. What if that's about the enchanted soldiers? They're unwillingly bound by the Ace-Lord's spell, forced to do his bidding."

Darion frowned thoughtfully. "That's not a bad guess. I wish the Prophecy included more about how to break the enchantment, if that's the case. Have you suggested that to the king? He seems to know the Prophecy pretty well."

"He does, but he's not sure either," Allie said with a sigh. The one person she wanted to talk to was Iriam. The Neutral could help them sort out some of their theories, and he may be able to help them understand the enchantment too. "I wish we had some solid answers," she said, frustrated. "The best I can do is come up with ideas."

"Well, they're not bad ideas, princess," Darion said.

"Just call me Allie," she corrected him with a smile, then added, "I just wish we could know for sure."

"Did you learn anything about the Prophecy in your studies? You said Iriam had you memorize it."

"Yes, but as luck would have it, he left to Mata City before I could ask him anything," Allie said wryly. "I doubt I'll be able to talk to him until after we've finished our mission to Wiverrun."

"Maybe we'll answer some of our questions ourselves," Darion mused.

"Maybe," Allie repeated dryly, but despite her doubts, she found she was glad the young ranger was here. This mission had given her a purpose, and she was encouraged by Darion's support. She was surprised to realize that in the last few days, her suspicions had faded away and she had come to consider him a friend.

"How long have you been a ranger?" she asked, moving away from the grim topic of the Prophecy.

Darion thought a moment. "I started training when I was eleven—ten years ago now, I suppose." He shrugged ruefully. "I started young. Kenneth—the Meadowlark, as you know him—had just finished training an apprentice, so he decided to take me on even though I was young."

Allie knew most children began apprenticeship at age twelve, so for Darion to begin training a year younger was unusual. "Did you always want to be a ranger?" she asked, interested.

"Oh, I think I decided when I was nine or so," Darion said. "There are only so many trades available in a small town like Wiverrun, you know. Did you always want to be the Heiress?" he added teasingly.

Allie rolled her eyes. "Definitely not. When I was little I wanted to run away and join the circus. Really," she added as Darion gave an incredulous laugh. "I wanted to travel the world and do fancy tricks with a sword."

"I wanted to travel too," Darion said. "That's one thing that made me want to be a ranger. Living in Wiverrun, you start to feel a little isolated."

Their conversation continued until they crested the hill and began yet another descent. The slow pace grated on Allie's patience, but she knew they couldn't risk injuring the horses. And so down they went, slipping and sliding on the gravel as the sunset glared in their faces.

By nightfall, they had reached another valley. A meadow of daisies and tall grass filled its basin. They tethered the horses and allowed them to graze, then set up camp.

Allie's whole body felt coated in dust, the scent of smoke clung to her hair and clothes, and dirt caked her skin and fingernails. She washed her hands in the creek, which was better than nothing, then sat next to Jan at the fire while they ate supper.

"Trail life agreeing with you, little Wildkid?" Jan asked her with a half smile.

"Better than studies," Allie said, flushing slightly at the name. Jan and Dandio had called her that when she was small. She didn't mind it in Caer Sia, but it was embarrassing to hear it here. "Speaking of Wildkids," she said, changing the subject, "Aryion and Mel said Dusty's group was heading to central Coonsia. I wonder if we'll run into them."

"We might," Jan said. "I would like to meet with them and discuss renewing our kingdoms' alliance."

"The Wildkids have returned to the Mainland?" Darion asked, surprised.

"Only recently," Jan told him. "A friend of ours—Dusty of the N'Tell—is working to ally the Clans. The Hummingbird brought us news of it a few months ago."

"I still don't know why they didn't just come to Caer Sia," Allie said. "We need to know if they're going to join the war or not."

"Aryion thinks they will come, eventually," Jan said. "I hope the same, but we must understand, they still consider many of the Mainland kingdoms their enemies. Dusty's involvement was a blessing, but she'll need to convince the Clans that the war is worth fighting in."

"Rygal's pretty sure Dusty can do it," Allie said, hoping he was right.

A slight commotion behind her drew their attention. Allie recognized one of the scouts, his tone urgent and uneasy as he spoke with General Arrex.

Jan stood and moved to them. Allie jumped up and followed, both curious and worried.

Arrex was talking as they approached. "… could be a trick of the light, but we must find out." He paused as Jan arrived. The scout glanced between the king and the general nervously.

"Everything all right, private?" Jan asked him mildly.

"Yes, sire. Sorry, sir," the scout stammered, glancing uncertainly at his general. "I—I don't know if I'm correct. But I've seen figures moving on the south ridge, headed downhill. They seem to be coming this way."

"How many?" Jan asked.

"Two for certain, maybe more. It's hard to tell in the dark," the scout admitted apologetically.

"I've sent some men up the ridge to investigate, sire," General Arrex said. "I know we have only just set up camp, but we may need to move to a different position."

"That would be wise," Jan agreed.

"Who do you think they are?" Allie asked.

"Might be nothing," Jan said, "or it might be Aces. Either way, better safe than sorry." He turned back to Arrex. "Have the men pack up the supplies, and let's move a half mile or so up this ravine, away from the main path. I will wait to see what the scouts report."

"I'll stay with you," Allie said, though she already knew what he would say.

Jan shook his head. "No. Go with the soldiers, and stay with them until we know what we face. It's not safe for the Heiress of Caer Sia to enter unnecessary battles."

"Not any safer for the High King," Allie protested.

"Now you sound like your father," Jan said with a half smile. "Go with the soldiers. I'll be there shortly."

Allie walked back to the campfire, irritated but knowing he was right. She was not here to fight; in fact, ideally, she'd finish this mission without ever needing her sword. She supposed that was a good thing, but waiting with no way of knowing what was happening was unbearable.

The fires were extinguished, filling the valley in shadows. Allie had just swung into the saddle when a shout from behind made her pause. General Arrex's voice drifted back to her, calling to the scouts uphill. "You caught them? Who are they?"

Allie dropped to the ground again, ignoring Darion's warning as he jogged after her. Far too interested to think about the danger, she ran back toward Jan.

There was a muffled reply from the scout she couldn't hear, then General Arrex' voice—he sounded amused. "Light above—sire, you had best come see this."

Jan appeared, Drisilas blazing golden fire in his hand, a puzzled look on his face. His eyes landed first on Allie, and raised an eyebrow in clear disapproval.

"They caught them, didn't they?" Allie pointed out.

Jan shook his head. "Quite a talent you have there, following orders."

"I get it from my father," Allie said.

"Who are they?" Darion wondered from behind her, looking uphill.

The scouts, both carrying torches, came into view. Two hooded figures walked among them, their faces hidden in shadow. The taller of the two removed his hood as they entered the camp. "I hope you haven't moved camp yet. We've been walking all day," he commented, in a familiar low voice.

"And I'm hungry," the shorter added.

"What in Orlell are you two doing here?" Jan asked in disbelief, moving forward to clasp Aryion and Mel's hands in turn. The two rangers bowed to him, and he shook his head. "None of that—we are comrades, and far away from such formalities."

"It's so good to see you," Allie said, her nervousness replaced by relief.

"You too," Mel said with a weary grin. "What are you all doing here?"

"I believe the king asked you first," Darion commented.

Aryion noticed him and gave a slight nod in greeting. "Blackbird. Good to see you, and congratulations on your new post. I trust Kenneth is well?"

"He is, yes," Darion said. He looked a little awed by the older ranger's presence; Aryion and Mel had become local legends after the quest for the Shards.

"Come and sit," Ĵan said, ushering them back into camp. The soldiers, reassured there was no danger, dismounted and settled down again. "I trust we have much to discuss. I thought you were both in Appledale."

"We stayed there for three weeks," Aryion said. "What are you all doing so far from Sia?"

"We're going to Wiverrun," Allie told him. "Darion brought word that the Aces are threatening the town."

Mel looked up with a frown. "You're going to Wiverrun? Then why…?"

Aryion's dark eyes turned to Ĵan. "I understand the situation has changed, then, to require the aid of the Red Dawn?"

"Situation?" Ĵan repeated, mirroring his confusion. "How do you mean?"

"We received your letter," Aryion said slowly. "That was six days ago now, and we've traveled hard and fast to get to Wiverrun as you asked. From what was implied, the Red Dawn would not arrive for several more weeks."

Allie looked at Jan, startled. Jan's brow was furrowed, a deep concern in his green eyes. "Letter?" he repeated finally.

"Yeah…" Mel said, looking more and more uneasy.

Jan looked between Aryion and Mel, shaking his head slowly. "I am glad you both are here," he said at last, "but if you came because of my request, then I'm concerned. I can assure you I never sent such a letter."

15

Deception

"You received no other news from this courier?" Jan asked. "No name, nothing else of where he'd come from?"

Aryion shook his head tiredly. Mel, sitting next to him, looked worried. Despite their long journey, the recent development had raised many concerning questions. Jan quickly explained all that had occured in Caer Sia, and Aryion in turn told of their time in Appledale, which had been interrupted by the letter.

They sat beside a fire on the edge of camp. Allie heard the muted conversations of the soldiers around them, and occasionally glimpsed a scout through the trees on the perimeter. Now that they were reassured there was no danger, the quiet of the woods and the warmth of the fire should have eased her nervousness. Yet Aryion's report had ruined any chance of that.

"He wore a courier's uniform," Aryion answered after thinking. "Average build, Caer Sian accent and badge. I don't think he was an imposter, even if the letter was."

"Do you still have the letter?" Jan asked.

Aryion opened the top of his pack and produced a folded page. Jan scanned it briefly; Allie could see his jaw tightening with every word. "They even produced a decent rendering of my handwriting," he said at last with a grim smile, passing it to Darion.

Allie read it beside him, her confusion and concern growing. "When did you say this arrived?" she asked.

"Six days ago," Mel said. "The courier came to my parents' house in the evening."

"Six days ago," Allie echoed, mentally counting back to the day. "Jan—that was the same day Darion brought his report. That was the first time we heard about Wiverrun at all."

"The same day?" Aryion repeated, looking at Jan. "Are you saying we received this letter *hours* after you first heard the news yourself?"

"That is exactly what we're saying," Jan said, his face serious. "Even our swiftest couriers would not have reached you so quickly. Not only did I not write this letter, there is no possible way it came from Caer Sia in the first place."

A worried silence followed the words, contrasted by the cheerful conversations from the oblivious soldiers around them.

"Hardly anyone knows about the danger in Wiverrun at all," Darion said finally. "I'm certain of that. The duke didn't want the news getting out that we were under threat."

"The same way he didn't want anyone knowing about Redeyes?" Allie asked.

"Yes." Darion paused, thinking. "Maybe the letter came from a concerned citizen."

"A citizen might be able to forge my handwriting and signature, but he couldn't have forged this," Jan said, showing him the bottom left corner of the page. "These seals are available only to those in official positions. It confirms that the letter came from the duke himself."

Darion looked shaken. "I—I don't understand why he would do this," he stammered at last. "The duke sent me to bring the matter to Caer Sia. Why would he send word to the Hummingbird?"

"Why resort to forgery at all," Aryion remarked. "This isn't just a misleading letter. This is forgery of the king's wishes, signature, and seal—which is considered high treason in times of peace. If the duke sent this, he'll be imprisoned at best and hanged at worst."

"He may not have acted alone," Jan pointed out. "He may have been pressured or bribed by the Aces." He shook his head. "Regardless, we will discover the truth of it. What concerns me more is the fact that whoever sent the letter knew where you two were—and thus, knew where the Stone was."

Mel's hand went to his pocket, protectively covering the small blue light. Aryion's expression was dark. "We must learn who sent this letter," he said firmly. "Whoever it is, they know far too much about us. Whether it's the Aces, or their accomplices, Mel and I will find out."

"I wonder," Darion said uneasily, "if that's what they want you to do."

Aryion turned to him. "You think it's a trap?"

"It might be," Darion said. "Whoever sent this message clearly wants you to get to Wiverrun. We don't know for what purpose, or even if the Aces are involved. But we do know that the Ace-Lord wants the Star-Stones—and we've currently brought both very close to Wiverrun."

Allie looked at Jan worriedly. Thus far, they had assumed that Wiverrun, though under threat, was not actively occupied by the Aces. But if Darion's guess was right, then the Aces had the duke under their control, and the garrison was walking right into the Ace-Lord's clutches.

"Do we... need to go back to Sia?" she asked.

Jan stared into the fire; Allie could tell he was thinking over their options. Finally he looked at Darion. "What other information has the duke withheld in the past?"

"Only the matter of Redeyes," Darion said. "He is loyal to Sia, sire—that much I'm certain of. He would never willingly surrender the town to the Aces, not without a fight."

"And why withhold the truth of Redeyes yourself?" Aryion asked. "Did your duke forbid you from bringing the news? Your account alone might have been enough."

His tone was level, but there was a subtle challenge there. Darion drew a breath, but Jan spoke before he could say anything. "Redeyes has long been considered a legend in the Magno regions, Hummingbird," he said. "Darion has explained the duke's reasoning. While neither of us agree with it, there is nothing we can do about it now, only try to make up the time we have."

"Then we risk going to Wiverrun now?" Aryion asked doubtfully. "Two Star-Stones in the same place seems dangerous and foolish."

Jan shook his head, looking at Aryion and Mel. "No. You are correct, it is a dangerous risk to bring the Blue Stone into a potential trap. I will send a few men south to Tinkeeyo to alert their warriors. If Wiverrun has been taken, they must be prepared. You and Mel will accompany them."

"Does that mean you're coming with us?" Mel asked. "The Aces want Isilas too."

Jan paused, and Allie noticed a split second glance pass between him and Darion. It was gone in an instant, and Jan looked at Mel. "I have promised to help Wiverrun," he said. "That is something I must do. I will not ask the rest of you to risk the danger, not if the Aces have deeper control of the town than we anticipated."

"Why?" Allie asked, sharper than she'd intended. "What are you planning that the soldiers can't handle themselves?"

Jan turned to her calmly. "I will tell you soon. But not now. Now, I need you to trust my plan." He looked at Aryion. "If you wish to accompany us to the outskirts of Wiverrun, I believe that is safe enough. But investigating this matter yourselves is not worth risking the Stone."

Allie could tell Mel didn't like this plan, but he did not argue, only looked to his mentor. Aryion nodded slowly. "Very well. We will travel to the edge of the village, but leave the investigation to you."

Allie looked at Jan, trying to read his face for any clues to his plans. There were none. His expression seemed as calm and measured as ever.

The nagging curiosity and concern she'd been pushing away for the last few days lurked in her thoughts. There was something else Jan wasn't telling her, and evidently, it was something he wanted to deal with himself.

. . . . . .

The following morning they began the climb up the last hill to Wiverrun. The winding road was less steep than the others, and the horses moved easier. Allie offered to let Mel ride, but he refused. A good night's sleep had refreshed him. He told her and Darion about the mission to Esile City, which Allie had only heard parts of. They both listened without interruption as Mel told them about finding the Wildkids, joining with a crew of pirates, defeating Terrax, and breaking the compass.

"The Wavers were controlled by the compass?" Darion asked as Mel finished his story.

Mel nodded. "I was there when the compass was broken, and I think some of the Ace-Lord's power was kept in the compass—that's what caused the Wavers to act the way they did. I wish we could have learned more about them, but they're gone now."

Allie was less concerned about the Wavers—her mind was focused on something else. "You said you heard the Ace-Lord's voice when it broke? What did he say?"

Mel nodded. "I did. He spoke out of the shadows—'*The signs are scarred, The Messenger has come, The Twelfth will rise*'—and then asked if we're sure about playing his game." His face was uneasy. "I didn't understand at first. It makes more sense now that I've read the Prophecy—if Redeyes is the Messenger, I bet the Ace-Lord used the magic from the compass to bring him back."

"That seems likely," Darion said, looking both interested and worried.

The voice from one of their outriders drifted down from the peak of the hill. "Wiverrun ahead, General!"

Allie looked up hopefully, tapping her heels against the horse's sides as the group picked up their pace. The crowd of soldiers blocked her view for an instant as they crested the hill, and she remained in the saddle to peer over the many heads.

They stood above a forested valley nestled in the crook of four slanting hills. The road led along the hilltop to her right, following the rocky crest north for a half mile or so before beginning the descent. Before and below them, a treeless patch marked the village. Allie could make out the rooftops of small wooden houses, the road winding past them before slanting to the left. Her eyes followed the road to rocky cliffs and hills. There lay the marble quarry, she assumed, remembering what she'd learned of Wiverrun's geography and resources. She peered past the rocks, trying to glimpse the ruin of Castle Droco in that direction. But she could see nothing besides the crests of more forested hills.

"There's the duke's manor," Darion said beside her. His face was lit with hope and relief as he studied his home village. "Just through those trees."

Allie followed his pointing finger. She could just make out a large, well-ordered house on the north side of town and a green square that marked a well-tended lawn. All appeared well. There was no sign of battle, nothing that showed the level of destruction the Aces were capable of.

"Where's the castle you mentioned, master Blackbird?" General Arrex asked.

Darion pointed south. "On the other side of those hills—up and around past the quarries. That's the road to Tinkeeyo."

"Up and around," Aryion repeated dryly. "In that case," he said, turning to Jan, "I think Mel and I might take a moment's rest in town before we start south."

"Of course," Jan said. He seemed in good spirits. The sight of Wiverrun waiting quiet and peaceful had reassured everyone. "Let's head down."

The road, though crumbling away from years of travel, was wider and less steep than before, and allowed them to ride instead of walk. Allie's heart leapt as they reached the valley and rode through the dense trees toward the distant village. A few farms marked the outskirts of the town. At long last, they had arrived, and her mission had begun.

"It's too quiet," Aryion said in a low voice. The ranger walked just in front of Allie's horse, his dark eyes scanning the wood. "I see no sign of the townspeople."

"We haven't quite entered the village," Allie pointed out.

"Exactly," Aryion said shortly. "I haven't seen a single farmer in any of these homesteads."

He nodded to a farmhouse. The fence behind it enclosed a small herd of goats, who glanced up with mild interest as the riders passed. There was no sign of their owner.

Darion looked uneasy too, studying the farms. "He's right," he said. "There's no smoke from any of the chimneys, either. Where is everyone?"

"Maybe there's something going on in town," Mel suggested, but he looked doubtful.

They continued through the trees. Allie strained her ears for any sound of civilization, but aside from the jingle of the horses' harnesses and the rhythm of hoofbeats as they rode, the forest was silent. An unwanted fear tightened in her chest.

At last, the road widened, the trees fell away, and Wiverrun came into full view before them. The riders stopped.

"Light above," General Arrex murmured.

Allie dismounted. Glass crunched under her boots, sprinkling the road from the shattered windows of every building around them. Empty houses hunched in place, doors hanging from splintered hinges, the ashes from their hearths strewn out as though caught by a mighty wind.

Wiverrun was empty.

White ice glittered in patches on the frames of the houses and crusted on the road. A few wagons stood abandoned along the roadside, harnesses broken, as if the animal had torn away in panic.

Slowly, the soldiers moved through the town. No one spoke. There was nothing to be said; the sights spoke for themselves, repeating one horrible truth: *Too late.*

It was Aryion's voice that broke the silence. "There's no signs of struggle, no bodies." He turned to Ĵan. "Even the Aces could not conceal a mass execution. Maybe the duke feared an attack and evacuated the village."

Some of the crippling despair faded as Allie realized he was right. Buildings and property had been damaged, but she saw no signs of death.

"Search the surrounding forest," Ĵan ordered. "If there is anyone left, we must find them."

The soldiers spread out, moving through the streets of Wiverrun. Aryion and Mel walked toward the duke's manor.

Allie remained in the square, unable to tear her eyes away from the chilling sight. It was not the destruction, the abandoned village, or even the icy mark that frightened her the most. The worst of it, she realized, was the silence—total, utter silence, as though the life had been physically drained out of the area. She knew that silence well; it had gripped Caer Sia when the Ace-Lord had taken over.

Darion knelt on the road, holding a piece of glass, his face drawn and pale with shock.

"I'm… sure we'll find them," Allie offered. Her words felt flat and meaningless.

It seemed a very long time before the soldiers regrouped in the square, confirming what they had already assumed. The town was completely deserted. There were no tracks in the surrounding forest to give any clue where the survivors had gone. The duke's manor had been stripped and looted of all valuables—likely, Jan guessed, by thieves and bandits following the town's desertion.

"The southern Magno is just as silent," Aryion said grimly. "Mel and I noticed that on our way here. There's something else here, some plot of the Ace-Lord we have not discovered."

"The townsfolk might be alive," Mel said slowly. "There's no signs of death. Maybe they managed to escape—or maybe they're being held captive."

"Captured isn't much of an improvement," Darion said, his voice hollow. "Not if the Ace-Lord plans to enchant them and add their small numbers to his forces."

There was a heavy silence. Allie looked at Jan, seeking some reassurance in his face. At last, the king looked at General Arrex. "The surest road lies to Tinkeeyo, a three day's ride southeast. If the inhabitants of Wiverrun survived, I would expect them to go that way. Either way, Tinkeeyo must be made aware of this. Send a third of your men there to bring the news and see if they've heard anything."

"Yes, sire," Arrex replied. His face was serious. "Should the rest of our company remain here?"

Jan let out a breath. "At this point, there is little we can do for the town. But I do not want to leave without investigating further, not after we have come this far. Set up a camp on the north side of town, a mile or so outside of the village, and wait for us there. We'll join you tomorrow morning."

"What do you plan to do in the meantime, sire?" Arrex asked.

Jan looked at Darion. "I will go with Master Blackbird to observe the quarry. There is a chance that the people of Wiverrun took shelter there, or fled further into the hills."

Allie looked at him, puzzled.

"Is that... wise, sire?" Arrex asked warily. "If this attack is a work of the Aces, they may still be in the area."

Jan smiled slightly. "I appreciate your concern, but it is unwarranted. If the Aces are near, I would expect them to be near the castle ruins. We will avoid that area. But if the townsfolk have fled to the quarry, we must help them."

"Let us come with you, at least," Aryion said. "Mel and I can offer some protection."

Jan studied him. "You would do better to join the force headed to Tinkeeyo."

"We have nothing to report to Tinkeeyo," Aryion returned. "Nothing that can help the inhabitants of Wiverrun. If the Aces are in this area, they likely already know we are here, with the Star-Stones."

"It might be better to keep the Stones together if the Aces are nearby," Mel added. "Otherwise, they could attack us each while we're seperated, and then take the Stones. If we're together, we can protect them both."

"I want to come too," Allie said hesitantly. "Please. I was supposed to investigate the enchantment—if the townspeople have been enchanted, that's part of my mission."

Jan let out a breath. Allie could tell he agreed with Mel, that separating the Stones now could be dangerous. Yet his hesitation lay not only in her own safety. He seemed to be considering something else, something that likely lay in his mysterious plan.

But he finally nodded slightly. "Very well. But I must ask this of each of you. You must follow my orders. Even if they do not make sense in the moment, even if they are orders you do not like, our plan will rely on your obedience."

Allie and Mel both nodded; Aryion's dark eyes were fixed on Jan's face, clearly seeking a reason for this blind path of obedience. But the king's face remained impassive. Darion's expression was uneasy.

Jan turned back to the general. "We will survey the quarries and search for clues, and meet up with your men tomorrow morning. If we are not back by noon tomorrow, you must head to Badwater, and get word to Lady Ajaha."

"Very well, sire," Arrex answered. Allie could hear the uncertainty in his voice, the same worry she felt. Worry for the civilians of Wiverrun, unease over what could have happened, and a growing confusion and fear over Jan's plan, which seemed far more secretive than usual.

But Arrex did not argue as he swung into the saddle, and with a final farewell led his men through the deserted village.

16

The Duke's Mistake

Despite the urgency to find the villagers of Wiverrun, Jan insisted they rest before moving on. Darion led them into the wreckage of the duke's manor. Most of the furniture, though overturned and battered, was still intact, so they sat in the once-fine parlor and waited.

Allie felt too worried to eat anything. Her emotions alternated between a desire to know what had happened and a dread of what she would learn. She tried to reassure herself that all was well, and the townsfolk had fled the town before the attack. But they had nowhere to go. The nearest city was a three or four day journey on foot, and if they had children and elderly with them, their progress would be painfully slow.

Aryion seemed unable to sit and rest, and paced the room, his dark eyes searching for clues. Mel followed his mentor outside after he'd eaten, and they went to survey the yard behind the house. Allie could hear their voices through the broken windows; Mel's questions, and Aryion's uncertain answers.

She waited in silence for a few minutes, until Jan's low voice drifted to her ears from one of the empty hallways.

"They must know the truth now. Other arrangements must be made."

Darion's voice answered, the words muffled. "…never meant for this. I can't go back on the deal, not now. But what about…"

His tone lowered. Allie, curios, moved quietly over to the hall, straining her ears.

Ĵan was speaking again. "I will not risk their lives for anything. I alone am bound by the arrangement, and yet we are all bound by the danger." He sighed heavily. "But it is unlikely that this chance will present itself again."

Darion's voice was low, but Allie could hear the bitterness there. "There's nothing I can do now. I don't think you can keep the truth from them much longer—the Hummingbird is already suspicious."

"It won't have to be kept for long," Ĵan answered. "We must proceed as planned. I need you to buy us the time we need. Can I trust you in that?"

"I don't know why you would still trust me at all," Darion replied, so quietly Allie could hardly hear him.

"I trust you with one thing more," Ĵan answered. "You must keep her safe, after I…"

The groan of a broken door muffled the rest of the sentence as Aryion and Mel re-entered the building. Allie drew back from the hall, trying to look casual, though her heart was pounding so hard she was certain everyone could hear it.

"More rubble in the back," Aryion reported. He glanced around.

"Where's the king?"

"I am here," Ĵan said, appearing from the hallway. "Did you find anything in the yard?" His voice was level and even, cleared of the worry Allie had previously heard.

"There were a few sets of tracks leading south," Aryion said. "Four or five of them, as far as I can tell. Who they are, your guess is as good as mine, but it seems they came from the manor."

"It might be some of the duke's servants," Darion suggested. He stood in the shadow of the hall, arms folded over his chest, scarred face half-lit by the daylight.

"Maybe," Ĵan said. "We will follow them, whoever they are."

The five companions left the ransacked manor and rode south, hooves crunching on the gravel road. The rocky white hills stood out from the endless green of the forest as the path began to climb again. Aryion and Ĵan talked in lowered tones. Mel was talking to Darion.

Allie rode in silence, her mind trying to make sense of the conversation she'd overheard. Ĵan had made a deal with Darion—they had some sort of plan, which she was yet to discover. The fact that Ĵan trusted Darion over her stung, almost as much as the fear of whatever Ĵan could be alluding to.

She hated all the secrets, hated the way her uncle's demeanor had changed the moment Darion had brought his message to Caer Sia. The tentative friendship she and Darion had developed on the road to Wiverrun was replaced again with suspicion. She studied Darion as he walked in front of her, leading his horse and listening to Mel's musings. Ĵan trusted him, she reminded herself. But Ĵan seemed desperate.

The quarry dropped away to their left, the road leading around the steep drop and up another set of hills. Allie kept to the edge of the road, away from the ledge. Even from this height, she could make out the glistening veins of marble and quartz in the stone. There was no sign of the quarry workers.

"Their tools and gear are gone too," Darion pointed out. "That seems like a good sign. If they were suddenly attacked, their equipment would have been left behind."

"That's not much help to us," Allie said. Darion glanced at her, clearly catching the edge in her voice. Allie was tempted to demand answers then and there, but Aryion's voice cut her off.

"Here, Ĵan—more tracks join the others." The tall ranger knelt just within the tree line a little ways ahead of them, studying a thin trail that wound south. The others moved to join him. Deer tracks marked the damp ground, but there were human prints mingled in, too.

"Are you sure that's the same group from the manor?" Allie asked uncertainty. "Why would they leave the main road?"

"Perhaps they were pursued," Aryion said, surveying the thin trail. "There are ten or twelve of them here, as far as I can make out."

"They were not warriors," Ĵan said, nodding to a set of tiny footprints. "There were children in this group."

"Either way, they headed uphill," Darion said slowly. "There's a hunting lodge a few miles from here—maybe they headed there."

"It would be a good place to look," Jan agreed.

The journey was much slower as they left the main road and headed uphill. The horses stumbled up the steep slope, and the companions were obliged to dismount and continue on foot. The tracks had reassured Allie of one thing. Some of the townsfolk had escaped the Aces. There were families in this group. Hopefully they were all right, wherever they were. She knew from experience that it was difficult to escape the Aces.

"There's no signs of soldiers," Mel panted as they toiled uphill. "It doesn't look like this group was being chased—and if it were Aces, we would have found ice."

"Can you tell how old the tracks are?" Allie asked.

"A few days, maybe. I can't tell for sure," Mel admitted.

"They must have fled from the attack," Darion said. "That means the Aces would have come days ago." His face was drawn. With every moment since finding Wiverrun in ruin, he seemed to have grown grimmer, his expression as much of anger as fear. Allie could understand that feeling. Yet on Darion's face, it seemed a deeper hatred. Almost of betrayal.

Evening fell quickly in the shadowed woods, and a steady rain began. They lit the lanterns and continued on. A biting wind tore up the slopes as they climbed the hills, and Allie was soon soaked to the bone.

The shape of the hunting lodge finally came into view before them, wooden sides shining with rain, mud streaked across the porch. There was no light in the windows. Allie's heart sank. They'd spent an entire day seeking the civilians, hiking up hills, trekking through the rain, for nothing.

"More tracks," Darion noted in a hushed voice, pointing at the muddy trail. "Quite fresh."

"Very fresh," Aryion agreed quietly. "And there's blood here, too." He moved his lantern closer to a fern overhanging the trail, showing a streak of red.

Allie looked at the cabin again. In the dim light, she could see the muddy footprints tracked over the steps of the porch and through the door.

"Carefully," Jan cautioned as they moved toward the cabin. "We have no idea if this is a group of civilians, or if they are with the Aces." He stepped forward and knocked shortly on the door. There was no reply from within. Slowly, he opened the door and led the way inside.

Frigid air filled the cabin, colder even than the night air outside. In the light of the lanterns, Allie could see simple wood furniture and supplies customary of a hunting lodge. A hearth was built on the far wall, with a small stack of fire wood next to it. White ash streaked across the floor.

A figure hunched beside the hearth, huddled in a cloak. An old woman, Allie realized, so frail she might have been blown away by the gale outside. She made no movement as the group entered, not even noticing their presence.

"Mel, light the fire," Aryion ordered, moving quickly to the old woman.

"There are others here," Darion said. Four figures huddled along the right wall. As with the first, they did not acknowledge the arrival of the five travelers.

Mel worked quickly, and soon yellow light flickered within the fireplace. Two of the ragged figures reacted blearily to the light; the others remained unmoving. Allie offered an old man her water flask, not sure what to say or do. "What happened, sir?" she asked softly, hoping to get some information from the ragged group.

The man held the flask but didn't drink, his face dazed and expressionless. He said nothing, only stared at the ground.

"Which of them is bleeding?" Mel asked, adding another piece of wood to the fire.

"Our friend here has a cut on her foot," Aryion told him. He was trying to rouse the old woman. "It's not bad. It looks as though she sliced it on the walk here."

"There are two more over here, dead," Jan said quietly. He stood by the table next to the door. Two still figures lay under it.

Darion knelt by the bodies. Allie tore her eyes away, trying to remain calm. "What about the children?"

"No sign," Aryion said heavily. "Their tracks lead here, but it doesn't look like they ever entered the cabin."

"They must have made it here," Jan said slowly.

"They're both ice-cold," Darion said in a choked whisper. "No injuries on either of them—but I recognize these two—"

He stood abruptly, swinging his gaze around the others in the room. Allie looked back at the three civilians sitting by the wall with the old man. A middle-aged couple and a woman who looked to be in her late twenties, but with the dirt and grime it was impossible to tell.

"Who were they, Darion?" Jan asked.

Darion was staring at the townsfolk by the wall; Allie could see true fear on his face. "Those two were believed lost," he said, nodding to the bodies. "They joined the Aces, I think—I thought they'd be enchanted now, not dead—she went with them," he added, pointing to the old woman by the hearth. "But she's not enchanted." He knelt down, studying the dull faces of the middle-aged couple.

"They are not enchanted," Aryion said slowly. "They are completely unresponsive. I can't get any word out of her." He took the old woman's hand gently and continued speaking quietly to her. She did not even react to his voice.

"They're not enchanted," Darion repeated, his voice shaking. "They're shattered, and that's a worse thing all together." He studied the comatose couple seated by the wall. Like the old woman, their expressions were vacant. No blue light shone in their hollow eyes, yet neither did they seem alive—their faces were completely devoid of thought.

"Shattered?" Aryion echoed, frowning.

Allie turned back to the old man, who still held the flask, unmoving. His shadowed face stared into space. "Listen, sir. This is important. There were children with you. Where are they?"

The man looked at her blearily. "The children," Allie reiterated, a little louder.

At the word, the old man straightened slightly. His rasping words came slowly, mechanically. "Gone. Taken with the others. That is the price."

"The… price?" Allie repeated.

Darion's voice, rising with tension, grew louder as he reached the young woman. "Freya—can you hear me? Where are the boys?" He took her shoulders, looking desperately into the dull face, his hands shaking. Jan stepped forward and drew him back. "My brother's wife," Darion stammered before Jan could ask, "she's my brother's wife—she should be safe, she wasn't supposed to be involved—"

"Involved in what?" Aryion asked, eying him carefully.

Jan had moved to the old man, turning his face toward the light. The man's expression was dull, but unlike the others, his eyes shone with pale blue light. And this face was familiar. "Light above," Jan breathed. "It's the duke."

"Enchanted?" Mel asked, stunned.

Allie's focus was still on Darion, who was staring from the duke, to the group by the wall, to the bodies under the table in turn. The look in his eyes was deeper than fear—it was dread. The same dread she had seen in her uncle's eyes back in Caer Sia.

Darion's haunted gaze swung back to Ĵan. "*They know,*" he whispered hoarsely. "They know—they're coming—"

"Who?" Allie asked, looking between Ĵan and Darion.

The sound of footsteps and clinking chainmail reached her ears before anyone answered. Five men entered the cabin; four armored guards, and their leader wearing a gray jerkin and a blue-plumed hat that shaded the top half of his face.

Aryion drew his sword in a flash, followed by Mel. Allie jumped to her feet, looking over at Ĵan. He had not moved, his green eyes narrowed as he studied the newcomers. Darion, closest to the door, had reached halfway for an arrow, but didn't draw it, only stared at the man in the hat.

"Welcome," the leader greeted them in the tense silence. His jerkin was finely made, his blond hair and beard neatly cut.

"Who are you?" Aryion demanded, taking a half step forward, the tip of his sword lowered at the man's neck. "What do you know of these people? Speak swiftly."

The man looked at him with a slight frown, as though puzzled. "We have come as requested. These four souls," he nodded to the ragged group by the wall, "were left alone until we could offer them hospitality, and so we have come to bring them home."

"Requested?" Mel repeated.

The man nodded. His calm, courteous tone should have reassured Allie, yet it only unnerved her further. There was something wrong here, something unnatural in the appearance of these five men.

"You haven't answered my question," Aryion said in a dangerously low tone, taking another step closer. "I will ask once more. Who are you?"

"Wait," Darion said suddenly, moving to stand between Aryion and the strangers. There was no sign of his initial fear. He spoke slowly but firmly, eyes fixed on the leader. "They are here as promised, Fargrin. Here to help Wiverrun."

The leader—Fargrin, as Darion had called him—barely reacted to these words. "You know my orders, Blackbird. There can be no witnesses here. Whatever they are here for, we must bring them."

"Bring us where?" Allie asked, turning sharply to Darion. "You know these men? Who are they?"

Darion ignored her, his eyes still on Fargrin. "They are not witnesses. I have brought them myself, just I was asked to." He paused. "Is… he… with you?"

"He will be along shortly," the blond man replied. His attention turned to the others for the first time. The fire crackled and flared, and Allie could see his face better now as he turned toward her.

The firelight reflected on clouded blue eyes that shone with a hollow light.

In an instant, her suspicions fell into place. The man's vacant expression, the methodical tone in his voice, the blue eyes—it was all too familiar. These five newcomers were enchanted.

"Darion?" she asked slowly.

"It looks as though you've succeeded, Blackbird," Fargrin commented, looking at Darion. "They will be pleased."

"For the sake of Wiverrun," Darion murmured.

The soldiers in chainmail moved forward. Jan drew Drisilas in a flaming arc. "Not here, Darion," he said. His tone was low, but the tension of his words heightened Allie's growing fear.

"You don't have a choice," Darion told him quietly.

"What choice?" Mel asked, his voice rising. "A choice to let these soldiers take us to the Aces?"

Darion didn't answer him, his eyes locked on Jan's face. An invisible conversation seemed to play out between the two of them, a meaning hidden behind every word. "It was their choice to follow you here. Against my warnings, but here we are. Back out now, and they'll all die."

For an instant, Drisilas' fire illuminated the unease, the regret, the anger on Jan's face. Then he nodded shortly and, to Allie's disbelief, sheathed the blade. "Do what you will, Blackbird."

The soldiers, who had paused, moved forward again. Allie stepped back, looking at Darion. "I don't know what deal you've made," she said, fighting to keep her voice as level and calm as Jan's. "But we came here to help them—to investigate the enchantment—you really think handing us over to the Ace-Lord is going to help that?"

"You'll have to see," Darion said, as though pleading with her to understand. "There's nothing to investigate in Wiverrun. You can trust me there. You'll have to look elsewhere for answers."

"Answers to what?" Allie snapped.

Darion opened his mouth to answer, but before he did, a low growl filled the room, and Allie's façade of calm was extinguished.

An uncertain dark shape crouched in the doorway, like a hulking cloud of black smoke. For an instant it appeared as a mere shadow, an extension of the night beyond. But in slow deliberation, it detached itself from the shadows on the edge of the room and prowled into the light of the fire.

The beast stood almost as tall as Allie, ashen gray fur streaked with black stripes. Numerous scars interrupted the glossy pelt, but clearly none of the wounds had affected the beast's strength. Its teeth glinted as it snarled. Yet it was its eyes that caught Allie's gaze, held her attention like a helpless animal before an approaching predator. The eyes were blood red, and a strange light seemed to leak from them like mist; two merciless, soulless pools.

The great cat padded into the room, its terrible gaze sweeping over each companion before locking eyes with Jan. They stared one another down.

"So you have come at last," the beast said finally, its voice deep and snarling.

Jan said nothing for a long moment. When he finally spoke, his voice was slightly strained. "What have you done to Wiverrun, Redeyes?"

"What was promised," Redeyes answered, sitting and curling his tail around his paws. "Its curse has been reconciled. Yours, of

course, is yet to be fulfilled."

Jan closed his eyes. "The Darkness' attack on Sia should have been more than enough."

"And yet you live," Redeyes replied shortly.

Allie's mouth was dry and her thoughts were too tangled to make sense of this interaction, but a new suspicion drove all else away, and she looked at Jan. His expression remained calm as he stared at Redeyes, but Allie saw the fear in his eyes, the same fear she'd noticed before.

Not a fear of Redeyes himself, terrifying though the beast was. Fear of what he would do. Fear of Redeyes' role, his task, his purpose.

Your curse is yet to be fulfilled.

The Messenger—the Marks—entire cities cursed to be destroyed by the Darkness, following the Marks of Redeyes—All along, Jan had been so insistent that he should go alone, not because he feared the risk, but because he *was* the risk, the very reason the Darkness had come again and again to Caer Sia.

No, she told herself, no, that was impossible.

And yet, at the same time, what else explained it? What else besides a curse, borne in secret by the king himself?

"The curse was reconciled twice over," Jan stated, as Aryion looked at him uncertainly. "You have no claim here. Nor do you have any claim over Wiverrun."

"My master takes only what was given to him," Redeyes answered. His gaze flicked to Darion. "I trust the Blackbird will acquaint you

with the truth. He has, after all, aided my master in claiming the Magno villages. What is Wiverrun, if not one more?"

Darion said nothing, his face white as he stared at the floor.

"Your deal?" Aryion said, spitting the words like a curse as he turned to Darion, gripping his sword. "*This* was your deal, traitor?"

"Lower your blade, Hummingbird," Jan ordered sharply, turning back to Redeyes. "The curse of Sia is reconciled. Any business you have is with me alone now."

Allie's heart plummeted in fear.

"It is too late for that," Redeyes said shortly. "The Ace-Lord wants all of you, and the Blackbird will deliver on his promise."

The words rang in Allie's ears. The Blackbird's promise. Darion had never been helping them. All along, he had been serving the Aces. Bringing them and the Star-Stones into the Ace-Lord's hands.

In an instant, her shock was replaced by rage. Her sword seemed to move of its own volition, slashing at the soldiers as they reached for her. The blade nicked over Fargrin's wrist; she saw the cut appear briefly before the skin knitted itself back together. The enchantment protected these men, and her companions wouldn't stand a chance fighting them.

Blue light flared from Mel's hand in the same moment. He held the Blue Stone out in front of him. "Stay back," he ordered.

Redeyes looked at him disdainfully. "Resist us, boy," he said, "and I will tear your friends' throats from their necks before the light leaves the Stone."

"No, you won't," Darion snapped. "The Ace-Lord needs them alive. Both Wielders, that's what he said—both Wielders are needed."

"He has said nothing about the other two," Redeyes said. His fiery eyes flicked between Allie and Aryion greedily.

"Do it, Mel," Allie barked, gripping her sword tighter. The contempt in Redeyes' gaze fed her growing fury, electrified the fire in her veins. She caught Darion's gaze; he gave an almost imperceptible shake of his head. He didn't want them to fight and die here—of course, that would damage the Ace-Lord's prize.

"I trusted you!" she shouted, flinging the words at him. "We would have helped you, and Wiverrun—but you've handed it over to the Ace-Lord yourself. Everything you told me was a lie!" She jerked her head at the unresponsive civilians. "You lied about them, pretended to care—you're the reason they're here, broken like this!"

She sensed her words had touched a nerve. Darion said nothing, but his pale face was suddenly drawn as though in pain. Then the moment passed, and his expression was cold again.

"Sheathe your blades," Jan ordered, raising a hand. "Aryion, Asescia, stand down. We cannot fight them."

Allie looked at him in disbelief. Jan held her gaze before turning to Redeyes. "But I will warn you. Harm one hair on any of their heads, and I will make certain you stay dead this time."

Redeyes gave a low chuckle. "Fierce threats for a man in chains. Come, Marked One. We have a score to settle."

Allie was hauled forward by the guards, out of the lonely cabin.

She barely felt the rain or the biting wind as they were marched back down the muddy road. The fate of Wiverrun, Jan's dark secrets, all of it paled in comparison to the burning fury in her chest. Because of Darion, she would once again face the Aces as a prisoner.

He had betrayed them all.

17

Bargain

Rain pelted down on the dismal party as they traveled the muddy winding roads. Despite the chill, all Allie could feel was hot rage as she was marched up another rise.

Confused and vengeful thoughts swirled in her mind. Darion had betrayed them. What had prompted him to do this, she did not know. How much, if any, of what he'd told her was true? Apparently he had been serving the Ace-Lord all along, even playing a role in handing over the helpless Magno villages. And she had played right into his little game, giving him information, showing so much care for his cause, believing his every lie.

She wanted to fight, despite the chains on her wrists. Loose the red fire crackling in her veins and blast their way out of here. Yet her own weariness held her back. She didn't doubt Redeyes' threat. He could—and would—kill them at any resistance. It seemed the Ace-Lord only needed Ĵan and Mel, as the Wielders of the Stones. She and Aryion were expendable. Their survival had been bargained for by Ĵan, for now, but there was no telling how long it would last.

Ĵan, her dear uncle, whom she had thought she'd known. All the secrets he yet concealed filled her with confusion and anger. Her mind could not make sense of his actions at all—and now, there were more pressing issues.

She tripped on a root and stumbled. Darion caught her elbow before she fell, and she pulled away sharply, glaring at him. "How much is your reward for bringing us in?" she hissed.

Darion said nothing, his gaze fixed resolutely on the path ahead of them. "You really think this is for a reward?" he returned quietly, then moved ahead of her on the trail.

Allie stared after him, confused. Darion had mentioned a deal with the Aces. What else but a reward would prompt such treachery?

And yet, as her mind replayed the scene in the cabin and Darion's reaction to seeing the silent villagers, the Aces seemed to have broken their part of the deal. They'd involved Darion's family and attacked Wiverrun.

She didn't understand it. She glanced at Fargrin, who marched beside her, sword pointed at her ribs. Well, this was one good thing about being captured, she thought wryly. If she wanted to learn about the enchanted soldiers as her mission had entailed, this would be about as close as one could get. Maybe she could learn more about the Aces, too.

Assuming any of them made it out alive.

The trail crested a hill, and a brief flicker of lightning lit the valley ahead of them. The land fell away before a deep gorge at least a mile wide. She could not see the bottom of the ravine, only darkness that seemed to go on forever. In the center of the ravine, the outline of a ruined structure was just visible, but it seemed to shimmer and shift in the uncertain light.

It wasn't just the light, Allie realized with a surge of interest. She recognized the filmy, watery covering as an illusion.

As they drew closer, the ruin shimmered into focus, and with it, the newly repaired Castle Droco.

Allie stared in awe. The palace stood tall on three massive stone columns rising above the canyon floor, its towers reaching toward the dark sky. Marble walls were covered in elaborate carvings depicting scenes and strange runes. Their pearly white color cut a striking contrast between the dark forest.

Back in Caer Sia, they had speculated, for a time, that the Ace-Lord might retake his old fortress, and yet the sight of this ancient palace took Allie's breath away.

Stretching away from the castle to the north and west were two massive marble bridges reaching to the canyon's edge. Those, Allie realized, were the only ways in or out of the castle, unless someone climbed down the columns to the ravine floor.

The idea of scaling the columns was banished as they crossed the bridge, and she risked a glance over the edge. The canyon was no longer a natural divide in the land—the Ace-Lord had corrupted even that, turned it into something far worse. Where she expected to see stone or water far below, she saw only darkness, impenetrable blackness dotted with a few pale lights far, far away. Castle Droco was surrounded by a void of black emptiness that yawned beneath its bridges, dropping away for miles.

The height dizzied her, and she edged away from the railing, heart pounding. Behind her, Mel gave a short gasp of fear. She glanced back and saw his face was pale and drawn. "It's all right," she said, hoping to reassure him of the height.

Mel shook his head rapidly. "No, it's not all right. That's a void, Allie. Just empty blackness full of sounds and visions until you hit bottom. Like in the Darkness." He closed his eyes tightly and allowed the guards to guide him blindly the rest of the way across.

Allie looked down again at the empty blackness. Mel was right. The rift of darkness filled the ravine like a molten liquid. A patch where the Dark Realm's powers had been allowed to leak through.

This emptiness, this blackness, was what the Ace-Lord planned for all of Orlell, she knew. She didn't realize he had already opened patches like this, and a chill of fear ran down her back.

Redeyes prowled ahead of them, leading them over the bridge and through the white marble doors of the castle. The doors fell closed behind them with an ominous boom that made Allie shudder, filling her with dread.

It was surprisingly quiet inside the castle. Soldiers and servants with pale blue eyes moved past them silently. She recognized orcs, a few goblins, and far too many humans among the enchanted. Strange howls and snarls echoed dimly from the deeper parts of the fortress, the sounds of animals she had never heard before.

She looked around. The castle was not built in stories and levels, the way Castle Sia was. Instead, the entire structure was built up into the towers. Countless staircases climbed up in a seemingly endless pattern, higher and higher.

Fargrin pushed her forward, and they began to climb. Darion, Allie noticed, was looking around with a fearful yet intense interest. Could it be that he had never been inside the Aces' fortress? That would explain his unease when he had spoken about the ruin before. The illusion would prevent anyone from seeing the truth.

They reached a second set of double doors. A single sentry stood before them. An Ace, Allie realized, but less solid than the Ace-Lord or his deputy. The guard floated ghost-like above the ground, purple-red eyes staring dully from the depths of its hood. Each of the Aces seemed a different level of decay. This one was little more than a shadow, though she had no doubt that it held the same power as its fellows.

"Open," Redeyes growled, and the Ace silently swung the heavy doors open.

The room was bitterly cold, lit with a pale white light. It was roughly the size of the throne room in Castle Sia, but the lack of furniture and the high ceiling made it look bigger. A tall figure stood on the far side of the room, back to the door, wreathed in black.

"Bow," Redeyes ordered. No one moved—the guards kicked the back of their legs, and the four prisoners fell to their knees on the hard floor.

The figure turned, armor clinking softly. This was not the Ace-Lord. Allie recognized this Ace at once. Half of his face had been destroyed, exposing a pale white skull on the left side. A smile flickered over his horrific features.

"Welcome back, Redeyes," the Ace-Deputy said, in the silky, cool voice that had haunted Allie's nightmares ever since she'd first heard it in Sia. "You have brought the prisoners, I see."

"They are the Blackbird's prize," Redeyes said irritably. "Why are you here? Where is our lord?"

"He is engaged elsewhere at present," the Deputy answered delicately, turning to the prisoners. "I hope you might forgive his absence. He bid me to welcome you, his honored guests."

Redeyes growled softly, clearly not pleased by the change in plans. But he stepped back, turning his terrible gaze to Darion. "Speak, Blackbird."

Darion stepped forward and bowed stiffly. "Sir. As requested, I have brought the Stones and their Wielders."

"So you have," the Deputy said. His purple-red eyes studied the four companions. "You have also brought two others. What purpose do they serve? Surely you understand the danger of unneeded witnesses; our location here must remain secret."

"I assumed we could use them as ransom," Darion said, glancing sidelong at Allie. "They are worth much to the Liznee cause."

"Ransom!" the Ace-Deputy echoed, chuckling softly. "Well. I will suggest this to my master. He shall decide their fate."

"When will he return?" Darion asked tensely.

"I am not privy to our lord's schedule," the Deputy told him. "There are a great many matters he must see to. This operation, as you know, has been entrusted to me now."

"Then was it your choice to take Wiverrun?" Darion asked. His tone remained calm, but Allie could hear the edge of fury there.

"Wiverrun was liberated," the Deputy said smoothly. "The same way we have liberated the villages you have handed over to us."

"Your master promised Wiverrun would be kept safe," Darion said hoarsely. "You know I only agreed to serve him because of that promise."

"I hope your emotions have not clouded your judgement, Blackbird," the Deputy said in a conversational tone. "Need I remind you that your reckless tongue is what earned you the scars upon your face? My master fulfills his promises. The inhabitants of Wiverrun *are* safe now, safe even from death." He laughed softly. Redeyes smiled. Darion's face was drawn with anger.

"Now," the Deputy said, "the matter of the prisoners. Take the New Blood and the king to the west tower, I will question them myself. As for the ranger and the girl, we have no use for them. Ransom is not our way. However… they may yet serve our conquest."

He turned thoughtfully toward the prisoners, and a chill of foreboding ran down Allie's spine. "Both of you are capable warriors. You have displayed great strength of mind. We might place the enchantment upon you, if you are willing."

Allie fought to keep her expression neutral, though her mind was racing. The Deputy's words confirmed her earlier guess. The enchantment had to be a choice. Though the Aces might threaten and bribe, the soldiers still had to choose it themselves.

"We'll have to pass that by," Aryion snapped, straining at the chains. "And you are certainly *not* taking the New Blood or the Stone he guards, not as long as I breathe."

"Is that so," the Deputy mused, turning away from Allie and looking into the ranger's face. "So you are the Blood Oath-bearer," he said softly. "I believe we have met briefly, during the disagreement in Kamon. You are free of the Oath, I understand? What occupies your days now?"

"Take off these chains and I'll show you," Aryion snarled, with more fire than Allie had ever seen.

"Ah, so you protect the New Blood," the Deputy said with a soft laugh. "How ironic, that you who sought to bring about death now guard this young life so devotedly."

He turned back to Allie. "What about you, young heiress? There is rage in you too, I can see. Does it anger you to have your king—your uncle, I understand—taken from you thus?"

Allie clenched her teeth. Of course it did. The same way it had angered her when they had taken her father, or when they had broken Sia's gates, or when they had executed so many valiant men. Her chest felt hot and tight with the restrained fury inside, and fire sparked from her fingertips as she glared into the cruel purple-red eyes.

"Your expression speaks for itself," the Deputy said. He looked at Darion. "Well, Master Blackbird, these prisoners may be useful after all. We will refrain from throwing them in the pit."

"What do you want with us?" Jan asked. "Surely your master's plan can be done without involving the innocents of Wiverrun."

"Innocents," the Deputy repeated dryly. "Who is to judge innocence nowadays? Those simple mortals now serve a higher purpose. As for your use, you are of great value to my master, as is the young New Blood. Your power over the Stones is unique, and if that power is to be unlocked, we will need your willing participation."

Jan gave a short laugh. "I think you overestimate your own abilities. You would do better to slay us now. Mel and I would die before we used the Stones' power for you or your master."

"Bold words for the one who has twisted Isilas," the Deputy said. "However, it will not be you who dies first." He looked at Allie and Aryion, and Allie finally understood. She and Aryion were to be kept here, used as incentive to force Jan and Mel to cooperate. Jan's face was pale as he glanced between Allie and the Deputy.

"Don't worry about us," Allie said, attempting to sound brave, but her voice trembled. "We'll be all right."

"She will die first, if you refuse to use the Stone," the Deputy informed him.

"No," Jan said. He took a breath, defeated. "You need not involve her in this. I will do what you ask."

"So will I," Mel said, while Aryion shook his head in defeat.

"On three conditions," Jan continued firmly. "You will not harm the heiress or the ranger. You will not move them to another prison, and most importantly, you will refrain from laying curses on any of our party." He directed the last statement to Redeyes, who growled.

"I am glad we have reached such an agreeable compromise," the Deputy said pleasantly. "Now, Captain Fargrin, show them to their cells."

"Wait," Darion said sharply. "What of our bargain?"

The Deputy turned to him. "Your bargain, unfortunately, was with the Ace-Lord alone, and I am unable to fulfill it. You will have to wait until he returns."

"You've already broken one part of our deal," Darion said through clenched teeth. "The least you can do now is free the ones I ask."

Redeyes snarled and stepped forward. The Deputy's cool smile vanished. "I warned you once of your hasty words, Blackbird," he said softly. "The warning will not come a third time. Before, you were bound to us by your word and your blood. Now you are bound by a curse far stronger. My master shall come when he is disposed to do so, and not a moment before."

Darion stood stock still, one hand gripping his bow, the other resting on the hilt of his knife. For one wild instant, Allie thought he would lash out to kill. He did not. He simply stood, trembling with rage.

"Await your next assignment on the third level, Blackbird," the

Deputy ordered shortly, then turned to Fargrin. "Escort our guests to their quarters."

"Yes, sir," Fargrin replied, bowing slightly before nodding to the guards.

Strong hands gripped Allie from behind, hauling her roughly to her feet and out of the room. The four companions were forced through the heavy doors and up, up, staircase after staircase, higher and higher into Castle Droco. The enchanted soldiers showed no sign of tiring as they climbed. Allie was out of breath when the guards stopped her and Aryion halfway up the tower. Two guards moved onward up the stairs with Jan and Mel.

An iron door was opened, and Allie and Aryion were marched down a dark hall, away from their companions. A single lantern shone pale light, illuminating the area only slightly. The left wall was lined with cells. The guards opened a door and shoved Aryion inside before locking the cell and continuing on down the corridor.

Near the end of the hallway the guards stopped, opened another cell, and forced Allie inside. She staggered and fell to her hands and knees on the cold, damp floor.

The iron door slammed behind her. The darkness and bitter cold wrapped freezing hands around her. The helpless rage she had fought to contain for hours burst to the surface. A scream tore from her chest, and she flung herself against the door, red fire blazing in her chained hands. The harsh iron bit into her shoulder. The door was unyielding.

With another cry, she let the fire loose. The red light lit the tiny cell for a few seconds before dying away, leaving only sparks of red.

Utter silence rang in her ears as she slumped, her back against the door, shivering from the cold and from the growing fear in her heart.

18

꙰ ꙰ ꙰ ꙰ ꙰ ꙰ ꙰ ꙰ ꙰ ꙰

The Cursed King

Allie had no idea how long she sat there, alone in the dark and damp. She might have dozed off at one point, though it was hard to tell. She felt utterly exhausted from both the trek and the dreadful events of the day. Her clothes, damp from the rain, clung to her skin. Her shivering only made her more tired.

Hours seemed to pass. At last, unable to sit still any longer, she stood and paced the small confines of the cell, trying to think. Her churning thoughts made it impossible to think clearly. There was too much unanswered, too much she needed to know.

Calm down! She sat down and took a deep breath. At least she was no longer in immediate danger. The Aces intended to keep her here, forcing Jan to cooperate. Evidently, the Aces needed both Jan and Mel to use the Star-Stones.

This made sense, she thought. The Aces could not use the Stones on their own; they could hardly touch them without being burned. By that logic, if the Ace-Lord wanted to use the Star-Stones to fully open the Dark Realm, he would need the Wielders to do it. Perhaps he planned to enchant Jan and Mel, she thought with a surge of fear. Except that couldn't be right—as Mel had learned before joining the

213

Shards, the enchanted soldiers had no more power over the Stones than the Aces.

Forget the Stones for now, then. What about Darion? He had betrayed them—for what, Allie did not know. Whatever the reward was, it seemed to be something only the Ace-Lord could give him. Yet in addition to the reward was his desperation to be free of the Aces. *Your word and your blood*, the Ace-Deputy had said to him. Did Darion bear a Blood Oath, then, binding him to serve the Ace-Lord?

She didn't want to think about Darion either. It only added to the angry confusion in her heart. Hard as she tried, she couldn't hate him. She wanted answers to every one of her questions, to demand why he'd done what he'd done, to know what plan he'd made with Jan.

And what about Jan? What was he concealing from her? Had she not earned his trust a hundred times?

The tears she had fought to contain burned behind her eyes. She huddled against the wall, taking shaking breaths.

The door opened unexpectedly. A tall figure entered, framed in pale light from the passage beyond.

Allie sprang to her feet as the door slammed shut, heart racing. "Stay back, Ace," she ordered, trying to keep her voice from shaking.

"I'll do that," came the quiet reply. "You have good reason to be angry at me."

The voice was not the Ace-Deputy's—it was low and measured, wonderfully familiar.

"Jan?" she asked timidly, hardly daring to hope, squinting in the dim light.

His hand rested on her shoulder. "Are you all right? Are you hurt?"

"No, I'm fine," Allie replied, relief filling her. Jan sat beside her, back to the wall. Their situation had not improved, but it was so much better with him there. She swallowed her tears and huddled against him, trying to warm up. "What happened?"

"He questioned us," Jan said. "Mel and I told him very little, but he didn't ask much of import."

"The Ace-Lord?" Allie interjected.

"No, the Deputy. It seems the Ace-Lord is still away."

"Where?"

"I am not sure. From the Deputy's implication, it seems he is near the Flats."

"Then what are the rest of the Aces doing here?" Allie wondered.

Jan paused. "I am only learning this now, Allie. I might be wrong. But I can tell you my guess." He thought for a moment before continuing. "I imagine you noticed the darkness below the fortress when we crossed the bridge?"

Allie nodded. "Mel said it was a void, like the Darkness."

"I believe he is right. It is a weak place between the mortal world and the Dark Realm, a placeholder for the darkness the Ace-Lord intends to bring here."

"How will he do that?"

"The Stones," Jan said. "The Ace-Lord needs the Stones to transform the patches of darkness into gateways, drawing the Dark Realm's powers into the mortal world."

"But hasn't he already done that? How else is Redeyes here?" Allie asked, puzzled.

"I do not know. Perhaps he was able to use the compass' magic to open a lesser doorway, and desires one of more power. Regardless, it is clear that is his intent. He will need the Wielders to use the Stones."

"So he's going to force you and Mel to use them," Allie realized. She had assumed as much.

"I believe that is his goal," Jan said.

"Is that what Redeyes was talking about?" Allie asked. "When he said your curse was yet to be fulfilled?"

A long pause. Allie could just make out the outline of Jan's face in the darkness. Even in the dimness, she could see a deep pain in his eyes.

"Jan?"

"No," Jan said finally. His voice was low. "No, it is not what Redeyes meant. He referred to another curse, the type that only he commands."

Allie looked at him, suddenly afraid to know any more. "The Marks, you mean?"

"Yes."

"But you don't have any scars. Redeyes didn't Mark you… right?"

Another long pause. Finally a small red flame flared in Ĵan's hand, lighting the cell. With his other hand, he pulled down the collar of his jerkin, exposing part of three long claw marks that ran down his chest under his shirt.

"He did," he said softly. "I have borne these Marks for years."

The red fire died away, leaving the cell in darkness again. Allie could not speak, overwhelmed with emotions for a moment. Disbelief, denial, shock, and anger rushed through her mind one after another. "You… when… why…" she stammered finally.

Ĵan took a deep breath. "After the Darkness attacked Caer Sia, I wanted nothing more than vengeance for the many fallen. No one knew how we would defeat the Darkness. The Star-Stones were a thing of legend, lost for centuries. Until the hama-dryads came to us, offering us an unexpected token of alliance—the Stone Isilas, gifted to the Liznees long before."

He spoke slowly, as though every word was torn from him. "The Stones were meant to protect, to guard life, and to serve the mortals, never to harm. I knew this, and yet I saw the Stone as the means of revenge—the means to defeat the Darkness. And so we had Drisilas forged, with the Star-Stone Isilas in its hilt. A weapon of war forged from a thing of peace."

He closed his eyes. "We attacked the Darkness, defeated it, drove it back into the depths of the Magno Forest. And then Redeyes appeared. For my actions, I was scarred, Marked. Cursed for corrupting the Star-Stone's magic and using it for harm. Even in death, Redeyes said that the curse of the Marks would be fulfilled one day. The Darkness would return to exact vengeance. I would pay for what I had done."

Jan paused. Allie said nothing, her mouth dry, her heart throbbing against her ribs. He finally continued. "When the Darkness reappeared, we held out hope that it was mere rumor. Your father in particular found it difficult to believe. But of course, the rumor made itself known as reality."

Allie nodded slowly, remembering those weeks of fear before the sword had been stolen. "You knew this was going to happen," she said at last. "You knew the Darkness would come back to kill you."

"I suspected it," Jan said, "but I hoped not."

Allie rubbed her forehead wearily, as though she could wipe away the tumult of emotions filling her. "What about… what about Darion?" she asked instead. "He's Marked too—pretty recently, if he told me the truth. Did you know he had the curse too?"

"I had a guess when he first appeared. When he brought the rumor of Redeyes' return as well, I knew it could be no coincidence, though I struggled to accept it," Jan said. "Once I did, I knew I needed the truth from him. And so together we formed a plan. There was much he had left unsaid in his initial report that he told me later."

"There was a lot he left unsaid," Allie said bitterly.

"True. And some of it must remain unsaid until you are out of here safely," Jan said. He lowered his voice. "This you can know. Darion told me everything in Caer Sia. He was bound in service to the Aces, swearing a Blood Oath and promising to help them gain the Magno villages in exchange for the safety of Wiverrun. The Ace-Lord deceived him and enchanted over half the population of Wiverrun—including, as Darion has told me, his own brother. Darion confronted the Ace-Lord for this, and for his insolence, and breaking his part of the deal, he was Marked."

He paused. "Darion was sent to Caer Sia to lie about the security of Wiverrun and to lure more warriors into the Aces' trap. Instead, he told me what was actually happening in Wiverrun, as well as the urgency to find the truth. I recognized his scars. I promised to help him, and so we formed our plan."

Allie shook her head in disbelief. "Don't tell me you still trust him."

"I do, because Darion trusts me. Our success and survival depend on his part of the plan now. If we are to learn more about the Ace-Lord's plot and what his warriors are doing here, they must be convinced that we are beaten. That is why I withheld this from you and the others. Your reactions during our capture needed to be legitimate."

"Then what are we trying to learn now?" Allie asked.

"Truth," Jan said. "The truth of what the Ace-Lord is doing, and why. How he was able to access the Dark Realm, and bring Redeyes back to our world. There are many secrets hidden here. This fortress was one. Darion is certain there are others. If the Aces are convinced we are captured and beaten, they will become careless—and *that*, I think, might reveal the information we are seeking."

"And you think it's worth getting everyone captured, including the Stones?" Allie said doubtfully.

"I hope. That was not exactly what we had planned for. The Aces discovered some part of Darion's treachery—only part of it, or else we would not be here. Our plan still stands. And I refuse to allow you three to remain here," Jan said, leaning back against the wall.

"And once we're out, you'll tell me everything?" Allie asked, not liking the separation he implied.

"Once you're free, everything will be revealed," Jan said. He let out a breath. "I am sorry for concealing it—for concealing everything. When I was first Marked, it was kept secret from nearly everyone. It seemed wiser than announcing to Sia that its new king bore such a curse. I see now that the uncertainty only added to their fear, and I am truly sorry if it added to yours."

Allie stared at the shadowed floor. The truth was darker and heavier even than her fears, but at least it had lifted some of the weight of her questions. Jan was not wrong. At a difficult time in her people's history, keeping the scars a secret was probably wiser than making it public knowledge. Still, that secret should have been told when the Darkness returned.

"What about Isilas, then?" she asked hesitantly, almost afraid to know the answer. "If you used its magic for a weapon, how will your curse be reconciled?"

"I do not know," Jan said quietly. "The Marks of Redeyes call for atonement, and the Ace-Lord demands death as the only way for it to be atoned. I do not know if there is a way to reverse the corruption of the Stone, or if my own life will be forfeit for failing to protect it."

"What about the Stars?" Allie asked, desperately seeking a solution.

"This curse is not of the High Light," Jan said, though he sounded uncertain. "I have heard that the Light alone may judge the mortals, but the price demanded of the Marks must still be paid. Nor do I know if the Stars will intervene, unless the curse contradicts the Prophecy's words." He let out a breath. "Either way, I can escape the Marks no longer. The curse will be fulfilled, and I refuse to let anyone else be harmed on my behalf."

"I'm not going to let the Aces kill you," Allie said fiercely, terrified by the finality in his words. "There has to be something else that will end the curse. You and Iriam taught me that the High Light grants forgiveness to any who ask it—maybe there's another way."

"I appreciate that," Jan said with a half smile. "But if my life is the only one the Ace-Lord requires, you must trust that choice."

"You won't have to make that choice," Allie said firmly. "We're going to get out of here somehow."

"Let's hope for that," Jan agreed. "For now, you should rest. I will keep watch for us both."

Allie didn't feel tired, but she knew she needed rest. She leaned back against the wall. Her mind swirled with thoughts and fears as she sat there in the darkness. Fears for herself, fears for her friends, fears for Jan. But eventually, she dozed off.

19

The Flight of the Hummingbird

Aryion had allowed himself a few moment's rest when he was first thrown into the cell. But the urgent need to get out and find Mel overrode his weariness.

He did a thorough examination of his cell, which was small, boxlike, furnished only by a narrow cot on the wall. But there had to be some flaw in this room that would allow for escape. This castle was ancient—surely parts had decayed over time, despite the repairs the Aces had done.

He wished Bryn were here. His sister would have found a way out instantly; she'd been a bounty hunter for years, and had always been good at escaping from tight situations. Of course, Bryn was probably miles away on a ship somewhere, unaware of the danger he was in here.

Aryion studied the floor in the dim light, feeling for cracks between the tiles. No luck there. Below the tile was more solid rock. He tried the walls—easily as solid as the floor, and the stone muffled any calls between prisoners. That left the door, but a quick survey told him it was secure also. The hinges were on the opposite side, preventing any tampering from within, and there was no lock for him to pick.

He sighed in frustration and paced for a few moments, thinking. No windows. Solid floor. Solid walls. Solid door.

"The whole place is solid, blast it," he muttered, falling flat on his back on the cot and staring up at the darkness. Anxiety and desperation to do something lurked in his mind. He needed to find Mel and the others and get out of here. The darkness seemed to press down upon him like a vice.

He finally stood, needing the movement more than anything else, and stared up at the ceiling. It was about eight feet high, he guessed, cross barred with a massive iron grating dividing the ceiling from the stone floor of the next level of the castle. It looked like some type of crawl space. He could probably touch it if he jumped and reached.

Interested, he peered up into the darkness. Perhaps if he could pull himself through the grating, into the crawl space. Not that there was anywhere to go after that.

Footsteps beyond the door drew his attention, and he returned to the cot, hiding his growing interest in the ceiling. One person, he guessed. Captain Fargrin, perhaps? Or worse—the Ace-Deputy here to question him. He sat still, his heartbeat quickening. The footsteps stopped outside.

"Are you there, Hummingbird?"

It was Darion Blackbird's voice.

Aryion leaned back against the wall, mildly surprised, but not willing to respond. That traitor. He must be trying to get information from him to appease the Ace-Deputy.

"Listen, I don't have a lot of time. Are you there?"

Aryion ignored him, adjusting the empty scabbards of the knives he usually kept in his boots. They had taken his sword too, of course. He felt naked without it. Getting it back would be his second order of business after escaping with Mel and the Liznees.

The door swung open. Darion slipped silently inside and threw him an exasperated look. "Did you hear me?"

"Did you think I would care to answer?" Aryion asked dryly.

Darion took a breath, carefully closing the door behind him. "Like I said, I don't have a lot of time. Listen carefully and do what I say. There's a way out of here and you need to take it when the chance arrives."

Aryion glanced at him. "What chance is that, then? When it's the best time for you?"

"I know where they took the boy," Darion said.

Aryion sprang up from the cot and crossed the distance between them in two strides, towering over the young ranger. His body trembled with the sudden surge of both fear and anger at the mention of his apprentice. "Talk, Blackbird," he hissed, inches from Darion's face. "Talk fast. That boy is more important than you know. Tell me where they've taken him before I lose my temper."

Darion, to his credit, didn't flinch. "He's in one of the upper levels. And no, you can't get to him through that crawl space, if that's what you were going to ask." He nodded at the ceiling. "But you can get to the Liznees. They're a few cells down the hall."

"And how does that help?" Aryion asked. "We'd be trapped in the crawl space instead of trapped in the cells."

"No, you wouldn't," Darion said, lowering his voice. "The crawl space connects every room of this level. You could get out of the cell block and drop into the hall."

Aryion took a step back, thinking. He still distrusted the young ranger. But there was a genuine concern and urgency in Darion's eyes. "How do I know this isn't another trap?"

Darion gave a small shrug. "Aside from trusting me, you don't. But I'll give you my word, for as much as it counts—I'm still on your side. The king's plan still stands. We need to learn what the Aces are doing here."

"Seems you would have learned that from working for them by now."

"I haven't. I've seen the void and some of the stuff they've got around the area, but this is the first time I've been inside the castle. You saw that it's concealed by an illusion from the outside."

"So you say," Aryion said uncertainly, but he was beginning to realize, as much as he hated it, that this was the best chance they had.

"You can go up there now if you want," Darion added, nodding to the ceiling. "It's only about two feet of room. You'll have to crawl. Make sure you aren't caught, but I doubt that'll be a challenge for you. Jan's trusting us to find our best route of escape."

"Our?" Aryion repeated doubtfully.

"Yes, our," Darion said irritably. "What, you think I'm still working for them? You saw what they did to Wiverrun. We needed some kind of cover. This is the closest we'll get to seeing what the Aces are up to."

"A capture in place of an investigation," Aryion said dryly.

"None of the investigations have found this," Darion said, gesturing around him. "I had a guess the Aces had hidden something in the ruin, but I had no idea it was this big. Whatever secrets they're hiding here, whatever they're planning—no one will find it unless the Ace-Lord allows it to be found, and by then, it'll be too late."

Aryion stared at him for a long moment, still not sure what to make of the young ranger. This was Jan's plan, apparently—allow them to be captured, if only to learn the truth of what was happening. The king was counting on the two rangers to find their way back out so they could bring the crucial news to Caer Sia.

Risky, yes. Aryion was fairly sure there was another reason Jan had allowed this, something that lay in Redeyes' cryptic mention of the Marks. But that question would have to be answered later.

"I'll see what I find," he said shortly, nodding up at the grate. "In the meantime, I need you to do two things."

Darion looked at him expectantly, and Aryion continued. "Get word to General Arrex. If they come looking for us, this entire plan will have been for nothing. Tell them to go south to Tinkeeyo. Send word of what's happened and ready the southern fiefs in case the Aces strike from the Magno Forest."

Darion nodded again. "All right. What else?"

Aryion smiled faintly. "Go find my sword."

The young ranger left the cell and locked the door behind him. Aryion sized up the grating, his mind already planning their escape.

. . . . . .

His mission through the crawl space was both fruitful and frustrating. As Darion had told him, the space above the grating allowed silent travel above the cells. It stretched out over the hall, allowing the faint pale light to penetrate the darkness. From his position, Aryion could see the guards stationed at either end of the hall, hollow eyes staring at nothing.

The guards would be a problem. Even if all four of them managed to escape through the crawl space, there was no way the guards wouldn't notice the empty cells. Then they would be caught before they were halfway down the stairs. They would have to escape between guard rotations, and hope that the new guards wouldn't notice which cells were occupied or not.

He found the Liznees in a cell near the very end of the corridor. Asescia was asleep, and Jan was seated beside her keeping watch in the shadows. For a moment, Aryion considered dropping into the cell and explaining his developing strategy. But that would be dangerous, with the guards this close. Any noise, any error, and the escape attempt would be over before it had even begun.

No, there would be time to fill the Liznees in on the plan later. For now, he would work with what he'd learned.

He made his way back to his cell and sat on the cot, waiting and thinking. There was no sign of Darion for several hours. The guards changed rotation, and Aryion wished he had a way to keep track of time. It would be important to know when the shift changed.

By the time Darion returned, Aryion had more questions for him. There was the quiet rattle of a key in the door, and Darion entered.

"Did it work?" was the first thing he asked, nodding at the ceiling.

"We'll fit," Aryion answered. "But I am not sure how we'll get the Liznees out unnoticed. The guards are watching their cell closely."

"I'm not surprised. They want the king more than anyone else here—except for Mel, maybe."

"Did you find him?" Aryion demanded.

"Yes, but it'll be tricky to make contact. He's under heavy guard. I know which cell he's in, but I couldn't get word to him." Darion produced a satchel. "Here are your weapons—hide them well. The Deputy is personally guarding the Star-Stones. To be honest, I don't know if we have a chance of getting out with the Stones."

"How many levels are in this castle?" Aryion asked.

"Twenty, thirty maybe," Darion said, thinking. "It just keeps going up. There's also some lower levels built into the supporting columns, too, mostly used as storage."

"Could you rappel down the column to reach the bottom of the canyon?"

"Maybe at one time. You can't now—you'll just fall into the Patch."

"The Patch?"

"That void-thing in the moat outside," Darion said, nodding in the direction of the main gates. "They call it the Patch."

"What's in there?"

"No one really knows. It's the one thing the illusion doesn't fully cover. The Aces go in and out of it fairly often, but I've never seen a mortal go in and come back out alive," Darion said. "It protects the castle more than the guards. You have to get over the Patch to go anywhere."

"And there's no other way out?" Aryion asked uneasily.

"Only the marble bridges." Darion thought for a moment. "I think the west gate is less guarded. Maybe we could escape that way."

"That would put Castle Droco between us and the road back to Sia," Aryion pointed out.

"I don't know if we can help that," Darion said. "I'll scout around a little more and see what I find." He stepped toward the door.

"Be careful," Aryion warned him. "The guards may notice you've been here frequently."

"They change shifts every three hours, so this rotation hasn't seen me yet," Darion said. "I've noticed the enchantment keeps them from questioning these sorts of things—they know I'm on their side, so they won't stop me."

"Every three hours, you said?" Aryion repeated.

"Yes. I sent word to General Arrex, by the way—the Aces took all of the duke's possessions, including his carrier pigeons. The birds should return to the manor. If the soldiers return to look for us, they'll get my message."

"Good," Aryion said, satisfied. "Well, if you reach Mel, try to let him know what we're planning. I want to know what he thinks."

"He's eleven," Darion said doubtfully.

"He's twelve, actually. And more importantly, he's beat the Aces before."

Darion nodded, conceding that point, then left the cell again.

Aryion sat on the cot in the dim light, thinking. The strategy seemed like a good one, but there were too many unknowns. This castle seemed to have been constructed to be incredibly difficult to escape. The Aces would not wait forever. Eventually, their questioning would turn violent, and the truth of their mission here might be revealed.

And so he sat in the darkness, worry lingering in his mind even as he planned their escape.

20

❧ ❧ ❧ ❧ ❧ ❧ ❧ ❧ ❧

Mortal Roles

Mel didn't know how long he waited in darkness.

After the soldiers had dragged Allie and Aryion down the long corridor, they had marched Mel and Jan up another three flights of winding stairs. At last they reached a cold iron room lit dimly by pale light. The Deputy joined them shortly after and began to fire questions at them both. Mel was surprised by the topics—the Ace-Deputy asked very little regarding the war or current events. He wanted to know how the Liznees had regained Isilas, where Drisilas had come from, if Mel had known about the Blue Stone before joining the quest for the Shards.

Mel was so tired he answered without much hesitation. No, he hadn't learned about the Stone before. No, he hadn't helped the Liznees get Isilas itself, just the sword. No, he hadn't been there when the sword was forged.

None of the information the Deputy asked for seemed terribly important. Most of the questions made him realize that the Deputy had very little concept of how time worked for the mortals. He seemed surprised to learn that Mel's knowledge spanned barely past the last century or so.

Eventually the Deputy stopped questioning Mel and turned his attention to Jan. Mel was taken from the room and up more flights of stairs. His legs ached with the continuous climb, and he was too weary to protest when the guards hauled him into another dark corridor. This level of cells was eerily quiet, without even the strange white lights to fill the room with light or sound.

The guards seemed to be able to see in the darkness. There was a creak as a door opened, then Mel was flung inside a cell. He heard the door slam shut, then the sound of retreating footsteps. Then all was silent.

Mel groped his way around the room, trying to get his bearings. It was so dark he could barely tell which direction the door was. The blackness was suffocating. For an instant, his mind spiraled into panic and he again hung suspended in the void within the Darkness. "Hey!" he shouted, stumbling forward. Nothing.

Shivering in the cold, he huddled against what he assumed was the door and tried to catch his breath, forcing the memories away. As his panic settled, reason reasserted itself in his mind. "Calm down," he whispered. "What do I do in a situation like this?"

Aryion's training filled his thoughts. "Find a way out," he murmured. "Gather information and see if there's any way out. Well, I can't see anything at all."

He figured he sounded crazy, mumbling to himself in the dark. But whispering the words helped ground his anxious thoughts.

He stood and felt his way along the wall, counting his paces. He reached ten paces before bumping into the back wall, and six across. The measurement helped him picture the room in his mind. That was something else Aryion had taught him, to use other senses when one was dulled.

"How high did we come up?" he asked out loud. "Ten stairways? Maybe five more after they separated us? So that's… fifteen levels?"

Fifteen levels up in a castle surrounded by a void of nothingness, with the only way out heavily guarded by enchanted, deathless soldiers.

He slumped back against the wall, an unwelcome hopelessness filling his chest again. Even if, by some miracle, he found a way out of his cell, how would he reach his companions and make it over the bridge?

Quiet footfalls reached his ears. A pale light illuminated the door frame from beyond. Mel scrambled back from the door, waiting for it to open.

The door did not open. Instead, the shadowy walker in the corridor reached the frame and ghosted into the room.

"Hello, New Blood."

Mel sprang to his feet. The Ace-Deputy strode forward, looking around the cell with mild interest. His armor gave off a faint white light that lit the room slightly. The light would have been comforting, if the Deputy were not its source.

"These are fine quarters," the Deputy said conversationally.

"Not bad for a prison," Mel shot back. "What do you want?"

The Ace-Deputy shook his head. "Temper, temper, child," he chided. "I only wish to talk to you. I am far more forgiving than my master; he is slow to forget the past. But aside from your rather… problematic… ideals, you have done me no direct harm. Thus, I hold nothing against you yet."

"Yeah, well, I definitely have things to hold against you," Mel snapped. "And if you're here to torture me, you won't learn much that your master doesn't already know."

"I assumed as much," the Deputy replied. "Yet you are useful in other ways. You are, of course, very powerful."

"Not really," Mel said. "That's the Stone's power, not mine."

"Ah, the Stone," the Deputy said, nodding. "I am impressed the Liznees chose you to be its keeper. Though, perhaps you were the most fitting. It is a role written in your prophecy, is it not?"

"It is," Mel said, a little confused by this route of questioning, and added flatly, "just like your defeat."

"Is it?" the Deputy asked. "Why can you not see that the Prophecy foretells the Ace-Lord's victory? We do not wish for so many to suffer. The only pain we have caused was, in fact, brought about by the mortals' resistance. The Prophecy's words spell out the glorious kingdom to come.

"Think, New Blood," the Deputy continued, his smooth tone filling the cell. "Think of the Prophecy's words. The first stanza, I have noticed, was fulfilled when you joined the Shards. My master offered you the chance to share his power then, you remember. You denied his offer, but have you not understood the message of the fourth stanza? *Beware the Twelfth who stands unnamed.*"

Mel remained silent. The Deputy shook his head. "And look who is mentioned in the seventh stanza, described in a similar fashion: *When nameless New Blood knows their call.* Do you not see, child, that your destiny lies with us? Do you not see how woefully the mortals have misinterpreted the Prophecy's words? And yet it was they who hid its truth for centuries. We cannot deny the Prophecy—we must follow its words, and thus our victory is sealed."

The words fed the doubt that lurked on the edges of Mel's mind. He forced it away, looking up at the decayed face. "You lie," he whispered. "Your master's plan is evil, and he has no part in the goodness of the Prophecy. Besides, I'm not the Twelfth Ace. Haven't you already given that role to Redeyes?"

"Ah yes, Redeyes," the Ace-Deputy said distastefully. "The butcher of death returned to the land of mortals. I had hoped my master's plans would lie elsewhere, but who am I to question the Dark Lord?" He studied Mel thoughtfully, a wily light shining in his purple-red eyes. "I had hoped he would choose someone wiser, cleverer, less obsessed with killing, for the role of the Twelfth. But alas, you threw that chance away."

"And I'd do it again," Mel said firmly. "Get to the point. Why are you here?"

The sound of heavy padded steps in the hall beyond reached his ears. The Ace-Deputy opened the door, allowing Redeyes to enter.

"Well, Messenger. I am glad you could join us."

"You requested my presence," the great cat snarled. His fiery eyes flicked over to Mel. "Does one require the Marks?" he asked with barely concealed excitement.

"Silence, beast," the Ace-Deputy snapped. "Speak not so of our honored guest. The boy has agreed to hear our offer."

"I haven't agreed to anything," Mel corrected him. "I just asked you to tell me what you want from me."

Redeyes stretched and sat down, curling his thick tail around his paws. The Ace-Deputy turned back to Mel. "Answer me this question, New Blood. Can you command the Stone's power?"

"It's not really a command," Mel said slowly. "Yes, I can use its power. But I can only use it for the right reasons. I can't control it or order it to do things."

"That did not seem to stop you when you used it against Terrax," the Ace-Deputy said silkily.

Mel faltered, caught off guard by the statement. He was not sure how the Deputy had heard about that, but it mattered little. He'd used the Stone in a moment of vengeful rage in Esile City, charging at Terrax and protecting himself with a shield of blue energy.

"That… that was different," he said, confidence shaken. "That's not the way you're supposed to use the Stones. You can't use them as weapons, like the Ace-Lord wants to."

"You misunderstand the Dark Lord's plans," the Deputy said. "He understands the Stones are not meant to harm, far better than certain mortals I could mention. They are tools, objects of power to be used for the welfare of the kingdom. That is exactly how he intends to use them. With the Stones, the power of the Dark Realm will fill Orlell, and the mortal will become immortal."

His voice grew low. "Think of that, New Blood. No pain. No death. Think of all who have died already in this pointless war. Think of your family. Will you see them die in such a meaningless way? Why should they die when, with the Dark Realm's powers, they will live forever, embracing the enchantment as our loyal servants?"

"You leave my family out of this," Mel hissed, rage and fear filling his heart.

"You brought them into it the moment you joined the Shards," the Deputy said coldly. "Should you refuse to cooperate, they will suffer for your decision. You may yet save them and serve my master's coming empire. Make your choice now. Tell me of the Stone's power. What must one do to command it?"

Despite himself, Mel gave a short laugh. "You can't even touch it. Good luck trying to command it."

"I will not," the Deputy said. "Redeyes will."

Mel looked at Redeyes, startled. Yet he had begun to understand. While Redeyes fulfilled the role of the Twelfth Ace, he was not physically changed. Per the Ace-Lord's interpretation of the Prophecy, the New Blood and the Twelfth Ace must be one and the same. "You can't," he said in disbelief. "I mean… you can't be the Stone's Wielder. It has to be a mortal Cantrian."

"I am not as mortal as I once was," Redeyes growled. "But neither was Captain Hagshrub, who surrendered his immortality in the same way I did upon returning to the living world. My powers are my own, and my Essence is Cantrian as it ever has been."

Mel looked between the two of them, shaken, not sure what to say.

"You have already refused my master's offer," the Deputy said. "The role must be filled by another. Redeyes fits the criteria far better than Hagshrub once did, and thanks to the Blackbird, we now have the Blue Stone. However, Redeyes must learn how to use its powers."

"So you want me to teach you to use the Stone," Mel guessed, shaking his head.

"You doubt my strength?" Redeyes snarled.

"Not really. I don't know what to tell you. You can't really… I mean, the Stone isn't something you learn how to command," Mel said slowly. "It's a gift. Its power isn't something to control. I can't teach you."

"Can't? Or won't?" the Deputy mused. "I believe you mean the latter. Whether or not I am correct remains to be seen."

"We will know soon," Redeyes growled. "If torture is meaningless against you as you claim, your love and care for others is a predictable weakness. Let us see if you are so sure after you have seen what is done to your mentor."

A cold dread seemed to seep into Mel's bones. Seeing his face, a hideous smile passed over Redeyes' features. "He is strong, I have no doubt. He will be less so after I am finished with him. One Mark bears the curse of a kingdom. Imagine the pain a thousand scars will cause." He yawned, his teeth glinting in the light. "Or, perhaps we will throw him into the Patch and allow the darkness to consume his Essence."

"Don't," Mel said, his voice hoarse. "Don't touch him—don't touch any of them."

"He does not have to," the Deputy said. "It is your decision, New Blood. Your life is the one we require, not theirs. Their fate will hinge on your choice."

Mel let out a breath. His duty to the Stone fought with his desperation to save his friends, and in this lonely pit of darkness, his friends won. "I'll try to teach you," he told Redeyes. "I don't know how I'll do it. I think… I think it might be better to wait for the Ace-Lord to come back," he added, with a glance at the Deputy. "He'll probably know more about this kind of thing."

"That is acceptable," the Ace-Deputy agreed. "We will fetch you when he returns."

"Remember, boy," Redeyes hissed, "any tricks, any attempts of escape, and I will shred your master's flesh from his bones. And I will do the same for your family if you resist. Your cooperation is their lifeblood."

Mel nodded shortly, unable to form words.

The two left the cell, and he was enveloped by darkness again. The horror of what Redeyes described, the threat against his family, and the overwhelming despair of their situation cracked his weak ruse of bravery. He hunched against the wall and wept.

. . . . . .

Distant sounds roused him.

Mel sat up stiffly. Faint gray light leaked from the corridor beyond. Daylight, he guessed. Had they been here only one night? It felt like far longer.

Low voices came from far away, echoing down the hall. He couldn't make out words. Footsteps drew nearer, heavy, purposeful footsteps. The door unlocked and swung forward, and a guard entered, empty blue eyes staring at nothing. He set a tray of food on the floor and left without a word.

Mel ate hungrily. The bread was stale and the water bitterly cold, but it soothed his churning stomach. At least the Aces did not intend to starve him into cooperation. That was good. Then again, the Ace-Lord needed him alive and whole for his plans.

His teeth met something papery as he bit into the bread, and he pulled out a folded slip of parchment tucked inside the roll.

Interested, he unfolded it and read the short words by the dim light beyond:

Black will come. Look high for Humming. I will find you.

Mel studied the brief message, his heart pounding with a new-found energy. The handwriting was slightly scrawled, clearly done in haste, but Aryion had taught him the art of code talk and riddles during his ranger training. Slowly, painfully, he read over the message, wishing for Misty's quick talent with words. He forced himself to slow down and process every word, seeking the meaning.

At last he understood. *Black* as in Blackbird. *Humming* as in Hummingbird.

Why Darion had chosen to join their side again, Mel had no idea, but the sheer hope of that last line drove the other thoughts away.

I will find you.

"Aryion," he breathed, almost crying with relief. Aryion and Darion were planning an escape.

Look high for Humming. Look high, his mind echoed thoughtfully. What could that mean? He looked up. The ceiling above was shrouded in darkness, but in the faint light brought by day beyond, he noticed a strange cross-barred grating that covered the ceiling. The space beyond was completely dark, but it was a space nonetheless.

There was a way out. Aryion would find him, coming from above.

Mel tore the paper into shreds and dropped them into the water cup, watching the ink blur and disperse. Whenever the escape happened, he had to be prepared. The message had both encouraged him and increased his desire to escape and warn his family. But there was nothing he could do for now.

He sat against the wall and waited.

Yet the faint daylight beyond had faded again by the time he finally heard footsteps—and the sounds did not belong to his mentor.

21

The Doorway

Allie drained the last of the bitter water in the cup and leaned back against the stone wall. Based on the fading gray light from the hall beyond, she assumed evening was falling. That meant they had been here a full day.

When would General Arrex realize their plans had gone awry? Would he come to help them? If he did, his entire squadron would be captured and either killed or enchanted. By the time anyone in Caer Sia found out what had happened, it might be too late to help the captives.

Allie tucked her knees up under her and glanced at her uncle. Jan was asleep, his chin resting forward on his chest. His face bore the bruises of the interrogation he had recently endured. The guards had come and jarred Allie out of her uneasy sleep, taking the king away into the winding castle. Allie had waited, tense with worry, for what felt like hours before the guards finally returned and shoved Jan inside.

The Ace-Deputy, it seemed, had questioned Jan, demanding to know more about Drisilas. Apparently, the sword needed to be unsheathed if the Aces were to access the Stone's powers. They could not remove Isilas from the sword's hilt, though Jan said they'd tried to, so their only option was to force Jan to draw the blade and remove the magic that protected it from any hands but his own.

That magic was neither the Stone's, nor Jan's. The spell guarding Drisilas from any hand but the king's had been laid upon it by the hama-dryads when it had first been forged. Jan had explained this, but the Ace-Deputy refused to believe him, growing increasingly angry and more aggressive as the interrogation dragged on.

"They will find a way to break the spell," Jan had told Allie wearily, as she cleaned the blood from his face. "They say Isilas' powers have grown weaker the longer it remains in the sword's hilt. The Aces' magic is a darker and stronger kind than the natural spells of the hama-dryads. It will take them awhile, but they will break it."

He had been so tired and sad. Allie urged him to rest, and he had finally agreed, which showed how worn out he was. The guards changed rotations twice. Someone brought water and a chunk of dry bread. Allie debated waking her uncle so he could eat, but decided against it, and set his paltry meal aside. She ate and drank slowly, spreading it out over a few hours to help the gnawing hunger and thirst.

As the dim gray light faded into their second evening here, she stood and paced the cell. So many questions had been answered in such a short time, and she was still reeling from the implications. Firstly, there was the matter of Isilas. Jan bore the curse for turning it into a weapon, which corrupted the Star-Stone's pure magic. Allie had no idea if there was any way to reconcile that curse, or if the corruption could be reversed.

Jan had allowed himself to be captured to atone for that wrong. Yet Allie knew, with sickening certainty, that the Aces would not remove the curse so easily. Every scar, every Mark, every sign that had appeared since—the attacks on Caer Sia over the years, the scars on Darion's face, the gashes on Glentree's back—they were all reminders, reiterating the fatal price the Ace-Lord required.

Yet the Ace-Lord needed Isilas, too. Perhaps he planned to enchant Jan, or force Jan to use the sword for his conquest.

"We'll escape before it comes to that," she murmured to herself, and sat down on the hard cot again.

Jan stirred at the sound of her voice. "Any change?" he asked hoarsely, blinking in the dim gray light.

"The guards changed post twice," Allie said softly, offering him the tray of bread. "I'd guess every three or four hours, but I can't tell."

Jan's eyes flicked to the door. "It is getting darker again. Are the guards still in the corridor?"

"Right by the door," Allie said bitterly. Jan had said their plan hinged on Aryion and Darion finding a way out. But that seemed less likely with every passing minute.

With a harsh clank, the door swung open. One of the guards stepped inside. "You are summoned," he said dully.

Allie's heart sank. The Ace-Deputy had roughly questioned Jan last time. Soon, he would turn to crueler tortures.

Jan stood stiffly, but the guard shook his head. "Not you. Her."

Allie looked at him, startled. "Me?" she repeated, taken aback.

"You have been summoned," the guard repeated tonelessly.

"Why? By whom?" Jan demanded.

The guard did not answer, but gripped Allie's arm and forced her towards the door. Red fire flared instantly in Jan's hands as he stepped forward to protect her.

"Jan, no," Allie said quickly. "I'll be all right."

It was an effort to hide her growing fears and keep her expression calm. The guard said nothing further as he marched her out of the cell. She glimpsed Jan's worried face before the door slammed behind her and the lock clicked in place.

. . . . . .

Aryion knew something had gone wrong.

Darion had been here three times—twice to talk, and the last time to pass Aryion's secret message to Mel. He had brought Aryion's sword and both the rangers' packs—concealed in his black cloak, the uncertain light in the halls worked to his advantage. He had promised to return and bring the rest of the gear after passing the message to Mel.

That was the last time Aryion had seen him. The guards had changed post twice, which meant it had been six hours. At the first interval, he had assumed Darion was unable to reach him. Maybe the young ranger was investigating the rest of the fortress, or better yet, getting word to the other companions.

But as the hours wore by, Aryion's concern grew. Darion had been gone far too long. Perhaps it had all been a trap, and he had gone to the Ace-Deputy. But Aryion doubted that. If that were so, the Aces surely would have doubled their guard, or come to question Aryion himself. No, Darion had not betrayed them. Despite his mistakes, Darion was working to right the wrongs he had caused, and their escape plan had been coming together.

Why then did Darion delay? It had to be growing dark outside. They had been here for a full day, and he sensed time was running out.

Aryion stood uncertainly by the door of his cell, straining his ears for any sounds of activity beyond, but heard none. The hall remained utterly silent.

He weighed his options for a few more minutes before deciding he could wait no longer. Under better circumstances, they might have the luxury of waiting for an opportune time, but they did not have that now. The Ace-Lord might return at any moment, which would put a stop to any escape attempts.

The Deputy they might manage to evade. The Lord of Death was a completely different matter.

He shouldered the packs and clipped his sword to his belt, then jumped and gripped the iron bars of the ceiling, pulling himself into the crawl space above.

Slowly, he crept along the grating, bracing himself against the wall on his left. Urgency gnawed on his nerves, but precision mattered more than speed. He must go slowly, burdened with the packs and weapons. Any sound or sudden movement could alert the guards to the secret escape route.

Finally, he reached the cell at the end of the corridor where the Liznees were held. Only one guard waited outside. The cell below him was dark, but he could just make out Ĵan's tall form, standing by the door.

As though he could sense the gaze upon him, the Liznee king looked up sharply, and his green eyes narrowed as he saw the shadowy form above.

Aryion lowered himself silently into the cell, motioning for quiet as he did. Not daring to risk a whisper, he gestured up at the crawl space. "Hurry," he mouthed urgently.

Ĵan shook his head and pointed back at the door. Aryion was about to argue, but realized he had missed something. He looked around the cell, hoping he was wrong, but no. He turned back to Ĵan. "Where's Asescia?"

"The guard took her," Ĵan answered, his worried voice just below a whisper. "I do not know where or why. We cannot leave without her."

Aryion let out a tense breath. This was bad. Mel locked in an upper level, Darion's disappearance, and now Asescia taken somewhere else—it further complicated their tedious escape. "We'll find her," he murmured. "They might have moved her to a cell in the upper levels. Mel's up there."

"Did Darion speak with you?" Jan asked.

"Yes, he mentioned this was your plan," Aryion said. He studied the Liznee's face for any sign Darion had lied, but Jan only nodded, looking relieved.

"Good. I am glad he reached you. You can trust him."

"I'll believe that when we're out," Aryion replied shortly. He climbed back through the grating and moved out of the way for Jan to follow. The king moved with a grunt of pain; bruises scored his face and his usually graceful movements seemed strained. But Jan didn't complain.

"Did Darion find out where the Stones are being kept?" Jan whispered as he climbed up.

"Not exactly—he said the Ace-Deputy is guarding them," Aryion told him quietly. "We don't know where, and I haven't seen him in hours." He paused. "To be honest, I think the Stones have a slightly better chance of surviving the Ace-Lord than we do."

"Then our priority lies with Allie and Mel for now," Jan said with a nod. "Lead on."

......

The guard led Allie up the winding stairs, further into the tallest tower of Castle Droco. They passed the doors of the upper prison levels, passed arched rooms that showed the once splendid wealth of Lord Kahlifis, and still they climbed.

The enchanted guard marched effortlessly up the stairs, showing no signs of weariness, and kept his crossbow pointed at Allie's back.

The crossbow, Allie thought dryly, was unneeded. She was exhausted, her breath coming in ragged gasps. She tripped on the top step leading to another landing and fell forward on her hands and knees. The guard, thankfully, didn't urge her up right away, which allowed her a quick glance to the left, over the edge of the balcony.

She immediately regretted it. The many staircases along the wall of the tower formed a seemingly endless spiral leading all the way to the ground floor, which appeared as nothing more than a small square far, far below her. Allie's head swam, and she pulled away from the balcony edge with a shudder.

The guard gripped her arm and pulled her to her feet, and they walked on, but not up more stairs. Instead they turned right, through a set of double doors. They reminded her, for a moment, of the doors outside the throne room in Castle Sia.

Except these doors were jet black, crusted with glittering white ice.

The guard opened the doors, but did not follow, only pushed her inside. Allie stumbled inside, studying the room she had been cast into. The tower room was long, with a high ceiling and pale walls, and her footsteps echoed around her as she moved slowly forward.

Several things caught her eye. The first was a huge silver archway that covered the back wall like a massive tapestry. Gray mist swirled within it like a curtain, yet the infinite blackness of the void beyond it sent chills down her spine.

Mel stood to the left of the archway between two Ace guards. To her surprise, he held the Blue Stone. Behind Mel, a battered figure in a dark cloak slumped against the wall.

Yet Allie's attention was immediately fixed on the other being in the room, towering in darkness, shrouded in shadows. A silver crown shone dully on his withered brow.

"I welcome you, Heiress," the Ace-Lord said, his low voice filling the room like fog. "Please, join us."

Allie tried to move back for the doors, but her legs refused to obey. The Ace-Lord's broken teeth glinted as he smiled. "I see you fear me. Where then is the fearless daughter of Sia I was led to expect? Did you not escape my forces when we entered your city all those months ago?"

Caer Sia. The attack. Towers toppled. Her parents imprisoned, her people killed, good soldiers executed as examples of the Aces' brutality.

Suddenly, her fear was gone. Fury coursing through her, she leapt forward, firing a blast at the Ace-Lord's face.

The Ace-Lord raised a hand casually and deflected the blow with his own pale ice. Allie raised her hands again. "You'll pay for what you did in Sia," she spat, fire flickering from her fingertips.

The Ace-Lord extended a finger at her outstretched hands. Chains of white ice appeared from thin air, binding her wrists before her so tightly they seemed to freeze her veins.

"There is the fire," the Ace-Lord said with a soft laugh. "Such passion. Such rage. It will serve me well." He motioned toward Mel. "Join your friend. Swiftly, now."

Allie stood next to Mel, trembling with anger and fear. "Are you okay?" she asked quietly.

"Yeah, I'm fine," Mel replied. He nodded down at the Stone, which glimmered in his hands. "I tried the same thing as soon as he let me have the Stone. He just blocked its power. I think that void thing makes him stronger." He nodded at the gaping archway.

"It is not a void, New Blood," the Ace-Lord informed him. "It holds far more power than the mere patches of darkness you have seen outside these walls. This is a gateway, a pathway between your world and my kingdom. Before, such a thing existed only through the Jewel's power. Thanks to the remnant of that magic remaining in the compass, I have created this." He laid a clawlike hand on the archway, staring into the shifting shadows with reverence. "Is it not magnificent?"

Allie and Mel remained silent. The Ace-Lord turned back to them, studying them thoughtfully. Allie tried to stare back defiantly, but the purple-red eyes seemed to penetrate into her mind, searing into her skull, and she looked away.

"My Deputy informed me of a strange tale," the Ace-Lord said at length. "A tale of a plot devised by the Liznee king and a traitorous servant, a plot to learn of my powers and escape after doing so." His piercing gaze fixed on Mel. "Tell me, New Blood, is this wretched servant indeed your friend?"

He gestured to the ragged shape crouched against the wall. The figure raised his head, staring up at them with hazel eyes filled with fear.

Allie almost started in shock. The battered stranger was Darion Blackbird.

Blood streaked the young ranger's face and clothes. He had been beaten; the whip had left welts on his neck and forearms. He glanced between Allie and Mel pleadingly.

"A strange tale it is," the Ace-Lord went on calmly. "Once before, this servant abandoned the task given him and defied the oath of servitude. For that, Redeyes has seen to his punishment." The look he cast Darion was one of no more interest than studying a broken tool. "Yet despite that mercy you defy me again. Think you that I do not know of your treachery? I know your intentions here, know you hoped to play both sides of this game."

Allie stared at Darion. The fear and anger churning in her mind made it difficult to think clearly. Darion, punished by Redeyes for failing his task… Darion, trying to help them escape… Darion, who had betrayed them…

"My Deputy believes you both to be involved in the Blackbird's schemes," the Ace-Lord continued. His eyes scrutinized their faces. Allie was not sure which answer he sought. Somewhere in the torrent of confused and angry thoughts came Jan's words about Darion aiding their cause. But they were drowned out.

"This is the first I've heard of anything," she said shortly. "If he was planning to help us escape, I doubt it was for our good."

The Ace-Lord glanced at her with mild surprise. "These are harsh words, Heiress," he said softly. "I am not one to take such sentiments lightly."

"I'm not lying," Allie said flatly. "He's not with us now, if he ever was."

The Ace-Lord nodded thoughtfully. "Very well. If indeed this is true, he is of no further use to anyone." He raised a hand, white ice shining on his fingertips, reflecting in Darion's startled and frightened eyes.

"No," Mel broke in. "Don't kill him. We had a plan. But he wasn't a part of it. It was my plan—my idea to escape. Don't kill him."

Allie looked at him in disbelief. The Ace-Lord smiled and lowered his hands. "You may be cunning in other ways, New Blood, but you are no master of deceit. I know you had no hand in any vain escape plan. Be silent."

Mel was quiet, still staring at Darion.

The Ace-Lord's words drew Allie's attention away from him. "I believe this is your uncle's sword, Heiress?" He held Drisilas before her.

Allie snatched the sword, holding it close. "What do you want with this?" she demanded. Somewhere in her mind, it dawned on her how strange this all was. The Ace-Lord had not harmed them. He had said nothing of torture, only of cooperation. He had given them both Star-Stones.

"What I want," the Ace-Lord said, stepping toward her, "will not be brought about by Star-Stones. At last I have foreseen this. I allowed you to come here, allowed you to see Castle Droco for what it has become, but that cost is acceptable. If you knew the rules of this game, child, you would understand that certain risks must be taken."

"All I know is that your plans will be ruined without the Stones," Allie shot back.

The Ace-Lord took her chin in an unbreakable grip, looking into her face. Allie tried not to shudder, to stare back with an equally angry and brave expression. But her fear drowned out her bravery.

"So very like your father, though not as skilled at hiding your fear as he," the Ace-Lord said with a smile. "There is a task laid before you, Heiress, a destiny you must embrace. The doorway, thus far, has served to return my servants to the mortal world, but it must become more. The Wielders shall use the Stones to open the door wide, and our worlds shall become one."

"I'll never join you," Allie replied, but her voice trembled.

The hand grew impossibly cold, as though her chin rested in a grip of ice. Cold spread down her throat, clutching her voice, reaching icy fingers toward her heart. Her pulse quickened, and her breath came in ragged gasps of terror. The fire of her Essence flared in retaliation, until she felt caught between burning cold and searing heat. Pale stars swam in her mind. The Ace-Lord's face focused in her vision, framed by the empty blackness of the doorway beyond.

Through the dizzying rush of fear she heard his voice, heard an ancient incantation in a tongue she neither recognized nor understood: "*Aranac, devariss, vey dovannon.*"

A pale light glittered behind her vision. The fear surged once, stabbing her heart, then she was left with anger, a helpless, boiling fury. The Essence in her veins grew hot as though her blood had turned to fire. She gave a choked cry but barely recognized her own voice.

Then the Ace-Lord pulled away.

Allie crashed to the ground, shaking, her senses assaulted by the sudden return to reality. Every sight and sound seemed magnified. The blackness of the void seemed darker, the light blaringly bright, the frantic voice of Mel far too loud. Her vision blurred at the edges. Colors seemed washed out. She shook her head, trying to clear her reeling mind and ringing ears.

"Peace, New Blood," the Ace-Lord ordered.

Mel was shouting—his words finally cut through the incessant ringing. "What did you do to her? What do you want with us? If you hurt her I'll use the Stone to destroy—"

"Silence," the Ace-Lord commanded. "She is unharmed. It is you I now have need of." He turned to the two Ace guards. "Bring them."

With that, he turned and strode through the archway, vanishing into the darkness beyond.

22

Battle on the Bridge

The Ace-Lord's silhouette was framed in the shadows of the void in the arch before he vanished. Gray fog swirled in his passing, then settled again. The archway gaped like an open mouth before Allie and Mel.

Cold hands gripped Allie's arms, hauling her upright. She stumbled, trying to get her balance enough to put up some resistance. She clutched Drisilas, wishing for Jan's power to wield the blade, but there was nothing she could do. She staggered helplessly toward the gateway.

Yet even as they moved closer to the arch, the deep-throated thrum of a bowstring sounded just behind her, and suddenly the Ace guard lurched forward with a hiss. An arrow sunk into its back.

The Ace gave a hissing snarl of anger more than pain and turned, ice gleaming on its claw-like fingers. Its companion raised its hands, but Mel slammed his shoulder into its thin chest and shoved it off balance.

Barely able to see what was happening but knowing this was their only hope of escape, Allie raised her hand, sending fire leaping from her fingertips. Blinding agony shot through her head, as though her body had gone from cold to hot in a matter of seconds.

She stumbled and fell to her knees again, clutching Drisilas, but the blast had set the Ace toppling back through the archway. As the second guard turned to her, Mel raised the Blue Stone. Vivid light filled the room, searing the darkness like fire, and a wall of energy radiated from its core. The Ace snarled, shielding its face. Another arrow plunged into its chest, and it finally retreated—not dead, Allie knew, nor even badly injured. Likely it would follow its companion into the void and alert the Ace-Lord.

She swung her gaze back into the room. Darion stood, a third arrow resting on the string. His scarred face was bruised, but in it was a determination that was far different from the fear he had shown the Ace-Lord. "You two all right?"

"Yeah," Mel breathed, holding the Blue Stone close. "We have to go—those two will be back."

Darion nodded toward the door. "We'll make for the main gate. Come on."

"Wait," Allie said, striding up to Darion. Fire crackled in her fist as she glared at him. "Why on Orlell should we trust you?"

"Allie, don't," Mel called behind her.

Darion spread his hands. "Not here. We don't have time. If the plan worked, Aryion's already got the king out, but we lost a lot of time when they moved you two."

Allie felt Mel's hand on her arm, pulling her away. "We have to go."

Anger still surging through her, she slung Drisilas' strap over her shoulders and took a trembling breath. The terror of meeting the Ace-Lord, his confusing words to them, and the ache in her head made it hard to think clearly, but she knew they were right. Jan still trusted Darion, that much she knew—and that would have to be enough for now.

They started toward the double doors. Darion had concealed their weapons within his quiver—Allie's sword and Mel's long dagger. She had just wrapped her hand around the familiar curve of the hilt when ice crackled behind them, spreading up the walls in razor-sharp darts. The two Ace guards had returned, frost crusting their knuckles as they raised their hands.

Darion shoved her and Mel towards the door. Allie ducked as a hail of icy darts raked the air behind them. Four enchanted soldiers, hearing the commotion, opened the double doors at the same time; Mel leapt forward, raising the Blue Stone and sending a shield of energy from its core, forcing the soldiers backward.

Allie reached the end of the balcony and skidded to a halt, her heart pounding. The landing dropped away before her, revealing the dizzying height. Spiraling stairs along the wall led down to the floor far below.

She pulled away and ran down the steps after Darion and Mel. Darion wielded his bow like a quarterstaff, swinging it into any guards who rushed to stop them. Down, down they went, and yet the distant gates to freedom seemed no closer.

A crossbow bolt whizzed past Allie's ear from behind. She turned—the soldiers in the upper levels had been alerted, and now they streamed down the stairs after them. She fired a blast back into their midst, unable to see if she'd hit anything. Ice crusted the stairs before them, and they slipped and slid down to the next landing. Allie risked another glance backward—the two Ace guards appeared as shadows behind the ranks of enchanted soldiers, ghosting toward them.

Red fire surged in her hands, blazing hot, crackling with an intensity that she attributed to sheer terror. She sent another blast back at their pursuers. The enchanted soldiers, startled by the fire, hesitated. White ice cut through the flames in a burst of steam as the Aces, unbothered, continued forward, speeding after their escaping prisoners.

Darion stopped at the next landing, where a door on the left led into the prison wing. He kicked open the door and braced himself in the opening. Allie sent fire down the stairs at the approaching soldiers. The effort took her breath away. "Any other way out of here?" she yelled over her shoulder.

"No—hold on!" Darion shouted back.

Mel raised the Stone, allowing a vivid plume of blue light to shield them for a moment and deflect the oncoming crossbow bolts. But in another instant the light faded and they stood unprotected. Allie swung back toward the Aces, knowing she was outmatched. The white ice would tear the Essence from her and her companions, killing them all in a moment. Fire crackled in her palms, and she fought to control it, to build it into one final, futile blast.

But she never had to let the shot fly.

A tall figure leapt from the doorway behind Darion and reached Allie's side, moving her out of the way. Red fire crackled from his hands as he shot both groups of soldiers simultaneously. The force of the fire flung the nearest guards from the stairs, sending them toppling to the floor far below.

Ĵan straightened and turned to her, concerned. "Are you all right?"

"Yes, I'm—fine," Allie managed to pant, pressing Drisilas into his hands. She hugged him tightly, too relieved that he was here to care about anything else.

Aryion appeared through the door as well, and Mel moved quickly to him, his face drawn with fear. "Aryion, they said they'll go after my family if we escape—I don't know what to—"

"We'll help them," Aryion reassured him. "But not here. We must get out of this fortress." He turned to Darion. "These stairs will slow us down. Any other way out of here?"

"No other way but down," Darion said. He had removed the arrows from his quiver, reaching inside. "And seeing as we're going down anyway…"

The soldiers, startled by Ĵan's fire, had quickly regrouped and were closing in again. Ĵan deflected a bolt of white ice aimed at Aryion, and looked at Darion. "Whatever you are doing, do it quickly."

Darion had produced a length of rope from inside his quiver, and began to fasten it to the railing. "This'll be faster," he muttered. "Better than going down all those stairs."

Aryion looked between the rope and the drop over the rail, his face falling. "We are going… down the stairwell?"

"Just hold tight and go as fast as you can," Darion said, handing them each a leather strap to protect their hands. He dropped the rest of the line over the railing. Allie heard the quiet thump as it hit the tile floor far, far below.

"I can hold them for now," Jan said. "The rest of you, hurry."

"I'm not leaving you," Allie said firmly.

Jan took her shoulders and pushed her toward the railing. "Go! I'll come as soon as I can."

Darion slipped under the railing, gripping the rope in front of him. "Let yourself fall and kick off the staircases as you pass them. Just hold tight." With that, he leaned back and dropped out of sight.

Allie gripped the line, trying not to look down. A blast of ice glanced off the railing, and the rising din of voices below told her the entire castle was now alerted to their escape.

She gritted her teeth and let herself drop.

Her heart seemed to leap into her throat as she fell. The rope bit into her tired hands through the leather, and the momentum swung her inwards. She kicked off and fell again. In slow, painful sections she descended, swinging forwards and kicking backwards, dropping as fast as she could stomach and slowing herself down again.

At last her boots slammed into the tile. She staggered, unable to unlock her fingers from the line. Darion gripped her arm and hauled her to her feet. "Watch our backs," he warned shortly. An arrow rested on his bowstring.

Allie turned. The Ace-Lord's servants had come, and the previously quiet castle seemed to have come to life in a swarm of voices and movement. Enchanted soldiers streamed from the staircases, orcs and goblins approached with cudgels, strange shadow creatures that bristled and snarled lurked just beyond the reach of light.

She spread fire in a glowing arch before her, creating a wall of red flames. In the firelight, she could see the glowing eyes of the pursuers, pressing forward, staying out of reach of the fire but prepared to leap forward the moment the flames died down.

Mel landed behind her, pulling the Stone from his pocket and holding it before him. Aryion landed next, light on his feet, sword half raised. "There's too many for us to take here, Blackbird," he warned.

There was a final flash of red from high above, then Jan descended down the rope, gripping Drisilas in his free hand. He had barely reached the ground before ice glistened down the line, shredding it in pieces. Allie could see the blazing eyes of the Aces above.

She looked back at the hoards of warriors, who still held back. *Why don't they attack?* The nagging thought inquired from the back of her mind. The companions were outnumbered and completely exposed. The Aces must want the prisoners recaptured alive—but why?

The soldiers had formed up before the north gate—Darion turned to the left, and the companions fled before the throng of hollow-eyed warriors. Allie ran, breathing raggedly, tightening her grip on her sword.

"This is the wrong way," Aryion panted. "We'll come out on the west, with Caer Droco between us and the road back to Sia."

"It's our only chance!" Darion called back. "There's too many guards at the main bridge."

They reached the double doors, and Aryion and Darion forced them open.

Rain fell in sheets, and a wild wind whipped through the hills around the valley. The marble bridge arched away into the night, a glistening pathway to freedom.

"Block the doors!" Jan ordered. He and Aryion jammed the doors closed in the faces of the oncoming soldiers, wedging them shut with a large stone beside the bridge.

"We're almost out!" Mel cried excitedly.

Allie had just set foot on the slick surface of the bridge when she saw them. A second group of soldiers had emerged from the opposite side of the gorge. A feline shape with blazing eyes prowled before them, fangs bared in triumph.

"Behind me!" Jan shouted, the tension evident in his voice.

Allie placed herself beside him, gripping her sword. This, she realized, was why the guards inside had made no real move to stop them. They must know this was their only way out, over the bridge above the gaping void.

She looked over the railing. Inky blackness surrounded the castle in a depth that seemed to go on forever. Yet it had an end, she knew. A hard ending after a long, painful fall.

They were trapped.

Redeyes snarled and sprang forward, leading the soldiers across the bridge. Allie gripped her sword, forcing herself not to think about the drop below. Aryion and Jan moved beside her. Behind them, she heard the guards pounding on the doors, forcing them open.

The warriors slammed into them in an onslaught of blades and bodies. Allie's boots skidded on the slick marble; half blinded by rain, she slashed at her opponent. Her sword made contact, but there was no cry of pain from the enchanted soldier. A second shape moved on her left, and she felt a blade glance over her unprotected left side. With a cry she stumbled out of the way, just in time—Redeyes' claws slashed, missing her back, and instead caught the soldier who had just cut her arm, flinging him from the bridge.

Drisilas flared between her and Redeyes. The blade left a trail of sparks beneath the great cat's whiskers, and for the first time Allie saw him hesitate. Redeyes snarled; fear gleamed in his terrible eyes at the fire, and Jan advanced, keeping the blade lowered before him.

"Stay close," he ordered over his shoulder. He sent a blast at Redeyes, who ducked under the blow with a hiss. Jan stepped between

Redeyes and the companions, holding a bolt of red fire like a buckler as he approached. Redeyes lunged, claws gleaming. The sheer strength of the beast almost knocked Ĵan down, but he kept his footing as the fire seared Redeyes' black fur.

Allie slashed at another enchanted soldier. Any wounds she inflicted were instantly healed by the enchantment. She managed to blast one off the bridge, but another soldier seized the back of her jerkin as she did so. An arrow slammed into his chest before he could strike, sending him careening off the edge.

Darion fitted another arrow to the string, his face pale. "You all right?"

Allie nodded, unable to form words. Ĵan forced Redeyes back, then swung Drisilas in a flaming arc, knocking two more soldiers down. For a split second, the pathway was clear again.

"Go!" Aryion barked. "We're almost there." Hope had lit in his tired eyes.

Mel looked back at his mentor's voice, and Allie saw the same hope in his face. Then, in an instant, Mel's eyes focused on something behind them, and his face went white. "Look out!"

Allie turned back to the castle. Standing on the bridge behind them was the Ace-Deputy, a cruel smile of triumph on his face as he flung a bolt of white ice at Aryion's back.

. . . . . .

Mel saw the Ace-Deputy raise his withered hands, saw the light of wicked triumph in his eyes, and caught the glint of fatal white that filled the bolt. There was death in that blast, a power that would strip the very Essence from Aryion before he could flee.

He cried out a warning and leapt forward, raising the Blue Stone as he sprang between the Deputy and his mentor. Aryion dropped low, out of the way, as the blast whistled overhead.

The deathly white ice collided with the Star-Stone, shattering into fragments upon the pure light. The force of it knocked the soldiers beyond to the ground and shook the bridge.

Mel was flung sideways by the blast, over the railing. He felt the sickening sensation of falling before someone caught his arm, holding him above the void. The sudden lurch shook the Stone from his fingers, and it fell, spinning and twinkling, into the darkness below.

Aryion gripped his arm. "Hold on—it's all right—hold on."

"The Stone," Mel choked, horrified. "I lost—"

"It's all right." Aryion's voice was tight with fear. Mel reached up and gripped Aryion's wrist as his mentor hauled him upward. Yet as Mel's fingers reached the edge of the bridge, a sword flashed across Aryion's shoulder. An enchanted soldier had come from behind, stabbing the ranger's exposed back.

Aryion fell forward onto his chest. Mel's fingers slipped on the wet marble and he fell again, clutching his mentor's hand. Aryion twisted onto his back, freeing his sword, and slashed up at the soldiers that rushed for them. The sudden counter attack caught them off guard. Jan shot a blast at the attackers, sending them flying back toward the Deputy, but he was cut off from the two rangers.

"Aryion!" Mel cried fearfully.

"Hold on," Aryion said hoarsely. Blood ran down his arm, making his grip slick. "Reach for the rail." He tried to get to his knees. A blast of ice hit him in the back, knocking him forward again. Mel dangled above the darkness, clutching Aryion's hand, unable to reach the edge of the bridge.

"Make your choice, New Blood!" came the Ace-Deputy's amused voice. White ice played over his fingertips as he watched the struggling pair.

Make your choice. The words echoed in Mel's mind, and suddenly, he understood. He looked down into the nothingness of the void below him. A life for a life. There was only one life the Aces required here, and it wasn't Aryion's.

"Hold on," Aryion repeated, his voice edged in fear. His bloodied fingers sought a tighter grip on his apprentice's hand.

Mel looked up. His mentor's weary face was drawn with pain, the dim light highlighting the desperation in his eyes. Lightning crackled in the sky above, momentarily lighting the scenes, freezing them in time and cementing them in Mel's memory.

He wished there was time to explain. To elaborate on what his last choice would be. To explain to this man, who had become as a second father to him, why he must make this choice. Why he could not allow them all to die here.

His mouth was dry, throat tight with tears. "I'm sorry," he managed to whisper.

And he let go.

Aryion screamed after him, clutching empty air after his apprentice. Mel heard the agony in his voice, saw the pain in his face, and felt a stab of grief deep in his heart. Cold air whipped past him as he fell. He had time to feel the sadness over all he would never do, over the people he had not been able to say goodbye to. He had time, too, to feel an odd sense of surprise that after everything, this was how it would end.

And then it was over.

．．．．．．

The glaring light from the Blue Stone sent fresh flares of pain into Allie's head, but she saw it all as it happened. She saw Aryion catch Mel, saw the soldiers attack the ranger, trying to break his hold. She saw the Ace-Deputy fling a second shot of ice that glanced over Aryion's back and flung him against the marble bridge again. She thought she heard the Deputy call something to Mel.

And then came a flare of lightning, fully illuminating the moment that Mel fell.

For an instant she could not believe what she had seen. Then the light vanished, thunder shook the valley, and she knew she had not imagined it.

Aryion was screaming his apprentice's name—he staggered to his feet, clearly intending to fling himself into the yawning void after Mel. Jan caught his arm just in time, pulling him back, his voice thick with emotion. "He is gone—he is gone, Aryion, you can do nothing for him now."

A volley of arrows clattered on the bridge around them. Jan generated a shield, protecting the remaining four companions from the onslaught. Redeyes sprang forward again, his claws slashing through the fire. One claw tore the front of Jan's jerkin—Jan swung Drisilas forward, forcing the beast back again.

"Go!" he ordered, and the companions ran forward again. The way was clear. Allie sprinted after Darion, her heart pounding in fear and grief. The enchanted soldiers drew back before them— evidently, Mel's life was all the Aces had required.

Yet even in that thought, she was wrong.

She was ten paces from the end of the bridge when an icy chain looped around her ankle, hauling her back. The Ace-Deputy had caught her, so close to escape. She fell to her knees, slashing desperately at the ice.

On the far brink of the gorge, she saw Jan turn back.

"No!" she screamed, her voice shrill with panic. This was what the Aces wanted—they only wanted the Wielders. "Go back! They want—"

The chain hauled her toward the castle. Jan sprinted up the bridge towards Allie, sending a blast of red fire at the soldiers that raced to intercept him. Drisilas blazed as he brought the blade down, severing the chain. He pulled Allie to her feet. "Run, quickly—we are almost—"

He was cut off as a massive bolt of ice slammed into the bridge beside them. Allie was flung forward by the force, sliding along the marble surface to reach the opposite bank. She landed in the bracken and jumped up again. Ĵan, a few paces from the edge, turned to face the approaching Deputy, whose hideous features distorted in a smile of satisfaction.

"No!" she cried, springing to her feet and racing back. But before she reached them, before she could stop what was unfolding, Ĵan dropped to his knees, slamming both hands into the marble bridge. The bridge shuddered under the fiery blast, then the marble gave way and cracked in two. A huge section broke before Allie, opening a chasm between Ĵan and the opposite bank.

She stopped at the edge, reeling from the shock and terror. "Ĵan!"

Ĵan stood, looking back at the Deputy, whose smile of triumph had been replaced by livid hatred. Ĵan slid Drisilas back into its scabbard and flung it to the opposite bank. It fell at Allie's feet. "Take the sword!" he ordered. "Protect the Stone. You must do as I say."

"Ĵan!" Allie screamed again, refusing to budge from the edge of the broken bridge. Knowing it was futile, knowing nothing would change what was happening, she flung a blast of fire at the Ace-Deputy, who deflected it.

Ĵan looked back at her once more. His face was tired and sad, drawn with the strain. His jerkin, torn by Redeyes' claws, revealed the scars that had Marked him for this fate. "Go, Allie," he said quietly, then sprang forward into the approaching soldiers. Red fire flashed again and again from his palms, knocking men off the bridge.

Redeyes lunged at him, snarling in victory. Jan generated another shield, blocking the vicious claws. But even as he did so, icy chains looped around his legs, dragging him to his knees. Another circled around his throat, hauling him forward.

Still he held the shield, teeth gritted, breath coming in ragged gasps, as more chains latched around his arms and wrists. Finally, the fire flickered, his strength spent, and he fell facedown on the slick marble.

Someone gripped Allie's arm, pulling her away. "No!" she cried, fighting blindly. "I can't leave him—we can't leave him here—"

The other voice came from far away, blurry through her fury and grief. The hand pulled her onward. They ran through the pelting rain, sprinting up the steep roads. Voices came from far away, voices of pursuers somewhere in the darkness. On they ran, cresting the first hill on the west ridge and starting the frantic descent down.

Allie skidded and lurched in the mud, clutching her sword in one hand and the sheathed Drisilas in the other. Fire blazed unrestrained in her veins, hate and fury whipped it into a tempest inside her. She wanted the Aces to follow. She wanted the chance to strike, over and over again, until they had paid for all they had done, all they had killed.

Eventually the wrath was replaced by exhaustion and fear. They stumbled down the steep draw into a gorge, where the wind tore through the boughs of the trees overhead and showered them with droplets.

Allie crashed to the ground. Her whole body was shaking. She managed to loosen her grip on her sword hilt, but retained her grasp on Drisilas, clutching it close.

Painfully, she started to rise. Darion's hand stopped her gently. "We're safe," he breathed. "We're safe. We'll rest here."

Allie looked at him. His face was streaked with mud from the frantic escape, yet she could see sorrow and regret in his eyes.

Behind him, Aryion gave a strangled cry of grief and sank to his knees.

The reality of the events on the bridge returned anew in her mind. She saw Mel fall, saw Ĵan shatter the marble, saw him turn back to buy them just the few minutes they needed for escape.

They were gone.

The full weight of it hit her in the chest. She crumpled to the ground, unable to stop the tears, while the rain around them slowed, then faded, then fell no more.

PART 3

The Wielder of Isilas

23

The Queen's Message

The bitter cold of morning roused Allie from her troubled dreams. She lay on the hard ground, shivering, partially wrapped in her cloak. Her hands felt frozen around the scabbard that she clutched to her chest.

Drisilas.

Fresh pain stabbed her heart as the horrific memories of their escape returned. The fight on the bridge. The storm. Mel, falling into the infinite blackness of the gorge. Jan breaking the bridge, fighting the Ace-Deputy, dragged down under many foes. Darion telling her to run.

She took a shaking breath, but no tears came. The grief lay stagnant in her heart.

She sat up tiredly, her head aching, and glanced around the silent glade. Aryion sat with his back against a tree across from her, wrapped in his cloak, his face hidden by his cowl. Darion sat a little ways to her right, keeping watch. Allie wished she could summon some of her earlier anger at him. Yet the emotional exhaustion of last night had drained her of the fury.

Darion noticed her sit up, and glanced at Aryion. "I think we need to get going," he ventured quietly.

There was a long pause. Aryion answered without moving. "Where to?"

"I… I'm not sure," Darion admitted.

Allie looked at him. "Why?" she asked, her voice hoarse from tears. "Why did you take us to the Aces?" She wanted to force her fire into the question, to find some wrath to fling at him, but as before, she felt nothing. Only a weariness that drained her entire body.

Darion was silent for a time, as if trying to find the right words. As if there were any words that would erase the grief and anger. "Jan believed it to be our best move," he said finally. "The investigations before have found nothing, even when they scouted around the castle. The Aces have concealed everything with their magic. No one except the enchanted soldiers know about it, and their minds are easy enough to erase."

"Then why did they trust you?" Allie asked bitterly.

"Because I had served them, for a time," Darion answered quietly.

"Why'd you stop?" Allie asked, catching the past tense in his words.

Darion stared at the ground. "They broke their word. I served them under the same conditions as most of their servants—that if I helped them, they would keep my family safe. So I bargained for the safety of Wiverrun. A Blood Oath, sworn to protect my family. In exchange, I would turn over the neighboring villages and farmsteads to them." He let out a breath. "Those villages trusted me, as their ranger. As the one who should have protected them. Instead, I sold them out to the Ace-Lord."

He closed his eyes. "That was the arrangement for months. Until one day I returned to Wiverrun and found half the town gone. My mentor, my family—enchanted, enslaved, or worse, as I'm still learning."

"And Redeyes gave you the scars then?" Allie guessed, remembering something the Deputy had said.

"I threatened to bring the news to Caer Sia, since the Aces had broken their bargain," Darion said. "But I was bound to them by my promise. To break the Blood Oath—to break my word to the Ace-Lord—that comes with a curse, one that Redeyes made clear." He rubbed the scar on his cheek, as if he could brush it away.

"Then why not let us help you? Why turn us in?" Allie asked, still not understanding.

"As I said, the Ace-Lord's magic around Castle Droco would have made certain you found nothing. We had to learn the truth somehow. That wasn't the goal of our plan, and we had hoped you three would have been kept out of harm's way."

"We?"

"The king and I," Darion said. He paused. "The plan was to go to Wiverrun, where I would turn Ĵan in to the Aces as they had ordered me. Ĵan knew Redeyes was after him, and he thought turning himself in would keep the Aces from attacking Caer Sia again." He glanced between the two of them. "He didn't want to tell you any of this or put you in danger. The Aces have ways of knowing the truth. It had to appear that you knew nothing at all."

Jan's words from the cell a few nights ago drifted through Allie's thoughts: *"The curse will be fulfilled, and I will not let anyone be harmed on my behalf."* Jan had known what was coming, as she'd always suspected. He must have known from the moment they were captured that he would not escape. Yet he'd bought them the time to flee.

"What curse did Jan bear?" Aryion asked slowly, his voice rasping. His face was hooded, but Allie could make out the glimmer of his eyes in the shadows.

"Isilas," Allie answered quietly, as Darion paused uncertainly. "Jan was Marked for using Isilas' magic as a weapon. He's kept it secret for decades—he only told me after we were captured."

Aryion closed his eyes and leaned his head back against the tree. Allie looked at Darion. "What part in this plan did you play, then?" she asked.

Darion let out a breath. "My task was to go to Caer Sia and try to lure the king and his entourage to the Aces. Then the Aces would kill Jan, and force the Red Dawn knights to join their forces."

"But you didn't?"

"I intended to. I had nothing left to gain from resisting the Aces," Darion said. "But Jan spoke to me after I brought the report. I thought I'd kept it secret, but he knew about Redeyes. He said he understood the curse I bore." He shook his head. "I didn't expect that. I decided to trust him, and follow the plan he laid out. I told him the truth of why I'd come, what I'd been sent to do. I told him what would happen if I failed." He gave a small, sad smile. "I suppose it doesn't matter now. Wiverrun is lost."

His account of Jan's kindness stabbed Allie's heart afresh. That compassion, that understanding, even to one sent to betray them… that was something unique about her uncle.

"That's why… he didn't want us to come with him," she guessed, remembering Jan's strange behavior and the secrets behind his eyes when they'd parted with General Arrex's group.

"That's why. I'd arranged to meet Captain Fargrin at the hunting cabin. Then I was to present Jan to the Aces as a prisoner." Darion's face was grim. "What we hadn't expected was that the Aces had taken the rest of Wiverrun, and that they had the duke under their control. That's what led to the duke sending a false letter, and luring the New Blood here." He glanced at Aryion, who said nothing, only studied him silently.

"I wish I had come to Caer Sia before," Darion said after a pause. "I wish I'd seen through the Ace-Lord's lies sooner, and brought the news, curse or no curse. Jan helped me see the truth, which is why I agreed to his plan. But that doesn't erase what I've done."

Aryion spoke, his voice low and toneless, as though he was just as drained as Allie felt. "It doesn't matter now. They're gone. Jan and Mel. Both the Wielders are dead."

A heavy silence settled over them. The despair seemed to press down on Allie, threatening to crush her.

Darion finally spoke. "I can't say anything to fix what I've done. But there might still be something I can do to help."

"Is there?" Aryion asked, his voice low and dull.

"Yes. I think the Ace-Lord has other plans for them. I think they're both alive."

A shock seemed to go through Allie, as though a fire had sparked to life in her chest. The dark grief faltered before the new hope. She sat staring at Darion in disbelief, not sure if she'd heard him right. The final word echoed over and over in her mind. Alive… alive… they might be alive…

Aryion stood, looking at him warily. "What do you mean? You told me no one comes out of the Patch."

"Well, no one ever has, except for the Aces," Darion admitted. "But it's not like the Darkness, which was a black force of death. The Patch seems to be one giant doorway, like the one the Ace-Lord showed you and Mel," he added to Allie.

"A doorway to where?" Allie demanded.

"That's what I don't know. Like I said, no one's ever gone in there and returned to tell of it. It might go to some other fortress of the Ace-Lord's. It might even go into the Dark Realm itself." Darion gave a slow shrug. "Either way, it can't just be an empty space. It has purpose, just like everything else in the Ace-Lord's plans. If the Ace-Lord wanted Jan and Mel to die on the bridge, he would have killed them while he had them captive."

The flickering hope in Allie's heart burned brighter, sparking in defiance of the despair. Jan and Mel could still be alive. All hope was not yet lost.

"How would we get him out of the Patch?" Aryion asked, still sounding uncertain. "If you can go into it one way, how do you get out?"

"I don't know that either," Darion said. "But I think we could find out. Once we did, we can save Jan and Mel, and regain the Blue Stone."

They might be able to rescue them.

Allie got to her feet, fresh energy filling her veins as she turned toward the road. "Then we have to go back."

"You can't," Darion said behind her. "The three of us won't stand a chance against the Aces alone."

"Neither will Jan or Mel," Allie snapped, turning back to face him. "We have to help them, now, before it's too late."

"And we will," Darion said, glancing at Aryion for assistance. "But they're the bait. We're the only ones who know about the gateway void, and how the Ace-Lord has brought back his servants. We have to get that news to Caer Sia, and wait until we have a better strategy."

"Have to?" Allie repeated, glaring at him. She knew he was right, knew charging blindly back to Castle Droco would probably get them all captured or killed. But her fear, distrust, and anger seemed to have boiled to the surface. "I'm the heiress. You can't *order* me to do anything."

Darion faltered. Allie took a step toward the road. "If there's a chance to save them, we have to take it. Even if it's a lost cause."

"It is not lost yet," Aryion said unexpectedly. "Darion is right. Any move we make now has to be carefully planned, for all of our lives, for Jan and Mel's."

"We've taken risks before," Allie argued, rounding on him. "You've taken risks. On the quest for the Shards—I've heard about it—there were plenty of risks, and it all worked out."

"It all worked out?" Aryion repeated, a dry smile appearing on his battered face. "Is that your view of these matters? A little adventure, a walk in the woods, and you'll swing your sword at a few villains and live happily ever after. That's far from reality. That quest was successful because people made sacrifices. People *died*, Asescia."

His voice was low, but the words cut deep. "This is war, highness. There will be losses, and there will be consequences to follow. You've only heard of the victory and assumed, in your blissful ignorance, that it came without cost."

Allie looked away, unable to meet his eyes. Hot shame replaced her uncontrolled emotion. She fought for an answer, for a retort, but she could say nothing to change the facts. They struck deep one after another, crumbling the romanticized version of events that she had come to imagine as reality.

"What do you think we should do, then?" she asked shortly.

Aryion looked at Darion, who thought for a moment. "Well… there aren't many options this side of Wiverrun. We're cut off from the roads south, and the path back to Caer Sia." He paused. "We might get to Mata City. I don't know how far we are. But if we made it, we could pass our news on to Caer Sia from there."

"Jan and Mel might not have that much time," Allie stated.

"Then we shouldn't delay here," Aryion said, turning to her again. "We can't order you one way or another, Heiress. The choice is yours to make. But in times like this I would consider what Jan would have you do."

Allie stared at the ground, unsure if the turmoil of thoughts showed on her face. The thought of leaving Jan and Mel behind, dead or alive, wrenched her heart. Part of her still wanted to return to Castle Droco and storm the gates, battle through foes, fight her way inside until she found and freed Jan and Mel. But she knew how that would end. The only reason they'd managed to escape the first time was because the Ace-Lord had kept the two he wanted. He had one out of two Star-Stones as well.

Her hands wrapped around Drisilas. Jan would know what to do. But Jan was gone. He'd entrusted the blade—and more importantly, the Star-Stone—to her. If it were lost, his sacrifice would be in vain.

She looked up at Aryion and was surprised to see the very same pain in the ranger's usually measured expression. His dark eyes were full of the same anger, the same grief, the same agony of unknowing whether someone he cared for was alive or not. Yet the wisest move they could make now was to press on. To use the time afforded to them as best they could and deliver the vital information they'd learned back to Caer Sia.

"All right," she said in a hoarse whisper. "All right. How far is it to Mata City?"

She saw a quick flash of approval in Aryion's slight nod before he turned to Darion. "Where would you place our position here?"

"I'd say around thirty miles from the coast," Darion replied, thinking. "The road to Badwater is farther east, but I don't think we should risk going back that way. There's another, less-traveled road leading north not far from here, leading to the Strait."

"As long as we find the Strait, we can follow it north to Mata City, right?" Allie asked, trying to recall the maps of Coonsia she'd studied. The Mata Strait ran between mainland Coonsia and the western half of the country, dividing it in two. At its northern mouth lay the Cooper kingdom of Mata City.

"Yes, if we can make it that far," Aryion said. "But we have very few provisions." He turned to the younger ranger. "Are there any towns between us and Mata City? Any villages or farmsteads?"

"None that the Aces haven't captured," Darion said heavily. He paused, brow furrowed slightly as a thought occurred to him. "Actually, there's one other group in the Magno Forest that I don't think the Ace-Lord has found. These are the lands of the Alfona. But I'm not sure if they're still here—the Aces may have driven them out of the Magno."

Aryion shook his head. "It's better than nothing. We will travel north, and hope the Alfona are still here."

As the morning sun peeked through dreary gray clouds, they began the hike up the western hills. The trip to Wiverrun had been difficult, but this walk was without a doubt the hardest Allie could remember. The bitter ache battled with stubborn hope inside her. Jan might be alive. But if he was, he was in the hands of the Aces, who might kill him anyway—or worse. She thought of what they had done to her father, what they had done to the broken villagers they'd encountered in the cabin.

Worse than those fears was her own helplessness. They were alone in the wilderness—two rangers and an inexperienced girl. They had escaped Castle Droco only because the Ace-Lord had allowed them to. He had the prisoners he wanted—the Wielders.

Her head still ached from the Ace-Lord's interrogation, and she rubbed a hand over her forehead to try to relieve it. The words he had spoken made no sense to her, only filled her with more fear and uncertainty. Was that another type of curse? Had she interrupted it when she'd collapsed?

There was no way to know.

The headache had mostly faded by the time they stopped at the crest of a hill. The sun had slipped behind the clouds again as the day grew old, and the chill and damp seemed to permeate into her bones.

Aryion was moving in visible pain, and several of Darion's wounds had reopened on his neck. They paused, looking down at the next valley.

"I think the Alfona lands are a little south of here," Darion said. "But I don't know this part of the forest very well."

Aryion nodded slightly, his face drawn.

"Can we stop here for now?" Allie asked. "You're both injured."

The two of them glanced at her, then at each other, as though remembering this for the first time. Aryion shook his head. "Not here. Too exposed on the hill top. We can rest in the valley."

With that, he began moving forward again. The road arched downward, and Allie tried not to slide in the mud. Last night's rain had made the path slick. Darion came behind her, surer-footed on these steep trails than the other two.

Rain began to fall as they reached the valley. The next hill loomed before them, but it was less steep than the last few. They had nearly reached the end of the foothills, where the land began to level out and the Magno Forest spread in a wooded carpet toward the Strait.

They settled down to rest and took stock of the few supplies they had. Darion had managed to gain Aryion and Mel's backpacks, but the rest of their supplies were lost to the Aces. The packs contained a small assortment of tools and gear, including flint and steel and a small blanket.

They shared the remaining water in the flasks between the three of them. It was bitterly cold, but the blanket would be little good. Allie cut it into bandages while Aryion inspected Darion's back, which was crisscrossed with whip lashes. The wounds, though painful and bruised, were not deep.

Aryion bound the injuries with a few strips of fabric to help stop the bleeding, then reluctantly allowed his own injuries to be treated. The gashes on his shoulder and upper arms were far worse than the cuts of a whip, inflicted by the soldiers when he'd caught Mel. There was also a deeper wound stretching across his shoulder blades from the Deputy's icy blade.

The longer, deeper cut needed stitches, Darion said, but they didn't have the suture supplies for that. He bound it with fabric and fastened a makeshift sling for Aryion's arm.

"You're hurt, too," he stated to Allie as he worked.

"I'm all right," Allie said with a small shrug. The motion jarred the cut on her arm, and she tried not to wince.

Aryion shook his head. "At least wrap it up. If it gets infected we can't do anything to help it."

"And then you'd have to cut it off?" Allie guessed with a faint smile.

"If it was bad enough," Darion said. "Sit here." He fetched more strips of fabric and carefully wrapped the cut. Allie sat in silence while he worked, not sure what to say. Her harsh words in the Ace-Lord's tower rang again in her ears.

"Does it hurt?" Darion asked when he finished.

"A little. It's not bad," Allie said shortly, and hesitated. "I'm… sorry. For what I said in the castle. I thought you were still on the Ace-Lord's side."

"I can't really blame you for that. You didn't know."

"No, but… Jan had mentioned some of it," Allie admitted. "I just didn't want to trust you."

Darion let out a breath. "I'm sorry too. I thought our plan would work. But I didn't know if I could trust you either."

The apology eased a little from Allie's mind, though she still felt burdened with fears and uncertainties. What they had learned in Castle Droco had raised as many questions as answers.

They settled down, and Aryion took first watch. Allie tried to rest, to forget about the fear and just allow herself to sink into sleep. But sleep did not come. Her mind circled over the scenes in Castle Droco, over and over, the Ace-Lord's voice echoing again in her ears as he spoke the strange spell.

She drifted in and out of dreams. When Darion roused her to take over watch, she sat on the edge of their small camp, partially sheltered from the rain beneath the massive trees. Aryion had warned them against lighting a fire, in case they were being pursued. This warning was unneeded—they had not been followed, and it was far too wet to light a fire anyway.

So she sat in darkness, staring into the shadowed woods. Without even the moon for light, the darkness seemed to close in around them. In an instant, it was as if she were back in the cell of Castle Droco, waiting in the blackness for something to happen.

Except Jan had been there then. Now all she had was his sword. She held it close, staring into the depths of the Star-Stone in its hilt. The blue glimmered slightly in the faint light, and she could make out her own reflection, her face bruised and muddy, hair disheveled.

"Trail life agreeing with you, little Wildkid?" She heard Ĵan's teasing voice in her thoughts, and a fresh stab of grief pierced her heart.

Wearily, she leaned back against the tree and looked up into the rainy sky. *Why?* That was the only word she could manage. Why did such darkness exist in the world? Why did hope seem so weak compared to it? Why must they place faith in a Prophecy that seemed only to promise more darkness?

She closed her eyes for a moment. A song swam into her thoughts, one sung in Castle Sia's halls on stormy nights.

'Ere the world was wrought from dust,
'Ere the dark woods cover us
'Ere the kings sit on their thrones,
'Ere foot trod on Elven roads,
They in the Land Immortal dwell.

Rain shimmered down on her face like the tears that would not fall. She whispered the words, joining the voices from memory.

When I fall where this road ends,
And lie in crypt beneath my lands
Don't weep for me, I'm not gone
I've flown away, but I live on
There in the Land Immortal dwell.

"Rise, child."

Allie jolted upright at the voice. A tall woman stood a few paces before her. Golden light glittered around her frame. Her proud eyes were fixed on the Star-Stone.

Allie stood, a hand already reaching to her sword hilt while the other gripped Drisilas. The woman raised a hand, shaking her head. "Stay your weapons. I am not come to harm. Be not afraid."

"Who are you?" Allie asked uncertainly.

"I am a messenger of the Lord of Light. I am called Cahadras in the tongues of mortals."

Allie stared at her. The name was familiar. "You're… the Queen of the Stars."

"I am." Cahadras regarded her carefully. "Are you well, child?"

"Not exactly," Allie answered honestly. "We don't know where to go or what to do. The Aces have the Blue Stone and they've brought some of the Dark Realm here, I think."

"I have heard of this. This is why I was sent."

Hope lit in Allie's chest. "The Stars are coming? Coming to fight?"

"No. Not unless we are commanded thus," Cahadras replied, her voice measured and calm.

Hope was gone just as fast. "But—we need you," Allie couldn't help protesting. "We're outnumbered in this war. We've already lost one Star-Stone. The Aces are growing stronger every day. We can't beat them alone."

"If that were true, the Prophecy would not say otherwise," Cahadras told her. "As such, we cannot interfere with what is foretold. Its words tell of many things, though its meaning may be veiled to your eyes. Yet it tells of the way the mortals will defeat Kahlifis and his forces, how he shall be destroyed by the very ones he seeks to conquer." She paused. "That will come in time. I am here only to bring a message."

"What message?" Allie asked.

"It is this. The Ace-Lord seeks to taint and twist the words of the Prophecy. He will create his own pawns to fit into the Prophecy's words, and use the Stones to his own advantage. He will use his magic to gift unnatural powers to those he has chosen for this purpose. It is imperative that this does not happen, child." Cahadras paused. "The Stone Isilas must be protected. Its purpose has been altered, and thus it is the easiest for the Ace-Lord to corrupt."

She reached out and touched the Stone in the hilt. For an instant, the blue light was drained and the Stone glowed pale white. Allie clutched the sword closer, and the blue returned.

With everything that had happened, she had almost forgotten what Jan had told her. His curse came from what had been done to Isilas—using the Star-Stone as a weapon. "How do we fix it?" she asked softly, suddenly feeling very young. "Jan wanted to hand himself over to the Aces to remedy the curse. Isn't there something we can do?"

"The curse involves Jan alone," Cahadras told her. "Its atoning lies less in the past and more in the future. However, the corruption of

Isilas is something you can help to further prevent. Protect it," she said again. "Its power comes from the Land Immortal, and that will be lost should Kahlifis succeed. Be wise in your actions. Hold your hope."

Cahadras stepped back. Flames flared from her crown, spreading down her tall frame before streaking away into the sky. She had vanished. The glade was filled with shadows again.

Allie blinked. She sat with her back to the tree, in the same place she had been while on watch. Pale light filled the valley, and she was unsure if she had dreamt it all. But lying where the Star Queen had stood were two silver packs.

24

The Warriors of the Woods

Far too eager to share what she had learned to wait until dawn, Allie woke both her companions. Aryion started awake instantly when Allie touched his shoulder, his hand flying to his sword hilt. "What is it? Are we in danger?"

"No, everything's fine. Someone came to me a moment ago," Allie told him, moving to wake up Darion. The young ranger sat up stiffly, grimacing in pain as he stretched his injured back. His hazel eyes landed on the silver packs a few paces away.

"Where'd you find those?"

"A Star came here," Allie said. "Cahadras—the same Star who was at the council in Flora, I think."

She looked at Aryion for confirmation. He raised his eyebrows, looking impressed. "Yes, that would be the same. She spoke to Mel in Kamon as well. What did she tell you?"

Allie told them Cahadras' message, trying not to leave anything out. Both rangers looked immensely interested as she spoke of the Ace-Lord's plan.

"We already know the Ace-Lord intends to twist the Prophecy's words," Aryion mused thoughtfully. "He'll need his own players for his plan to work."

"Can he do that?" Allie asked uneasily. "Can he give people that power—make his own Wielders?"

"He'll try," Darion said.

"If he can, he will have a far easier time gaining the Star-Stones," Aryion said grimly. "We have seen the Ace-Lord twist the magic of the Stones—he may intend to warp the mortals in a similar way."

"He said something like that in the tower," Allie said slowly. "That what he wants won't be brought about by Star-Stones." She frowned. "But doesn't he need the Stones to bring the Dark Realm's power here?" All this time, they had assumed gaining the Stones was the Ace-Lord's strategy. But the Ace-Lord's words in the tower made her wonder if he had altered his plans somehow.

What his new strategy could be, she had no way of knowing. But it sent chills of foreboding into her heart.

The grim questions were left unanswered as Aryion opened the silver packs and assessed what they had been given. The contents were encouraging. There were flasks of fresh water, pale loaves of some type of flatbread, and a small satchel that contained dried, brilliantly red petals.

"Is that what I think it is?" Darion asked, studying the satchel with interest.

Aryion inspected them carefully, then nodded. "Fireflower. We'll need to use them sparingly."

"Fireflower?" Allie repeated in disbelief. She knew the plants were incredibly rare, growing in small amounts in the harsh mountain regions of northern Coonsia. When steeped, they possessed potent healing powers—once, she knew, they had saved her father's life.

"I admit I'm unfamiliar with them," Aryion said slowly, "but I'm nearly certain that's what they are."

The flasks were made of a lightweight steel, and they set one beside the fire to boil water. Once it was hot, Aryion steeped a small pinch of the fireflower, then applied the mixture to each of their injuries. The warm petals seemed to grow even hotter as they touched Allie's skin, but she could feel them penetrating into the cut on her arm.

They split one of the little loaves among the three of them. Despite the small portions, the pastry was surprisingly rich, and Allie felt satisfied after finishing it. With food and water, and the ache in her arm gradually fading, the road ahead of them seemed less daunting.

They shouldered their packs and began the walk north. The thick cover of gray clouds broke around midmorning, and sunlight lit the trail.

They spoke very little as they walked. Despite the gentle light, the overgrown road and the densely grown tunnel of trees made it difficult to see far ahead. Thick underbrush entangled the towering evergreens, and ivy stretched over the branches like a massive web. Strange birds called through the trees, their cries echoing through the forest.

This part of the Magno, Allie could tell, was rarely travelled. With the main road from Wiverrun farther north, this path must have been abandoned years ago. She wondered if they should make for the main road, but that idea vanished with a quick look around her. It would be unwise to leave this path, overgrown or not.

She tripped over a trailing vine of ivy and stumbled forward into Aryion, who had stopped abruptly.

"Look at this," Aryion said before Allie could apologize. He knelt and brushed the leaves aside, revealing a cord stretched over the trail. The thick rope was coated in mud, blending in with the trail, further concealed by fallen leaves.

"Is it a trap?" Allie asked. It looked similar to the snares she'd seen used for hunting back in Caer Sia. But those traps were made of wires, not rope. Beside that, the rope didn't seem to be attached to anything particular.

Darion crouched beside Aryion, studying the cord. "If it's a trap, I doubt it was laid by the Aces. If they wanted to trap us, they'd do something more..." he frowned, searching for the word, then said, "dramatic."

"Would they?" Aryion asked dryly.

"You've seen the castle, haven't you?" Darion pointed out with a sarcastic grin.

Aryion thought for a moment, then nodded, conceding that point. "Fair. I agree that this is likely not the Aces' work. Stand back," he added, rising and motioning the other two behind him. Carefully, he nudged the rope forward with the tip of his sword. Allie waited for a net or trap to spring forth, but instead, a low thrum sounded from the nearest tree, like a massive stringed instrument.

"Why did you do that?" Darion asked, exasperated. "We've clearly announced our presence to Light-knows-what now."

"I think they already know, whoever they are," Aryion answered. "This is not a hunting trap. This is a warning system of some kind, which means whoever they are, they are as wary of strangers as we are. I think we may have entered the lands of the Alfona."

Allie looked around the dense forest. The woods appeared the same. The thick underbrush and shadowy trees limited visibility. "What if it's not?" she asked uneasily.

Aryion gave a wry smile. "If not, then they think they have the element of surprise since we've tripped the warning. We'll prove them wrong if so."

He stood, brushing the dirt from his knees. "Be alert, and keep your weapons ready."

"Don't try to fight them," Darion said. "The Alfona already distrust outsiders, probably more so with the Aces nearby, and they're better warriors than the three of us can fight. We'll need to approach them as friends."

"Not till we figure out who's actually here," Allie said, loosening her sword in its scabbard.

They continued on along the overgrown path. Allie strained her eyes for any signs of movement, but there were none. The bird calls continued in the distance, their wild cries mingling with the quiet of the woods.

By the time Aryion called a halt again, it was near midday. They had seen no sign of Aces nor Alfona.

"We need a heading," Darion said uncertainly. "If we continue on like this, we might miss the tribe entirely, and be on our own until Mata City."

Aryion let out a breath. "I know. Rest a moment, and let me think."

Allie's newfound energy from the morning had long faded, replaced by worry. She sat on a stump near the trail and shrugged the pack from her shoulders. "How's your back?" she asked as Darion sat nearby.

Darion stretched experimentally. "Hardly hurts at all now," he said in surprise. "What about your arm?"

Allie rolled up her sleeve, noticing the residual ache had gone. So had the wound, she saw—a pale, freshly formed scar was the only sign of the cruel gash.

Darion raised his eyebrows. "That was potent fireflower—but I imagine it came from the Land Immortal itself."

Allie stared at the scar, glad the pain had gone. Seeing the injury healed reassured her that perhaps they might just make it out of this safely. "In Caer Sia, people say fireflowers only grow where souls have been laid to rest," she said thoughtfully. "I suppose that explains why they're so rare."

"And why there have been more growing nowadays," Darion pointed out grimly.

Aryion stood on the trail, arms folded over his chest, brow furrowed. "We may try to bear farther west," he said finally. "We've been on a northernly route all day."

"We could try that. I'm not sure where the tribe lives now," Darion admitted. "I'm nearly positive that these are their lands, but they may have moved after the Aces took over."

"Have you ever met the Alfona?" Allie asked.

"A few times," he answered. "They used to come through Wiverrun and trade goods on market days. My mentor and I used to meet with them at their trading post and exchange information, too."

"Used to?" Allie repeated.

Darion looked at the ground. "I... I haven't been in contact with them for months. Not since I joined the Aces. The Ace-Lord wanted me to find them and turn them in too, but I never did. I don't know if they're dead or not. Their trading post just disappeared."

Allie frowned, concerned. She had hoped the Alfona still inhabited these parts. If they had all been killed or driven away, the Aces had total control of the Magno Forest, and it would be a long, treacherous road north.

Darion noticed her expression and forced a slight smile. "Don't worry. That alarm system we found makes me think they're still here, somewhere."

"I think you're right," Aryion said suddenly.

He stood in the center of the path, head tilted slightly as he listened. Allie drew breath to ask what he meant, then realized something had changed. She turned, scanning the woods, trying to place it. The trees appeared as grim and watchful as ever. The clouds had shifted, sending sunlight streaming to the forest floor.

Their surroundings hadn't changed, but there was something else—a sound. Or rather, as the realization hit her, the lack of it. The repetitive wild cries of the distant birds had disappeared.

"What's—" she started, but was interrupted by a sharp command in a strange language from the woods to her left. As she swung to face the sound, three arrows slammed into the dirt inches from their feet.

Aryion drew his sword, and a fourth arrow skipped expertly off the tip of his blade before he could make another move.

"The next shot will have your head, *Ana'i.*" It was a man's voice, grim and wary. Shadows moved in the bracken, and Allie could make out at least thirty warriors moving forward. Brush crackled behind her—she risked a glance over her shoulder and saw more figures cutting off their retreat. In an instant, they were surrounded.

"On your knees," the voice ordered.

Allie reached for her sword. The sudden arrival of the warriors and the deadly accuracy of their arrows overtook her reason for an instant, and she drew the blade halfway.

"No," Darion said quickly. "They're Alfona—at least, they're speaking their dialect."

Aryion sheathed his sword and held up his hands. "We are not here to harm you or your people. We are only passing through."

"Passing through to where? And for what purpose?" the man shot back. The archers continued approaching. Patches of sunlight lit their forms, showing tawny buckskin clothes that blended with the dull browns and grays of the brush. Their faces were chiseled and tan, their hair long and black. The skin of their forearms and legs was darker and hardened, like the bark of the trees. Black markings covered their brows and cheeks, unique to each warrior.

The leader, who wore a beaded band of eagle feathers on his head, barked a short command and the warriors formed a perfect circle around their captives.

"We are going to Mata City," Aryion answered, keeping his tone calm and measured. "As for knowing our purpose, that depends on whom you serve. I am known as the Hummingbird. With me is the ranger known as the Blackbird—you may know him."

The Alfona leader paused, looking carefully at Darion. "Your face is familiar," he said finally. His tone gave nothing away. "It was said you had joined the Aces."

"He is on our side," Aryion said, as Darion hesitated. "I can vouch for his loyalty."

"Your name is known here, Hummingbird," the warrior replied warily. "We hold you in respect. But to vouch for one believed to be a traitor, your own honor must be questioned."

"Question it if you will," Aryion said. "We are no allies of the Aces."

"Hold, Wolfsbane," a new voice said behind them, before the Alfona warrior could speak again. A younger voice, with a far different accent than the Alfona's and a slight note of amusement. "I assure you the Hummingbird does not serve the Aces."

Aryion's face showed both confusion and a hopeful light of recognition. Allie turned slowly. The warriors behind them were not Alfona. In the shifting green light they appeared human enough, with shaggy hair and piercing green eyes. They seemed to be clad in furs. But as her eyes adjusted, she realized she was wrong—the fur was their own, as were the catlike ears and tails that flicked lightly through the bracken.

"Wildkids?" she said slowly.

At the word from the Wildkid, the Alfona leader paused, his face showing more confusion than hostility. The brambles rustled behind Allie as the Wildkids moved forward. One of them, a tall youth with black fur and curly hair, strode forward with a smile.

"I take it your mission back to Esile was successful, Master Hummingbird," he said.

Aryion's tense expression relaxed into a tired smile. "Joesp? So your warriors did make it into Coonsia after all."

"Of course," the Wildkid replied. "The warriors of the Mara-N'Tell have joined the Alfona." He looked at the uncertain warriors. "Be at ease. These are *Ak'is* of our sister."

The tall tribesman lowered his spear and inclined his head in greeting. Allie looked at the Wildkid called Joesp. There was something familiar about his appearance. That dark curly hair, those vivid green eyes—they were very reminiscent of the only other Wildkid she'd met.

"You're Dusty's brother?" she guessed slowly, and looked at Aryion. "You met them before?"

"Indeed," Joesp replied, nodding to Aryion. He studied Allie. "We have not met, but my sister speaks highly of you. You are the heiress?"

"I am," Allie said, blushing a little at the praise. She'd fought beside Dusty against the Darkness when it had attacked Caer Sia. That felt like decades ago, even though it was just over a year. So much—so many strange, terrible things—had happened since.

The Wildkids emerged from the shadows, at ease now that they were assured there was no danger. The Alfona warriors relaxed slightly, but they were still hesitant. Allie couldn't blame them— from what Darion had said, the Alfona had barely escaped the Aces.

The Alfona leader, Wolfsbane, looked at Joesp. "These are the ones you told us of?" he asked. "The one who guards the Stone?"

"He guards its keeper, at least," Joesp said. A slight frown crossed his face as he regarded the three companions. "But I do not see the New Blood."

Aryion's relieved expression vanished as though dissolved in the sunlight. "Mel... the New Blood, as you call him..." He stopped, unable to finish. Memories of Castle Droco filled Allie's mind afresh, and she could not speak. The realization settled afresh on her chest like a weight.

Darion, sensing neither of them could bring themselves to answer, spoke quietly. "The Aces have both the New Blood and the High King in their fortress. Whether dead or alive, we aren't sure, but we're hoping to launch an attack and free them."

A murmur of concern ran through the listening Alfona and Wildkids at his words. Joesp looked at Darion in disbelief. "The Aces have taken them? When did this happen?"

"The day before yesterday," Darion told him. "We escaped, and we've been hoping to find your chieftain and speak with him," he added, turning to the Alfona leader.

Wolfsbane nodded. "It is not our custom to bring strangers into our dwellings. However, I fear the times require it. Come quickly."

The Alfona warriors slipped into the woods to the left of the trail, leading the way before them. Allie followed, walking beside the two rangers. Behind them, the Wildkids slipped through the trees, guarding their backs, silent as a coming storm.

25

❦ ❦ ❦ ❦ ❦ ❦ ❦ ❦ ❦

Allies of the Alfona

The Alfona led them off the overgrown trail and into the dense brush. The woods sloped down slightly, and Allie could hear the babble of a creek in the distance, mingling with the whisper of wind through the towering trees.

The tribesmen seemed to disappear and reappear before her eyes as they moved forward. Their bark-like skin reflected the deep shadows, the black markings on their limbs and brows blended them into the brush, and they walked so soundlessly that they seemed as much a part of the wood as the trees themselves.

Behind them came the Wildkids. They too seemed to shift in and out of the trees, but less shadowy than the Alfona. Rather, they moved with the grace and silence of creatures of the forest, stealthy as foxes, their dappled fur mingling with the light.

Joesp walked beside them, speaking quietly with Aryion. Allie listened with interest to the conversation. She knew Dusty's group of Wildkid warriors had joined Aryion and Mel during a fight with the Crime Rings in Waypath. After that, they had parted ways, with Aryion and Mel sailing to Esile City and the Wildkids heading further north to gather information about the Aces.

"We travelled due north, as Dusty determined," Joesp said. "Through the prairies of Daffodalion. We were delayed by a group of Dwarves near the North Gulley caves—thankfully, we learned they were not on the Ace-Lord's side before there was a fight."

"There are a few tribes still loyal to the Liznees," Aryion told him. "I'm glad to hear the Gulley area is guarded by them."

"Yes, well, we rested there for five weeks until the snow had cleared," Joesp said. "After that we started north again. It was no easy feat to find the Alfona, and we only recently learned that the Aces are in this area. Dusty can tell you the whole of it."

"Did the Aces drive the Alfona out?" Darion asked. "Their trading post was deserted months ago."

"They did," Joesp said grimly, "and I expect Chief Kadryion can tell you more. The important thing is, the Aces do not know where the Alfona are now—nor, as far as we can tell, do they have any idea that our people are here too. We've been in the Magno a little less than a month."

"Well, I'm glad you're here," Aryion said. "We had begun to worry your warriors would never make it into Coonsia."

Joesp flashed a fierce smile. "Then you underestimate the Mara-N'Tell. Our journey was not easy, but we have come, as we said we would."

"Where are the rest of your warriors?" Aryion asked. "And your siblings?"

"Of those who fought in Waypath, we have all made it here," Joesp said. "Nellioh was hurt crossing the mountain passes, but he will recover. Dusty and the others are with Chief Kadryion."

"Have you got the evidence you need now?" Allie asked. "We heard that your mission was to convince the other Clans to help fight. If you've seen the Aces, is that proof enough?"

Joesp sighed heavily. "It might be, Heiress, but it may not. In truth, we have not seen the Aces at all, only heard rumors. I fear Wildkid blood must be spilled before our Clans are persuaded to fight alongside your people."

"The Aces will have a difficult time spilling it," a young Wildkid girl piped up behind Joesp.

"They will, but we should hope it won't come to that," Joesp chastened her.

The girl nodded, but Allie could still see the fiery determination in her eyes. It reminded her of Dusty. This Wildkid was younger, perhaps around thirteen or fourteen, with silver fur. Many of the Wildkids were quite young. Then again, Allie thought, she and Mel hadn't been very old when they'd joined this fight, either.

"This is my sister Graysil," Joesp said. "This is her first mission, but she is showing some promise yet." Despite his teasing, Allie could detect the pride in his voice as he looked at his younger sister.

The land sloped into a shallow ravine, where a slender creek streamed beneath the ferns. On the opposite bank, etched into the hillside, was an earthen cave.

Two Alfona warriors seemed to materialize from the woods as

they approached, stepping forward with spears. Wolfsbane called softly to them in their own language. Whatever he said caused interest to light in the guards' eyes, and they stepped aside and allowed the group to enter.

It wasn't a cave, Allie realized now, but a tunnel, carved into the hill and leading further down. The ceiling brushed her hair, and most of the warriors had to stoop. Allie felt her way down the tunnel wall, stumbling forward in the dim light. The Alfona warriors walked with ease, clearly having come this way a thousand times.

Finally a greenish light appeared before them, and the tunnel levelled out. They stood in a massive cavern, nearly as tall as the towers of Castle Droco, and wider than a courtyard. Sunlight streamed through the gaps of the huge interlocking roots that formed the ceiling, and firelight filled the chamber within.

Allie was reminded of the bustling streets of Caer Sia as she watched the people milling through the cavern—that is, if a large earthen dome had enclosed the streets of Sia. Six tunnel openings lined the cavern walls, leading to other parts of the underground colony. To her right, a channel lined with stones allowed part of the creek to fall in a cascading shower to a large basin. A great fire burned brightly in the center of the cavern, casting elongated shadows over the earthen walls.

"I've seen the Alfona trading posts," Darion said quietly behind her, his voice filled with the same awe as she felt. "But I've never seen anything like this."

Wolfsbane gave a smile of pride. "The Aces may have taken back their ruined kingdom, but these lands belonged to the Diné long before Kahlifis came here, and we will be here long after his time."

He gave orders to the other warriors, then turned to the newcomers again. "Wait here. We must report our findings to our chieftain before you are allowed within."

He disappeared down a tunnel to the left.

The Wildkid warriors had spread out inside the cavern, some speaking with Alfona tribesmen, others fading into the tunnels. Allie stood beside Darion, feeling a little lost, her eyes following the flow of activity. Several Alfona villagers studied them carefully, seeming neither welcoming nor hostile. The fear of the Aces was evident in their eyes.

Wolfsbane reappeared. Striding behind him was a Wildkid warrior with dark fur and curly hair, her green eyes filled with relief as she saw them.

Allie felt herself relax—this, at least, was a familiar face. "Dusty— it's so good to see you!"

"You as well," Dusty greeted her, giving her a light hug. The Wildkid's features bore the signs of long travel and difficult days. There were tired lines on her face, and a recent scar on the side of her neck. Her hair had been cut shorter since the last time Allie had seen her—it now brushed her shoulders. She greeted Aryion; Allie saw her face register that Mel was not here, and guessed that Wolfsbane had told her briefly of their news.

Wolfsbane's deep voice interrupted the hurried reunion. "My chieftain wishes to speak with you. Please follow." With that, he led the way down the center tunnel.

The companions followed, along with Dusty and Joesp. Three Alfona warriors flanked them. Dusty was talking quietly to Aryion; Allie could hear snatches of their conversation. "We may be able to lead a company back to the fortress, and attempt to free them. There are seventy warriors with me here, and the Aces know nothing of our presence."

"And so it must stay," Aryion answered. His voice was slow and grave, as though the words came from far away. "The Aces will expect any such attack, and are prepared to counter it. We would be captured, and most of us would probably be killed. If Mel is still… alive… such an attack would not help him."

"Unless we managed it," Joesp pointed out.

"I can't ask you to risk that," Aryion said. "If we are to overtake Castle Droco, we will need a better strategy."

Allie kept her eyes down, trying not to show that she'd been listening. The Wildkids were willing to attack Castle Droco and find Jan and Mel. Yet as much as she wanted this, she knew Aryion was right. The Wildkids didn't have numbers enough, not against the hoards of enchanted soldiers. With the void opened, the Ace-Lord's forces would be virtually unlimited. The Wildkids would be killed either by the sword, or by the deathly white ice.

Any attack must be well-planned, coordinated, and timed accordingly. They must wait patiently for that time to come.

They reached a large chamber at the end of the tunnel. A fire burned brightly in the center of the room. The pale green of daylight had vanished, and the ceiling was made of stone, much lower than that of the great cavern. While it gave the chamber a boxed-in feeling, it also made her feel more secure.

She turned her attention to the people within. Four Alfona guards sat cross-legged around a crackling fire. Sitting between them was a tall man clad in the same simple buckskin as his warriors. A wolf pelt was draped over his thin shoulders, and a feathered headdress rested on his head, the vibrant red and gray feathers contrasting with his silver hair. The bark-like plating on his forearms and knees was as gnarled as the ancient trees of the forest. His face was lined and weathered, and there was a keen and wise light in his dark eyes.

"My friends," Wolfsbane said, "meet you Kadryion, chieftain of the Alfona." He bowed, and the three companions did the same.

Kadryion inclined his head to them. "Welcome to Alfona, *Ak'is* of the Wildkids." His voice was deep and measured, and reminded Allie, strangely, of Iriam's voice. "Please, sit." His dark eyes studied each of them in turn, resting on Darion. "It is good to see you, young Blackbird," he said. "It has been many weeks since we have heard from you or your master."

Darion looked down. "I am to blame for that, sir. I have only recently left the servitude of the Ace-Lord." He let out a breath. "My mentor was taken to Caer Droco when the Aces came for the duke and his entourage. Dead or enchanted, I don't know yet."

The guards eyed him uneasily at these words, and a frown passed over Dusty's face. "You served them, Blackbird?" one of the guards repeated with evident suspicion.

"For what purpose?" Kadryion asked. His face was still calm.

"To help them gather soldiers," Darion answered. "That's the only reason the Aces are here, you know. These villages—most of them are too remote for anyone to notice if they're gone. I can tell you, at least, that the Ace-Lord doesn't know where your people are."

"How certain can you be of that?" the guard inquired warily.

"If I was wrong, the Aces would have already found you," Darion said quietly. "This village is well-hidden from them."

"And yet we allow you here," the guard said, his voice edged with hostility.

"Peace, Tarro," Wolfsbane ordered. "The Hummingbird vouches for his honesty. The Blackbird has forsaken the Aces."

"For that, I am glad," Kadryion said. He studied Darion a moment longer, but not in suspicion. At last he turned to the others. "Tell me your tale. There is much in it I wish to know."

Between Aryion and Darion, the story was told. They did not linger on certain details—Jan's plan, Allie realized, and the Marks, were topics they avoided. It would raise far too many questions that they did not yet have answers to. Yet Kadryion seemed unsurprised, almost as if he knew something of their story already. He listened to their account of the escape from Castle Droco, the flight through the forest, and Cahadras' message. Aryion also mentioned the little

they had learned of the Ace-Lord's plan and power, and the compass'
destruction.

"We plan to go north, to Mata City," Aryion said as he finished.
"From there I hope we can return to Caer Sia. But we're nearly out
of provisions."

"That can be attended to," Kadryion said, looking thoughtful.
"These are dark times, and there is little hospitality we can offer.
Nevertheless we offer it to you, for however long is needed. What
the Blackbird has said is true—the Aces do not know where we
make our fires now."

"I hope that lasts," Aryion said. "We can't stay here long. We know
they are after the sword," he nodded to Drisilas, still slung over Allie's
shoulder, "and we do not wish to lead them to you."

"The Aces will find us eventually," Kadryion said. He stared into
the fire, watching the swirling smoke. "The time has passed for the
Diné to dwell in the shadows. Already the dryads are wakened, and
the trees are restless. If it is time to act, the Alfona will ride."

Two of the guards exchanged uneasy glances at these words, and
Allie realized that not everyone shared their chieftain's view of the
situation. The Alfona had remained safely out of the fight till now,
avoiding the Aces and their servants.

"Surely we may offer hospitality without such risk," the guard
called Tarro said slowly.

"From now on, there is always risk," Wolfsbane told him. "Our
allies," he nodded to the Wildkids, "know it is time to act. If indeed

the void of darkness has been opened, the power of the Ace-Lord will be unchecked."

"We have scouted that valley and seen nothing," the guard replied bluntly.

"It's covered by an illusion," Allie chimed in, unable to keep silent any longer. "The Patch is the only thing it can't fully cover, but you wouldn't know that unless you were right on top of it."

"If you deem it wise, my chief, allow me to scout the valley further," Wolfsbane said. "Perhaps there is some way to destroy this Patch."

"I think the Star-Stones are the only thing that can do that," Darion told him.

Kadryion thought for a moment, his eyes seeming to see far away. "Our people have spoken of such voids in the past," he said. "It was said they might be closed by fire, but they cannot be destroyed, not fully. In the same way that the Ace-Lord's magic was returned to him when the compass you spoke of was destroyed," he added, looking at Aryion, "it is believed his power will only be moved to another place. Not until the Ace-Lord is gone, I believe, will the voids also be gone."

"In that case I suppose we had best decipher the Prophecy," Aryion said, but his expression was grim, and Allie saw the same helpless frustration that she felt reflected in his eyes.

Her hand closed around Drisilas as she looked at the Stone in its hilt. Perhaps it was only the faint light of the cavern, but she was nearly certain the Stone appeared paler than before, its color leaking away with every moment it remained corrupted.

26

SSSSSSSSS

Fear and Rumors

Life had begun to fall into a pattern in Mata City, and there was hardly a day Rygal was not occupied. Settled in the barracks with the Guardians of Gayrile, his time was filled with meetings, training exercises, and plans for battle.

Mata City had practically transformed overnight from a simple coastal city into a key military position. News came up and down the Strait from both directions, and it was the task of Lord Roan's couriers to pass it along to their allies. The Guardians, meanwhile, were occupied mainly with patrolling the northern waters or repairing the sea wall along the edge of Mata City, which, in years of peace, had begun to weaken.

Rygal managed to find time to continue practicing magic. No yellow fire yet burned from his sword, but the bright sparks blazed for a longer time than before. Slow progress, but progress all the same.

A meeting between Caer Sia's spies and the Elven delegation from Elimar was arranged to take place in three day's time. Mata City was neutral ground for both parties, and Lord Roan would oversee the meeting. The couriers of Sia would present their findings to the Elves, showing the seriousness of the situation with the Aces. With that report, Elimar might be persuaded to join the war. Lord Roan had explained the situation to Rygal that afternoon, while Jarus drafted up a letter to Elimar to reassure them they would not be pressured into the war without their consent.

"They still have a choice," Lord Roan had said gently, when Jarus had voiced his irritation with the Elves. "To send their warriors into battle to die for a cause that seems lost—that is something they must choose of their own will."

Rygal could understand this, but it still irked him.

After the meeting, Jarus had invited him to come home for dinner, which he'd gladly accepted. Once their discussions with Lord Roan was over, they set off through the network of canals to the Puddlepaw's house.

"House" did not accurately describe the Puddlepaw's lodging—like most Coopers, they lived in a finely made stone hut with a rounded dome. It appeared as rocky and weathered as a cave carved by the sea, but inside, it was lit by firelight and filled with comfortable wicker furniture.

Maya greeted them at the door, her sky-blue eyes twinkling, a few spots of ink staining the blonde fur around her paws. She kissed Jarus, then turned to Rygal with a smile. "It's been too long—how have you been?"

"Pretty well," Rygal answered, kneeling to hug her. He noticed her eyes lingered with concern on his face, as though trying to read the lines that grief had left. "I hear you've been busy," he said to avoid any questions on that topic. "Something about ship designs for the navy?"

Maya ducked her head in embarrassment, but her smile only widened. "Oh, yes. It hasn't just been me, of course—I've been studying for the last few years, and my team is mainly old classmates. We've been working on new sail designs, and they might eventually get picked up by the navy."

"That's wonderful," Rygal told her.

A small furry paw had grabbed the edge of the door, hauling it open with an effort, and Rygal glimpsed a pair of bright blue eyes peeking out. Maya turned and nudged the door open. "Ella, come out here. But don't go jumping in the canal again."

A tiny Cooper, hardly larger than a kitten, emerged from the house. Her eyes were the same blue as her mother's, but her fur was a darker shade, the color of fresh honey.

Rygal knelt down with a smile. "Hello, Ella. Glad to finally meet you."

A bashful smile lit the child's face. Her blue eyes seemed almost too large for it, made wider with fearless curiosity. Her voice was similar pitch as a toddler's. "Hi. You know Daddy?" she asked, glancing at Jarus.

"I do. I know your mother, too," Rygal said.

Ella seemed intrigued by this statement, but her attention was quickly caught by the sword at his belt. "I see?" she asked hopefully, reaching one small paw up to grasp the air.

"Not now, Ella," Maya intervened. "Come along inside."

Rygal smiled as he straightened and walked inside after them. "Got an interest in weaponry, does she?" he asked Jarus.

Jarus shook his head. "Oh, Light above, no. She likes shiny things, the little magpie. That's the only interest or use she sees in a sword."

His smile had faded slightly, and a bittersweet tone had entered his voice. Rygal could understand the feeling. There had been a time when he, too, could not understand the true need for a sword. When he'd seen only a beautiful and noble blade, something a hero would brandish while his portrait was painted. Now he knew better, had experienced the purpose of a sword, seen the blood on its blade.

Perhaps this was yet another reason they must fight this war. To protect the innocence of the next generation, so that they'd never know the darkness and terror that brought the need for such weaponry.

Maya had prepared a savory fish soup and mashed potatoes. Ella chattered eagerly throughout dinner, hindered only by spoonfuls of soup her mother coaxed into her mouth. Jarus filled Rygal in on life in Mata City. Jarus' mother Ada had retired from her job as informant to the Guardians of Gayrile a few months after the quest for the Shards. She and Carus were taking a well-deserved getaway to West Coonsia.

"Finally persuaded them to take a vacation," Jarus said, then added in a quieter tone, "plus, it's safer over there. The Hyenins have the area protected on that side of the Strait, and with luck, the Western settlements will be kept out of the war."

Rygal nodded, hoping he was right. "How safe is Mata City, then?" he asked.

Jarus started to reply, but a knock on the door interrupted him. Maya left her seat and padded over to open it. Her voice was surprised but pleased. "Lammar—good to see you, come in."

The Siren's lilting voice filled the house as he entered. "Sorry to interrupt your supper. Ah, it smells delightful in here, Maya."

Lammar stood a little taller than the Coopers padding on all fours. Instead of fur, his skin was smooth and green, mottled like the swamp he hailed from, marked by a large scar just under his right foreleg and crossing his chest. The Sirens had always reminded Rygal of large salamanders, except for the cunning and intelligent light in their eyes, and their uncanny powers of shapeshifting. But Lammar wore his usual guise today.

"There's more soup, if you'd like some," Maya offered.

"Ah, don't tempt me," Lammar answered with a smile, then turned to Rygal and Jarus. "I'm afraid I'm here to call you two back to business. Nothing dangerous," he added, clearly seeing the worry on their faces, "but urgent all the same."

"Is it about the Aces?" Rygal asked, reaching for his sword—even if there was no immediate danger, he'd never go anywhere without it.

"No, and try not to bring *them* up in front of the little one," Lammar said witheringly, with a nod to Ella. The little Cooper had stopped fingerpainting in her mashed potatoes upon his arrival, squirming in her chair.

"Uncle 'mar! Can you turn into a—a—" She looked around for inspiration, before challenging, "Spoon!"

"If you bribe him with food, he might," Rygal told her.

"Not tonight, Ellie dear—perhaps I'll be back for breakfast," Lammar answered with a wink.

"We'll be back," Jarus said, kissing the top of Ella's head before following Lammar and Rygal outside.

The three of them guided the flat boat back through the canals toward the castle. The soft sound of the paddle slipping in and out of the water was joined by hundreds of others filling the city. On a quiet spring night like this, Mata's canals were full of Coopers fishing, swimming, or paddling to nowhere in particular.

"What's going on, Lammar?" Jarus asked quietly.

The Siren looked at him. "Lord Roan wanted your help drafting a proposal to the governor of Bridgeport. The humans are concerned about the blockade on the Strait, and how it may affect their trade."

"War will always affect trade," Rygal said, shaking his head. "They have to know that."

"Yeah, well, it might not be fun telling them that," Lammar said wryly. "Jarus'll manage the telling more tactfully than either of us."

Jarus started to argue, stopped and thought about it, then shrugged, conceding that point.

"What do you need me for?" Rygal asked.

"We're meeting with the Red Dawn delegates. They got here an hour ago."

"A delegation?" Rygal repeated, puzzled. "From Caer Sia?"

"No. From Badwater. Lady Ajaha is here to speak with Roan and Iriam." Lammar glanced across the water. "Iriam asked us to come."

Rygal studied the Siren's face, confused by this piece of news. Ajaha, he knew, was leading the investigation regarding the Aces. She was not expected to arrive for the council for several more days.

Out of nowhere, a horrible sense of foreboding gripped his heart like icy claws. He kept his eyes on the rocky cliffs above them as Castle Mata grew closer. Surely everything was fine, he told himself firmly. There were no Aces in Badwater. How could anything drastic have happened in the two weeks since leaving Caer Sia?

Of course, the last time you thought that, Caer Sia was attacked by Aces, a nagging voice reminded him. He forced it away—that thought wouldn't help anything. But he could not shake the unease, which he found revolved around his ever-present thoughts for Allie.

After what felt like a very long time, they entered Castle Mata. Cooper soldiers waited outside as before, along with several Liznees clad in the colors of the Red Dawn. They would have escorted Ajaha here.

Lord Roan, Iriam, and a handful of Guardians were waiting in the council room. Ajaha stood beside Iriam, still clad in her jacket and travel skirt. Rygal studied her elegant face, trying to read any clues in her expression, but there were none.

"Good evening, gentlemen," Roan said gratefully. "Jarus, I'll join you in my study in a few moments. Would you mind looking over my response to Bridgeport in the meantime?"

"Yes, sir," Jarus said, but he gave Rygal a look that said, "Fill me in later!"

"You men are dismissed for tonight," Lammar told the other Guardians. "Go get yourselves some supper. We'll meet in the barracks this evening."

The warriors nodded and left. A short tense silence fell over the waiting group.

Ajaha finally spoke. Her face remained calm. It was her voice that gave her away, the slight hesitation, the faint tremor in her words as she spoke. "Forgive me for interrupting your evening. I just—I have news that you must know."

She let out a breath. "The king disembarked with a delegation to Wiverrun a week ago, with the intention of meeting with the duke. Four days after his departure, three civilians reached Badwater with the news that the Aces had attacked and claimed Wiverrun, and taken the townsfolk into captivity." Her voice faltered as fear clutched her throat. "The civilians had no report of ever seeing the delegation from Caer Sia, though I expect the king would have arrived after the devastation occurred."

"How?" Lammar asked, as she paused. "How could we not have known this?"

"The Aces are very skilled at remaining hidden, if it suits their purpose," Iriam answered. There was an edge of unease in his voice that scared Rygal more than anything else.

He finally managed to find words. "Then—you think the king's been captured? With the garrison?"

"It is as much as I can hope for," Ajaha said. Her voice was hollow with fear. "He has been captured, with the Stone Isilas… and with Allie."

The perfectly maintained mask of calm and reserve crumbled at the last word, and one hand flew to her mouth to stifle the tears. Allie. The foreboding in Rygal's chest turned to true fear, like a knife to his heart.

"Sit," Iriam said, taking Ajaha's hand and gently helping her into a chair. "There may yet be hope." He let out a long, weary sigh. "I do know, at least, what Jan had intended by going to Wiverrun. He shared his plan with me before we disembarked to Mata. But I was concerned it would bring Asescia into danger." He shook his head. "I fear I was correct."

"There's more, Iriam." Ajaha straightened and took a breath, looking up at the Neutral grimly. "One of the survivors was the duke's scribe who confirmed that his master has been enchanted by the Aces. His last task was to pen a false report to send to Appledale, to draw the New Blood to the Aces."

For the first time since Rygal had known him, fear showed on Iriam's face; fear and helpless rage. The knife twisted again in his heart, until he could hardly breathe from the dread. His hand gripped his sword hilt so tightly it hurt.

"Did the rangers go to Wiverrun, then?" Lammar asked—he seemed the only one able to form a question.

"We don't know," Ajaha answered hoarsely. "I have contacts in Flora who may have seen Aryion and Mel if they passed through town. But their response will not reach me for at least another five days."

Iriam clenched his fists. A thin layer of indigo ice coated the table top in front of him. When he spoke, his quiet voice showed no sign of anger. "In that case…we can assume the Ace-Lord has one, if not both Star-Stones. Attacking Wiverrun will not change that, especially not if the Aces have hostages."

"Then… is the war lost?" Rygal asked. He could hear the helplessness in his own voice.

"Not until the Wielders themselves give up the Stones," Iriam answered. "We can assume this has not happened, as Orlell yet breathes. If the Wielders have resisted thus far, we must act quickly." He frowned slightly as a different thought occurred to him; he spoke softly, half to himself. "Yet the Ace-Lord surely has ways to make them comply. Why then has his plan shifted away from using the Star-Stones? What is his new strategy?"

"We have to get them out of there," Rygal said. He wished he could hide the worry in his voice, wished he could speak in Norrin's calm, reassuring tone. But his voice was not Norrin's, but the voice of a young warrior, angry, afraid, and so weary of grief.

"Why didn't we know the Aces were in Wiverrun?" he demanded of no one in particular. "How could we have missed that?" Another thought struck him, and he turned to Iriam. "Wait—you knew Jan's plan? What was it?"

"That is a discussion for another time," Iriam replied. "A time when there are fewer lives at stake. We must act, that much is certain, but we cannot attack Wiverrun blindly."

"Then let us scout it out," Lammar said immediately. "I'll take a group of Guardians down the Strait and investigate the western side of the Magno Forest."

"And should you encounter Aces?" Iriam inquired.

"We'll run like the *Red Canary* back to Mata City," Lammar answered.

"You might try to reach Dandio too," Ajaha said, as Iriam paused, actually considering this plan. "His ship has joined the blockade in the north. What's more, they will have firepower."

Iriam sighed. "Under no ordinary circumstances would I consider this a wise strategy," he told Lammar. "But this situation is desperate. Set sail as soon as possible."

"I can send a ship to Dandio while you prepare," Lord Roan offered, and Iriam nodded gratefully.

"I'm coming," Rygal said. The words felt strained, his throat tight. No one argued—not that they had reason to. But he would have felt better if Iriam had ordered him otherwise, if only to hear the usual note of authority that was now lost from the Neutral's voice.

27

A Day in Darkness

Earthy darkness filled the Alfona village, and conversation and movement in the great cavern had faded away as Allie and the two rangers joined the Wildkids to talk.

Dusty and her four siblings brought them to a small chamber which reminded Allie of the council hall of Castle Sia. Golden light of many torches filled the room, yet the shadows of uncertainty remained in Allie's thoughts. She sensed Dusty had realized they had left some matters unsaid when they'd reported to Chief Kadryion, and braced herself to explain the truth of Jan's curse and the Marks.

Thankfully, the Wildkids did not ask about that. Dusty filled them in on their journey to the north. As Joesp had mentioned, they had spent time with the Dwarves before beginning the trek through the mountains. While the roads were clear, dense snow and ice had filled the pass, making the journey a treacherous one. Nellioh had broken his ankle sliding down a frozen embankment. But they had pressed on, and encountered Alfona scouts shortly after entering the Magno Forest.

"The Alfona have been scouting farther south," Dusty said. "Chief Kadryion hopes that the village will remain hidden, both for safety and because this is a prime position to keep an eye on the happenings nearby. The dryads are stirring, and *they* haven't been wakened for centuries."

"Why not?" Allie asked.

"No one really knows. They simply faded into their trees after the Dividing War, as our stories say," Dusty said, shaking her head. "It was said that the Druids of Old joined their knowledge to the dryads and led them in the fight against Kahlifis."

"We met a dryad on the way here," Darion said thoughtfully. "I know they've inhabited the Magno Forest for… well, since time began, I think. But that's the first I've heard of them fighting alongside us."

"Jan mentioned the Druids, too," Allie murmured. That conversation felt so long ago. Back then, she'd still been confident they would protect Wiverrun and the Aces would be easily defeated. She had since learned otherwise.

"I have heard of the Druids," Aryion said, stroking his beard thoughtfully. "In ancient times, they brought the High Light's messages to the mortals. It was said their magic came directly from the Land Immortal, bestowed upon them to be used to protect."

"I've heard of that too," Joesp said. "The story-weavers of the Clans still speak of them, but more as legend than reality."

"I wonder," Aryion said with a wry smile, "if there's more truth in those legends than we realize."

"What about the Aces?" Nellioh asked, folding his arms over his russet-furred chest. "Do you believe they'll pursue you?"

"They might," Aryion answered, nodding to the sword slung over Allie's shoulders. "We have Drisilas. The Ace-Lord needs the Star-Stones, and he'll come for Isilas eventually."

Allie slid the sword from her shoulders and held it before her. "Are we sure that's true?" she asked softly.

She sensed the inquiring eyes of the others as they turned to her. "You think otherwise?" Joesp asked.

Allie let out a breath, trying to sort out her ideas. "Just… something I've been thinking about. The Ace-Lord gave Mel and I the Star-Stones before we escaped—that doesn't make any sense."

"Perhaps he hoped you would join him," Newuel suggested.

"But we'd already refused him at that point." Allie said shook her head tiredly. "Besides, Ĵan is the Wielder of Isilas, not me. If the Ace-Lord really wants the Star-Stones… why give us the chance to take them at all?"

"What did he say when he gave them to you?" Aryion asked, his brow furrowed.

Allie racked her brain for the answer. The interaction by the shimmering archway in Castle Droco's high tower, and the questions it had raised, had been put aside by worry for Ĵan and Mel. But now she thought it over, reliving the memories.

"He said… he said he doesn't want the Star-Stones," she said slowly. "At least, not yet. He said he'd realized that certain risks have to be taken."

"For what purpose?" Dusty asked, concerned. "We know the Star-Stones will fully open the Dark Realm. The Patches are weaker voids, not the real thing. Why would the Ace-Lord delay?"

"Maybe it's not a delay at all," Darion said. "Maybe he's figured out a quicker way to gain the Star-Stones—something that we can't counter." He looked at Allie. "He said something like that, remember? He said he'd foreseen a different strategy."

"Whatever that is, we need to find out," Aryion said firmly. "He would not return the Star-Stones without some ulterior motive, not after fighting so hard to gain them." There was another pause. Aryion finally straightened, seeming to brush the unanswered questions aside. "Whatever their plan is now, our goal is to get Mel and Jan out of there. Once we send word, the Red Dawn must be prepared to attack."

Allie figured she should have rallied at his words. After all, she was the one who'd originally wanted to storm Castle Droco. But at the moment, she felt too tired to feel any real excitement. For the first time, she wanted the war to be over, for life to return to boring studies and sparring in the rain and lighthearted conversations with Jan.

. . . . . .

Allie slept fitfully that night, nestled on a pile of pelts in a small cavern. She awoke in earthy darkness, stiff but feeling rested for the first time in several days. Last night's conversation and questions entered her mind afresh, yet this time, she felt a surge of energy. Now was the time she had waited for—the threshold of battle.

Battle, her mind echoed, and a thrill of both excitement and fear coursed through her. Not the first battle in this war—that title probably applied to the Ace-Lord's attack on Caer Sia. But it would be the first definite strike back at the Aces, the first offensive in the second stage of the Prophecy.

She pulled on her jacket and boots and slipped through the curtain that separated the tiny alcove from the cavern they had talked in last night.

Darion was seated cross-legged on the floor, an oil lamp and a few pieces of paper stacked beside him. The soft scratching of the quill as he wrote was the only sound.

"Morning," Allie greeted him.

He looked up, registering her presence for the first time. "Morning. Hope I didn't wake you."

"You didn't." Allie tilted her head to the side, trying to make out the words he'd written. "What's this?"

"It was your uncle's idea," Darion said, hesitating slightly. "When I met with Jan, he said one of our main problems is we don't have many solid answers about the Aces—most everything is speculation. I'm not sure it'll make much difference, but…" He shrugged. "I'm trying to compile a record of our mission to Wiverrun. The enchantment, the shattered townsfolk, the lay of the castle. Once completed, this report could be sent across Coonsia, maybe even across the Mainland, and persuade more people to act."

"Not a bad plan," Allie said. "Maybe Dusty could take that report to the Wildkid Clans, too."

"Yes, she suggested that this morning," Darion agreed.

Allie sat down beside him. "What have you got so far?"

"Quite a bit. I'm recording the gateway with the void now," Darion said. "I hope I've described it all right."

"*'Tall, arched doorway with a shadowy curtain beyond,'*" Allie read off the page. "That's pretty accurate to me." She picked up a discarded page and skimmed his hurried handwriting. It was messy, but legible. The couriers could produce a more formal version to distribute, of course. "The Shattered?" she read, tapping the words. "What are they?"

"We don't really know. I've only seen them a few times. You saw them, in the cabin," Darion said. His eyes remained fixed on the paper. "Not the enchanted ones, the ones who just seemed… empty. Unresponsive. Whatever the Aces have done to them, their minds are completely broken. Whether we can fix it, I don't know."

Allie set the page aside. "Your brother's wife," she said slowly. "She was one of them, wasn't she?"

"Freya." Darion said nothing further, his face strained.

Allie moved away from the painful topic. "Do you have any ideas for how the Aces do it? Shatter minds?"

"I think they have to touch you for it. Some of them are powerful enough to read minds, you know," Darion said. "If you aren't prepared to resist it, they can read your thoughts." A shadow had come over his face. "I found that out in Castle Droco, from the

Deputy. He caught me outside Mel's cell block, after I'd passed Mel the message. Didn't ask any questions."

"So that's how the Ace-Lord knew," Allie said softly. A sudden chill ran down her spine. "Do you think that's what he did to me? Did he read my mind in the tower?" Fear filled her as she remembered the Ace-Lord's frigid grip on her face, the strange words he'd spoken. If he had read her thoughts, what terrible secrets might she have revealed?

"I don't think he did," Darion said. "The Aces don't have to speak to be able to enter your mind. It was some sort of spell, I think. But it looked like it hurt." He shook his head.

"It's all right," Allie reassured him, a little awkwardly. "I'm fine now." She thought a moment. "Maybe he was trying to… to shatter my mind, or something."

"I don't know if the shattering is something you can resist," Darion said with a frown.

"Do you think he did it?" Allie asked, putting a hand to her head involuntarily.

"I don't think so. You're still here," Darion said with a faint grin. "Like I said, once you're shattered, you're completely unresponsive. Broken. A shell of a person."

Allie could not decide if that fate was worse than the enchantment. One was a curse, binding you to fight for the Aces. But the alternative… to be emptied of who you were, of all your memories…

Footsteps sounded in the corridor, and Dusty peeked in. "Good morning, you two. Breakfast is ready if you want to join us."

Between the constant stress and adrenaline and the days of hard travel, Allie felt half-starved. She and Darion followed Dusty into another cavern, slightly larger than the last. A crowd of Wildkids stood grouped around a small fire. Several of them had already eaten, and moved to Dusty to receive their orders for the day. Dusty directed them in their native tongue.

Breakfast consisted of seasoned venison and a sweet corn mash. Allie ate hungrily, seated with the two rangers and Dusty and her siblings.

"Wolfsbane wants to patrol the southern woods again," she said to Allie once she had finished giving orders. "We're looking for more signs of the Dal-kerri."

A chill ran down Allie's spine. "Dal-kerri?" she repeated incredulously. "They're… real?"

"Real as the Aces, it seems," Aryion said, giving her a wry smile. "You've heard the stories, I assume?"

"Just a little," Allie said. Every child this side of Coonsia had grown up knowing the scary tales of the Dal-kerri. The name was whispered around a fire, echoed in the voices among Allie's friends growing up. It was a word out of mythology and lore, practically a joke— *"Better listen to your mother, or the Dal-kerri will come for you!"*

Dal-kerri were shadow creatures, lesser wraiths taking the form of fierce predators. Hounds with chilling howls, great cats with blazing eyes, wild boars the size of carriages that crushed soldiers underfoot.

They were said to have filled Kahlifis' forces during the Dividing War, but their existence was mostly speculation.

"Wolfsbane told me about their findings last night," Darion said. "He found tracks he didn't recognize three days ago—strange tracks, burned into the ground. There's been reports of shadowy creatures in the forest nearby, too." His hazel eyes were filled with concern. "If the Aces can access the Dark Realm through the gateway voids, who knows what sort of delightful creatures they're bringing into our world."

"Redeyes is Dal-kerri, isn't he?" Allie asked slowly, as the realization occurred to her for the first time.

"Probably," Aryion said. "But I think he is something more, if the Ace-Lord intends to make him the Twelfth Ace."

"We have heard of Dal-kerri in Kasabren, too," Nellioh said thoughtfully. "We call them Winterbeasts. But I thought them no more than a myth."

"Seems a lot of myths have come to life lately," Darion said. "The real problem is, if the Dal-kerri are real, we'll be badly outnumbered."

A solemn silence followed his words.

"We are still gathering allies," Dusty pointed out. "As soon as we have proof to send to my father, the Wildkids will come to help."

"I thought being captured by Jenna would be enough proof that it's dangerous," Graysil muttered into her plate.

"I'd have thought so too," Joesp said with a trace of anger. "But I suppose Father must do what is best for the Clan."

Allie looked at the young Wildkid girl, surprised. "You were taken by Jenna?"

"A few months ago," Graysil said, not sounding much concerned. "They would have sold me to who knows where. The one called Bryn freed me," she added, with a glance at Aryion.

"The fact that you got captured, of course, has nothing to do with the fact that you had snuck away during a Clan mission," Dusty pointed out.

"No. No different than you getting taken by those pirates when you went to fight the Hazes. And you were younger than me, too," Graysil said in a matter-of-fact tone.

"That was different," Dusty said. "I wasn't looking to join the fight."

"Of course you weren't," Newuel said. "You just happened to sneak onto a merchant ship that was conveniently heading north."

Joesp and Nellioh snorted with laughter. Graysil looked triumphant. Dusty glared at them, but Allie could see she was hiding a smile.

"Even if I *was* looking to join the fight," Dusty said loftily, "it worked out very well. *If* you don't remember, I was the one who killed Kado, so if I hadn't stowed away, who knows what would have happened."

"*You* killed Kado?" Aryion inquired innocently. "Rygal told that story very differently."

Dusty's glare swung to him, but there was a glint of humor she could not quite conceal in her eyes. "Did he? I'll kill him."

Even Aryion could not hide his smile, and Darion and Allie joined the laughter this time. It was good to laugh, Allie thought. Everything had been so dark and grim lately that she had almost forgotten the sensation.

"So, what's our plan now?" she asked as they finished their meal.

Aryion thought for a moment. "We need to get to Mata City, ideally in the next few days. We need to plan our departure above ground well, to avoid risking exposing the Alfona's location."

"At least you've thrown the Aces off your trail for now," Joesp said.

"Either way, time is crucial now," Aryion said. "The Aces have the Wielders. I am sure they have ways to force them to comply." The happiness had vanished from his face. His dark eyes were grim and sad again.

"At least we know he needs Jan and Mel alive," Darion ventured, but his optimism sounded painfully forced.

"And he does not seem focused on the Stones at the moment," Dusty added. "At least, he let you escape with Isilas. No matter how marred its magic is, there must still be a way to save it."

"That doesn't explain why the Ace-Lord let us take it," Allie said. "He wouldn't care if Isilas has been marred, he'd probably be happy that…"

She stopped as the thought struck her.

If Mortal heart remains unmarred; The spell that bound leaves deeper scars; Than the Shadow that awakened.

Marred. Twisted. Warped from its true purpose by darkness—

darkness whose greatest strength lay in fear and death, and if that fear ran deep enough, the darkness would go with it…

"Light above," she breathed.

"What would make him happy?" Darion asked, puzzled.

Allie didn't answer. A light seemed to have lit up her thoughts, illuminating the truth in horrific detail. The Marks, the scars, the curses, the waiting Patches of darkness—it all served a greater purpose, something the mortals could not counter. It relied on the simple truth that fear dwelt in every heart, the one common weakness that the Ace-Lord could corrupt, use, distort to serve him.

And the things one would do to combat that fear… the bloodshed, the false promises, the betrayal… it transformed into a darkness in the heart of a mortal that played directly into the Ace-Lord's hand.

Your futile battle sealed your doom.

She felt as though something huge and black had sunk its claws into her chest, and for an instant she could not breathe.

"What are you thinking?" Dusty asked slowly.

Allie looked at her, acutely aware of her pounding heart. Her voice came haltingly, so much calmer than she actually felt. "The Ace-Lord doesn't need the Stones—not yet. He's realized by now that we won't join him willingly. What he's going to do now… what he's been doing from the start… he's going to corrupt us with fear. *That's* what he's foreseen—that we can only resist for so long, before the fear and grief and darkness consume us."

She looked at Aryion, her thoughts spiraling. "Mel said they threatened his family, so Mel took himself out of the game *for them.* Jan thought his death was the only way to reconcile the curse, so he would have *let them kill him.* The civilians of Wiverrun—most of them thought they were protecting their families, so they *chose* to take the curse, and the others—the others were shattered—"

A light dawned in Aryion's eyes. "The Prophecy. The stanza about the unmarred mortal—how does it go?"

"*If mortal heart remains unmarred; The spell that bound leaves deeper scars,*" Darion quoted. He gave a low whistle. "*If…* That's what the Ace-Lord's plan is. He'd corrupt us all to the point that we'd actually believe his lies. It's a risk, but I can't argue that it's a dangerously good one for him to take."

"It's a very good one," Dusty said. Her voice was tense. "If the Ace-Lord can craft a curse like the Marks—an accusation so weighty that people would do anything to be rid of it—there's nothing keeping him from convincing the mortals that the best thing to do is to give up."

"And we'd hand him the Stones ourselves," Allie breathed. "No resistance, just like he wants." She gripped her head in her hands, reeling from this implication. "All he has to do is corrupt the mortals."

"I thought he needed the Star-Stones," Nellioh said, clearly confused.

"Oh, he does," Aryion said grimly. "But he has plenty of time to gain them. All he has to do is drag this war out, beat us down one by one, until eventually the Wielders' own grief and fear corrupts them so that they obey him."

The Ace-Lord's words in the tower echoed in Allie's mind like a breath of frigid air: *"What I want will not be brought about by Star-Stones."* He had turned time itself against them. As Aryion had pointed out, the Aces could drag this war out as long as they needed until the mortals at last surrendered. No matter how much they resisted, eventually all hope would be worn away.

And the survivors would bow to Kahlifis.

She could practically sense the fear making its way through Orlell, a disease that rotted the very core of hope.

"Then what's the Ace-Lord planning?" Joesp wondered.

"Redeyes," Darion said, his voice grim. "This adds a whole new layer to Redeyes' purpose, doesn't it? He's not just here to lay curses—those curses mar people, make them desperate." He shook his head. "I can tell you that much for certain."

"Glentree said the Ace-Lord's bringing a wraith," Allie said. Her hands were shaking. She could practically feel the fire crackling in her veins, her Essence churning with the surges of emotion. "Drisilas was the only weapon that could stop the Darkness, but the Stone is corrupted." The sheer extent of the Ace-Lord's plan overwhelmed her. Not only had Jan twisted the Star-Stone's magic, the curse ensured he must atone for it, thus removing the one person who could wield such a weapon against the wraith of shadow.

Aryion turned sharply to Darion. "When you made your plan with Jan, did he say anything about trying to reconcile the curse?"

"No," Darion said wearily. "He barely went into details about his curse at all. He said there was something he had to deal with, that he'd been cursed by Redeyes, but he never told me why. I thought it was just because the Aces wanted him dead, but…"

"If Jan warped the Stone, then Jan's the only one who can fix it," Allie said, getting to her feet. "We have to get him out—quickly— before the Aces—"

"We will," Dusty said, her voice level. She stood and took Allie's hands gently, trying to calm her. "We will. We have Drisilas, and the Ace-Lord can do little without it."

"He can still torture Jan," Allie said, her voice catching. "You didn't see what the Aces did to Caer Sia—what they did to my father—"

"We'll rescue Jan and Mel before that happens," Aryion said, standing before her. "Take a breath. The corruption is not complete yet. We have time as long as we have hope."

Allie exhaled slowly, controlling her emotions with an effort. The fear remained, a cold weight in the pit of her heart. "We need to get to Mata City," she said. "Aryion—we need to go as soon as we can. Please."

The ranger nodded. "I agree. I will speak with Kadryion." He looked at Dusty. "Will your warriors accompany us?"

"I think we'd better," Dusty said. "We can hardly return to the east now."

Allie sat down. Her heartbeat felt far too fast. Unrestrained fire blazed in her veins, and she fought to push it down.

Frantic voices beyond dispelled the momentary calm she had gathered like a candle abruptly blown out. Someone was calling out in the Alfona language—the words were muffled, but the tone was unmistakably fraught with panic.

The Wildkids leapt to their feet. Dusty started for the tunnel mouth, but before she reached it, Wolfsbane stumbled inside, out of breath and streaked in mud—and blood.

"What is it? What has happened?" Dusty demanded immediately, but Wolfsbane spoke over her questions.

"My friends, the Dal-kerri have found the tunnels. The Aces have found us. You must flee."

28

Flight to the Strait

Wolfsbane's deep voice, though urgent, remained so calm that it took Allie a moment to register his words. The Aces had found them. The Dal-kerri were here.

"Where are they?" Aryion asked, a hand going to his sword hilt. "We cannot leave your people here to fight alone."

"I thank you, Hummingbird, but it is your group they are after," Wolfsbane answered him. He wiped the sweat from his brow with a hand streaked in blood—too dark to be human. The blood of the Dal-kerri was the color of umber, like bones scorched in flame. "You must flee, and protect the Star-Stone."

The Star-Stone. Isilas.

Allie's hand went to her shoulder, reaching for the strap she knew was not there. "Drisilas—I left it in my room," she gasped, sickened by her own foolishness. "I'm going to get it."

"I'll come with you," Darion said immediately, moving to join her.

"Go quickly," Dusty warned. "We'll head for the tunnel leading west and meet you outside."

Allie was already halfway out of the cavern, running down the short tunnel. Muffled sounds came from the grand cavern ahead of her, and as the tunnel ended, she skidded to a halt.

Crowds surged past her like a swirling tide. The great fire in the center of the room had been extinguished, and pale green daylight leaked through the tree roots interlocking the ceiling, casting odd shadows on the fleeing people below. People ran laden by their few belongings, small children stumbled after their families, men carried the elderly on their backs. There was little sound—the fear was silent, tense as a bowstring, filling the room like acrid smoke.

"This way," Darion said, taking her arm. They edged forward against the tide, backs to the wall, until they reached the next tunnel.

Allie ran inside, feeling along the wall until she found cold steel. "I've got it—come on."

They returned to the large cavern, joining the crowd. Wolfsbane stood with his warriors, blades drawn, standing by the doorway. Allie watched as the last of the tribe members streamed out of the cavern, until only the warriors remained beside their chieftain.

Kadryion stood beside the smoldering remnants of the fire, tall and rugged as an old tree. His dark eyes landed on Allie and Darion, and he gestured to the right. "The tunnel leads to the road north. Do not stop until you are above ground. Follow the road until you reach Mata City."

Allie hesitated as she followed Darion toward the indicated tunnel. "What about all of you?"

Kadryion raised his hands, murmuring words in a strange tongue. Above them, the roots of the great tree uncoiled like snakes, stretching down the wall until they interlocked over the tunnels, sealing them from the inside. A faint smile crossed the chieftain's face as he turned back to Allie. "We will endure. Now go, Heiress."

Dusty stood beside the tunnel entrance—relief crossed her face as she saw them. "Good—now hurry. I don't know how long those roots will hold them."

They ran into the tunnel. The gradual curve blocked the light behind them in moments, and they were left in blackness. Allie could vaguely see Dusty hurrying ahead of them, her eyes better equipped to seeing in the dark. Darion came next, feeling along the wall. Allie gripped the back of his vest with one hand while the other clutched Drisilas. Her heart pounded against her ribs as she ran. The darkness seemed to press in on her, as though the tunnel were collapsing.

"How far does this tunnel run?" she managed to pant.

"I'm not sure," Darion whispered back. "I think this tunnel goes underneath the hill, and opens out not too far from the Strait."

"And how far from there to Mata City?"

"Twenty miles, I'd say?" Darion guessed. Allie could hear the tension in his voice. Twenty miles of open, desolate country, with the Dal-kerri at their heels. For a moment, exhaustion slowed her pace, but a sound behind her sent a fresh surge of adrenaline through her body.

Panting. Something far behind was panting, snarling as it ran in the darkness. Allie heard it snuffling and growing as it pursued them.

Dusty checked her speed slightly—Allie heard her inhale sharply, scenting the tunnel. "How many?" Allie whispered.

"Too many for the three of us," was the reply. "Hurry." She dropped back behind them. Allie heard the soft whisper of steel on leather as Dusty drew her knife and continued running.

They picked up their pace. Allie gripped Darion's elbow, trying to ignore the snarling and huffing far behind them. She had never run this far before, nor felt her heart throbbing this way. Sparring practice, exercise in Caer Sia—that was nothing to this, this raw fear that clawed her heart, the primal urge to flee before unseen predators.

Gradually, inevitably, the panting grew closer, louder with every moment. Allie's breath came in ragged gasps. Faint light reached her eyes far, far ahead, and a surge of relief gave her new strength to continue running. Twenty paces to the end of the tunnel. Ten.

"Watch your back!" Dusty shouted behind her.

The creature snarled behind them, and teeth snapped at Allie's heels. She heard Dusty slash wildly behind them. Their pursuer snarled again—Allie put on a final burst of speed, and she and Darion stumbled into daylight. Dusty, her knife streaked in dark blood, turned to face the tunnel even as they sprang to safety.

Something else sprang after them.

Allie stumbled into a creek bed, icy water splashing her face, hardly noticing the muddy forest they had emerged in. Her attention was fixed solely on the Dal-kerri.

The beasts chasing them stood in a pack just inside the shadow of the tunnel. They were wolf-like, but longer and lankier, their eyes hollow blue, their mouths open as they bared fangs like a viper's.

Dusty held her knife before her, and Darion brought his bow back to full draw; Allie, gasping for breath, raised her hands and unleashed a crackling blast of fire. It slammed into the first Dal-kerri's side, flinging it off its feet. It writhed in the stream, snapping at the red flames.

"Couldn't have done that earlier?" Darion asked.

"I couldn't see anything earlier," Allie told him.

The pack of Dal-kerri growled, advancing slowly down the short hillside toward the stream, their glowing eyes fixed on their retreating quarry. One of the hounds leapt forward, teeth bared—an arrow struck it in the shoulder, forcing it aside.

"Up here!" came Joesp's voice. He and the Wildkid squadron stood on the ridge across from the tunnel. Darion let his arrow fly as Allie turned and sprinted uphill with Dusty. Behind her, the splashing and rustling told her that the hounds had crossed the stream. She turned and fired another blast. The fire caught the two nearest Dal-kerri, searing their bristling fur. The Wildkids' arrows dispatched the rest.

Joesp took her hand and pulled her to the crest of the hill. Allie's lungs ached as she fought to catch her breath. The terror of the race and the strain of unleashing the fire made it impossible.

"More will come," Aryion warned. His sword was streaked in umber blood.

Dusty nodded. "Keep to the north. There's better visibility up on this hill." She organized her warriors into a tight arrowhead formation, and they started off at a brisk pace.

Fog filled the forest, and pale sunlight leaked through the trees. This part of the Magno, Allie noticed, grew thinner than the eastern side. The trees here were shorter, their trunks narrow and ashen, and the tangle of undergrowth was replaced by spindly sagebrush and waist-high brambles.

The woods were eerily silent as they hurried on. Mist doused the wood in a hazy embrace. Allie was drenched in sweat by the time Dusty finally ordered her warriors to halt. She sat down on a fallen log beside Darion and tried to steady her pounding heart.

"We're nearly out of the forest," Nellioh said. He was favoring his injured ankle.

"That means we'll have less cover soon," one of the warriors pointed out grimly.

"Travel will be faster, all the same," Dusty told them. "And the lighting will be better. I don't like this fog."

Graysil's young voice reached them—the girl had walked a little ways into the woods to the left. "We've reached the Strait!"

The others stood and headed down the hillside toward her, sliding in the underbrush. Graysil stood on the rocky edge of the Strait. Sea water lapped the stones at her feet. Miles across the water, Allie could make out the arching mountains of West Coonsia.

"How far would you put us from Mata City, Blackbird?" Dusty asked.

"Maybe fifteen miles, maybe less," Darion replied. A relieved smile had spread over his scarred face.

But the words had barely left his mouth before a haunting, wild howl rose up behind them, echoing through the foggy trees. It was answered by another cry, then another, still far off but gradually growing closer.

"Form up and keep moving," Dusty ordered. "We must reach Mata City." But her face showed her weariness.

"Could we cross the Strait?" The question came from a young male Wildkid with spotted fur, not much older than Graysil. "We might swim across it and escape the Winterhounds."

"We can't swim that far," Joesp said wryly. "And if the legends are true, the Dal-kerri can swim as well. Fire is said to be the only thing they fear."

"Fire," Darion echoed, his eyes lighting up. He slid his pack from his shoulders and rummaged through it until he produced the tinderbox. "I doubt it'll slow the Aces down much," he said as he clicked the stones together, sparking a flame to life. "But a decent blaze might keep the hounds back."

"It might," Dusty said doubtfully. "It might also set the entire Magno Forest up in flames around us."

"We're almost out of the wood," Darion answered. "The land between the forest and Mata City is mostly flatlands. The fire will burn brightly, but it won't spread."

"We can test that once we're out of the forest," Aryion said.

Another round of haunting cries filled the forest behind them.

Darion passed out torches to the warriors. Armed with fire, they resumed their brisk march. A thin trail led alongside the Strait, weaving through the trees. Allie forced herself to breathe calmly, to slow her heartbeat and ease the burning Essence in her veins. The fire felt hotter, wilder, harder to control, though she assumed it was just the terror of the chase.

As the trail wound into the forest and the Strait disappeared from view, Allie had the uneasy sensation that they were going the wrong way. What if the Aces had altered these trails to lure them back to Castle Droco? What if they were lying in wait somewhere in the foggy trees?

She gritted her teeth and gripped her sword hilt so tightly her knuckles whitened. The fear in the tunnels had gone. All she had left was rage. *Let the Aces come*, a part of her mind challenged. *Let them attack us, after everything they've done, all they've killed.* Drisilas thumped lightly against her back as she walked, like a second heartbeat.

On and on they went. Gray clouds swept over the sun. Deep fog filled the forest, and condensation clung to Allie's face and clothes. The air grew colder and colder. Another presence, another darkness, stirred in the wood, sending chills up her spine.

She glanced at Darion and Aryion, who walked on either side of her. The look on their faces told her they had sensed it too. "Aces?" she whispered.

"Little else explains this cold," Aryion replied quietly.

Dusty glanced back at him, her face drawn with worry. She had never fought the Aces, Allie realized, but she knew Dusty's fear was not for herself. No, Dusty feared for her followers—this little band of warriors, most of them very young, some whom had hardly ever seen battle.

Joesp noticed his older sister's expression and spoke in a low voice. "They all knew the risk when they joined you. We are all prepared to do what we must."

Dusty nodded shortly, but the fear remained etched on her face.

The trail dipped down into a narrow draw. The trees tilted forward, branches interlocking overhead. Allie could barely make out the opposite side of the valley through the fog. But she sensed the darkness, felt the cold.

"I can smell the wolves," the young spotted Wildkid said softly.

Through the mist, Allie saw lanky creatures stalking through the sage to the right of the trail, hackles up, teeth bared, blue eyes glowing.

"Raise the torches," Darion said—his voice was hoarse.

The torches spat in the heavy fog, but the flames cast a comforting golden light over the gray woods. Allie allowed the fire to crackle at her fingertips, trying to generate the flaming buckler that Jan had used in battle. All she could manage was a gauntlet of red fire that ran up and down her forearms, spitting red sparks.

The group edged down the draw. The hounds snarled as they

passed by, but hesitated at the sight of the fire. Only two of them paced forward, teeth bared; the Wildkid archers dispatched them quickly. The rest of the pack waited, growling.

The trail began to angle up again, out of the draw. Allie retreated slowly, eyes on the Dal-kerri, fire blazing hotter and hotter in her veins.

"You fools, attack!"

A cold, snarling, and horribly familiar voice barked the command to Allie's left. She turned quickly. Figures emerged from the fog behind the Dal-kerri, jogging through the underbrush, their armor clinking, swords and crossbows drawn. Enchanted soldiers, led by Captain Fargrin.

Behind, sweeping through the forest, ice crusting the ground beneath him, was the Ace-Deputy, a satisfied smile on his face.

At his voice, the Dal-kerri snarled and leapt forward. Arrows felled the nearest hounds, but four of the beasts made contact, tackling the Wildkids to the ground. Allie let the fire fly from her hands, knocking two of the creatures back. She turned toward the Ace-Deputy—he was still moving steadily forward, as if there was no reason to hurry at all. The sight of his smile brought all her rage rushing back. She fired a blast at him; he deflected it easily and continued on.

The torches trailed golden light as they ran up the slope. The trees had thinned out before them, allowing better visibility. Packs of Dal-kerri skirted the woods around them, yipping and snarling.

Dusty shouted an order in the Wildkid tongue, and her warriors swung into a semi-circle formation, loosing a volley of arrows at the charging Dal-kerri.

The enchanted soldiers did not pursue. Then again, Allie thought, they must know the Wildkids had nowhere to go. Mata City was still miles away.

It was Aryion who called a halt in a wide, grassless clearing speckled with large boulders. The ranger turned to Dusty. "We can't keep this up. The Aces must know we mean to reach Mata City. They'll run us to exhaustion, then attack again."

"We can hold for now," Dusty replied through gritted teeth, fitting a fresh string to her bow—her previous one had been cut by a hound's claws.

"For now," Aryion repeated pointedly. "You will run out of arrows eventually. Your mission was not to die in the wilderness."

Darion spoke slowly. "We can't keep running. I don't think an all-out attack would end well, either."

Dusty sighed, leaning on her bow, and looked at him. "What do you rangers have in mind?"

Darion pointed down the trail. "The rocks are our best cover. We can shelter behind these boulders and stave off the next attack. Then we'll light a fire perimeter," his finger traced a line across the trail, "and keep running. If we light a new fire every half mile or so to slow down the Dal-kerri, we might make it."

"Not a terrible plan," Dusty admitted. A little hope had returned to her eyes, but she still looked wary. "That is a strategy we know, at least. But what about the Ace?"

"I'll face him," Allie said. "I know I'm not Jan or Iriam," she said quickly, as all three opened their mouths to argue, "but none of you have Essence to slow down the ice."

Aryion let out a long breath. "That's… oh, very well. But when Dusty gives the command to run, you must run."

Allie nodded. She expected to feel fear, but there was none. Only the anger. Only the fire in her veins, growing hotter by the second as if to sear her heart.

The Wildkids gathered bundles of brush to burn, and lay it across the trail. Five warriors had been injured in the last attack, but they could still walk—Dusty ordered them to keep moving north, then took a position behind a large tree with her siblings. Allie joined Aryion and Darion behind a boulder on the opposite side of the trail.

The first pack of Dal-kerri stalked over the rise, panting, muzzles in the air as they scented their quarry. Ten enchanted soldiers came behind them, moving slower, hollow blue eyes scanning the glade. Their movements were not like Rygal's description of the Serventiri's shuddering motions, nor how Mel had described the Wavers' stumbling gait. The enchanted soldiers moved in a smooth, calculated, uniformed rhythm, puppeteered by their master's will.

The hounds charged forward with bone-chilling howls.

"*Arriss!*" Dusty shouted, and a volley of arrows launched from the group behind her. As they did, the next group of archers stepped forward and loosed their shots, followed immediately by a third group that moved to protect them. Watching the Wildkids, Allie could tell this was a strategy they must have practiced over and over, perfecting it until they could execute it flawlessly.

But there were always factors they could not control. The moment the archers showed themselves, three soldiers raised their crossbows. Two missed, but the third dart slammed into a Wildkid's shoulder—he fell back behind the rock with a stifled cry.

Aryion's sword cut down a hound that lunged at their hiding place. Darion loosed an arrow next to him. Allie forced her attention away from the battle, watching the ridge, waiting for the Ace-Deputy to emerge.

"*Bentra!*" Dusty ordered.

Three Wildkids rushed forward, dropping torches on the line of tinder laid across the path. Fire flared up before the Dal-kerri; they sprang back, yelping.

The Wildkids sprinted down the trail. Allie ran with them. Crossbow bolts whizzed over their heads. Two bolts found their mark, striking one Wildkid in the calf and another in the back. The first stumbled but was pulled along by his comrades, the second fell soundless and lay unmoving.

"A little further!" Joesp yelled from the front of the group.

The trail dipped down again. The forest was all but past them now—only a few slender pines stood before them, overlooking the desolate land like sentries. The Mata Strait stretched on to the left—to the right, rocky hills arched up into the Magno Forest back toward Wiverrun. They were trapped between stone and sea, with steel behind them and a long road before them.

"Calvi!" Dusty ordered breathlessly. The Wildkids split into groups, hiding behind boulders, preparing for the next attack. Allie stood beside Darion. Aryion had joined Joesp and Nellioh, and Dusty waited with Graysil and a squadron of archers on the other side of the path.

They had barely got into position when the next attack began. There was no pretense of waiting this time. Crossbow bolts thudded into the trunk of the tree Aryion sheltered behind and skidded off stone with a screech of steel. The Dal-kerri charged forward—Dusty gave the command a second too late, and the hounds lunged upon the archers. The Wildkids defended themselves with their curved daggers, but Allie saw them giving ground. Three bodies lay unmoving when the hounds had finally been defeated.

Darion nudged her suddenly. "He's here."

Allie looked back at the trail. Through the fog came the Ace-Deputy, black cloak swirling around him, tarnished armor gleaming, purple-red eyes glinting in hate and triumph. He raised his hands—ice crusted a boulder before him and shattered it as if it were made of glass. The archers behind it fled; white ice flashed and two of them crumpled unmoving, their Essence destroyed from within.

Allie stepped out behind the rock and let the fire fly from her hands. The Ace-Deputy intercepted it with a blast of ice, and she saw him smile.

"It was wise of you to stop running," he informed her, as casually as if they were speaking of the weather.

Allie blocked a bolt of ice, generating a shield in front of her. The force of his blast punched the air from her lungs, shoving her backward with unbelievable force. Gasping, she set her stance just in time to dodge the next icy bolt the Ace-Deputy sent at her. It struck the tree behind her, showering her in bark dust and icy fragments.

"All we ask is the Stone, Heiress," the Deputy continued calmly. "Why ask your friends to perish protecting it? Should they, too, die with the New Blood and your uncle?"

He's lying, Allie told herself, *they're not dead, he's lying*. But the words destroyed any attempt to react calmly. The fury was back, blazing hot, crackling uncontrolled. She had never felt so much power before, so much raw fire and fury.

The blasts flew, one after another—the Deputy deflected them easily, as though they were troublesome gnats he waved out of the air.

Dusty shouted the order to run again, but Allie didn't retreat, continuing her advance on the Deputy. She thought she heard Aryion shouting, heard Darion calling her name, but she did not run. The rest of the battlefield had drained away. The blood was roaring in her ears. Her head hurt as though it would split in two, but still she kept attacking.

And then she heard someone scream.

The young, female voice, so close by, snapped her attention away from the Ace-Deputy for an instant. Graysil. The small silver Wildkid had fallen to the stony path, scooting away from five enchanted soldiers who advanced on her, swords and spears raised. Her face was frozen in terror.

"Graysil!" Dusty's voice was raw with panic as she shouted her sister's name.

The Ace-Deputy flung another ray of ice—Allie generated another shield just in time, and the force sent her staggering again. Graysil got to her knees, her little knife gripped in her hand as she slashed at the hands of the soldier who reached for her. Yet as on the fight on the marble bridge, Allie saw the wound heal itself, and the soldier continued, unbothered.

"Graysil!" Dusty screamed again, running back for her. She flung herself between the soldiers and her sister, her dagger in one hand, a broken arrow in the other, slashing and stabbing at the five soldiers. Over and over again, Allie saw the blades make contact, but the soldiers barely reacted.

At last, one of them struck Dusty across the face with the flat of his sword. She staggered back, blood running beneath her black hair—Graysil leapt to her feet, but one of the soldiers slammed the butt of his spear against her temple, and she collapsed like a ragdoll.

They knelt there, the two Wildkids, Dusty clutching her sister's small form close to her as though to shield her with her body, as the enchanted soldiers closed around them like a vice.

Allie could never explain what happened next, nor would she understand it till much later. She was conscious only of a new type of heat, a new fury crackling from her veins, blazing from her fingers as she turned away from the Ace-Deputy and sprinted to the two Wildkids.

Red fire blazed in her hands, waves of heat blew into her face and hair, crimson sparks scattered on the ground like drops of blood. She struck again and again, blast after blast. Her vision seemed heightened, honing in on her targets. A shot to the heart, there. A blast to the head, there.

A bolt of ice glanced across her arm, flinging her sideways. Her sword went spinning from her hand. She felt the searing cold for an instant before the fire overwhelmed it. The Ace-Deputy swept toward her, towering over her, yet there was something in his withered face she didn't understand. Confusion, surprise—and fear.

He raised his hands, white ice glistening on his palms. Allie reacted out of instinct more than anything else, reaching behind her, her fingers closing on a hilt and wrenching the blade from its scabbard on her back. Her other hand deflected the ray of deadly ice just in time, shattering it, showering the glade in white shards.

Abruptly, her vision refocused.

She barely registered the other things—the Ace-Deputy drawing back slowly, reluctantly; the Dal-kerri whimpering and snarling; the bodies of the enchanted soldiers—bodies—dead—they were dead, their chests smoldering where the red fire had struck them, empty eyes wide open in surprise at that last pain they must have felt.

She didn't notice any of it. All her focus was drawn to the cold hilt of the sword in her hand and the crackling heat on her face as Drisilas blazed white fire.

29

The Fight at the Fort

Allie stared at the white flames crackling along the blade of Jan's sword, her chest heaving with the strain of the fight. The white fire reflected off the blackened blade, glaring in her eyes.

Drisilas, blazing unsheathed in her hand.

It was heavy, so much heavier than her own sword. She slid it back into the scabbard with an effort. The Star-Stone in its hilt was pale blue, not as white as the flames that had just lit it.

"Asescia!"

Aryion's shout rang behind her. With an effort, she picked up her discarded sword and forced her legs away from the battlefield. She tripped over a body on the ground—an enchanted soldier, face blackened by the red fire.

For an instant, shock and confusion overwhelmed her, and she felt sick. She stumbled after the retreating Wildkids, her mind a whirl of thoughts. Dead. By her hand. How had she killed them? The spell had not been broken, that much she knew. She had seen the hollow blue light in their eyes even as her fire had killed them, and they'd crumpled like toy soldiers, as if an Ace had stripped them of their Essence.

Drisilas hung heavy over her shoulder. They must have done it. The Ace-Lord had broken the hama-dryad's spell that protected the sword from any hand but Ĵan's. Had they simply killed him, and through some strange event the blade now answered to her? No, she told herself fiercely, that didn't make sense at all. Ĵan's death would not automatically release Drisilas. Something told her no one—not even the Ace-Deputy—had expected any of this to happen.

Someone took her arm as she stumbled—Darion. "Are you all right?" There was deep concern in his voice.

"I'm fine," Allie replied. Her voice sounded oddly cold, and calmer than she currently felt.

Darion looked back, then to her again, disbelief evident on his face. "You can kill them—the enchanted soldiers," he stammered. "How long have you been able to do that?"

"Maybe a minute or so," Allie answered shortly.

"No one can kill the enchanted soldiers," came Newuel's stunned voice to her right. "How…"

"As if I know!" Allie snapped, sharper than she had intended. She took a deep breath. "I'm fine. I don't know what happened back there. We have to keep moving."

But they had only gone about a hundred yards when the group stopped again. About a third of their number were wounded, Allie saw. Several lay lifeless back in the glade where the white ice had struck them.

Dusty wiped a streak of blood from her forehead, kneeling beside

Graysil. "She's alive. Still out cold. Help me," she said to Nellioh, who lifted his unconscious sister from the ground as though she weighed no more than a baby.

"How much farther?" one of the Wildkids asked worriedly.

"I don't know. We can hardly make it to Mata City like this," Dusty said. She glanced at Allie with a small frown of concern. "Are you all right?"

"I'm fine," Allie repeated. Shock, confusion, and fear made her tone irritable. "But I don't know if we can survive another fight like that."

"With better cover, we might," Aryion said. He pointed toward the Strait. A cluster of rock walls, crumbled with age, stood overlooking the water, the ruin of an old fort. The walls were not much taller than a man, but built up on the hill, it offered higher ground to shoot down from. "We can set up there. The wounded can rest for a moment, and we can stave off the next attack."

"For how long?" Joesp asked wearily. "If we stop running, we will eventually be cut off."

"If we keep running, they will continue pursuing us," Aryion told him. "We'll keep our escape route clear, to begin running north again when we're ready. But for now, we must stand and fight."

There was a long pause. Dusty finally sighed. "Yes. Do as he says."

The Wildkids entered the fort, bracing themselves against the walls facing the road and nocking arrows to their bowstrings. The wounded were set on the seaward side of the fort, where they would be better protected from the onslaught and could flee if needed. Not like they were in any condition to flee, Allie thought grimly. But she set herself against the wall, eyes on the road thirty yards before them.

Aryion spoke quietly beside her. "Has that ever happened before?"

Allie glanced at him, knowing what he meant. "No. I don't know why my fire could… do that this time."

"And you've fought the enchanted soldiers before?"

"I did, a little. When we fought the Aces in Caer Sia," Allie replied. "And I could never—it never happened then."

"What about the sword?" Aryion studied her carefully, his dark eyes searching her face.

Allie turned away from the penetrating gaze. "I don't know," was all she said, wishing he would stop asking questions. He had to know that none of her sudden powers had happened before. If she'd been able to kill the Ace-Lord's soldiers, or wield Jan's sword, surely he would have heard about it by now.

But it had never happened before. Not the inferno of fury, not the white fire of Drisilas, not the deaths of the deathless soldiers.

"They're coming," one of the archers called, her voice tense with nervousness. The enchanted soldiers and Dal-kerri hounds had regrouped. Allie could hear the yips and howls accompanied by the clinks of armor and rhythm of iron-shod boots.

"Two volleys, then let them draw closer," Dusty said. "Aim for the Dal-kerri. We can't afford to waste arrows. Wait until they're in range."

Allie counted the Wildkid archers by the walls. Twenty-two. Around twenty more waited with daggers drawn. But many others lay with the wounded, or back with the smoldering bodies of the enchanted soldiers.

How many had she killed? Just the five that were attacking Dusty and Graysil, or others? She hadn't had time to count.

She watched as the figures came into view. The Dal-kerri approached slowly, cautiously. They must have finally realized that their quarry could bite back.

"Hold," Dusty ordered, her voice low.

The enchanted soldiers had seen them. Shouting, they beckoned the Dal-kerri forward. The wolflike beasts snarled and stalked toward the fort.

"Draw," Dusty commanded. Twenty-two bows bent back as the Wildkids sighted on their approaching targets. The Dal-kerri, seeing that the hated flames were gone, doubled their pace.

"Release," came Dusty's quiet voice.

The bowstrings thrummed, and the volley leapt away, slamming into the oncoming hounds. Several of them reeled back with snarls of pain, but more and more came from behind, creeping from the foggy edge of trees in a black mass.

Allie ignored the Dal-kerri, watching over the oncoming heads for the Ace-Deputy. There was no sign of him. Perhaps he was waiting for a lull in the battle. But surely she would have seen him by now?

"Here come the soldiers," Darion warned beside her.

A second volley of arrows launched at the enchanted warriors, but they continued onward, unhindered.

"Save your arrows!" Allie called to the Wildkids. She forgot the Ace-Deputy for now. Fire crackled in her hands as she leapt down from the fort. Again, her vision fractured, focused on the approaching threat. Red lightning tore across the plain, and this time she saw it strike, saw it pierce the bodies of two soldiers, saw the pain and shock on their faces as the life left them.

Dusty's shouted commands penetrated the fog of wrath that filled Allie's head. "Bows down—they're falling back." She was right—the soldiers had retreated uneasily at the sight of Allie's fire. Slowly, Allie walked back to the fort.

Dusty looked at her. "Can you hold them off?"

Allie nodded briefly, setting herself in front of the fort. The soldiers were advancing again, albeit more slowly than before. For a moment, the unease on their faces made her hesitate. Her mission had been to find a cure for these people. They were entrapped by the Aces. She was not supposed to kill them.

But the fury overcame that thought as darker memories took its place. Caer Sia, walls blackened, people slain, her father covered in ash and blood, weakened from his time as the Aces' prisoner. Her city, torn and tattered. Mel, falling from the bridge. Jan, dragged back by icy chains.

And her fire continued, again and again, striking her targets as they charged forward. Not until the enchanted soldiers retreated into the fog again did she lower her hands, winded and light-headed. She'd never used so much power before, and never like this, with the fear and red-hot rage flowing from her.

"Easy," Dusty ordered the archers. "They'll hesitate to attack after that." She looked at Allie as she re-entered the fort, her expression both impressed and unsettled. "Catch your breath," was all she said, and moved to stand by Aryion again.

Allie took her place beside Darion. He did not look at her, his face drawn and pale. Again, the reality of what she had done entered her thoughts. How many of those soldiers had Darion known as friends before the Aces had taken them? How many had she killed?

She did not want those questions answered. Instead, she contented herself with the idea that those men had chosen their fate, that they were mercenaries who'd joined for reward. She heard Captain Fargrin shouting, trying to organize his stricken band.

The sudden silence rang in Allie's ears. So quiet. After the constant shouting, screaming, and clashing of battle, the quiet was jarring. Yet tension shivered in the air like a clock counting down the seconds.

Through the fog came a black-robed figure.

Allie raised her hands instantly, ready for the blast, but the Deputy's ice was not aimed at her. Instead, he raised his hands and sent a sweeping wave at the ancient walls.

The crackling fire shield caught the ice sidelong, and Allie was flung backwards against the fort. The stone walls buckled under the blow. Shards of ice and stone flew through the air. A massive cloud of dust joined the fog. The walls shuddered, but stood, balancing precariously on the edge of the hill.

Allie spat out a mouthful of dirt, gasping for breath as she forced herself up again. Four Wildkids lay unmoving to her left—dead or unconscious, she couldn't tell. Their comrades pulled them to safety. A hail of crossbow bolts rained down on the crumbling fort, dancing off the stones, striking the exposed archers.

"Down!" Dusty was shouting, her voice raw—"down, all of you!"

The plodding of heavy boots on the road snapped Allie's attention back. The enchanted soldiers, taking advantage of the distraction, now charged towards them. She sprang forward, fire tearing from her fingers, and killed three of the soldiers before they had time to shoot. Blast after blast launched from her hands.

Out of the corner of her eye, she saw the Ace-Deputy raise his hands again.

"Allie, *get down!*" Someone tackled her sideways as the white ice flew at her. The second blast of ice struck the walls, and this time the ancient brick gave way, showering the Wildkids in dirt and stone.

Allie tasted blood in her mouth. Loose soil covered her face. She coughed and spat, struggling to her knees. Darion gripped her shoulder, holding her down as the fort crumbled around them. Another blast of ice exploded the air behind her, destroying the wall the wounded had sheltered behind.

"Are you mad?" Darion choked. "You think yourself immortal now, because you can kill the enchanted?"

"Let me up!" Allie yelled back. "We don't have any cover!" Blood streaked her hand as she wiped her face, and she felt a large gash on her chin. There was blood on Darion's face, too, and he lifted his bow with an effort.

"Listen," he croaked, coughing. "We're out of—"

"We're not giving up," Allie snapped at him, trying to stand—her knees shook so badly she fell again. All around her were cries, frightened voices, voices of the many injured—she heard Dusty yelling, desperately trying to regain order. Aryion was shouting too, though Allie couldn't see where he was. She took a breath, and leaning against the wall, started for the battlefield.

Darion caught her hand, pulling her back. "Wait, Allie. We can't—"

"We're not giving up!" Allie repeated angrily. "We can't lose the Star-Stone, Darion—we can't let them take it, Ĵan trusted me to—"

"We have no arrows!" Darion gripped her shoulders and flung the words into her face. Behind him, the quivers of spare arrows had been crushed beneath the rocks. Splintered shafts littered the ground. Several bows lay snapped in two where they had fallen.

For the first time all day, a cold despair engulfed the fire in her heart.

"Down here, you two," Dusty called, her voice heavy.

Darion nodded meaningfully down the rise, and they headed

down. The remaining warriors huddled beside the tranquil water of the Strait, covered in dust. Most of them were bleeding. Aryion knelt by Newuel, quickly bandaging a gash on the young Wildkid's shaggy head. He looked up as Allie and Darion joined them, his face grim.

"This is the plan," he said, in a low tone that brooked no argument. "You two are to go with the wounded and try to reach Mata City. You must get the Star-Stone away from the Aces. We'll buy you time here—with any luck, the Aces won't immediately realize you're gone."

"No!" Allie cried immediately. She knew arguing was pointless, but she didn't care. "I'm not just giving up. Darion can take the sword. You'll need me here—I can kill the soldiers, I'll buy you more time than you'd buy us."

"The sword is useless without you," Dusty said tiredly. "Allie, can't you see? Through some magic or devilry, you are now the Wielder of Isilas. You are as crucial to the Aces as Mel and Jan, and if you're captured or killed, we've lost the war."

Allie heard the truth in her words, but her heart refused to accept it. "I can't just—"

"Asescia," Aryion said, in an even quieter voice. He said nothing more, only looked at her, the same way he had when she'd wanted to attack Castle Droco. His weary yet firm expression spoke the same. *Don't fight me*, his eyes said, so filled with weariness and grief that it snuffed the reckless fire within her.

Allie nodded wordlessly. It took great effort to turn her back on the little group, to take the first steps away from them and toward the distant refuge of Mata City.

Yet they had only taken a few steps when a deafening blast caused her to clap her hands over her ears, shrinking back.

Boom! Boom! Boom!

The shots came in rapid succession, splitting the silence like rolls of thunder, vibrating through the ground. The Wildkids dropped down, covering their heads. Answering thuds came from beyond as heavy missiles pounded into the battlefield.

Cannon fire.

Gliding down the Strait from the north were two ships. The first, smaller, bore the simple yet utilitarian design of a Garilian frigate, with a stocky build and no cannons. Allie could make out many figures swarming the decks, men loading into rowboats, and thought she saw yellow fire illuminating their weapons.

But her attention was drawn to the second ship. Tall and lean, her silhouette so familiar through the haze of dust and fog, the smoke from her cannons filling the air. The red and black banner of Caer Sia snapped in the breeze behind her as she fired again and again to shore.

The *Gryphon*, the flagship of the Caer Sian fleet, her father's pride and joy. A sob of relief tore from her throat.

The Guardians of Gayrile reached them first, springing from the rowboats, splashing through the salty water until they reached shore. They carried swords and staffs, and she saw in awe that her guess was correct—fire indeed lit their blades, yellow and red and vivid blue. They charged amid the Dal-kerri, who fled at the sight of the terrible multi-colored flames.

Allie climbed up the rise to the ruin of the fort, watching as their rescuers attacked with practiced skill. The enchanted soldiers hesitated, but another round from the Coonsian warship and they retreated back into the trees. The Ace-Deputy had vanished.

A tall warrior clad entirely in black armor stood at the head of the attacking force. "Form up! Protect the wounded!" His lilting voice was unfamiliar to Allie, but her attention was drawn to another—a tall young warrior sending yellow sparks dancing from his sword and shield.

Rygal turned, and she saw his eyes searching the ragged group on shore until they rested on her. He jogged over, relief evident in every line of his face. "Are you all right? Where are the others?"

"Here—we're here—most of us," Allie replied haltingly, trying to catch her breath. Her eyes landed on the yellow sparks glowing on the ground behind Rygal, and she forced a grin. "Essence channeling? When did you learn that?"

"I'll have to tell you about it later," Rygal answered with a smile of relief. But the concern remained on his face as he looked at her, as though trying to assure himself she was unharmed. "You're... all right, then?" As if unable to stop himself, he reached out and lightly brushed the blood from her cheek, then pulled back.

"Yes, I'm all right," Allie answered, realizing, for the first time, how much she'd missed him.

Rygal stepped aside with a short nod, moving first to Dusty, then Aryion. By that time, the *Gryphon* had drawn near to shore. Allie saw the gleaming armor of the Red Dawn warriors as they jogged to land. Most of the Dal-kerri had fled at the arrival of the Guardians, but a few hounds still lingered amid the carnage of the battle. One of them sprang at an injured Wildkid—a tall Liznee caught the hound with his sword before it could attack. He swept the dead Dal-kerri back into the bracken, then turned, the brilliant flames of the Guardians illuminating his face.

The breath caught in Allie's chest. Her legs propelled her forward— she stumbled over the stones, but kept moving until she fell forward, caught in her father's arms.

Dandio held her so tightly it almost hurt. She felt a sob building in her chest, clutching her throat, but it did not come. She could feel the vibration of his voice as he spoke, though she couldn't make out the words, and pulled back.

"Are you all right? Are you hurt?" he demanded, looking her up and down.

"I'm fine," Allie answered. Her voice was raspy from the dust and smoke. Relief spread over her father's scarred face, and he held her tightly again. For a moment, she allowed herself to rest there, to pretend she was five years old again and he was comforting her from a harmless nightmare.

But the deeper ache of guilt and grief in her chest caused her to pull away again. "Dad… something happened… Jan—"

"Not here," Dandio said hoarsely, pulling her in again. He whispered the words into her hair. "We received a report. Tell me this only. Did they kill him?"

"I don't know," Allie replied. "They captured him, him and Mel."

She could feel him tense, and wished her news could have been anything but that. If only their report had been victorious. If only she could turn around now and, by some magic, all would be well, and Jan would join their embrace, and Mel would be smiling by Aryion's side as he always was.

But she knew better now. Such things happened only in storybooks, not in the grim reality of war.

Dandio released his embrace, but kept her hand gripped in his as he directed the men. "Load the wounded at once. Lammar, might your warriors set up a perimeter?"

The black-armored warrior nodded, calling the Guardians to search the woods and be certain the Aces' forces had gone. Rygal went with them.

The Wildkids headed gratefully for the rowboats. A tall, burly figure waited on shore, talking with Dusty. He turned, and a wide smile spread over his broad face as he saw Allie. "Well, lass, how do you like this adventuring business?"

"Glentree!" Allie breathed in relief, embracing the giant warrior. "It's good to see you back on your feet."

"Couldn't have missed out on all this for long," Glentree remarked with a shrug. He seemed to regret it, and winced. "Blasted thing still bites. But there's much to do, and no time to be sittin' in bed."

Allie looked at Dandio, interested. "Much to do? Do we have a plan?"

"I think you had best rest from the first mission before beginning the next," Dandio said gently. "We are headed to Mata City now. This mission is over, and our next move is still being decided."

Allie nodded, secretly relieved. The fateful mission to Wiverrun, at last, had ended.

And yet, she thought, as she held Drisilas before her, the mission had raised more questions, more problems, more mysteries than it had answered.

30

ᔅ ᔅ ᔅ ᔅ ᔅ ᔅ ᔅ ᔅ ᔅ ᔅ

The Voyage North

Allie took refuge in the shadowy cabin below the *Gryphon's* decks, seated on a cot. After the tension and terror of the day, it took her a long time to slow her breathing and quiet her restless thoughts.

The medic checked her injuries, which were nowhere near as severe as most of her companions'. After reassuring him that she was fine, just sore, the medic left to work on the others. Her whole body ached. The Deputy's blasts had flung her about as if she were a ragdoll. But she was alive and conscious, which was more than most could say after a fight with an Ace.

Dandio sat with her. She had braced herself to tell the whole story, but he didn't ask for that. He knew her well, knew this was not the time for an interrogation. The questions he asked could be answered simply. No, Jan had not been killed on the bridge. Yes, Darion had known Jan's plan, or at least most of it. No, Jan had not told her about the curse before, or any strategy to be rid of it.

She shared her theory about the Ace-Lord's new aim—corrupting the mortals so thoroughly that the Stone's magic would be corrupted as well. She could tell from Dandio's grim expression that he didn't enjoy the thought, but he agreed it was likely.

"They probably would not have let you leave with the Stones otherwise," he said. "And it adds more cause for them to lay the curse on Ĵan." He let out a breath. "Tell me. Did Cahadras offer any solution to the curse?"

"She said… she said it's up to Ĵan," Allie said slowly. "She said something about the atoning lying in the present, not the past. I don't know what she meant." Doubt filled her. Ĵan had twisted the Stone's magic, and she was sure the Stars did not take that lightly. Yet it was the Ace-Lord who accused him, not the Stars nor the High Light. Was there a way to free Ĵan from the curse he bore? To stop the corruption of Isilas?

There was no answer to those questions.

Dandio went back on deck, leaving Allie to rest. After a few minutes, she could stand the silence and solitude of the cabin no longer. A small mirror on the shelf across from the cot caught her reflection as she stood. Her hair was tangled and greasy, and though she'd washed her face, it was still streaked with mud. Grime clung to her skin no matter how much she'd scrubbed it.

Evening was falling, and the cool air refreshed her tired body. The *Gryphon* cruised up the Mata Strait, the gentle rhythm of the rowers propelling her onward. The soft creaks and groans of the timbers were familiar, homely sounds. She'd made many childhood memories here: joining her father on a short voyage to Cattrick Fief, while he taught her the art of navigation and reading the maps written in the stars;

accompanying her mother on a mission to Badwater; slipping away on a hot summer day and reading in the shade of the mizzen mast.

A small crowd stood on the stern. Dandio was speaking with Dusty, who was giving her report of the Wildkids' journey and mission to the Mainland. Aryion and Darion stood nearby, along with Lammar and Rygal, who were listening to Dusty's words with interest.

"I'd been hoping you would make it this far north eventually," Lammar said as Dusty finished. The Siren, as Allie had learned upon meeting him, was the interim leader of the Guardians of Gayrile. Lammar had shed his previous guise of the black-armored warrior, and now wore his usual skin, smooth green scales glistening in the twilight.

"I'd hoped we'd be more help than this," Dusty replied wearily.

"Don't worry about that for now," Dandio said. "Let your soldiers rest for a time. We will gather our forces in Mata City. I've already summoned my generals for a war council with Lord Roan."

Allie looked at him, interested. "War council? Does that mean we're going back to Castle Droco?" Why did that idea sound so appealing? Shouldn't the idea of returning to the Ace-Lord's fortress fill her with dread? But there was no fear, at least not for herself.

"As soon as we can," Dandio replied. A familiar fire blazed in his green eyes. "We must recover the Stone and—more importantly— rescue Ĵan and Mel. The main challenge will be gathering the forces to do it."

"The men will follow you," Glentree said with a slight frown.

"I don't doubt that," Dandio agreed dryly. "But bringing the entire Red Dawn to Caer Droco might end badly. We have been single-handedly protecting the northeastern fiefs for months."

"What about the Elves of Elimar?" Allie asked.

"Still bickering over the Narivo Agreement. Your mother has gathered evidence of the Ace-Lord's plans, and the Elven delegates from both Elimar and Tinkeeyo will attend the meeting in Mata City. But I think your report might be what convinces them." Dandio nodded to Darion.

That was better than nothing, Allie knew. Their first-hand account of the darkness in Castle Droco would hopefully persuade Elimar that the situation was dire. But if it didn't… if it didn't, then there would be no one to protect the northeastern borders, and that might affect whether or not they were able to rescue Jan and Mel. They needed Elimar's warriors to guard their backs before they attempted any rescues.

Dandio noticed her unease and gave her a tight smile. "We'll figure it out soon. For now, try to rest. We are not far from Mata City."

Dusk had fallen, and twinkling lights from thousands of carved stone windows reflected on the water as they drew near the town. Lights glowed from the skiffs and boats that cruised the canals as night approached. Allie had only been to Mata City in passing, never for more than a few hours. Yet the cheerful firelight, the distant rolling thunder of the ocean, and the lapping seawater in the canals seemed to welcome her in as though she were an old friend.

They sailed into the city. The gradual hills rose on either side of the Strait, like the winds of some great bird. In the dim light, Allie could make out the stone dwellings, the ships headed down the Strait, Coopers guiding their wooden paddleboards on the water, and figures walking the stone byways alongside the canals.

There were many piers and harbors, but the one they sailed into looked to be the largest, set in the heart of the city. Many other ships were docked here—single-mast sailboats, slender skiffs, and several warships, built with the distinctive twin triangle sails of Mata City's navy.

A few crowds still milled the streets around the harbor, humans and Coopers alike, and Allie sensed the curious glances as the two warships docked at the pier. But Allie's eyes were drawn to a small group waiting on the other side of the harbor. As the ship slowed, they hurried toward the pier.

Allie's heart caught as she saw her mother and the deep concern on her usually calm face. A tall figure robed in black waited behind her—Iriam.

A Cooper led the group, and moved aside as the gangplank was lowered. "There, what did I tell you, Lady Ki? They're all right."

Ajaha, disregarding every protocol that likely demanded her to stand calm and serene, ran down the pier and embraced her daughter. Allie could feel her shaking. "I'm all right," she managed, her voice muffled into her mother's shoulder.

Ajaha pulled back, looking her up and down several times before her face relaxed. "Good. Oh, Asescia." She hugged her again. The familiar embrace brought to light the fear of the last few days, the horrors she had seen. The tears rose in Allie's throat again, but she forced them away.

"I thought you were in Badwater," she said as the others disembarked.

"I was. We received news of the capture of Wiverrun. Most of us feared the worst," Ajaha replied, moving to Dandio.

"Ain't much good news they've brought," Glentree remarked grimly, "but the good news of it is, they're alive. And there's hope yet we'll free the others."

"And you have guarded the Stone," Iriam said. His face was as unreadable as ever, but Allie heard the relief in his voice.

"Drisilas is safe," she replied, not yet able to explain the unbelievable power she'd wielded today. Though perhaps she did not have to. Something changed in Iriam's expression as he studied her—something remarkably similar to the Ace-Deputy's reaction. Confusion and surprise… and a hint of fear.

She decided she was imagining it.

Jarus greeted them—despite his confident reassurance to Ajaha, he was clearly relieved to see them alive. He noticed Mel's absence first, and Allie saw pain and concern enter his eyes. "Is there… any hope to save them?" he asked slowly, while the sailors loaded the injured Wildkids on stretchers bound for the hospital.

"There's always hope," Dandio said, but his face was grave.

Dusty argued to give her report to Lord Roan at once, but eventually she was persuaded to go to the hospital with her injured siblings. Rygal and Lammar left to tell Lord Roan that their mission had been successful. Allie was left with her parents and the two rangers.

"There's an inn a few blocks from here," Jarus said as he led them to a small sailboat. "But I assumed you'd want somewhere more private. You're all welcome to stay the night with us."

They thanked him and agreed. Allie was grateful for the offer. Jarus seemed to know just as well as she did that news travelled fast from local inns. She had only just brought herself to answer her father's questions, and she didn't want to answer the questions of strangers.

Worse, what would happen if word got out about her strange dark powers?

"Are you well, child?" Iriam's quiet voice came from behind. Allie hadn't realized he was still there.

"Yes, I'm fine now. Just tired," she answered. There was something familiar in the way he'd asked that question, but she couldn't place it.

Iriam nodded slightly, but his thoughtful red eyes remained fixed on her with concern, like she were made of glass and might suddenly shatter before him. He joined them on the boat, which ferried them through the canals to the Puddlepaws' home. Only after they were safely escorted inside did he bid them goodnight.

"We have two guest rooms," Jarus was saying as he opened the door. "One's a little cold—we're still working on building a fireplace in there, but hopefully it won't be—"

"It's perfect, Jarus. Thank you," Ajaha said with a smile.

Maya met them inside, greeting them cheerfully. Dandio and Aja-ha still wanted to hear the details of what had occurred in Wiver-run. Allie didn't feel much like talking; the exhaustion seemed to have drained her. She followed Maya gratefully to the room.

"It's good to finally meet you," Maya told her, blue eyes twinkling kindly. "Rygal's told us all about you."

"He did?" Allie asked, as a little thrill of interest replaced her grim thoughts for a moment.

"Don't worry, it was all good," Maya replied with a smile. "Here's the guest room—let me know if you need anything."

Allie thanked her as she left. The room held a cot and a mat with woolen blankets. Though small, it was warm and cozy. Allie set her battered pack on the mat and changed into the spare clothes her mother had brought for her. She heard conversation resume in the parlor—the others were sharing their adventures with the Puddlepaws.

Wearily, she lay down on the mat and pulled the blankets over her, trying to rest. But the darkness persisted into sleep. She dreamt of marble bridges, of chasms filled with infinite blackness, of a face with purple-red eyes reciting words in an ancient tongue, as icy chains closed over her chest and encased her heart.

31

Refuge

The following morning felt blissfully uneventful. Allie remembered, with a bitter smile, the way she had begged for a task back in Caer Sia, to be involved in the coming war. After the events of the last few weeks, the peaceful breakfast in the Puddlepaws' home was a wonderful change.

Her mother had already left by the time Allie was awake. As Dandio explained, the last group of informants had returned from Yamo with their reports, which both Ajaha and Lammar wanted to hear. Dandio himself left shortly after to meet with Glentree.

"What do you need me to do?" Allie asked him before he left.

"Stay here, and enjoy the quiet," Dandio answered, a faint smile on his face. "I will return and tell you our plans as soon as they are decided."

Aryion went with him. The ranger looked grimmer than usual, and the dark shadows under his eyes made Allie suspect he hadn't slept much. She couldn't blame him for that. Being here, safe and sound, likely only heightened his concern for his lost apprentice.

She tried to distract herself from her own worries. She helped Maya tidy up after breakfast and played with little Ella, who was more interested in drawing on the tabletop than on her paper. Maya sat across from her, a small notebook open, pencil in paw as she scanned the pages.

"That won't work," she muttered a few times, scratching something out. She looked up at Allie with a wry smile. "Word of advice, Asescia—never enter an ever-changing profession. These sail designs worked well five years ago, but now, some designer across the Strait has created a new sail rig, so everyone wants their ships fitted that way."

Allie managed a smile. "Do the old designs still work?"

"Oh yes, they work fine. But it's the principle. If something is new and improved, everyone'll want it." Maya shook her head, but Allie could tell she thoroughly enjoyed creating the new and improved designs.

Ella pressed down so hard on her page that her pencil broke, and Allie got her a new one to avoid interrupting Maya's work. When she returned to the table, the Cooper was studying her with a mixture of curiosity and sympathy. She glanced away quickly as Allie returned her gaze. "Sorry—I'm just curious. Aryion mentioned your… skills… last night."

"What did he say?" Allie asked, a little irritated at the ranger.

"Nothing much, he told us to ask you about it ourselves," Maya reassured her. "All he said was that you're able to wield Drisilas, and to… break the enchantment."

The slight hesitation before the second statement told Allie that

Aryion had likely provided a more graphic description of what she could do. Break the enchantment. Well, that was technically true, but it wasn't in the way she'd hoped. Nor could she be sure that was the best way. Darion had been so sure that the enchanted soldiers were pressed into service, bound to the Ace-Lord just as he had been.

And she'd killed them without thought. Worse still… she had almost enjoyed it.

"I don't know any more than that," she answered finally. "It all happened so fast. It felt different than when I've fought before—the fire felt hotter. It felt…" she trailed off, searching for the right word. "Wrong."

Ella was still scribbling on her paper, ignorant of the grim conversation. Maya brushed a streak of gray graphite from her daughter's fur, her face thoughtful. "I'm sorry," she said at last. "I wonder, though…"

"Wonder what?" Allie asked, as she trailed off.

"Well… I don't know if it works like this. But those powers… they might be used for good, too," Maya said. "You can break the Ace-Lord's enchantment. I wonder if other forms of Ace-magic might be broken too." She shrugged slightly. "Something to think about. But you might try making use of what you have—it's an unexpected advantage, but it might be a good one."

Allie had not thought about it like that before, not in the slightest. Thus far, her concern had been on the how and why, seeking desperately for the reason behind this new, unnatural strength. Maya's suggestion that it could be used for good was a completely new outlook. She could defeat the enchanted soldiers. She could wield Drisilas. What else could she do? What was the extent of this power?

And, she wondered, with a surge of excitement, could it be used to free Jan and Mel?

In an instant, the spark of an idea flickered to life, and there was only one person she wanted to talk with.

By the time Darion returned some time later, accompanied by Jarus, Aryion, and Rygal, Allie's idea had transformed into a crackling blaze of hope. Maya left to meet with her fellow ship-builders after putting Ella down for a nap, and the other three were deep in discussion over the impending blockade at the north mouth of the Strait.

Allie caught Darion's elbow and led him into the hallway. "I need to talk to you."

He followed, confused but clearly interested. "About what?"

"If someone wanted to get into Castle Droco, where's the weakest point?" Allie asked.

A faint smile crossed his face. "Someone?"

"The weakest point's the Patch, isn't it?" Allie asked, ignoring his question.

She had his attention now—the smile vanished, and he looked concerned. "I…suppose so, but we wouldn't know that, because you'd only be trapped in the Patch."

"What if I wasn't? What if I could go in and out of it as easily as the Aces?"

"What gives you that idea?"

He listened without interruption as Allie told him about her discussion with Maya. "I don't know what I *can't* do at this point," she finished, her voice almost shaking with excitement. "But Darion—if I could get into the Patch—I might be able to find Jan and Mel, and get them out. You yourself said that the Aces seem to travel through the Patch—maybe I can, too."

Darion's scarred face was difficult to read—he seemed to be considering it, but looked unsure. "I hadn't thought of that," he admitted finally. "There's no way to test it. Who's to say you won't simply be killed, or lost in there forever?"

Allie hesitated, casting about for an answer. Drisilas pressed against her back as she leaned against the wall—after the incident at the Alfona's village, she refused to leave it even for a moment. She clutched the strap as the answer came to her. "I can use Drisilas. The Star-Stones can penetrate the illusions—Mel said so after he joined the Shards. He said the Blue Stone shone through the illusion and showed what was really there, and I'm willing to bet that Isilas works the same way."

"The same way as what?" came Dandio's voice. He stood at the end of the hallway, studying them with a slight frown. The hallway was rather cramped—she and Darion were standing very close.

Allie flushed. "I—didn't know you were back."

"Clearly." Dandio looked Darion up and down.

Allie edged out of the hallway, flustered, trying to gather her thoughts to tell the new plan. "Dad, we've been thinking that—"

"I heard you," Dandio said. With one last searching glance at Darion, who looked very uncomfortable, he turned away. "Come out here and tell it to the others all the same."

They sat at the table. Iriam had come with Dandio, which lifted Allie's spirits—if anyone could tell her if her idea might work or not, Iriam could.

"I think—I've been thinking that I might be able to—to get them out, using the Patch," she told them. Why did her voice have to come so haltingly? Her excitement seemed to tie her tongue in knots.

"Jan and Mel?" Jarus asked. "How do you know if they're in the Patch at all?"

"I don't, but—Maya and I were talking. She mentioned that I might try to use these new powers for our advantage. I might have more control of the Ace-Lord's magic than we think," she said. *Control* was a generous term. She could hardly call the wild, unrestrained fire something she had controlled. But then again, she might learn to tame it. "I might be able to go into the Patch, to wherever they're keeping them, and rescue Jan and Mel myself," she concluded.

She kept her eyes on Dandio—as she expected, he was shaking

his head before she finished. "No. I think that is far too risky. You have no idea what is in the Patch, or if it leads anywhere. If our plan is successful, the Red Dawn will rescue the prisoners during the attack."

"You know it won't be that easy," Allie argued.

"It rarely is," Iriam conceded. "But we are prepared to make the needed sacrifices to rescue the captives."

"But what if those sacrifices don't have to be made?" That was Darion. He still sounded unsure, but clearly supported Allie's idea, and she could have hugged him for it. "What if she can get into the void as simply as walking through a door, and bring Jan and Mel back through with her? The Aces have no reason to guard the Patch—no one's ever come out of it."

"We don't know what's in there," Rygal pointed out. Considering he was usually willing to try any plan, no matter how risky, his doubt cut deep. "It might just go on forever. You could be lost in the void for Light knows how long."

"Isn't that risk better than the deaths of who knows how many soldiers?" Allie shot back, looking desperately at Dandio. She noticed his expression was not doubtful that her plan would work, but more a fear for his daughter's safety.

"The point is, we don't know how your powers work at all," Rygal countered. He sounded torn between hearing her out or siding with Dandio. "For that matter, none of us know how the enchantment works, either."

"We didn't exactly have time to investigate that," Allie snapped.

Rygal spread his hands. "That's not what I meant. I meant that it could be better to wait until we have more information."

"Jan and Mel might be dead before then," Allie said. "If I can wield Isilas, the Ace-Lord doesn't need Jan. All he needs to do is to force Mel to use the Blue Stone. I know that'll be hard," she added, as Aryion drew breath to argue, "but we don't want it to get to that point, do we?"

"I do not believe such powers should be used at all," Iriam answered. His deep voice filled Allie with doubts. "Such strength cannot come without a price. Whatever that may be, I would suggest avoiding using it all together."

"The fact remains we don't know enough about the voids," Dandio said. "If you want to fight, then your place is with the Red Dawn charge, not in the void."

"The charge?" Darion repeated, looking at him in disbelief. "Those enchanted soldiers are people. You'd have your daughter at the head of the fight, killing them?"

"They haven't given us much reason to believe they have any humanity left," Rygal said grimly.

Darion raised an eyebrow in a familiar smirk. "Oh, of course. And neither did the Hazes."

The words sank into silence. Allie looked at Darion in shock, then at Dandio, whose face was rigid.

The Hazes. Kado's immortal soldiers, pressed into his service.

Ordinary people from Gayrile and Coonsia, friends and brothers. Rygal had told her about them often enough, and about how hard he and his companions had fought to find a way to cure them. Evidently he remembered that also—he avoided her eyes.

"Wiverrun is dead," Darion said hoarsely. "Their duke sold them out to the Ace-Lord, the same way I handed their neighbors into his hands. The same way Safacon betrayed the people of Gayrile. And now, when those people need help, your only solution is slaughter." His gaze swung to Allie. "You never came along to find a cure for them. You wanted to fight—wanted revenge for what they did to Caer Sia." A slight, mocking smile appeared on his face. "I suppose I can't blame you for that."

"Quiet your tone, Master Blackbird," Iriam said, his voice low but firm. "Accusations and arguments will gain us nothing, nor will it undo what has been done." He looked at Allie, his eyes searching her. "These powers are an unnatural thing, Heiress. If you will use them, or shun them, the choice must be yours. But I would caution you, there are always consequences to twisted magic."

Allie looked down, fresh unease chilling her heart. Darion leaned back in his seat, studying the floor. A tense silence followed.

Dandio finally spoke, his voice slow and quiet. "If there is a way to save the civilians of Wiverrun, you must know that we will take it, Blackbird. The attack on Castle Droco will not end the war. Nor would I have Allie kill at all. Her fire need not kill them—she might save many lives without ever needing to draw blood."

He looked at Allie. "As for the voids, no one has ever gone inside one and returned, save for Mel, and I think that was only because the Ace-Lord wanted the Darkness destroyed. But the Patches of darkness, the Ace-Lord's illusions—those were in Sia, too, during the occupation."

"I thought the civilians were kept in the city," Aryion said slowly.

"The civilians were," Dandio answered. "The generals, the government officials, hated enemies of the Aces—they were kept in the castle. A void of ice and madness."

His eyes were distant, his voice seeming to come from far away. "There are worse things than pain and death. The voids become your fear. Sights and sounds, jarring scenes from your darkest memories, voices of your loved ones screaming in pain. And, eventually, the Aces come to break you. When your mind is numbed by fear, they read your thoughts. Resist, and you will be shattered."

Dandio let out a breath. His face had turned pale, seeming to accentuate the black scar left by the Darkness long ago. Other, recent scars showed on his skin too. Though it had been almost a year, every now and then the spark of green would fade from his eyes, and they would turn grim and cold as though he had never been freed from the Ace-Lord's prison, as though the darkness and horror were a part of him.

She had never asked him about that time. Never dared ask about the weeks he had spent as the Ace-Lord's prisoner. The little he had told them had to be pieced together like a puzzle—the wounds covering his body, the way he seemed to have aged twenty years, the way he no longer enjoyed the darkness and solitude of a quiet night.

Allie tried to speak, but there were no words to be said. For the first time, the reality of what had happened to him—her father—seemed to strike her. Who knew how many others were suffering too?

Yet all she'd wanted was revenge. How selfish she had been. What Aryion had said before was true—her view on this conflict was far too narrow and simple, a mistaken belief that all she needed was revenge to make things right. Her face felt hot with shame.

Dandio straightened and squared his shoulders, as though in defiance of the pain and darkness of the past, and looked at Iriam. "Regardless of the risk, I agree that such powers could be used to our advantage. If this is her choice, do you believe her plan could work?"

Allie looked up in disbelief. Iriam sighed. "If she chooses to do so. She will likely have a better chance of success than anyone else." He looked at Allie. "Isilas will protect you from the illusions and madness within the void, but you must be aware of other dangers—particularly the ones surrounding your new... powers."

Allie nodded, stunned that they had agreed to her plan. "I will—I'll be careful." She paused, looking at Iriam. "Do you think... what do you think those dangers are?"

"I am unsure, and that is risk enough," Iriam replied. "As I have said, there is always a consequence to corrupting magic. These powers do not come from the High Light, which leads me to believe they were bestowed to you by the Ace-Lord. For what reason, I do not know, but there is undoubtedly a dark purpose at work here."

Again, a cold fear sent shivers down Allie's spine like chains brushing her skin, but she only nodded slightly.

"He'll regret ever giving her that power, no matter what he intended it for," Rygal said firmly. "And we can protect her on this side of the void, right?" he added, looking at Dandio.

"We will ensure your retreat," Dandio agreed. He rubbed his chin thoughtfully, then turned to Darion. "I'd like a word with you later—I need to know more about this castle. Could you provide a layout?"

Darion nodded. "Yes—and I have notes. Jan had me write down what we saw in Wiverrun."

"Of course he did," Dandio said, a small smile touching his face at his brother's name. "Likely, to help persuade me."

"When will we go back?" Allie asked hopefully.

Aryion spoke. "It sounds as though the council will meet tomorrow. You two will attend with the others, and likely, embark on the journey back to Wiverrun shortly afterwards."

Darion glanced at him with a frown. "You two?" he repeated. "What are you planning to do?"

Aryion let out a long breath. "Mel… before he fell, he mentioned that the Aces had threatened his family. Whether or not this was an idle threat, I can't take that lightly. If the Smallbuttons were captured by the Aces, they might be used as leverage to force Mel to cooperate—or worse." He paused. Allie could see he wanted nothing more than to charge into Castle Droco himself, fighting through Aces and Dal-kerri alike until Mel was free. But this choice must be made.

"You can't go all the way to Appledale alone," Darion said doubtfully. "And what about Mel?"

"There's nothing I can do for Mel now. Asescia alone has a chance of saving him," Aryion said. His voice was heavy, but there was a firm determination there, too. "If his family were taken, rescuing Mel would only become more complicated. And I won't be going alone. Dusty's coming too, with around twenty of her warriors to escort the Smallbuttons to Caer Sia."

Dandio nodded. "We planned it this morning," he said. "Mel is determined, and the Ace-Lord knows it. His devotion to his family— particularly his sister—is well-known too. We can better protect his family if we can get them to Caer Sia."

"And I will trust you to get Mel out," Aryion added. His dark eyes scrutinized first Dandio, then Allie.

She met his glance with a nod. "We'll get him out," she said firmly, "and meet you in Caer Sia."

Aryion returned her nod. A few weeks ago, Allie thought, he had doubted her decisions—and rightly so. Yet now, after all that had happened, she had earned his trust. She felt her promise settle on her shoulders like a weight.

A small voice cried out somewhere in the house. Jarus rose and padded down the hall to his daughter.

"Well," Dandio said briskly, standing. "I now have an attack to plan. Darion, I hope you'll lend your observations. And you, Aryion, if you could look over my notes before you leave, I would value your insights into our strategy."

Slowly, the group filtered toward the door. Dandio lingered as the others left, turning back to Allie. "I trust you know your strength, as well as your limitations," he said quietly, taking her hand in his. "I don't doubt your skill, Asescia. I never have. But know, too, that I have seen what the Aces are capable of."

Allie looked down. "I know. I—I'm sorry." The words were not enough to erase the pain he had endured at the hands of the Ace-Lord. Not enough to banish the fear and doubt in both their minds. But for now, they were enough for her father.

He smiled slightly. "Jan would be proud of you. As am I." He turned toward the door. "I will return tonight, after I have finished the details of our strategy. I expect we will discuss both that and other matters at the council."

Allie nodded as he left. Iriam was the last to leave. His red eyes studied her, and again she had the sensation he could see right through her. She braced herself for more warnings about using the powers, and the dangers he alluded to. But all he said was, "Think not of voids and darkness tonight, Heiress. Think on the Prophecy."

The Prophecy. Of course. How had she allowed it to slip so far back in her mind? "Well, I did have other things to worry about," she reminded herself.

But if what Iriam said was true, and the Prophecy spoke of their victory, then she would read it with fresh eyes tonight.

PART 4

Ice and Madness

32

∽ ∽ ∽ ∽ ∽ ∽ ∽ ∽

A Council of War

Aryion had already left when Allie awoke the following morning, headed east with the company of Wildkids. Jarus and Dandio had both gone to see them off. Sailing in a small but fast Caer Sian ship, the Wildkids would likely reach Cattrick Fief in a few days, then ride hard and fast inland to Appledale. While that area was believed to be secure, Allie couldn't help worrying. Aryion and Dusty's small group would likely be outnumbered in case they came across the Aces or their warriors.

"I doubt they'll see much of Aces," Maya said, though clearly she was worried too. "After all, we haven't heard any reports of the Aces being in that area."

"Their forces would have to travel past Elimar to get there," Dandio added. "While Elimar might not want to fight, they'd hardly overlook a troop of Dal-kerri marching past their villages." His typical trail clothes had been replaced with the full armor of a Red Dawn Commander, which clinked slightly as he leaned against the kitchen doorframe. Allie could see the same restless energy in his eyes that she felt.

She took a sip of the tea Maya had given her, trying to dispel her

401

nerves. There were too many things to worry about this morning. First, of course, there was Aryion's mission to protect the Smallbutton family. They would have no way of knowing if anything went wrong, or if Aryion and the Wildkids needed help.

She tried not to worry about that. Dandio was right. The border between Coonsia and Daffodalion was well-monitered, and those who dwelt there would be warned of the Dal-kerri in today's council.

The council. There lay her second source of unease. Darion would bring the report of what had happened in Wiverrun. Would the Elven councilors believe him? Worse, would they trust him at all, after hearing of Darion's treacherous past? Then, of course, there would be her father's plan, which would subsequently reveal the truth of Allie's own powers. She had no idea how the others would react to the reality of what she could do. Even if she were to use her new strength for good, that wouldn't stop fear and suspicion from spreading.

"Time to be off, then," Dandio said, straightening. "Jarus and Glentree will be waiting for us."

Allie finished her tea and followed him outside. The air was fresh and brisk, but a warm breeze blew in from the sea. "Have you planned the charge?" she asked as they walked. "How are we going to get to Castle Droco? And when will we leave?"

"We'll discuss that after the council," her father answered, a familiar half-smile on his scarred face. "How would *you* plan to get to Castle Droco?"

"By sea, maybe," Allie said slowly. "Sail upriver from the Strait. Wouldn't that be fastest?"

"Perhaps under normal circumstances, but your mother's reconnaissance teams found evidence that the Salem Flats are under control of the Aces now," Dandio said. "We will likely have to go over land instead."

"The Flats?" Allie asked. There was little in the matter of cities or civilization in central Coonsia—only miles of desolate wasteland. "What are they doing there?"

"They have claimed the ruins of Ar-Salem, as they did in the first Ace-rise," Dandio answered grimly. "Thankfully the Hyenin people have kept their side of the Strait safe. Their warriors have intercepted a few raiding parties and Dal-kerri, and learned valuable information. I expect we'll discuss that today."

The council was not to be held in Castle Mata, as Allie had expected. Instead, a large, square building that better accomodated the visiting delegations awaited them near the main harbor. A few groups of soldiers, clad in the different colors and uniforms of their respective kingdoms, stood outside, and Allie could see the masts of the visiting ships over the rounded rooftops.

Jarus was waiting for them at the door. "Oh, good, Dandio. Lord Roan was about to send me to fetch you. The meeting hasn't even started, but it's already getting heated in there."

"The Elimar Councilors, I expect?" Dandio inquired.

"That's right," Jarus said tiredly. "They're here for Lady Ki's report, of course, but the delegation from Tinkeeyo is here with more pressing news than that, so now everyone's upset by the change in schedule."

"Tinkeeyo?" Allie repeated hopefully. "Did General Arrex make it there?"

"He and his men reached Tinkeeyo three days ago," Jarus answered with a nod. "Worn out, but all alive. They received Darion's message and passed it on to Quinn—he rode like mad to get here last night."

"Good. I'm glad he is here," Dandio said, satisfied. Allie had met Quinn Fireleaf, the ranger of Tinkeeyo, briefly during the fight with the Aces in Caer Sia.

"I'm glad, too, but as you'd expect, he's not impressed by the whole argument about the Narivo Agreement," Jarus said wryly. "Elimar and Tinkeeyo have clashed for generations—now the delegates from Tinkeeyo believe Elimar to be cowards—"

"Not exactly wrong," Dandio commented under his breath; Allie stifled a laugh.

"—and the Elimar councilors say Tinkeeyo has no right to judge them, since they aren't involved in the war either," Jarus finished with a weary sigh. "To be honest, that's why I came out here to wait—Lady Ki is handling it better than I could."

"She is quite good at that," Dandio agreed.

They entered the foyer. Muffled but angry voices came from within the doors to the council chamber. Rygal and Glentree stood next to the doors, and came forward with relieved expressions when they saw Dandio.

"Good to see ya, sir," Glentree said with a brief salute. His usually cheery face was grave. "Bad news. The Direns won't be able to make it here—sounds as though the rebels have launched an attack on Flameton just this morning."

"Rebels?" Allie repeated, startled.

"Rebel Direns," Rygal explained. "They want Gayrile for themselves, and they want to dethrone King Casper. They've been causing trouble ever since Deathcap, but now it sounds like they're taking advantage of the Ace-War to revolt."

"But they're mortals," Allie said, uncomprehending. "They'll die with us if the Ace-Lord wins. Don't they know this fight is more important?"

Someone yelled from within the council hall, and Glentree sighed. "Tell that to the Elves. Lammar's gone to see to the Direns—he might manage to convince them to stop fighting."

Dandio shook his head, irritated. "Rebel Direns and arguing Elves. Seems this war council is off to an agreeable start."

Darion arrived, only hearing the very end of this statement. "Agreeable? Good. Do you think they'll agree to our plan?"

"I suppose we'll have to see," Dandio said, and led the way through the doors.

Sunlight streamed through two large windows on either wall of the council room. Its shape reminded Allie more of a court room than a meeting hall. Rows of chairs were set on each side of the room, looking up at a dais. A short aisle divided the room in two.

To the left, at the back, sat Joesp and the Wildkid warriors. Across from them were ten or twelve Hyenin delegates, who looked more tired than irritated.

A party of russet-haired Elves clad in the green and gold of Elimar sat in front of the Wildkids. They were glaring at the Elves on the other side of the room, who wore the chainmail and jerkins of Tinkeeyo archers. One of their number, a tall blond Elf, was speaking in a heated tone.

"You've heard of the severity of these matters, and still you delay," he said as they entered the room. "The time to act is now."

"Have you lost brothers, Master Fireleaf?" one of the Elimar councilors replied curtly, his voice low but clearly angry. "Sons? Our countrymen have paid with their lifeblood for far too many battles before the days of the High King, some battles caused by Caer Sia."

"Gentlemen, please. This matter is not what we have come to discuss," Lord Roan interrupted from the dais. He spoke calmly, but Allie could see the frustration on his furry face.

Quinn Fireleaf looked over as Dandio entered. His long blond hair was pulled back from his face, and mud streaked his clothes from his long journey.

The Liznee soldiers came to attention before their commander; Dandio motioned for them to sit. "Good morning. It seems Lammar will not be here today, he has been called away on urgent business to Gayrile."

There was a worried murmur around the room. Everyone had

heard the rumors about the unrest in the far north.

Allie joined Dandio, Rygal and Darion as they sat down behind Quinn's group. The Elven ranger gave them a quick smile of greeting, but his face was drawn.

Lord Roan nodded to Ajaha. "Well then, let us begin. Please, tell your report, Lady Ki."

Ajaha stood at the left of the dais, a small notebook under her arm, her shoulders back to accentuate her height. "I fear it is certain now that the Ace-Lord has gained Ar-Salem, reported by three separate teams scouting the Salem Flats. He has even rebuilt the ruin there, using it as his fortress."

"Why Ar-Salem, and not Castle Droco?" The question came from one of the Hyenins. "We have heard that Castle Droco, too, has been rebuilt. Is that not a far more strategic location for the Ace-Lord to begin his conquest?"

"Perhaps, but perhaps not," Ajaha answered. "Remember, Caer Droco was the domain of Kahlifis while he was mortal. After the Dividing War, he chose the Salem Flats, turning the village of Tiravale into Ar-Salem and thus creating the Eleven. We wonder if his powers are stronger in Ar-Salem."

"And they may well be," came Iriam's deep voice. He stood in the corner, his face thoughtful. "Kahlifis would loathe all memories of his mortal past. It is my belief that he has a different plan for Castle Droco all together."

"And what plan would that be?" Lord Roan asked.

Iriam's red eyes flickered briefly in Allie's direction. "The gateway void. The dark magic Kahlifis commands must be strong in Caer Droco, if he is also to draw the Dark Realm's powers through the void he has opened. On this, I ask the ranger Darion Blackbird of Wiverrun to speak further."

Darion stood and came toward the dais. Allie noticed the slight nervous tremor of his hands as he pulled out a sheet of parchment. But he stood calm, and his voice was steady as he spoke. "Good sirs and ladies. To best understand the predicament of Wiverrun, I must begin at the very beginning." He paused, then began. "The Ace-Lord reached the city at the beginning of winter, nearly four months ago now. He enlisted several of Wiverrun's warriors forcefully to his cause, stating that to protect our families and village, we must swear the Blood Oath in servitude. With this false hope of protecting our village, many joined the Aces. I was one such servant."

His voice did not falter as he stated the facts. Only his hazel eyes betrayed the pain of the memories. "Bound by a Blood Oath, I served the Aces for a time. But they broke their bargain, and my family was taken. I tried to resist, but in breaking my oath, I was punished with the scars of Redeyes, the Messenger of the Ace-Lord. Then—"

He was cut off by a chorus of voices raised in both doubt and fear. "Redeyes was slain," one of the Hyenins scoffed. "Do not mock us with these northern legends, Blackbird."

"Slain, was he?" Glentree boomed, folding his brawny arms over his chest. "An' I was brought down by an oversized tabby cat, was I?"

Lord Roan called for silence again; it was largely unneeded, as the doubters had quickly grown quiet at Glentree's voice. Darion kept talking, unmoved by the disbelief. This was what he had come to do. Allie could see it in his stance. His previous hesitance, the mask of nonchalance he usually wore, had been cast aside.

His voice was firm as he continued. "I was scarred by Redeyes. My assignment was to lure King Jan to the Ace-Lord, and thus bring him the Star-Stone Isilas. Upon my success, the Aces said they would leave Wiverrun and free those they had bound by the enchantment. But instead, the king offered a different plan, as he too bore the scars and curse of Redeyes. He would—"

Again, he was drowned out by voices. These were raised in outrage, from the Liznees especially. "Lies, Blackbird!" one of the generals cried. "Our king bears no such curse. You disgrace his name."

Iriam's low voice quieted them. "If any of you question Master Blackbird's account of King Jan," he said, "then I will tell you the truth of it. It is as he says. Jan has indeed borne this curse for years. In crafting Drisilas, the magic of the Star-Stone was warped into a weapon of war. He has promised to reconcile this curse, and he must do it soon, before Isilas is corrupted beyond repair. He shared his plan with me before embarking to Wiverrun. I fully verify the truth of Darion's tale."

Complete silence greeted his words. Allie could see the shock on the Liznees' expressions; several of them were shaking their heads wordlessly. Ĵan was a popular king. To know he bore such a curse cut deep. Allie remembered how she had reacted upon first hearing about it herself, and she couldn't blame them.

Darion went on. "We travelled to Caer Droco together—Ĵan, with the intent of reconciling his curse and thus protecting Sia, and I with the intent of learning the Ace-Lord's plan for Caer Droco. Unbeknownst to us, the duke had sent a false letter to Appledale, luring the New Blood and the Blue Stone into his grasp as well. Both the king and the New Blood were kept in the depths of Castle Droco, along with the Star-Stone. However, I managed to escape with the heiress Asescia and Aryion Paya. Asescia has guarded Drisilas herself until now, keeping it from the Aces."

He glanced up, giving Allie a faint smile. Allie smiled back.

"Then your mission to Wiverrun was in vain," Quinn said slowly, dismay in his voice. "One Star-Stone lost, and the king and Mel as well."

"Not entirely," Darion said. "We did find out what the Ace-Lord is hiding in Castle Droco. He has opened a void to the Dark Realm, a silver gateway of darkness in the highest tower of the castle. Through it, he has brought Redeyes and other Dal-kerri wraiths. We believe he intends to bring another wraith, similar in power and strength to the Darkness, out of the void as well, to annihilate any opposition."

"For what purpose?" one of the Elves inquired. "Does he not need the Star-Stones?"

"Not yet," Darion said slowly. "I believe his plan has shifted. If he can corrupt the mortals—break us down, further the unrest, divide and corrupt us so thoroughly we can't resist—then he'll have gained the Star-Stones as well. The fight will end before it's begun."

"If Mortal heart remains unmarred; The spell that bound leaves deeper scars; Than the Shadow that awakened," Iriam mused, as Darion paused. "It would explain why the Ace-Lord allowed you to escape with Isilas at all."

Darion nodded, folding the page quietly. The silence that fell told Allie that everyone had been listening intently. She could sense the interest, the concern, the anger as palpably as she felt her own.

"Whether or not the plan was mine, I bear responsibility for those lost in Castle Droco," Darion said after a pause. "I cannot ask forgiveness. All I can do is strive to reconcile my own curse—and, I hope, find a way to break the enchantment binding the survivors of Wiverrun."

With a short nod to the assembly, he returned to his seat.

"That was perfect," Allie whispered to him. "Elimar must agree to join us now."

"They can't argue against the evidence," Rygal agreed quietly, clapping Darion's shoulder lightly. Darion nodded with a small smile, but said nothing.

"What is to be done now?" Lord Roan asked. "Surely any attack upon the castle will end badly. We have no way of reaching the prisoners, not if they are within this void that Master Blackbird describes."

"We might," Dandio said. Anticipation filled Allie as her father moved slowly to the front of the room. His tarnished, battle-worn armor glinted like the fire in his green eyes. "People of Orlell. The Ace-Lord's dark magic was turned against him during the Dividing War, when his attempts to divide the Elven nations failed," here he glanced at the Elves on either side of the room. "His magic was turned against him again when a mere boy of eleven joined the Shards last year. If the Ace-Lord seeks to corrupt us in this war, that plan will be turned against him yet again. He himself has gifted us a key to enter the void."

He held out a hand, beckoning Allie forward. Slowly, she stood. Drisilas hung heavy against her back as she moved to the front of the room and stood beside her father. For a moment, her courage faltered before the confused and skeptical faces before her. But she felt Dandio's strong hand on her shoulder, and the fire in her heart crackled to life in response.

"I don't know how or why," she said, keeping her voice steady. "But I've been… given… the power to wield the sword. I think the Ace-Lord wanted to make me his Wielder, instead of Jan, and use me to open the Dark Realm. I'm also able to destroy the enchanted soldiers… I don't know why, yet." She kept her eyes on Darion's face. Any of the doubt he had shown yesterday was gone. He gave her a very slight nod of encouragement, urging her to continue.

Taking a deep breath, she concluded. "I think, since I can use Drisilas, I may be able to enter the void unharmed. If I did, I may be able to find where the Aces are holding Ĵan and Mel, and free them."

As before, voices rippled through the room. But this time, they were more wondering than skeptical. "You can wield the sword, you say?" one of the Elimar Councilors asked.

Allie reached behind her and wrested Drisilas from its scabbard, as she had done when she had fought the Dal-kerri in the woods. Its white flames lit the faces of her audience, shocked and awed.

"Sheathe the blade, Asescia," Iriam commanded. Surprised, she did as he said. "I do not know why the Ace-Lord has granted you these powers. I admit it makes me uneasy. It is no natural thing, to break the laws of the Star-Stones and bestow its power upon a new Wielder."

His doubt, and the underlying unease in his voice, sent a chill of fear through Allie. But Iriam shook his head. "Nevertheless, I believe this plan may work. With the Star-Stone, the Ace-Lord's illusions will retreat before you, and you will be able to resist them."

"I'll go into the void," Allie said. "I'll find Ĵan and Mel, and the Star-Stone with them, and get them out."

"How do you intend to escape?" Ajaha asked slowly. "The Aces will soon realize what you are doing. I doubt they will let you flee with their prisoners."

"They will have other things to worry about," Dandio said, a fierce light shining in his eyes. "As soon as Allie enters the void, we will attack the castle. Our strike will draw the Aces' forces away from the void. Not only that, but we have noticed that the Dal-kerri fear fire, just as the Aces. The Red Dawn will march with the Guardians of Gayrile and set fire to the Ace-Lord's fortress."

"But the castle is stone," Darion said uncertainly. "That won't burn."

"Dal-kerri burn," Dandio answered. "We found that out a few days ago. We'll smoke the Aces out of their hole and buy Asescia the time she needs to rescue the prisoners."

Glentree chuckled. "Oh, I *like* this strategy, sir. Like the old days. Fire and swords and the like."

"Lammar left the Guardians under my temporary command," Dandio added. "They're eager to join our fight. We can handle the assault on Castle Droco, but the north must be protected."

Ajaha looked at the Elves. "I understand your hesitation to join our fight," she said. "Many lives have been lost in the wars of the past, yet this war is unlike any before it. If the world is to survive, your aid and alliance is needed. Just as your forefathers put aside their disagreements to join forces in the Dividing War, I ask—no, I implore you, to join this cause, now that you know the gravity of our situation. Join us, and fight for the sake of Orlell."

Silence fell, thoughtful and tense. Allie stood beside Dandio, watching the Elves. They may not agree, and if they didn't, they all would be left vulnerable, and the assault on Castle Droco would be too dangerous to risk. She remembered Mel's account of the Esile Council, about their selfishness and the way the danger was not enough to persuade them.

But today, Ajaha's words would be enough.

The Elimar Councilors spoke quietly among themselves for a few moments, then an Elf with silver hair stood and nodded slightly. "On behalf of the Elimar Council," he said, "I, Llio Tarash, pledge our support and aid in the Ace-War—in memory of my sons, who fought and died for this cause."

"And so pledge the Elves of Tinkeeyo," Quinn said, rising.

Allie felt her face relax in a smile. Several people cheered. She saw her parents exchange smiles of victory, saw Iriam nodding his approval, saw Rygal and Darion grinning as they watched. It was a small spark of light and hope in the midst of several very dark weeks.

Lord Roan moved to the dais again as the Liznees sat down. "This is a monumental day," he said, a smile on his furry face. "I pray it to be the start of many such agreements and alliances." He studied the crowd. "This council is officially dismissed. Our discussion, I fear, must now turn to the preparation of war."

33

Dandio's Strategy

Though eager to learn about the Red Dawn's plans for battle, Allie knew she would be little help, so she returned to the Puddlepaws' house after Rygal promised to tell her everything they discussed.

It was good to see everyone in such high spirits. Jarus was practically skipping as he led the way, bounding down the sidewalk, and Darion was smiling so widely his scars seemed to fade. "There can't be any argument now," he said, as he and Allie walked behind Jarus. "The Elven kingdoms are allied—well, I suppose they've been allies under Caer Sia for a while, but it's been centuries since they worked together—they'll protect the northern fiefs and guard our backs while we're gone. And we'll return to Sia with the prisoners. Prisoners you'll have freed yourself, don't forget!" he added, nudging her lightly.

Allie had to smile—she'd never seen him look so happy. "It was your report that convinced them," she said. "But what did you mean when you said you had to reconcile your own curse?"

The happiness faded, like a candle puffed out. "Whatever I've done, I broke the oath to the Aces," he said slowly. "More than that, I am responsible for handing the Magno villages over to the Ace-Lord.

I need to find out a way to free them—break the curse, free the captives. And hopefully, break the enchantment."

Of course. Allie had nearly forgotten about his own curse. The price for breaking his oath to the Aces, and for selling out his countrymen. The best way to reconcile it, she knew, would be to free those bound by the spell.

"I'm sorry," she said quietly. "I promised to help you learn about breaking the enchantment, and I haven't. You were right yesterday, you know." She gave a slight, bitter smile. "I was more concerned with revenge than anything else."

"Maybe," Darion said, "but I shouldn't have said it. Whatever you did, you saved us all back at the fort."

"I'm going to learn about the enchantment now," Allie said firmly. "As soon as Jan and Mel are free, we'll figure out a way to break the enchantment together."

He smiled again, though she could still see the worry in his hazel eyes. There was no telling how they would break the spell, even if such a thing was possible. The only thing they'd learned for certain about it on the disastrous mission to Wiverrun was that the enchantment was voluntary. You had to choose the enchantment, or be broken in the attempt. Shattered.

"Your family," she began slowly. "Your brother's wife was in the cabin. What about your brother? Do you know if he's… still alive?"

Darion gave a short nod. "Yes. He's alive. Enchanted, but… I suppose that's better than the alternative."

Allie didn't press him further. She could not imagine how complicated the matter was—to fight against your own blood, knowing they were not themselves, but watching them serve the Aces nonetheless.

Her mind returned to thoughts of the void, of the swirling blackness and whatever awaited within. Between what Mel said before, and what her father had told her yesterday, it was filled with illusions—sounds and visions that attacked your mind and weaponized the truth.

Drisilas would be her shield, but that wouldn't stop the attacks of the Ace-Lord's illusions.

She and Darion ate lunch with the Puddlepaws. Quinn stopped by to greet Jarus and discuss the renewed alliance between Elven kingdoms. Allie knew the agreement was monumental—though both Elimar and Tinkeeyo were allied under Coonsia, there were centuries of hatred and disagreements between the two. But now they had agreed to set the past aside and aid the fight against the Ace-Lord.

"There will still be some arguments," Quinn said, gratefully accepting a cup of coffee from Maya. "We have historically been enemies with the sons of Delkir, and the hurts will be slow to heal. But I imagine war makes trust necessary."

"You Elves and your arguments," Jarus remarked, only half joking.

Quinn shook his head, smiling ruefully. "Yes, well, perhaps now the arguments can be forgotten. King Jan will be glad to hear it."

The name sent Allie's thoughts spiraling back to the void and her upcoming mission.

Dandio and Iriam arrived after Quinn left, accompanied by Rygal, Joesp, and Glentree, who were deep in discussion over a battle strategy. Joesp had assumed command over the Wildkids in Dusty's absence, and would lead their part of the attack. Iriam was talking to Dandio in a quiet voice—Allie only caught the words "illusions" and "Wielder" as they entered, and could guess what or who the conversation was about.

Whatever concerned Iriam worried her too. Uncertainty was so out of place on a face that always seemed to know exactly what to do. It wasn't just the unexpected assets of Drisilas or her new powers. He seemed to suspect something more.

Any such fear was hidden from his face now as he gave her a slight smile and sat down. "Your report was well-received, Master Blackbird," he said to Darion. "I hope you are pleased with the outcome."

Darion glanced down, but Allie could tell he appreciated the words. "Yes, well, hopefully it helps. I feel I should have said more about the void—I only had a few notes about it."

"Any information about the void will be needed mostly for the charge," Dandio reminded him. "I'd like that piece of our plan to be known by as few as possible. We have arranged the northern barricade, so we will now discuss battle strategy."

They gathered around the Puddlepaws' table, as they had done the day before. There was no uncertainty or hesitance of the coming strike. A plan was made. Dandio spoke firmly and concisely, a war commander laying out the strategy.

"We will come from the north," he began, spreading a chart depicting a detailed interior of Castle Droco on the table. "The Wildkids will accompany Darion and Allie to the edge of the void. You will take up your positions here, but remain out of sight, with a clear path to the marble bridge. Our forces will circle around and launch our attack from the west." He tapped the chart. "Once that attack begins, Allie, you must enter the void as quickly as you can."

Quickly would be easy enough, Allie thought dryly, if all she had to do was jump off the bridge. She decided against saying that aloud.

"Here is where our timing must be perfect," Dandio said, tracing two lines with his finger as he marked the two bridges. "Rygal, you will lead your force of Guardians across the north bridge, while we cross the west. We will regroup at the stairs that lead to the tower. There, the bulk of our forces, led by Glentree, will remain on the lower levels of the palace. Glentree's objective is to protect our way out—if the northward doors are blocked, we will be trapped."

"What are you going to do?" Allie asked.

"We will go up the stairs," Dandio answered. "Forge our way up until we reach the doorway, and protect it."

Iriam spoke. "I believe the doorway in the Ace-Lord's tower is likely connected somehow to the Patch outside. The Patch, as you have told us, is not a gateway as much as it is an empty space. Wherever that space shall lead, I am unsure. It is the doorways that will likely lead you to other places—perhaps even other worlds, if the Ace-Lord has used them to access the Dark Realm."

"If I'm going into the Patch, why protect the tower doorway?" Allie asked, not sure why this mattered.

"Because I fear the Patch will not allow you back out of the place you enter," Iriam said. "I believe it is a one-way path. Rather than the portals between worlds, I believe it will lead you to a sort of middle space, as the Druids of old wrote of. However, the doorway in the tower evidently leads somewhere."

The realization finally dawned on Allie. "So I'll go in through the Patch, then have to find the Ace-Lord's doorway to get back out?"

"Unless you find you can easily retreat back the same way you came in, in which case, our assault will be over very quickly," Dandio said. "I doubt it'll be that easy. Once you find Jan and Mel, and the Star-Stone, you must find a doorway that leads back into Castle Droco's tower."

Rygal nodded. His face, though concerned, was determined. "We'll hold the doorway for you until you're back out."

Allie smiled slightly, but she didn't like the risk they were all taking. There were so many variables. What if Iriam was wrong, and the voids were unconnected? What if she was trapped inside with Jan and Mel? Worst of all… what if they were already dead, and she died the minute she leapt into the Patch?

But there was no other way. If circumstances were different, and their places were switched, she knew Ĵan and Mel would both take the risk for her. She must do the same for them.

"What's our plan to get out of the castle?" Darion asked. "Once Allie's rescued Ĵan and Mel, I doubt the Ace-Lord will just let us escape."

"I doubt he will," Dandio said. He turned to Joesp. "As soon as Allie is out of the void, we will escape back down the stairway and bear for the north bridge. I have no idea how many of us will still be able to fight, so we will rely on you and the Wildkids at that point. As soon as we have crossed the bridge, we will destroy it to prevent any pursuit."

Joesp looked uneasy. "My warriors can handle Dal-kerri, but I am not sure about the Aces."

"I will deal with the Aces," Iriam replied calmly. "Your goal is to return to Badwater and board the ship to Caer Sia."

"You plan to face them alone?" Rygal said incredulously.

"If it is necessary. I believe the fires will slow their pursuit." Iriam looked at Dandio. "Have you any plan to close the voids?"

Dandio hesitated. "No… I did not think of that. What would you suggest?"

"I am not sure. It is said that fire will close the Patches, but the gateways are another matter altogether. Their power, I fear, will not fully vanish until the Ace-Lord is defeated." Iriam leaned back in his chair thoughtfully. "I must think on this."

"When do we leave?" Rygal asked.

"Two days from now," Dandio replied. "I must wait for Admiral Dessian to return before we set out—his blockade must be in place to protect both Mata City and Caer Sia."

Two days. Two days before the attack began, and she would learn what awaited her in the void.

Allie tried to summon the fiery energy, but could think only of the swirling darkness of the void, and a chill of foreboding filled her heart.

34

The Night Before

Shadows filled the tower like liquid, dripping from the walls and diluting the pale moonlight drifting through the windows. Through the dappled stained glass, the silver Flats were visible even in the dark of night.

The great gateway the Ace-Lord had crafted stood ominously in its place. Light glinted off its silver frame but could not penetrate the darkness within it. Even the shadows in the room paled to the darkness of the void, which swirled and shifted like a curtain.

The shimmering curtain was drawn aside now as a figure walked through, and the Ace-Deputy stepped into the palace of Ar-Salem. The glaring moonlight stung his purple-red eyes, and he shielded his ruined face with a hissing curse. Confound the Flats and the way the light seemed to radiate off them. He immediately missed Castle Droco, and the shroud of darkness cast by the towering trees.

But of course, the news must be delivered. The Ace-Lord had recently returned from his work within the void, from preparing the great wraith he had tamed. The Deputy had seen the brute before, in a lifetime past. It was far different than the shadowy giant that had been the Darkness. This wraith was a monster—a sub-breed of

Dal-kerri, perhaps—primed and prepared for killing.

The Ace-Lord's absence had allowed him to delay bringing his report. But now, the Deputy had been summoned to Ar-Salem to tell the news.

Redeyes had come as well, stepping out of the arched void as he had all those months ago when the Ace-Lord had first summoned him back. Yet this time there was a glimmer of fear in the great cat's hollow eyes. He, too, feared his master's reaction to their information.

The Ace-Lord awaited them in the high tower. His form shifted and shimmered as they approached, the illusion of the great lord he had once been—a tall figure clad in gleaming silver and misty shadows.

The Deputy and Redeyes bowed before him. "My lord," the Deputy said, pleased to hear no trace of fear in his own voice. Any unease he felt must be disguised, an illusion just like the Ace-Lord's appearance. "I hope your time away was fruitful."

The answer was a short, quiet laugh, which caused his calm to wither. "You are looking unwell, my Deputy," the Ace-Lord commented. "For what reason do I receive your anxious report?"

The Deputy looked up at him as the Ace-Lord sat down in the carved chair. He'd ordered a few enchanted craftsmen from Wiverrun to fashion it for him. It was a crude thing compared to the one he'd once had, but it did have an effect—dark and menacing, wrought of silver and blackened steel.

"I am fine, my lord. I have strange news." The Deputy paused, preparing every word. He must be careful, yet concise. The Ace-Lord hated rambling. "As you requested, my forces pursued the Star-Stone Isilas to bring it back to Castle Droco. The mortals fought to keep it and fled up the Strait. We would have killed them, except…"

He trailed off, already dreading the reaction to his next statement.

"It seems the girl can Wield," Redeyes said as he paused.

The Ace-Deputy threw him an angry, fearful glance, then looked back at his master.

There was no anger, no fear, no confusion as the Deputy had anticipated. Only an intense interest glimmered in the purple-red eyes. "Wield?" he breathed at last, leaning forward.

"Yes, my lord," the Deputy said. It had been decades since he had felt mortal fear, but the Ace-Lord had a way of stripping away any illusion of courage. "During the fight, she drew and used the sword against our forces. Not only that, her fire pierced the enchanted soldiers and killed several of them, despite the spell keeping them from death."

The Ace-Lord stood and turned away slowly, stroking his chin in thought. The Deputy waited, not daring to voice the many questions burning in his mind. Redeyes was less tactful. "How is this possible?" he growled. "Wielding aside, if she can kill the enchanted we are all vulnerable."

"Do you still fear fire, Redeyes?" the Ace-Lord asked with a quiet note of amusement.

Redeyes snarled softly but said nothing, staring at the floor.

The Ace-Lord turned back to them, and the Deputy saw something in his expression he had not expected to see. Satisfaction. "I have told you both my plans of conquest, have I not? How we must corrupt the mortals, until they embrace the darkness I offer willingly?"

"Yes, my lord. But what about our operations in the Magno? What about the wraith?" The Deputy fought to keep his voice calm, to hide his growing confusion. "Surely the wraith can kill the mortals and win the war for us."

"You misunderstand, Deputy. I do not wish to rule the dead. Not any more." The Ace-Lord's face was thoughtful, his eyes seeming to see far away. "The mortals believe they can resist the fear we spread with their foolish hope. Thus, instead of fear, we must break them. Loss, despair, anger… those are the truest ways to destroy a mortal's heart."

"I do not understand," Redeyes growled. "Was I not brought here to kill?"

"Indeed you were, and soon you shall," the Ace-Lord informed him. "But the sign of your marks, the weight of the curse—that is the true purpose for which you were returned to the land of the mortals." He turned. "I must enter the Dark Realm again. The wraith is nearly prepared. Await my return in Caer Droco."

"And if the mortals attack us?" the Deputy asked. "If the girl has these powers, I expect she will attempt to free the prisoners."

"I believe she will. You need not hinder her," the Ace-Lord replied calmly.

The Deputy stared after him, thoroughly confused. "My lord, I do not doubt your plan. But I do not understand. Why grant the girl such powers? Will it not ruin all we have built?"

The Ace-Lord turned to him again, and this time, he smiled. "Tell me, Deputy, do you know the gambit of the Life-Blood Spell?"

The Deputy stared at him as the words faded into silence. At last, he understood. For the second time that day, he felt a mixture of fear and awe at his master's cunning. "Yes, my lord. I do."

"Then you will know that this part of the game is won," the Ace-Lord told him. His voice grew low and soft, the illusion hiding his decayed face fading as hatred and triumph shone in his eyes. "And know, too, that no actions of the mortals can change that now."

. . . . . .

Twilight was falling as the *Gryphon* docked in Badwater, and Allie wondered again if the hours could pass any slower than they seemed to now. The last two days that she and her companions had spent in Mata City seemed to have flown by in comparison, a brief moment of peace and quiet before they would return to Caer Droco.

Returning to Caer Droco. Into the lion's den, as Glentree had grimly remarked that morning. The voyage to the neighboring coastal city of Badwater had been uneventful. Even the choppy sea, stirred by the warm breeze, seemed only to urge them onward, pressing them forward, carrying them toward the darkness waiting in the heart of the Magno.

Once they'd docked in Badwater's harbor, though, time seemed to slow to a crawl. The other two ships that had accompanied them—Admiral Dessian's *Blue Moon* and another called *Sea Bear*—had to be unloaded, and their passengers must disembark. The soldiers needed to be gathered under their respective companies, split into groups by Dandio. There were around three hundred troops, less than standard for an attack like this. But, as Dandio had pointed out, they needed to move quickly. A larger force would take days to make their way up and over the hills.

"The road's shorter from this direction, at least," Darion reassured her as they stood watching the Red Dawn soldiers. "The hills are smaller, and there's less distance to cover."

"Why didn't we come this way when we first escaped the Aces?" Allie wondered aloud. Badwater was much closer to Wiverrun than Mata City.

"The same reason we couldn't go back to Caer Sia, remember? The northern road was cut off to us," Darion reminded her. Of course. If they could have returned to Caer Sia, it would have saved them a difficult four day's journey. But then, they wouldn't have had the aid of the Alfona, or the Wildkids.

She saw Joesp's group assembled a short distance from the regiments of soldiers, illuminated in the yellow lantern light of the brick buildings of Badwater. They stood uncertainly, tails and ears twitching, raising their faces to the sulfur-scented wind. They seemed out of place and painfully small compared to Dandio's siege force.

At a word, three companies of soldiers turned and headed down the road. Despite their size, they moved quickly and quietly. These were no common foot soldiers who would blunder through the forest—these were Red Dawn strike forces, the best warriors of their regiments, trained to move silently. They faded into the woods with only the soft sound of shifting leathers.

Two other groups headed into the trees after a final word from Dandio. Allie spotted Glentree among them; he would lead one of the charges. The only troops left in Badwater's small square now were the Wildkids and the small group of Guardians.

"Looks like we'd better join the others," Allie said, and she and Darion left the cover of the awning to walk over. It was raining gently. The shimmering droplets helped douse the ever-present stench of sulfur, which came from the nearby pools that had earned Badwater its name.

Dandio was talking to Dessian. The Liznee admiral had the same athletic build as Dandio, but leaner, with blue eyes, a hawk-like nose, and a small dark beard on his chin. "It may be better to retreat back this way," he was saying to Dandio as Allie approached. "If your plan goes awry, you can try to escape at sea."

"It'd be a good retreat route under regular circumstances," Dandio answered, "but I don't want to lead the Dal-kerri into Badwater. We will meet you at the mouth of Hotspring Creek."

"Very well, Commander," Dessian agreed, but Allie could tell he was still worried. He saluted briskly, then strode back to the *Blue Moon*.

Dandio turned to face the remaining group before him. Comprised of Wildkids and Guardians, along with Allie, Darion, and Iriam, they numbered around fifty warriors. Allie couldn't help feeling a chill of fear as she remembered the hoards of Dal-kerri and soldiers swarming the lower levels of Castle Droco. What if their plan didn't work, and they were overwhelmed and killed the moment they crossed the bridge?

"The regiments have been sent ahead," Dandio said. "They have a longer distance to go, but they should be in place on the ridge by tonight. I'll join them once you all are in position." He nodded to the shadowed road. "It won't get any lighter. On we go."

Heavy tree branches overshadowed the road winding steadily uphill. Allie's legs were burning as they marched up the hills, but she was glad to notice that she was not quite as winded as last time. How long ago had that been? She tried to think. Two weeks, probably? Maybe more? Time had blurred since she'd left Caer Sia. Even the events of that morning had swirled by. Packing up. Bidding the Puddlepaws farewell, and noting the worry in the Coopers' expressions. Boarding the ship.

The unwelcome thought entered her mind of how many she had not been able to wish goodbye. Ajaha had seen them off—she would remain in Mata City another day, assisting with negotiations in Gayrile before she'd return home to Sia. But the others? Glentree, Aryion, Dusty, and so many others she might not see again, if she didn't make it out of the—

"Stop it," she whispered to herself, forcing her mind not to finish that sentence.

She turned her attention to the road ahead, which was difficult to see in the evening light. Dandio cautioned them against too much light, so only the warriors in the front and rear of the party carried torches. Thankfully the high ridges allowed them to keep an eye out for any signal fires from their comrades, if they were attacked.

The opposite ridge on her right was no more than a black outline against the starless sky. No warning fires. That was good. They'd hoped to save their fuel to keep the Dal-kerri at bay. Then again, suppose the Aces simply extinguished the fires with their deathly ice…

"Might I inquire into your thoughts?" Iriam's deep, quiet voice brought her back to reality. She hadn't realized the Neutral was beside her, silent in the rear of the party. He seemed to glide soundlessly through the night, and she could only make out the glitter of his eyes in the shadows.

"It's the plan," she replied softly. "Do you think it will work?"

Iriam seemed to consider this. "What of it do you doubt?"

Now it was Allie's turn to consider. There were variables, as there always were. Anything could go wrong, but could she narrow it down to one flaw? No, her father's strategy was sound. It was not that she feared.

What she feared was within the castle, waiting in a tall tower shrouded in shadow, always one step ahead of them, enjoying this game he had laid for the mortals.

Her head ached as though the Ace-Lord's hands still grasped it.

"It's not the plan," she said finally. "I think it will work. But what after that? Will it just go on and on like this, fighting and running and protecting the Star-Stones, until… what? We've killed the Aces?"

There was a pause, filled only with the soft rustling as the group moved through the forest.

"You fear the Ace-Lord?" Iriam asked her quietly.

"No," Allie said immediately, then, hearing the lie in her voice, lowered her head and whispered, "Yes."

"You would be foolish not to." Iriam was silent for a moment. "To answer your question, this war must not go on forever. We would be crushed, beaten down the longer it is drawn out. But the Ace-Lord cannot be killed as his followers can; he is corrupted so completely that death means nothing to him."

"So we're fighting for nothing," Allie said dully, as cold futility filled her heart. "There's no way we'll win?"

"That is not what I said, Heiress." Iriam's tone was gentle, but she heard firmness in his voice. "No mortal method would kill the Ace-Lord. But in his corruption, he is bound by chains far stronger than any mortal blade. He calls himself the ruler of death, but it would be better said that he is death's warden. Yes, even the Ace-Lord must submit to the High Light, though unwillingly. He thought himself above that task, and thus he rebelled."

"During the Dividing War?" Allie asked. She'd heard the story before, studying it regularly under Iriam's tutelage in Caer Sia.

"Indeed," Iriam said. "The Ace-Lord seeks to break those chains and extend his kingdom of death into the mortal world. This is the purpose of his conquest. He cannot die. But he can be defeated, bound, locked in the Dark Realm for all of eternity."

"How?"

Iriam gave a slight, almost sad, smile. "That, child, will be revealed only in time."

Allie let out an impatient breath. "We're running out of time."

"Perhaps, perhaps not. The Prophecy secures our victory, should we follow its words," Iriam answered. "It too binds the Ace-Lord. He must act only within what is foretold in the Prophecy, or risk the fury of the High Light."

Allie looked at him, interested to hear this. "Does that mean the High Light will send someone to atone again, like the Old Stories say? Or will He send the Stars into battle?"

"That is not for us to know," Iriam replied with another mysterious smile. "For now, we must complete the task set before us, written in the Prophecy."

The Prophecy. Allie had studied its words so many times, yet she could not see the hope there that Iriam spoke of. Why did the words reveal only death and pain to her? Even the parts surrounding the mortals seemed bleak: *Though Mortal be unwilling; A spell has made the binding; When the Shadow has arrived.*

Whatever those words spoke of, it seemed as dark and tangled as the forest around them.

Don't think about that, she told herself, letting out a breath. *Don't think about the Ace-Lord either. Think about Jan and Mel.* She pictured Jan, his steady voice reassuring her, the way his eyes twinkled when he concealed a smile. The fire in her chest blazed afresh at the memories, crackling through her veins. But this time, she felt control over it.

She would not charge into this fight as she had when she'd fought the Ace-Deputy. This time, her energy, her rage, her longing, would finally be put to use.

35

Beginning the Strike

Dandio woke them just before dawn, and their silent journey south continued.

Heavy fog spread over the ridges like a blanket, stifling all noise as the warriors continued onward. Despite the morning, the valley was cloaked in dim gray light. It reminded Allie all too well of the occupation of Caer Sia, when the presence of the Ace-Lord seemed to prevent even the sunlight from reaching within.

Dandio risked a torch signal to contact the warriors on the other side of the valley. There was a tense pause before Allie saw the answering signal through the fog, waving in acknowledgement. Even the firelight was darkened by the mist.

"They're in position," Dandio murmured. "All seems well. But I do not like this fog."

"Will the fires still light?" Rygal asked uneasily—his dark hair was damp with condensation.

"I'm less worried about our fires and more about visibility," Dandio replied. "Battles are chaotic enough. But we can barely see a pace ahead, and who knows what illusions the Ace-Lord has planned. Our way into the castle might be even more difficult than I had feared."

"They won't expect a full on attack," Darion reminded him. "Hopefully there won't be too many illusions outside."

"Be on your guard, all the same," Dandio said. He turned to Allie. "Are you ready?"

In contrast to her fear yesterday, Allie felt calm, as though the truth of what she was about to do had yet to sink in. She managed to nod.

"The castle's on the other side of this ridge," Darion told them. "We won't be able to see it through the illusion, and the fog should shield us from view."

"The Aces don't need to see us," Rygal reminded him dryly. "They can sense our fear."

"Indeed," Iriam said. "Be mindful of your thoughts. Do not allow the Aces to gain an advantage over your mind."

"Let's get going, then," Dandio said shortly. "We'll split ways at the top of the ridge."

They began the final climb. Allie's mind, tangled and fearful last night, felt strangely clear. No more contemplating the Prophecy, no more worrying over the Ace-Lord. Her thoughts had centered on her mission into the void, as though drawn to it by a powerful wind.

They reached the top of the ridge. Joesp's uncertain voice carried over to them. "I cannot see the castle."

"It's hidden," Darion said. "Behind the illusion. Walk downhill a little ways and it should come into view."

Dandio squeezed Allie's hand lightly. "We will do all we can to keep your way out of the void clear," he said quietly. "You will make it out of Castle Droco. I promise you."

Allie nodded. Her mouth felt too dry to manage words.

Dandio, Iriam, and half the group of Guardians headed towards the ridge to the right, vanishing into the fog. Allie sat on a fallen log and stared ahead. The trees partially concealed the valley floor from view, but she could see the darkness lurking there, inconspicuous as a shadow amid the greens and browns. Not even the illusion could fully conceal the Patch.

Rygal was talking quietly with Darion. "The townspeople didn't know this was here, I assume?"

"No. No one comes here. The locals believe this place is cursed." There was a wry edge of humor in Darion's voice. "I suppose it is, in a way."

"When did you learn about it?"

"When I first swore to serve them," Darion answered. "I was never allowed into the castle—sometimes I met with them outside in the courtyard, but no closer than that." He edged down the slope. "If you get close enough, you can see through the illusion, like a mirage." He walked a few more paces, peering through the trees, then nodded and beckoned to Rygal. "Stand here, and look this way."

Allie walked downhill with Rygal to where Darion stood. Her eyes followed the ranger's pointing finger, and saw the spires of Castle Droco flicker into view through the fog.

She'd seen it before, but the pale towers still sent a chill down her spine.

"Blazes, that'll be a lot of stairs," Rygal muttered as he studied it. "Every staircase will be its own battle, you know—we'll waste time climbing them, which gives anyone above us time to prepare."

"Can't help that," Darion said. "Though if we need to take the upper tower, the staircases will be the least of our troubles."

Allie's eyes had travelled down to the mass of darkness at the base of the supporting column. It seemed to have grown larger and blacker, spreading over the valley floor, but maybe that was just the angle.

Rygal looked at her, and she saw the concern in his eyes. "Do you have a plan to get in?"

"Not really," Allie said. "I sort of just… planned to jump."

Rygal raised his eyebrows. "That seems risky, even for you."

"We could try to lower you," Darion suggested.

"With what?" Rygal asked wearily.

"I have the rope we used to get out—oh, never mind, I forgot the Aces destroyed that. I can borrow another line from the Wildkids, though." He moved to Joesp's side.

Allie rolled her eyes after him. "Are either of you seriously planning to stand on the bridge and lower me down? You'd be completely exposed."

Rygal shrugged. "Might be preferable to jumping straight in."

"The attack is starting," one of the Wildkids warned.

Allie turned her attention back to the castle. Movement flickered through the trees on the opposite ridge as the regiments moved swiftly for the westward side. Her heart leapt into her throat. Somewhere in that rapid rush of bodies was her father.

"Time to go," Joesp warned.

Allie tore her eyes away and jogged with the others toward the north side of the castle. She strained her ears for any sounds of struggle in the distance. There were none. The Liznees probably hadn't reached the bridge yet, she reminded herself. That thought did nothing to ease her racing heart.

The Wildkids moved silently, flitting like sprites through the forest. She nearly collided with a warrior running downhill. Darion was just behind her, and she could hear Rygal's low, tense voice as he directed the Guardians into position.

Abruptly, the woods fell away at her feet and the void gaped before her.

She skidded to a stop. The main bridge arched up to the castle twenty yards to her left, larger than the one they had fled across during the escape. The soft rustling on the hill behind her told her the Wildkids were nearly in position, hiding in the trees overlooking the bridge.

She turned back as Darion stepped through the trees behind her. His face was pale as he looked down into the empty darkness, then he seemed to snap into action. "Well. This is probably better than the bridge. Let me tie the rope."

Allie smiled faintly. Despite what she'd said earlier, she was glad to avoid a sickening drop into darkness.

The Wildkids' ropes were woven from plant fibers, tough and wiry. Darion knotted it around Allie's waist in a makeshift harness. Allie watched his hands as he tied the knots wordlessly. The cool detachment from before was gone. Cold sweat had broken out on her face, and her heart was pounding so hard it felt like it would burst.

"I'll hold you here," Darion said, looping the rope around a stout tree. He hesitated. "If you change your mind, I can pull you back out."

"I think it's too late for that," Allie said. Her voice was hoarse with fear. She stepped back toward the edge, staring into the swirling darkness.

"Probably," Darion agreed. He looked at her for a long moment, as though seeking some words to reassure her. Finally he shook his head. "Whenever you're ready."

Allie took a deep breath, gritted her teeth, and leaned back. One foot swung over the edge, then the other. Slowly, she started down, the toes of her boots against the side of the pit. Down, down she went. The darkness yawned below her. She strained her eyes for the bottom, but saw none.

Abruptly, she stopped moving, hanging above the darkness. She looked up and only then realized how far down she had come. The edge of the ravine waited at least thirty feet above her. Darion's head appeared; he called down as loud as he dared.

"That's the end of the rope!"

The end? Allie groaned softly. Darion waited. Did he think she'd have him pull her up again, since the rope had failed? He had to know she couldn't do that. Not when this entire mission hinged on her.

"I'm cutting loose," she called back. Her hand trembled slightly as she reached behind her and unsheathed Drisilas. The white flames blazed in the darkness around her, and gripping the cold hilt, she felt braver.

With one last glance up at Darion, she swung the sword. The blade cut through the rope as though it were made of butter, and in the next instant, she was falling.

. . . . . .

Rygal knew Allie was gone the moment he saw Darion's face. The young ranger reappeared through the fog and dropped down behind a tree in front of where Rygal crouched. On the hillsides around and behind them, the Wildkids waited in the shadows. Rygal could hear Joesp's low voice issuing orders.

He looked at Darion. "She's in?"

Darion nodded slightly, his face drawn. "I tried to lower her, but she had to cut the rope to fall the rest of the way."

"The rest of the way? So she made it into wherever place is inside the Patch?"

"How would I know that?"

Rygal bit back the retort on the tip of his tongue. Arguing would not help the situation. Darion was worried for Allie, just as he was. Despite their banter earlier, Rygal could sense a camaraderie forged between them, both determined to help and protect Allie however they could.

"What's the plan now?" Darion asked.

Rygal nodded at the marble bridge before them. "We're going in that way as soon as Dandio's group makes it in. If we're there too early, we'll have to fight the Dal-kerri all by ourselves."

"Might not end well. Has Dandio's group reached the bridge yet?"

"No," Rygal answered. He looked to the right, back toward the ridge where they had parted ways. The westward bridge should be there, probably a quarter mile away. Broken by Jan, Allie had said, though Iriam could probably repair it with a simple layer of indigo ice. But he could see nothing in the fog.

He took a deep breath, trying to settle his nerves. This was exactly what Dandio had been worried about. If they couldn't see each other, they wouldn't be able to time their attack correctly.

"How many men are with you?" Darion asked.

"A little over forty," Rygal answered. It was a ridiculously small number considering the masses of Dal-kerri awaiting them inside. Not to mention the enchanted soldiers—and those warriors couldn't be killed. "Our main objective is to clear the path this way," he said. "Dandio thinks most of the Aces' forces will be focused on fighting the bulk of the attack on the west bridge."

"Let's hope for that," Darion agreed. He rested an arrow to his bowstring, fingering the fletching anxiously.

Rygal peered through the fog to the west, trying to make out the other bridge. His chest felt tight with worry. This was not something they had planned for. Once Dandio realized they couldn't see, would he still continue the attack? Most likely he would—retreat was not an option now.

He leaned against the tree, tightening his grip on his sword hilt while his other hand rested on the strap of his shield. If Dandio meant to continue the assault, this way needed to be cleared, which meant Rygal needed to lead the Guardians forward at the right time. How they would know that time, there was no guessing. He usually didn't have to worry about the details of a plan—normally, Dandio would be with him to strategize, or Lammar. Or Norrin.

"I can sort of see the bridge from this angle," Darion said slowly. "At least, I think it's the bridge. There's a line of white that keeps appearing through the fog."

Rygal squinted in the direction he was pointing. "You can? Do you see the Liznees?"

"No. I'm seeing the railing, I think. It's brighter white than the rest." Darion moved cautiously out from under the branches, standing on the edge of the road that led to the north bridge.

Rygal slid out from the cover of the trees and followed him. He could just make out what Darion was pointing at—an arching white line. It was the same color as the shifting mist, and seemed to vanish if he looked directly at it.

He called quietly to Joesp, and the Wildkid came down the slope. "We can't see if Dandio's made it to the bridge," Rygal told him in a low voice. "Can you hear or scent anything?"

Joesp frowned. "The air here is very acrid—it seems to mask everything." He listened silently for a few moments. "I can hear them, very faintly. It sounds as though they are still in the woods."

"Still in the woods? Shouldn't they be at the bridge by now?" Darion asked tensely.

"Do you hear sounds of fighting?" Rygal asked.

"No. But that means little; I can hardly hear anything. Curse this fog," Joesp spat, glaring into the emptiness.

Rygal exhaled, trying to settle his thoughts. A decision would have to be made. "If we don't see anything in the next five minutes, we're going in. If there are Dal-kerri, we'll have to hold this side of the doors until Dandio's group arrives."

It was not a good plan. But it was the best one he could come up with. He figured it would be better to be a little early than to arrive too late.

"Look!" Joesp said suddenly, pointing.

Rygal swung back to face the foggy divide. In the distance, as though drawn by an invisible hand, the outline of the west bridge appeared. The fog had not cleared—Rygal could see the bridge glittering in dark blue ice.

"Iriam," he breathed in relief. "He must have realized we couldn't see."

Even as he watched, he saw the swirl of movement as the Liznees left the trees and charged over the westward bridge. Yet from the castle came haunting howls, and they could hear the first clatter of steel on steel.

"Or he's reminding us they need help," Darion said grimly.

"Let's go!" Rygal called to the Guardians. No one needed to be told twice. He could see the same nervous excitement in their eyes. Fear of what awaited them, but an urgent desire to fight.

He drew his sword and charged down onto the bridge. The battle had begun.

36

∾ ∾ ∾ ∾ ∾ ∾ ∾ ∾ ∾

The Patch

Allie fell.

Frigid air whipped past her, tearing at her clothes and hair. Her teeth were clamped shut, and her heart pounded in her throat. White fire sputtered from Drisilas' blade as though freezing hands had closed around it. The white flames spun into empty air above her as the seconds ticked on, and still she fell, plummeting downward.

I'm going to die. The dull thought repeated itself in her mind. How could she have thought this would work? This void was exactly as Mel had described it when he'd crossed the bridge—empty space, black, cold, stifling air filled with sounds and illusions, before the fall ended in a brutal stop.

She tensed, clutching the sword tighter, bracing herself for the inevitable end. Gradually, she realized the assumptions were wrong. She was falling, yes, but there were no sounds, no visions, nothing for Isilas to shield her from. The silence was as impenetrable as the darkness.

When she felt the stone beneath her boots, it took her a moment to register that she had stopped falling. There had been no lurch, no

447

jarring thud that should have broken bones after that fall.

Allie dropped to her knees, trembling. Stone. Cold stone was beneath her hands, or something that felt like it. It was smooth and slate gray, illuminated by a faint light.

She stood, taking in her surroundings.

She was on a wide bridge, a straight, flat bridge spanning away in both directions. Below it was nothingness, a darkness blacker than the void itself. Above and around her glistened white stars, twinkling as far into the blackness as she could see, as though she was inside a massive globe. Cold air drafted up from below.

Where was she? Certainly not Caer Droco. Neither Dark Realm nor mortal world seemed an apt description for this place. A middle-world, as Iriam had called it. An empty space. She gripped Drisilas tightly, and the Star-Stone glowed pale white, illuminating the way before her.

She glanced over her shoulder. The bridge spanned away into nothingness; she could only make out the reflection of the pale stars on it far, far away. Dim light shone ahead of her from a silver archway at the far end of the bridge.

There was no going back. She couldn't see where the strange bridge went—if indeed it went anywhere. Onward it was.

Slowly, she started forward. The soft thuds of her footsteps filled the quiet. For the first time, she became aware of another noise, a consistent sound filling the background like a rushing wind. A voice—was it the Ace-Lord's? It breathed and whispered, the words overlapping until she could make them out.

Vessel... vessel...

Allie stopped, straining her ears. "What?" Her voice echoed away into the darkness. No reply. The whispering voice continued, and she could catch other words now.

Vessel... Life-Blood... Mortal bound, bound, bound...

The last word urged her forward, her heart pounding, looking wildly for the speaker. There was no sign. No glowing purple eyes, no ghostly face, as Mel had described the place within the Darkness. But she must be in the same place. The silvery stars and misty blackness matched Mel's story of the void.

At last she reached an archway at the end of the bridge. Swirling shadows filled the interior like a curtain. She reached inside hesitantly, but her hand met only frigid air. This doorway looked almost identical to the one in the Ace-Lord's tower, but there was no knowing where it led.

Yet it was her only option. If Jan and Mel were on the other side of this archway, she needed to find them.

Taking a deep breath, she stepped through.

There was a rush of wind that took her breath away, and she seemed to be shoved forward, back into the mortal world.

Dazzling daylight slapped her in the face. Allie blinked, eyes watering. Sunlight. It streamed through a large stained glass window before her. Totally confused, Allie swung around, taking in her new surroundings.

She was not in Castle Droco, that much was clear. She stood inside a throne room she had never seen before, with a high vaulted ceiling. A throne made of twisted ebony and silver sat at the far end of the hall. The Ace-Lord's banner hung above it, triangular emblem gleaming as though streaked in fresh blood. The stained glass depicted a tall lord with silver hair and purple-red eyes, standing in a benevolent pose over a group of bowing mortals. The sight of it turned Allie's stomach with hatred.

She could make out little of the land outside through the window. But the brilliant sunlight told her she was no longer in the densely shadowed, fog-filled Magno Forest. The light reflected off a wide expanse of flatlands.

She remembered her mother's report—that the Aces had settled in the Salem Flats. Was that where she was now? Ar-Salem?

If the Red Dawn spies had learned the Aces' location, they knew nothing of this palace the Ace-Lord had wrought. She moved away from the arched doorway, looking around in fearful awe. The blanched white towers of Castle Droco were lovely in an ancient sort of way, but this castle put even that to shame. Its glossy walls glittered black and shone with veins of silver. The bright colors of the stained glass windows contrasted brilliantly against the darkness.

Distant voices echoed faintly down the halls, snapping her focus back. She was not alone here. Quickly, she sheathed Drisilas and headed down a winding corridor towards the voices. The passage slanted downward, and daylight soon vanished behind her. Torchlight came from below. Two voices were speaking—harsh voices, with strange, gravelly accents.

"He won't like it. They don't like the fire, you know." That voice was high-pitched and harsh, like the cawing of a crow.

"Well, too bad. I need to see." The second voice was deeper and dripped in sarcasm. A goblin and an orc, Allie guessed, which explained why they were speaking Liznaeic. Most of the tribes spoke their own dialect, but nearly everyone in the north used the old Liznee tongue as a default. She found herself very grateful that her mother had made her learn it.

"He'll be back soon. Didn't you see what happened last time? Old Vashkag lit a torch and the Deputy turned his chest into an ice block. They don't like fire." The goblin's voice was nervous and pleading.

"He's not here now," the orc replied, unconcerned. Allie could see firelight reflecting off the glossy walls. "Didn't you pay attention at the briefing? The Deputy's in Caer Droco, getting things all ready for the Bruin, while the Ace-Lord's off to summon it. Them's the plan."

The Bruin, Allie thought, with a chill of curiosity and unease. What sort of creature was the Bruin?

"I don't care. The Ace-Lord just knows things, he won't have to be here to know you've disobeyed orders about fire." There was a rustle as someone stood. "I ain't sticking around to get my chest frozen. You play with fire around the prisoner, I'm going to get some grog."

Footsteps approached from below. Allie froze as the slender figure of the goblin appeared before her. His toad-like eyes widened as he saw her, then he reached for his knife. Allie seized his skinny arm; he jabbed the blade across her hand as she slammed him back against the wall, muffling the cry of alarm just in time. The unconscious goblin slumped to the ground.

Allie shook her hand—blood streamed between her fingers, but the blade hadn't done any serious damage. She pressed the cut against her shirt and kept moving, her heart pounding. *You play with fire around the prisoner,* the goblin had said—which prisoner awaited at the end of this slanting passage?

"Gorif?" The orc's uneasy voice called up the hall. He must have heard the scuffle—if he found his fallen comrade, he'd sound the alarm. Allie picked up her pace and ran forward. Her focus was fixed on the yellow light of the lantern on the floor, so that she crashed right into the orc's muscular frame. The orc guard gripped her by the neck—his eyes glowed hollow and blue. "What's this?" he snarled in her face. "Who are you?"

The fire, crackling in Allie's veins since she'd entered the void, now burst to the surface. Her hands glowed hot as she raised them. A blast of fire shot from her fingers into the orc's chest. He gave a horrible strangled cry and slumped backward, a smoking hole smoldering in his chest.

His last cry echoed up the passageway. Someone would have heard that.

Trembling, Allie looked around. The floor fell away, sloping sharply down into a cavern. A cistern, she guessed—a deep round pit, carved from the rock. Stone steps led along its edge, circling into the pit. The faint slosh of water below reached her ears. She picked up the lantern and headed down slowly, her eyes straining in the shadows.

The firelight reflected off a deep pool of water below her, off the silver chains suspending someone just above the surface, off the dull green eyes as the figure raised his head.

"Jan," Allie whispered, and in another instant her relief was replaced with horror. The king was alive, as far as she could tell, but his eyes were half-open, unfocused. His face was covered in blood. The water was up to his chin, so that it partially submerged his face as he tired.

Allie hesitated, not sure what to do. The glittering chains seemed to be secured to the ceiling high above, where his captors could raise and lower him at will. She edged into the water cautiously. The stairs ended, dropping off into the deep pit, but she managed to reach out and take the chains. With her free hand, she drew Drisilas. Any other blade would have broken upon the cursed chains, but Drisilas hewed through them as though they were rotted ropes.

Jan dropped downward, no longer suspended. The sudden weight nearly pulled Allie forward into the frigid water. She lurched, keeping her grip on the chains, refusing to let him fall into the blackness. With every bit of strength, she threw herself backward, hauling the king up onto the stairs.

Jan lay on his back in the shallow water, coughing weakly—she couldn't tell if he was conscious or not. His eyes were open, but he seemed to see nothing. The chains wrapped around his chest and shoulders. Two cruel hooks had pierced his inner arms, so that any motion he made while suspended drove them deeper in. She removed them carefully.

Jan's hand locked on her throat so fast she didn't even have time to flinch. His eyes squinted feverishly in the shadows. "Who are you?" he rasped. "What do you want?"

"Jan—" Allie choked, touching his hand. His skin was ice-cold.

His grip lessened, and she saw his face register her voice. "Asescia?"

"I'm here. It's me, I'm here," Allie said, catching her breath.

Jan sat up slowly, painfully, leaning his back against the wall of the pit. Allie took both his hands in hers. He was so cold, his wet clothes in tatters, and he was bleeding from multiple wounds. But he was alive. Alive. Relief took her breath away, and she hugged him tightly.

"Allie?" Jan asked again, his voice a little stronger. He looked around blearily, as though she had just roused him from sleep. "Where are we?"

"I was hoping you could tell me that," Allie said with a weak attempt at laughter. "I think we're in Ar-Salem."

"Ar-Salem?" Jan repeated, truly confused now. "I thought—didn't we—we were in Wiverrun, we went to Castle Droco…" He trailed off, clearly trying to remember the rest. His eyes landed on Drisilas, laying on the damp stone beside them, pale flames still spitting from its blade. "You can draw the sword?" he said, looking at her in disbelief.

"Yes, I can," Allie said, lifting it. It seemed wrong to wield it now that he was back. "Take it—it's yours." She pressed the hilt into his freezing hands.

Jan squinted in the brilliant blaze, but holding the sword seemed to return a little of his strength. "What happened to the fire?" he asked.

"I don't know. The Ace-Lord tried to make me the new Wielder of Isilas—he did it before we escaped Castle Droco, and now I can wield the sword," Allie said miserably.

But to her surprise, Jan smiled. "You can? That's—that's very strange—I wonder what brought that about. That's incredible, Allie."

"It is?" Allie asked, taken aback. Her uncle's familiar smile, that glitter of almost boyish curiosity that filled his eyes on the rare occasions he was truly surprised, finally made her smile too.

"It's good," Jan said. "Hopefully, you can wield it until I am stronger. Help me up."

Allie took the sword, then stood and hauled him to his feet. He staggered, bracing himself against the wall, looking around. "How many hours have I been here?" he asked dazedly.

"Hours?" Allie repeated. "Jan, it's been almost a week."

"A week!" Jan shook his head. "Well, I will worry about that later. Where is Mel?"

"I'm hoping he's somewhere else in the castle," Allie said. Distant voices came from above them. Soon, the bodies of the guards would be discovered. "Come on—we have to hurry."

Jan leaned heavily on her shoulder as they made their way up the stairs and out of the pit. He stared at the dead orc. "Was that your handiwork?" There was no sign of the incredulous smile as he beheld this side of her new powers.

"Yes." Allie avoided his eyes. "Let's go."

Jan said nothing more as they extinguished the lantern and climbed the sloping hall. Allie gripped Drisilas, scanning the area as they emerged in the throne room again. Muted conversations came from other parts of the palace, but they had not yet been discovered.

Jan looked at the archway. "Is this how you came through?"

"Yes. I'm hoping that's how we'll get back out," Allie told him, scanning the room. Several hallways led out of the main chamber. A set of double doors stood directly to her right. That probably led out into the courtyard, she guessed. The arched opening of the hallway next to it led up, while the hall next to that slanted downward.

"Is the Ace-Lord here?" Jan asked. He still looked dazed, but she could almost see a plan coming together in his head.

"No. I heard the guards talking," Allie told him. "He's somewhere in the void, getting ready for a creature called the Bruin."

She watched her uncle's face for any sign of recognition at the name, but he only looked concerned. "I have not heard of the Bruin outside of legend. They were said to be creatures resembling great bears that lived in the clouds and created thunder."

"I think it's some type of Dal-kerri wraith," Allie said. She remembered Glentree's report when he'd come to Sia—how long ago that felt—and his message about the Ace-Lord bringing another wraith into the world. That, she guessed, was probably the Bruin. Directed by Redeyes, it would bring about more death.

But they'd have to deal with that later. "Dad and Rygal are leading an attack on Castle Droco right now," she said. "Hopefully, we can get out at the same time that they reach the upper towers. Then they'll accompany us back out to reach Admiral Dessian at the coast."

Jan nodded slowly, digesting this. "Good. We will have to hurry. Where do you imagine they have taken Mel?"

Allie eyed the hallways. The one leading down echoed with orc voices—far too many for her and Jan to take by themselves. The upward slanting hall was silent, and she could see a winding staircase leading further up.

It would be better than battling orcs. If Mel was not there, they would have to search elsewhere.

"Let's go," she said, and gripping Drisilas, she and Jan headed up the winding stair.

37

The Fallen

The upper tower was filled with shadows, utterly silent. The surrounding darkness made it difficult for Allie to make out much else of the Ace-Lord's palace. The quiet reminded her of the void and the arching bridge. That strange middle world would be waiting for them once they escaped.

As soon as she could find Mel.

They climbed more stone stairs, moving as silently as they could. Jan walked behind her, carrying Drisilas again. The fire still shone white, as pale as the killing bolts of ice the Aces used.

Had Isilas already been corrupted? A small glimmer of blue still shone in the Stone, deep in its depths. Even though the Stone had been returned to the rightful Wielder, Allie could see Isilas was not what it had been. Perhaps it was too late to save it. Perhaps the Stone was already corrupted beyond repair, and there was nothing Jan could do to fix it or reconcile his curse.

She tried not to think of that. But she could tell from Jan's grave expression that similar thoughts were running through his mind.

The winding stairs ended as they reached the top of the tower. A set of double doors stood before them, made of the same glossy black stone as the rest of the palace. Obsidian, maybe? But obsidian did not feel so cold to the touch. These walls had come from another place, wrought by another power.

She reached for the doors. Jan stopped her. "Careful. There may be someone inside," he whispered.

"I don't hear anything," Allie said.

He arched an eyebrow. "We seldom do. Stay behind me."

Allie stepped aside. Jan pushed open the doors, allowing them to swing inward.

A low snarl came from within. Redeyes stood in the shadows of the room, hackles raised, tail lashing the air. Another stained glass window stood behind him, bathing the room in vivid red light. Framing the back wall was a second archway, smaller than the one in the throne room below, but filled with the same swirling darkness.

Redeyes crouched beside a small table. The Blue Stone sat upon it, glimmering pure blue in the darkness.

"Stand aside," Jan ordered, lowering Drisilas. His hoarse voice was firm and cold. "We are here for the Stone."

A satisfied smile spread over the monstrous face. "I expected you would be," he growled, and lunged forward.

Allie leapt between them, knowing that despite Jan's strong words, he could not fight in his current condition. Red fire crackled in her hands as Redeyes sprang at her. His claws locked on her shoulders, hauling her forward as his teeth opened to receive her throat. Allie let herself drop down, feeling the beast's hot breath on her face. Fire flashed from her hands as she shot upward blindly.

Redeyes snarled and stepped back as Allie crawled free, trembling in pain and fear. Jan leapt forward, white fire joining the red as he brought Drisilas up.

Redeyes avoided the sword and sprang again, claws gleaming. Allie saw them make contact with the king's chest, shoving him backward. Jan fell back through the double doors and down the curving stairs.

Allie sprang to her feet, her fear and rage turning her fire hot. She sent a blast glancing over Redeyes' back as he dropped low, sparks glittering on his black fur. As he drew away, Allie snatched the Blue Stone from the table, gripping it tightly. Redeyes came again, his claws tearing her cloak and dragging her toward him. She fired another blast, searing the polished tabletop, and spun away, putting the table between herself and the snarling cat. Her breath came short and panicked—despite her fire, she knew without a doubt that Redeyes was stronger and more skilled.

Redeyes stared at her, tail lashing, hackles bristling. Allie braced herself for his next attack, but he didn't move. She could tell every part of him desired to lunge and tear her apart, yet something held him back.

"Be grateful, vessel," he spat at last, "that my master still finds you useful."

And with that, he turned and sprang through the arching void, vanishing into the shadows.

"Asescia?"

Jan's voice came from the stairs, tense with fear.

"I'm all right," she called.

Jan stumbled through the doors, looking around. The front of his jerkin had been torn by Redeyes' claws, but the leather had prevented a more serious injury. "Where is he?"

"He went into the doorway," Allie replied, nodding to the arch. Her voice was steadier than she felt. Her shoulders ached where Redeyes had seized her. That terrifying moment when Redeyes had hauled her down, feeling his breath, waiting for his teeth to tear at her, replayed in her mind. Knees suddenly unsteady, she leaned on the table, holding the Blue Stone.

"You're all right," Jan reassured her, placing his hands on her shoulders. "You're all right. Breathe."

Allie took a deep breath and straightened. "We don't have time. We have to find Mel."

Jan studied at the swirling void. "Do you suppose he is in there?"

"I'm not sure," Allie said uncertainly. "From what Iriam told me, the gateway voids are used more as passageways than as prisons."

She looked around the room. Another hall led away to her right, narrow and dark. There was something similar about this tower—the darkness, the high ceiling, the artistic design—but she couldn't place it.

Jan had moved to the arch, peering uncertainly into the curtain of shadows. "I wonder if the voids only lead to certain places," he said finally. "This one is much smaller than both the Patch in Caer Droco and the archway we passed on the lower levels. Perhaps it is some sort of entrance for the Ace-Lord and his servants."

Allie finally placed the familiarity of the tower. "I think you're right. This room—this must be the Ace-Lord's quarters. It looks almost exactly like the one in Castle Droco, where he took Mel and I before we escaped." *When he gave me these powers,* her mind added. But she didn't say it aloud.

"Then I imagine this is our way back to Castle Droco," Jan said, and frowned slightly. "The question I would like answered is why the Ace-Lord is not here to stop us."

Allie looked at the Stone in her hand. "Redeyes was here to guard," she pointed out.

"Redeyes retreated," Jan said slowly. "That is not something he does willingly. Why would the Ace-Lord allow us to escape with the Blue Stone?"

An uneasy chill ran down Allie's spine. Jan was right. Even if the Ace-Lord's strategy was to corrupt the mortals, why would he let them take the Stone? "Maybe he just… made a mistake," she suggested, knowing the words sounded flat.

Jan shook his head, but said nothing more. "We will have to discuss it later. For now, we must find Mel. Search down that hall," he said, nodding to the narrow corridor to the right. "I'll stay here and be sure Redeyes does not return."

Allie nodded, heading down the short hall. No windows lit this passage. She allowed a small flame to rise from her palm, blinking as her eyes adjusted to the darkness.

The passage ended in a small room. Allie ignited a flame on the palm of her hand. Red light glowed off the shiny black walls inlayed with silver, the arching ceiling above her, and there, before her, a figure suspended.

Allie stepped back, her heart lurching in horror.

Mel hung in the air in front of her, held up by black, ribbon-like restraints. His ginger hair floated off his pale face, covered in wounds. Allie's fire lit his eyes, half-open and staring at nothing.

"Mel," she breathed, forcing herself forward. *Don't be dead*, her mind begged, *oh, Light above, don't let him be dead.* "Oh, what have they done to you." Her weak, terrified voice was the only sound. She launched a blast of flame at the restraints, letting the red fire sever the shadowy ropes.

Mel fell forward like a puppet whose strings had been cut. She caught him, stumbling under the limp weight, and lowered him to the ground. Her hands shook as she felt for a pulse.

It was there, beating faintly against her fingers.

He was still alive.

But what was wrong with him? He was cold—so much colder than Jan had been, completely unresponsive, and showed no improvement upon being freed as Jan had. A corpse with a heartbeat, she thought, and her fear intensified.

"Jan!" she called quietly, her voice trembling.

Jan jogged down the passageway. "What is it? Have you found him?" He stopped in his tracks as he saw the unmoving body, his eyes filling with horror.

"He's alive," Allie stammered. "But he won't move—he won't wake up—I don't know what's wrong –" Her voice shook. She had expected both Jan and Mel would be in bad shape when she found them. But once she'd freed Jan from the dreadful black water, he'd come to his senses and seemed himself again. She had not expected to find Mel barely alive.

Jan knelt beside her, gently lifting Mel's body. "He is alive. We can better assess his injuries once we are out of here." He stood. Mel hung lifeless in his arms, and it cut to Allie's heart.

"What do you think…" she started.

"The Aces have many means of torture," Jan said shortly. "They asked me no questions in the pit. It seems they did more to Mel." He headed down the hall, holding the limp body close.

Allie followed, trying to steady her thoughts. Mel would be all right, as soon as they made it out of here. "We'll… we'll have to go through the gateway void," she said. "I'll hold Drisilas. The Stones should protect us from any illusions."

Jan nodded. Allie took the sword, then gently placed the Blue Stone against Mel's chest, pressing his cold hand over it. The Stone was said to have healing powers. Perhaps it would help.

She took a deep breath and looked up at Jan. "I sure hope this leads to the right place."

Jan gave her a weak smile. "It can hardly be worse than here, can it?"

Allie didn't feel like answering that question. Instead, she turned and led the way into the shadows of the arch.

. . . . . .

Rygal found Dandio at the base of the staircase.

Thus far, their plan had worked perfectly. The Liznees had successfully entered the castle. Rygal's group had met them not a moment too soon, exactly where they had planned to meet. In fact, the only issue had been the sheer size of the Aces' forces.

Dal-kerri were everywhere, snarling, snapping, and loosing their bone-chilling howls. A pack of them had sprung upon the Liznee archers, killing several and inflicting terrible wounds. A circle of flames protected the Liznee forces now, keeping the Dal-kerri at bay. But other creatures filled the hall too—orcs and goblins, eyes glowing pale blue with the Ace-Lord's enchantment. They did not fear the flames, and swords were useless against them; the best they could do was force them back. Glentree had already lifted two orcs by their collars, tossing them back into the fray as though they weighed no more than dolls.

There were humans, too. Some of them, judging by their simple attire, had come from Wiverrun, but there were many others, from all across the country. The Ace-Lord had been busy.

Rygal summoned the Essence, sending sparks flashing down his blade. He could not yet create the pinwheels of fire like Norrin used to, but sparks had effect. The Dal-kerri hated them almost as much as the flames.

"Where'd you learn to do that?" Dandio asked, looking impressed, as they paused at the base of the stairs. Dark blood streaked the tall Liznee's sword and armor, and his eyes were alight with battle rage.

"He has been learning quickly," Iriam told him—he stood steady behind Dandio, dark blue ice shining on his fingertips.

Rygal shook his head, but he was pleased by the Neutral's praise. "I still can't make fire," he admitted.

"Shame," Dandio said absently, sending a blast of red at a Dal-kerri before it could attack.

Darion stood beside Rygal. He was out of arrows by now, and wielded his long-bladed dagger. His scarred face was drawn with both weariness and determination. "Are we taking the stairs now?"

Dandio let out a breath and looked at his towering deputy. "What do you say, Glentree? Up for more?"

Glentree bared his teeth in a fierce grin. "We'll hold the way out. Take the tower."

Without another word, Dandio and Rygal started forward, followed by a troop of Red Dawn soldiers. They sprinted up the steps, swords flashing, fire blazing before them into the attackers that rushed to meet them. Behind him, Rygal heard Iriam's low voice murmuring incantations in a strange tongue. Deep blue ice spread up the stairs before them, guiding the way ahead.

Up they went, running up the stone stairs. Dal-kerri leapt down upon them, howling and snarling. Rygal caught one against his shield, saw the golden sparks gleaming along the rim as the hound retreated. Teeth snapped on his sword arm, and Dandio's fire blasted the attacker just in time. Rygal swung to dispatch another hound before it could leap on Darion's turned back, and saw the young ranger shove an enchanted orc from the stairs.

And up they went, higher and higher into the spiraling fortress. His heart pounded against his ribs in battle cadence. This was what he had waited for. Weeks, months of inactivity, of letting his tension and grief and hatred against the Aces sit stagnant, now boiled to the surface. He felt no weariness. Sparks danced from his sword and shield as he slashed again and again, and the attack became a rhythm. Slash twice, three steps up. Slash again, another step forward.

Screams, crashes, howls, and cries filled the air around him. He stood back to back with Dandio, watching the yellow sparks mingle with the Liznee's red fire. In an instant, his mind returned to a time when he was twelve years old, when he had stood with Dandio to face the Hazes. He had been bleeding from his arm then too, and they had been forced to flee.

This time it was different. This time, he felt no fear. And this time, there would be no retreat.

"Upward!" Dandio shouted, springing up the next flight of stairs. The warriors continued, pressing forward, an impenetrable wall of fire and steel. Deep blue ice spread before them. Iriam hung suspended by his own indigo light, frost glittering on his fingertips, a deeper light glowing from his red eyes. Only once before had Rygal seen the Neutral's power unveiled, yet even that was nothing compared to the might he saw now.

On and on they went, until at last he and Dandio stood on the balcony. Dandio shouldered the doors open, blasting down the Dal-kerri that sprang from within.

White ice flashed behind him, a deadly dart aimed at the Liznee's heart.

Iriam's ice intercepted it just in time, shattering the bolt and sending shards in all directions. The Ace-Deputy stood across the room, his half-decayed face drawn with hate. With a snarl most unlike his usual smooth tone, he stepped forward, sending another blast. Iriam generated a shield, catching the bolt. The force of the Deputy's blow slid him backward, but he did not falter.

"Protect the archway," Iriam ordered, eyes fixed on the Deputy.

The archway stood unharmed at the end of the hall. Chills ran down Rygal's spine as he beheld it. Allie's stories, Darion's detailed description, neither had prepared him for the total darkness and evil leaking from the void. Yet it must stand. That was Allie's way out. Hopefully it could be closed after Allie had escaped through it.

He moved forward with Dandio.

Seeing the movement, the Ace-Deputy snarled and broke away from Iriam, giving up the battle as he fled through the archway. Rygal sprinted to follow—Dandio caught his arm and hauled him back. "No—we can't go in that way."

"Allie's in there!" Rygal reminded him, hearing the fear in his own voice.

"Allie has the Stone. You do not," Dandio told him firmly. "Take the other side of the arch. We'll hold here."

Rygal did as instructed, trying to catch his breath. Iriam stood on the landing looking down, sending an occasional ray of ice down the steps and protecting their way back down. That was good. They'd need that way cleared, especially if Allie was—

"He's coming back!" Darion warned suddenly, raising his dagger. His eyes were fixed on the archway.

Rygal and Dandio both set themselves before the doorway. Iriam moved forward, hands raised.

Rygal saw the shadowy figure of the Ace-Deputy coming slowly into focus through the shadows. He saw the swirling black robes, the glittering silver armor—armor that was finer made than the Deputy's. He saw a crown on the withered brow. And he saw the purple-red eyes as a face older than darkness smiled out at them.

He stumbled back in horror.

Shadows gathered around the towering form, following the figure like a veil as he stepped into the light.

"Mortals," the Ace-Lord breathed softly. "How very predictable you are."

38

The Bruin

The Ace-Lord stood before the frightened warriors in the room, a cold smile on his wrecked face. Rygal knew him only from the reports of his companions, yet the towering lord before him was more terrifying than words could describe. In the gleam of the purple-red eyes shone a cruel contempt, not just of their lives, but of their efforts to overthrow him. The attack was in vain, for at the end of it all stood the Lord of Death himself.

"Steady, men," Dandio ordered, as the Liznees of the Red Dawn edged away fearfully. Rygal was impressed he could form words—his own throat was dry with terror.

The Ace-Lord laughed softly. "Will you yet order them to their own demise, Commander? Such a ploy is not in your nature. Your heart I know well."

Red fire crackled in Dandio's hand as he stepped forward, raising his sword. He was tall, but even he was dwarfed by the Ace-Lord, who stared down at him as if amused. "If you know my heart," Dandio hissed, "then you'll know my rage. I'll give you one chance to go back through that doorway."

"You are in no position to demand such things," the Ace-Lord told

470

him coldly. "This ill-advised attack cannot alter the events set into motion."

A flare of ice shot from his hands, sweeping the warriors aside as though they were troublesome flies. Dandio and the other Liznees were tossed backward like toy soldiers. The ice caught Rygal across the legs, and he fell, raising his head to see the Ace-Lord stride through the hall.

One figure still stood before him, unmovable. Iriam. The Neutral stood wreathed in deep blue light, robes billowing around him, indigo ice glittering in his hands.

The Ace-Lord paused to study him, and Rygal saw a flicker of interest on his face. "The Neutral," he said softly. "So you still stand in the torrents of mortal matters. Do you not weary of it?"

For answer, Iriam raised his hands and sent five blades of ice flying at the Ace-Lord's face. The Ace-Lord swayed slightly to avoid them, deflecting the final bolt across a gleaming white blade that appeared in his right hand.

"I am not weary of protecting the good," Iriam answered in a low voice. "Leave this place, Kahlifis. The Prophecy has secured your downfall."

Rygal saw the interest turn into hatred on the Ace-Lord's decayed features. He raised his hands again, sending a bolt of white flying at Iriam. Rygal saw a rapid flash of movement as Iriam tried to generate another shield—the white ice struck him, flinging him backwards, over the railing and into the darkness beyond.

"Iriam!" he shouted hoarsely, too late, again—and in another instant, it was no longer Iriam's name he was crying, but Norrin's, and he was back in the foggy glade on a day long past, watching the man who had raised him crumple lifeless to the ground.

Sparks were flying from his blade, hot as the helpless fury boiling in him. Without thinking, he sprang to his feet, leaping forward to face the Ace-Lord, the killing spell from the book tearing from his throat as he lowered his blade. *"Devrando!"*

A ray of sparks shot from his sword, glowing white-hot.

The Ace-Lord raised a hand, allowing the blast to strike his palm, and watched with skeptical amusement as the deathly curse was absorbed into his blackened flesh. "Did it escape you, boy," he said softly, looking down at Rygal, "that I cannot be killed, much less by my own enchantments?"

Rygal took a step back, chest heaving, hands shaking so that he could hardly hold his sword. Fear, crippling fear had replaced his blind fury.

The Ace-Lord raised his transparent blade, slashing a lightning-fast strike. Rygal managed to parry it—the force jarred up his arm and back, like frosty claws sinking into his flesh. The yellow sparks were extinguished in a single blow. The magic he had worked so hard to learn was gone. He was only mortal, shaking in fear, drenched in Dal-kerri blood, helpless before the Ace-Lord.

The Ace-Lord struck him with a wave of ice, catching him across the chest and heaving him back against the wall. He felt it lock on either side of his body, trapping him there.

"How the greats have fallen," the Ace-Lord mused softly. "The legends of old had far more power than you, and yet you believe yourself worthy to stand before me where they have stood." His face spread in a smile, revealing every broken tooth in his decayed mouth. "At least now, the opposition is but a simple matter to defeat."

Something rumbled to Rygal's right. The silver arch shuddered as though something were pressing against it from inside.

"You chose to attack my fortress," the Ace-Lord said. "Now, you will watch its final moments."

Rygal squirmed in the icy grip, fighting to free his arms. He tried to summon the fiery sparks of before, to send them leaping down his blade and thaw his bonds. But it was in vain.

A low, rumbling growl shook the room. Something slammed against the arched doorway from within. Prowling from the shadows came Redeyes, his hackles prickling, ears back. "They have taken the Stone, my lord," he growled softly.

Rygal raised his head, hope suddenly filling him. The Stone—Allie had taken the Stone—Redeyes had said *"they,"* which must mean she had Jan and Mel with her too—

But the Ace-Lord only nodded. "I imagine they have. It is of no matter. Are you prepared?"

A sickening satisfaction replaced the anger in Redeyes' expression, and he stooped in a bow. "The Bruin awaits my orders."

The growl came again, echoing in Rygal's ears, deep and brutish.

Another blow landed on the other side of the doorway. Fragments of silver chipped from the arch, scattering across the floor, and through the curtain of shadows, Rygal saw a pair of eyes glowing white.

"Let it come," the Ace-Lord said. "Let it bring this wretched ruin of a castle to its defeat, and let my kingdom rise from Ar-Salem. I will have no reminders of the past."

There was one last blow, one last crunching groan, and the archway gave way, the steel warping, pressed open wide as the massive beast lurched into the mortal world.

A wraith of ice and shadow, but not like the Darkness. It seemed to have some substance to it, to be able to shake the room. It slammed against the walls, snarling, the size of a cottage, filling the tower. Icy claws broke the marble at its feet. Its huge back scuffed the ceiling. It raised its head and let out a deep, reverberating roar that rattled Rygal's teeth.

Redeyes bounded before it, dwarfed by the massive, bear-like beast. Rygal glimpsed the Ace-Lord's final smile before he vanished in a streak of shadow. The Bruin lurched forward, its shoulder striking the wall above Rygal's head. The blow vibrated down the wall, and he shrank back, shaking.

Toxic black fog followed the Bruin like a cloud, the same deadly mist that had shrouded the Darkness. It engulfed three Liznee soldiers who were unable to retreat in time; Rygal saw their lifeless armored forms fall to the ground with a clatter. The other Liznees had stepped forward, red fire blazing from their hands. The Bruin turned its huge head toward them and roared again, sweeping icy claws and felling more warriors.

The ancient castle shuddered before the Bruin's strength. Ice spread up the walls, tearing apart the marble, dousing the fires that had spread to the upper levels. Huge chunks of stone fell from the ceiling as the Bruin shouldered its way through the room. With a snarl, it slashed upward at the offending ceiling beams, swiping the stone and marble aside. Watery sunlight streamed within, as though to fully illuminate the end of Castle Droco.

Pressing both shoulders against the doorframe, the Bruin heaved upward with a roar. Ice crystalized the marble at its breath, shattering the stone. The tower ceiling lurched, and with one final groan, it broke into three pieces and gave way.

Rygal was showered in dust and debris. The floor shuddered beneath the falling ceiling. Rygal coughed, desperately fighting to break the ice. There was no sign of Dandio or the Red Dawn knights. Had they all been killed, engulfed by the toxic fog or crushed by the falling stones? Was he alone here, left to listen to the screams of horror as their forces outside were caught by the hulking Bruin? It would all end here, in a room full of rubble.

Allie would not come, even if she had, by some miracle, rescued Jan and Mel and gained the Star-Stone. The doorway had been destroyed by the thundering wraith. They would be trapped in the void.

Gritting his teeth, he wrenched an arm free of the icy bonds. The crunch of shattering marble and the screams of dying men filled his ears from the stairway. Fury filled his chest again, and he screamed a wordless challenge at the Ace-Lord's name, half hoping the Bruin would hear and come finish him off. Anything was preferable to this helplessness.

"Hold *on*, I'm coming!"

Rygal turned sharply. One of the Bruin's blows had opened a gap in the marble floor, a gaping hole that dropped all the way to the ground floor. Darion clung to the edge, covered in dust, fighting to pull himself up. Rygal had not seen him—he must have fled back this way after Iriam had been hit—but in that moment, he had never been more relieved to see anyone.

Darion managed to grip the stone, hauling himself out of the hole and crawling forward on the floor.

"Take your time," Rygal said wryly, clawing at the ice securing his chest.

Darion ignored this comment as he stood and moved over, studying the ice. "I don't think we can cut through it. Maybe…" He struck the ice with the pommel of his dagger. A few chips broke off, but it did not yield.

Another shattering crunch came from beyond—the Bruin was probably breaking the staircases.

"Allie's in the void," Rygal panted. "She's stuck in there—the doorway's destroyed—we'll have to get her out another way."

"It didn't fully destroy the void," Darion told him. "The archway's broken, but the void's still there."

Rygal looked to the other end of the hall. The silver arch had been warped beyond repair, broken in two and bent in either direction. But Darion was right. The swirling curtain of darkness remained, spilling into the room, dusting the pale floor in black.

There was a loud curse from the other side of the room. A blast of red fire split through the wall of rubble dividing the room. Dandio stumbled forward, covered in dust. "Light-blasted death-lord," he snapped, stepping over the chunks of broken rubble. The surviving members of his squadron followed him, some supporting their injured comrades.

Dandio moved to Rygal. "Hold still," he ordered shortly, and pressed both hands over the ice. Red fire shot from his fingers, sputtering on the cold, and Rygal felt his restraints give way. The ice split apart, and he staggered forward.

"Your orders, Commander?" one of the soldiers asked uncertainly behind Dandio.

Dandio nodded toward the door. "Get downstairs if you can, before that beast destroys our escape. Regroup with Glentree at our rendevous and stay out of the Bruin's way. We will reach you as soon as we can."

"Dandio—Iriam was—" Rygal started, his chest tight with fear and grief.

Dandio let out a breath. "We can do nothing for him at the moment."

He turned back to his men. "When you reach the ground floor, hold the north bridge as long as you can, but don't wait for us."

The captain frowned. "Sir…"

"That's an order, captain," Dandio said firmly. "I will not have you all consumed by that blaze-cursed beast while you wait around for me."

The captain hesitated only a moment longer before nodding, and led the surviving soldiers slowly toward the door.

"What are we going to do?" Darion asked.

Dandio looked at him, a familiar determined set to his exhausted face. "We are going to hold down the void. Allie's counting on us to be here, and so we must be here when she makes it out."

. . . .

As before, it seemed to take a long moment for Allie's body and mind to adjust to the complete darkness inside the void. Once she did, she quickly noticed that this was not the same strange middle-world she'd entered within the Patch. There was no arching bridge, no white stars, no quenching silence. Nor did the space seem to go on forever.

The space inside the tower doorway was a new world all together. It resembled a long hall, but what would be the walls and ceiling warped above her head in swirling shadows. Wind blew in her face and hair, pressing her back. Other rifts filled the space around her, smaller doorways of darkness. She wondered where those could lead.

She paused, trying to get her bearings. The wind and swirling shadows played tricks on her eyes, making it hard to see, and caused a claustrophobic sensation. She focused ahead of her. A black pathway led forward, bringing all the voids to a central location. The faint silver of a doorway glimmered ahead—a quarter mile, perhaps, though it was impossible to tell.

"There," she said, pointing. There was no need to raise her voice. Aside from the rustling of the wind, it was not much louder in here than it had been in the castle.

Jan stood behind her, holding Mel's still form. She could tell by one glance that the king was affected by the void; his face was drawn as though in pain, and he was squinting against the tugging wind.

She took his arm. "Look at the Blue Stone. I can see our way out."

Jan nodded and cast his eyes down at the soft blue light as he began moving forward. "Do you… hear it too?"

Allie paused, glancing back at him. "Hear what?"

Jan gave a slight shrug, taking a deep breath as they walked onward. "I imagine they are different for you… they're different for each person. The voices, the sounds… can you see the illusions?"

Allie frowned, confused by what he was talking about. Aside from the whisper of the rushing wind, she saw and heard nothing. "No, I don't see any illusions."

Jan's brow furrowed—whether from the illusions he seemed to see and hear, or from confusion over this statement, she wasn't sure. "That is strange. I suppose… it is because you carry the sword."

Allie nodded slowly, satisfied by that explanation, even though her reason argued against it. That made no sense. Jan was carrying the Blue Stone, and thus should be shielded by its powers. He was close enough to be protected by Isilas' powers as well, and yet the illusions still affected him. Why did she not see and hear them too?

"Let's just get out of here," she said. This was not the time to worry about the illusions. All the same, this discovery confused her. Perhaps it was just one more layer to the Ace-Lord's spell, making her invulnerable to the Ace-magic.

The thought should have been reassuring, but it terrified her. The spell—whatever it was—was all around too good to be true. The Ace-Lord wouldn't have given her all these new powers without reason. He must know she would never act as his Wielder—and with the power she now possessed, she might actually be a threat to his plan.

There was another reason, she knew. A darker purpose behind these new powers, a purpose that served the Ace-Lord's conquest. She was not sure what it could be, and that unknown filled her with the same dread she had seen in Iriam's eyes in Mata City.

She kept her hand on Jan's arm, pressing forward. Drisilas' fire sputtered in the wind, but the white flames burned steadily. Progress felt painfully slow. The rushing wind seemed to hold them in time. Were they moving at all? Were they trapped here, doomed to toil in this dark void forever?

She shivered and quickened her pace. They were almost there. She could see the doorframe outlined more clearly now, and a chill of foreboding filled her chest. The arch was broken in two, each side warped in separate directions.

Allie pressed a hand to the archway to steady herself. "It's broken," she whispered. "Jan—the door is broken."

Jan raised his head painfully, wincing as he focused on the archway. "Will it function?"

"I don't know," Allie said. Was their way out destroyed? What if that was what the Ace-Lord had wanted—to lure her in, then close the door as soon as they'd entered, trapping them?

Cautiously, she slipped a hand into the swirling shadows. There was no difference in the air beyond, no clue that might inform her if this way was the correct one.

She drew her hand back uncertainly, looking at Jan. He leaned against the archway, face drawn and pale, his eyes staring dully into the distance, seeing some terrible illusion Allie could not. Every second here was torture to him. But there was no telling if this doorway was the right one, or what would happen if they entered the damaged void.

She glanced around, casting about for an answer. There was no alternative. They would have to take the risk.

"Hold onto me," she said. "I don't know if this door still works, but we'll have to try."

Jan said nothing, only shifted Mel's still form to his shoulder and took Allie's arm with his free hand.

Allie took a deep breath and stepped forward.

She felt as though she had stepped off a precipice. Cold air tore at her face. A wild blast shoved her backward, holding her in place. Jan's grip tightened on her arm as she stumbled back, frantically trying to keep her forward momentum.

The void refused to yield them. She could feel its icy claws around her, hauling her back. Could almost hear the Ace-Lord's triumphant laugh somewhere in its depths.

She groped blindly into the darkness with her free hand, seeking a handhold. There was none. She was falling again, falling backward into the deathly wind-strewn hall with the friends she had tried so hard to save.

Until, abruptly, something caught her frantically reaching hand.

Allie squinted into the torrent, unable to see what held her. Someone had her hand, pulling her forward, forward to safety.

Jan's grip loosened. The winds, the illusions—it had been too much, too taxing on his already spent strength. She saw him falling, knew he would be lost in the void.

Not again, a voice screamed in her mind. She would not lose him a second time.

Fighting the tearing winds, she wrenched Drisilas back into its scabbard and gripped her uncle's cold hand in hers. For a moment, she felt herself suspended between worlds, a hand tugging her in both directions. One pulling her to light and safety, the other dragging her back into the darkness. She gritted her teeth and clung to both, refusing to let go.

For an instant, she wondered if she would be torn in two. Then the person on the other side of the door gave a mighty heave, and she was hauled into light, back into life. Jan staggered in from the doorway behind her, still clutching Mel. The Blue Stone cast brilliant light around a ruined hall.

Allie collapsed, gasping for air. A familiar embrace caught her, holding her tightly.

"Allie? Allie?"

Dazed, she raised her head, looking into her father's worried face.

"Are you all right?" That was Rygal, out of breath. He must have helped pull them through.

Allie nodded breathlessly, looking around. She was in the upper tower of Castle Droco, exactly where Iriam had predicted she would emerge. The once elegant hall was strewn with large heaps of rubble. The marble floor was cracked in numerous places.

Dandio moved quickly to Jan. His evident relief to see his brother alive vanished as he saw the unmoving form in Jan's arms. "Mel— what happened to him?"

"We don't know," Allie managed to reply. The struggle in the doorway had left her utterly exhausted.

"He's ice cold," Rygal said in a hollow voice, touching Mel's hand lightly. "Is he still…"

"He is alive," Jan told him. His voice was rasping, but Allie could hear his strength returning now that he was on this side of the doorway. "We must get him out of here." He looked around, taking in their ruined surroundings for the first time. "Light above, is this your handiwork?"

Dandio let out a breath, clearly almost as exhausted as they were. "This battle is far from over. With the Stones, we might have a chance to escape the Bruin."

"The Bruin?" Allie repeated. She'd all but forgotten the conversation she'd overheard before she'd rescued Jan. "What's—"

As if on cue, a thundering roar below them shook the castle. The floor lurched, the framework of the tower groaning as it balanced precariously.

"You'll find out in a moment," Dandio said grimly. "For now, we need to leave before this tower collapses."

39

Atoning

Signs of battle were written upon every part of Castle Droco. Fires blazed below, searing the white marble. Bodies lay broken and strewn across the ground floor; Allie could see them far below as they made their way down the stairs.

Yet nearly all fighting had ceased. Their attack had ended abruptly with the arrival of the Bruin.

Allie had never seen a Dal-kerri of this size before, if Dal-kerri the creature was. It raged below, tearing holes in the stone walls as though they were made of cloth, shattering the stairs and passageways around it. A dark feline shape darted around its feet, goading it into action like a sheephound snapping at its flock. Redeyes. The Messenger of the Ace-Lord, the harbinger of destruction, leading the Bruin forward.

"It's… it's tearing apart the castle," she stammered finally, her mouth dry as she watched. "Why would the Ace-Lord let it destroy his fortress?"

"The Ace-Lord has no more purpose for the castle," Rygal said. "He mentioned something about destroying the past. This place, it seems, is nothing but bad memories for him."

"This way," Dandio called.

The spiraling stairs bore the brunt of the Bruin's descent—the finely crafted railing was gone, wrested from its place, and the steps were broken in several areas. But they still stood, leading down from the crumbling tower.

Darion, surer-footed than the rest of them, took Mel's unmoving form over his shoulder and followed Dandio. Allie came next, keeping close to the wall, avoiding looking over at the dizzying drop on her right. Dark blue ice glittered on the steps, and with a pang of alarm she realized someone was missing. "Where's Iriam?"

She looked at Rygal—his face was pale. "I don't know. He was fighting the Ace-Lord. I saw him fall this way."

Allie looked down, trying to make out the lifeless forms on the floor below. It was impossible to see from this height. Iriam could not be dead, her mind argued desperately.

"We will find him once we are downstairs," Jan said behind her. "We can do nothing from here."

His low, calm voice slightly eased Allie's racing thoughts. She was so glad he was here, alive and whole. Yet his tone held a heaviness that revealed his concern.

Halfway down, Allie could make out a few survivors. A group of Red Dawn warriors formed a semi circle around the north door, their path to retreat at their back. A ring of yellow fires surrounded them as the Guardians held back the remaining Dal-kerri. Allie could make out Glentree's hulking form, striking attackers left and right. But his group was badly outnumbered, and the enchanted soldiers pressed relentlessly forward.

"That's our way out," Dandio called up to them, pointing at the north gate. He moved faster. Allie could sense his desperation to rejoin his weary men.

She picked up her pace, half jogging down the ruined stairs, sidestepping holes and jumping over the gaps left by the Bruin's ice-hewn claws. The bodies littering the floor became recognizable as they headed down. Broken Dal-kerri, their fur still burning. A few goblins, Black Dwarves, and desert dwellers, who must have refused the enchantment. But far too many bodies wore the colors of the Red Dawn. Still more of them were no more than withered husks, the life stripped out of them by the black fog swirling around the Bruin.

She focused on the stairs beneath her feet as the ground floor drew closer. The Bruin did not see them, far too busy destroying the castle, its snarls echoing off the stone walls, raging and lumbering as its claws ripped apart the ancient fortress.

If it left the castle, it would wreak havoc on the cities of Orlell. She remembered the damage the Darkness had caused, remembered those who had been killed, and felt a chill of fear. "How do we stop it?"

Dandio paused on a landing, allowing Darion past, and looked back up at her. "Once the bridges are destroyed, it should be trapped here. Or, better yet, it will fall into the Patch with the ruins."

The Bruin roared and slammed its shoulder into the wall across from them. The castle shuddered, and an ominous groan came from above. Hairline cracks spread over the tower ceiling.

"Quickly…" Ĵan's low voice urged from behind.

At the front of the group, Darion hesitated at the broken edge of the stairs. Cautiously, he lowered Mel's still form to the other side, then dropped down after him. Dandio came next—Allie saw his green eyes move up to the ceiling above.

"Go!" he urged. "Go now—the tower—"

A resounding crack split the air around them. The stairs shook as another piece of marble landed just behind Allie. She dropped down to the next step after Darion, not daring to look back. Out of the corner of her eye she saw Redeyes leap around the Bruin's claws, urging it to greater destruction. The Bruin let out a rumbling roar and barreled against the wall again, and the ceiling crumpled around them.

"Leap clear!" Ĵan shouted behind her.

The tower gave way, crashing down into the castle. Piles of marble and stone thundered to the ground floor, crushing the ruined walls, shattering the flights of stairs. The wall at Allie's right bowed inwards, and for an instant she wondered if it would fall and flatten them. Instead, it lurched back again and broke in pieces. The remaining stairway went with it, and Allie felt herself falling.

She sprang to the left as the wall crumbled, falling with the rubble to the ground floor. Stones crashed around her as she fell to her side.

Winded, she crawled for cover. Her side ached where she'd landed, but she'd made it down to the ground floor. Gasping for breath, she raised her head, looking desperately for her companions.

Castle Droco was littered in rubble. Only the remains of the walls still stood, a quarter of their original height, surviving only because the Bruin seemed to have tired of smashing them. With the open air and the tall walls framing the rubble, the space appeared as a large courtyard.

The dust settled around her. Darion, she saw, had managed to leap onto one of the rubble heaps, where he sat with Mel. He'd maintained his grip on the unconsious boy, protecting him from the drop, but he had clearly landed awkwardly. One leg was stretched out before him, and his face was twisted in pain.

Dandio crouched near him, his face pale, his eyes rapidly scanning the area. Jan and Rygal had both fallen behind Allie. They were plastered in dust, and Rygal was bleeding from a cut on his scalp, but they were both alive.

"It is finished, master!"

The triumphant voice rang out over the ruin. A familiar hatred lit in Allie's chest as she heard it, and she peered through the destruction, seeking the speaker. She had not known that the Ace-Deputy had returned.

The Bruin stood, huffing and heaving, its huge head nosing through the rubble. The archway to the north bridge was abandoned, and Allie could just see the group of soldiers waiting on the bridge outside. They seemed torn between escaping with their lives or entering the castle to help. Dandio noticed them and gestured firmly for them to go. They would be little help now—their best hope was to race to Badwater, get word to Admiral Dessian—

"Castle Droco is no more," the Ace-Deputy announced, his voice echoing over the stones. He stood by the opening that had once led to the main gate. His pale armor shimmered in the fog, his half-decayed face alight with victory. "The last remnant of my lord's past defeat has been erased from the mortal world. Our conquest begins anew!"

He practically shouted into the sky, as though the Ace-Lord could hear him from wherever he was. The tone of his voice was almost desperate, as though he were pleading for approval or notice. It had to hurt his pride, Allie thought, that the Ace-Lord could not be troubled to witness the Deputy's victory here.

"Go to the bridge," Dandio ordered quietly, getting to his feet, "now, while they are distracted."

He took Mel from Darion's arms. Rygal moved to join him, supporting the injured ranger. Allie stood up stiffly, forcing her legs to move. They were almost out. Almost out. How familiar this was, she thought bitterly, just as it had been the last time here, when they'd run desperately for the exit, while fear and rage crackled in her veins and Jan carried Drisilas behind her.

"Be freed, Bruin of old," the Deputy cried, raising his withered hands. The beast's huge head swung to face him, its hollow eyes riveted on him. "Follow the Messenger from this place, and bring the mortal world to destruction."

A smile crossed Redeyes' face. The Bruin gave a low rumble, and began to move toward the entrance.

"No!"

The firm voice split the silence. Allie swung around. Jan strode into the center of the ruined castle, Drisilas blazing white flames in his hand, facing the Deputy. "That is not how it will be," he stated. "Your business is with me alone, not the people of Orlell. It is I who bear the curse, I who warped the Stone—and it is I who will atone for it."

Something heavy seemed to hit Allie in the chest, and she fought for a breath. "No!" she cried, feeling afresh the bitter remembrance of their last escape. She would not allow him to stand alone this time.

Jan stepped toward the Ace-Deputy, his head held high. His voice, calm yet strong, filled the castle, as though the very stones were listening to his words. "I corrupted the Stone, long ago, in an act of vengeance. For this act I was cursed. I have come now to reconcile it."

Redeyes gave a low purr of pleasure and stalked forward. The Deputy stopped him. "Atone for it, High King?" he repeated with a short laugh. "The price to rid the curse is death, death alone. Do you believe your life will save your feeble subjects, that they will be permitted to leave here?"

Allie stumbled forward, forcing her weary legs to run faster, to weave around the heaps of rubble. Her feet slipped on the broken rock, and she fell forward.

But Jan shook his head, a slight, sad smile on his face. "I believed once that death would end the curse. I believed there to be no other recourse, after my actions. Yet I have come to understand that such a curse holds no weight, not without true judgment. And so death it will be," he said, raising his voice. "Death it must be, as the Prophecy demands. But not by your terms, but by the will of the High Light alone." He cast Drisilas aside. The blade struck the stone floor, lying smoldering quietly on the ground.

Allie watched in both fear and awe. Cahadras' words seemed to echo in Jan's voice, and this time she understood.

Redeyes growled in hatred. The Deputy's face turned livid. "Fool," he hissed, striding forward. "Do you forget your crimes? Your actions that bind you to this curse?"

Jan did not flinch. "You may take my life," he said calmly. "But it does not change your fate. You are bound to it, as you are bound to the Prophecy."

"Bound?" the Ace-Deputy snarled, seizing Jan by the throat and hauling him close. Allie got to her feet with a cry, fire blazing in her hands, but she was too far away—too late. "Do you know what I believe is best to reckon with such bonds? I believe we must break them—cast them off—if my master seeks to act within the Prophecy, I am not the one to question his plan—but as for me, I will act as

I see fit, and my master will behold the victory I bring when the bonds are broken. Just as I shall break you."

White ice glistened on his fingertips—Allie launched herself forward, hearing Dandio's shout of rage as he ran to Jan's side—too late, her mind repeated bitterly, too late to help. Jan would die.

"No mortal is innocent," the Deputy hissed, as Jan gasped in pain. "For your actions you will atone, and for their actions, they will bear a similar curse, and all Orlell shall bow before the weight of the Ace-Lord's judgment."

He raised his free hand, preparing the fatal blow.

"Stop!"

The deep voice thundered icy cold over the castle, chilling the air where Allie stood. A voice she had heard so many times, in a tone usually so calm and gentle, comforting in its certainty—yet now that voice stopped her in her tracks, and she turned.

Iriam strode forward through the wreckage, covered in dust so that he appeared almost ghostly, a single line of his violet blood streaking his face. Ice shattered the stones at his feet as he raised a hand, pointing at the Deputy. "You cannot break those bonds," he stated. "Your master is wiser than you, if you believe such ties can be severed."

The Deputy flung Jan back and rounded on the Neutral. His voice, usually so smooth and persuasive, was nearly shrill with hate. "This will be my victory!" he shouted. "We need not wait for the corruption of the mortals, not when they can so easily be cursed by their own actions. The Bruin will rise, and destroy the mortal world you have sought so long to protect. There will be no protection from the curse, no promise of the Prophecy, not without you to guard it, Neutral."

The Deputy raised his hands again. But a rare smile had flickered over Iriam's face like firelight, sending hopeful chills down Allie's spine. The air suddenly crackled with expectancy.

"I," Iriam said, "am not the only one who guards the promises of the Light."

A trumpet blast shook the air. Allie covered her ears, wincing, but not in fear. Redeyes' ears flattened to his skull. The Ace-Deputy looked up sharply, his face white.

Plumes of fire rained from the sky, streaming down like liquid gold. Descending upon the ruin was an army of Stars, golden flames alight on their brows and palms and shining on their blades. They landed on the heaps of rubble, alighted on the walls, launching fire from their hands as they attacked the Bruin.

Allie heard the Ace-Deputy screaming orders, thought she saw Redeyes snarling and slashing, but they were far outnumbered. The Dal-kerri turned tail and fled before the unexpected fiery army. The enchanted soldiers stood confused and uncertain for a moment, shielding their hollow eyes from the dazzling light, until at the Deputy's command, they retreated through the gate, springing into the shadows of the Patch below to escape the pure golden light.

Redeyes hesitated a moment longer, his hateful gaze on Jan. For an instant Allie saw him tense to spring and tear her uncle's throat—but his fear of fire won, and he bounded for the bridge and the void below.

The Ace-Deputy retreated slowly, reluctantly, white ice shooting from his hands. He struck down two Stars; Allie saw them fall lifeless, but he was far outmatched. A tall Star landed before him, fire blazing from her hands as she clashed with the white ice. Cahadras' fierce gaze was fixed on the Deputy's, her fire crackling and searing his withered skin. At last the Deputy broke away and sprang into the Patch.

Only the Bruin remained, bellowing and slashing at the fiery warriors. It trampled over the piles of rubble, blundering into the crumbling walls, claws raking the air.

Allie kept her eyes on the huge beast as she ran forward to her uncle. Jan knelt where the Deputy had stood, watching the Stars in disbelief and awe. Allie dropped down next to him, staring at the blazing warriors. The brilliant light dazzled her weary eyes, but she could not look away.

Glentree still waited on the bridge with a handful of soldiers, staring spellbound at the army of Stars. At Dandio's order, he fell back. Rygal and Darion reached him; Allie saw a soldier carry Mel to safety.

Dandio crouched beside Allie and Jan, staring at the Stars. "Never thought they would come," he breathed. "I never thought… they would be sent to fight."

"They must uphold the Prophecy," came Iriam's voice behind them. The Neutral stood watching the fiery battle. "To claim the right to judge the mortals, to use the Bruin to exact such judgment—that defied the Prophecy's words, and for that, the High Light will have justice."

The Bruin staggered, icy fangs snapping at the Stars, then, with one last groan, it collapsed in a cloud of toxic fog. Iriam stepped forward, generating a shield of deep blue ice, protecting the three Liznees as the fog wrapped around them. Allie huddled beside Jan, listening as the massive Dal-kerri's roars faded away into echoes.

Then all was still.

The Stars stood in the ruined courtyard. The fire still blazed around their heads like golden crowns, but the battle had been won. A few tended to their fallen, for despite their strength, the white ice of the Aces had claimed some lives.

"Come," Iriam said quietly, standing. "You as well, Asescia. There is something we must do."

Allie got to her feet, walking toward the waiting Stars. She felt very small beside the two Liznees and Iriam—small, and exposed somehow before the shining beings.

Cahadras stepped forward to meet them, clad in gleaming armor, her piercing eyes studying them each in turn. Jan bowed low before her. "My queen. I have come to reconcile the curse."

Cahadras studied him. Her tone held neither gentleness nor accusation; she simply stated the facts. "There was a time you hid the truth, son of Galaruel. A time you sought to rid yourself of the curse through other means."

"I did," Jan replied. "Ironically, it was the Aces themselves who revealed to me the truth. Their plan to corrupt the mortals begins with our scars. To be rid of that curse, the mortals would do anything—anything the Ace-Lord wished. I can understand that now," he added, with a small, sad smile. "But though the Ace-Lord would have had me pay for the curse with my life, I will not do so. Not on his terms, but through the High Light's plan, if my death is required."

Allie looked at him worriedly. Cahadras' eyes scanned Jan's face. "You indeed bear a curse, a curse for which you are not innocent," she informed him calmly. "It is you who turned the Stone into what it was never meant to be."

Jan bowed his head. "I cannot excuse my actions."

"I can," Dandio said, stepping forward. "My Queen—the law of the High Light is good and just, and demands atonement. But it also speaks of mercy, and of wrong being redeemed for good. My brother twisted the Stone's magic at a time where we both desired vengeance. But since that moment, he has used those powers for Isilas' true purpose—to protect and defend the innocent."

Cahadras' gaze flicked to Iriam. "Is this true?"

"You know it to be true, Cahadras," Iriam replied. "Though wrong has been done, right has come about through it, as the High Light wills."

"I cannot defend my actions," Ĵan said. "My task was to guard the Stone as its Wielder, not to turn it into a weapon of war." He lifted Drisilas, studying the white fires. "If there is yet hope to right those actions, please, tell us."

"That will be revealed in time," Cahadras answered. "The Prophecy is set into motion. The second stage is completed; the third has now begun. For that, I believe, the burden falls to another."

Her piercing eyes regarded Ĵan for a moment. "The damage inflicted upon the Stone is irreversible, High King. I trust you know this."

Ĵan bowed his head. "I know it."

"The price to be rid of the curse cannot be changed," Cahadras said. "To twist the magic of Isilas, to corrupt it into a weapon—that bears a great price, a price I cannot alter. Your life indeed is forfeit."

A stab of fear went to Allie's heart. She saw the color drain from Dandio's face; one hand went to his sword. Iriam looked very grave. Ĵan raised his face, his expression calm and measured.

"A price must be paid," Cahadras said again, quieter. "A price, High King, that you have paid many times over. What your brother has said is true. Though it was you who first corrupted the Stone, it is you who have sought to redeem that choice. Isilas has been used, once again, to protect and guard your people. You have spent your life keeping it so, though the struggle is great, and there are many you have lost."

She touched the blade of the sword lightly. "Yes, you have paid for the curse with your life, as the Ace-Lord would require. If the Stone is to be made whole, it is you who must right those wrongs."

Jan studied the sword. Drisilas' fire played on his face for a moment before he held it out to Cahadras. "Take it, then. Take the Stone from the blade, that its purpose might be used again for good."

Allie watched wordlessly. Cahadras laid her hand upon the Star-Stone, drawing it out of the hilt as easily as if it answered to her touch.

Drisilas' fire went out abruptly, and it lay in Jan's hands, a blackened blade streaked in ash and blood. He slid it back into the scabbard as gently as though laying a loved one to rest.

"The curse has been atoned," Cahadras said. In her hand, the Stone shone pale white. "For the corruption to fade, the words of the Prophecy must yet come to pass, lest another price be required of you." A case made of liquid fire formed around the Stone, solidifying in solid gold. The soft glow of the Stone reflected on its golden casing. "Return the Stone to Sia," Cahadras said, laying the case in Jan's hand. "Let it remain untouched, protecting and shielding your people until winter comes. In that time, the role of the Wielder must again be filled, or the Ace-Lord shall forge his own to claim Isilas."

"How?" Dandio asked uncertainly behind her. "Who should that be?"

"The choice will be clear in that time," Cahadras replied calmly.

"The Prophecy goes before you." Her eyes scanned the group of survivors retreating for the gate. "Now, where is the New Blood?"

"Mel yet lives," Ĵan said. "He still has the Blue Stone, but he will not wake."

"The Aces have many ways of harming the mind," Iriam said. "But he might be healed by your hand."

Cahadras was silent a moment. "I will tend him," she said finally, a soft smile touching her serious face for a moment, "as I tended the mortals in the elder days. He must protect the last Star-Stone, if there is yet any hope."

Iriam and the two Liznees bowed to her, and Allie quickly did the same. Dandio straightened, studying Cahadras hesitantly. "My Queen—might I ask a question. I know the Stars joined the mortals in the Dividing War, allied with us against the Aces. Might a time such as this require the same?"

Cahadras looked at Ĵan. "The alliance is renewed by the events of this day," she said. "But our forces will not join you in battle, not, at least, until we are commanded thus by the Lord of Light. This war, and the promises of the Prophecy, are not for us to interfere. If such a time comes that we are commanded here, know that we will fight. In the meantime, there are other allies, other peoples who have yet come, other Messengers of the High Light who will make themselves known at last."

Allie looked up, interested by this implication. Ĵan bowed to her. "Then we look forward to that time."

"Thank you, Cahadras," Iriam said, and with a final bow he headed toward the bridge.

Allie hesitated as the men moved away. "My lady," she said finally, unable to hold back the question. "When you met me in the wilderness—you said that the Ace-Lord will be defeated by the very ones he seeks to conquer. How will we do that?"

"That is not for me to say, child," Cahadras answered. "Seek your answers in the Prophecy. But know this, at least—it is by his own magic that the Ace-Lord will be defeated, and in his own spells will he be snared."

Allie thought this over, unsure what it meant, but sensing, for the first time, the hope in her words. "Thank you, my lady," she said, knowing better than to ask any more questions.

After all, she knew, it was unwise to anger a Star.

<h1 style="text-align:center">40</h1>

ㅇ ㅇ ㅇ ㅇ ㅇ ㅇ ㅇ ㅇ ㅇ

<h2 style="text-align:center">Mortal Bound</h2>

The time has come, time has come, time has come

The heart betrays what must be done.

Hope and death, victory and destruction, interwoven in equal parts in the words. Allie's mind dwelt on them, mulled over them, thought back on them until the rhythm was stuck in her head. It gave her something to think about on the slow journey back to Caer Sia, helped distract from the lingering horror of battle.

When Nameless New Blood knows their call,

If mortal heart remains unmarred,

When Lord of Death brings life to all,

The spell that bound leaves deeper scars,

Than the Shadow that awakened.

Bound, her mind echoed. The Prophecy bound the Aces, and it bound the mortals. Were they not all tied to this fate regardless? With or without the Prophecy's words, they were bound to fight this war through, bound to play the Ace-Lord's game. She could almost feel the icy chains wrapped around her, crushing tighter and tighter.

The stuffy quarters of the *Blue Moon* rocked and creaked around her, seeming to press down on her. In a flash, her mind returned to the void, as she fought against the tearing wind and struggled between two worlds.

Needing air, she climbed out of her hammock, careful not to wake the resting soldiers. Most of the wounded were on Dandio's ship, the *Gryphon*, but there were a great many who could not fit there. Several still bodies lay at the far end of the berth deck, clinging to life. The medics had done what they could do to help them until they returned to Caer Sia; Allie heard the faint groans of pain from a few restless injured.

Chilly wind blew her hair back from her face as she walked on deck. Sailors and soldiers milled about; she heard Admiral Dessian calling orders from the helm. To her right, the coastline of Coonsia stretched away, rising in the craggy mountains that surrounded the valley of Sia.

She peered across the water, trying to make out any details. How long had it been since she'd seen home? Three, four weeks? She wasn't sure. So many times during this trip she'd feared she'd never return. Languishing in the Ace-Lord's dungeons, fleeing through the forest from the Dal-kerri, toiling through the void—they were all interwoven with that fear of never returning home to Castle Sia.

Jan stood near the rail, looking towards the distant peaks, and turned as she approached. "Good morning. Rest well?"

Allie nodded. "Are you feeling better today?"

Jan smiled slightly. "Thanks to you. Mel and I owe you our lives. How did you learn you can pass through the voids?"

"I didn't really know for certain," Allie admitted. "It was mostly a guess, and a hope."

Jan shook his head, but she could tell he was impressed. "A reckless decision, maybe, but I am grateful for it all the same."

"How's Mel?" Allie asked fearfully. Mel's still form lay aboard the *Gryphon*. Cahadras had promised to heal him once they reached Caer Sia, but Allie had begun to fear he wouldn't last that long.

"No change thus far," Jan answered. "Actually, he may have improved slightly thanks to the Blue Stone. But I fear only Cahadras will be able to help him."

Allie tried to ignore the worry in the pit of her stomach. Mel was alive. He would awake in Caer Sia, and then Aryion would come with the rest of his family. Or perhaps Aryion would return before Mel woke up, so that he'd awake with his family beside him. That thought almost made her smile.

It had been two days since the battle at Castle Droco. They'd rested in Badwater, grateful there was no threat of pursuit from the Aces. Castle Droco remained a rugged ruin, rising above the dense tangle of wilderness. But the Aces no longer lurked there, though the Patch around the ruin was unchanged. "It will close when the Ace-Lord is defeated," Iriam had assured them, when Dandio had voiced his concern about it. "Until then, I fear, the void will remain."

The illusion around the castle had faded when the Aces left, leaving the broken white walls visible. It was lovely, in a haunting sort of way.

Clouds hung heavy in the sky over Caer Sia as the *Blue Moon* and *Gryphon* coasted into the bay. Watery sunlight glinted from the windows of Castle Sia and the arching structures in the heart of the city. The clamor of day-to-day life reached Allie's ears from the harbor; the shouts and calls, the clatter of thousands of carriages, the voices from countless conversations.

How strange it was that life continued so normally here, when elsewhere, people fought and bled and died to maintain this peace. Even stranger that she had longed for that very fight only a few weeks ago.

A garrison of soldiers met them by the harbor, and set to work helping transfer the wounded into carriages bound for the nearest hospitals. Mel would be treated in the healing rooms of Castle Sia, allowing for more privacy and care.

A familiar foxlike face with golden eyes caught Allie's eye as she walked down the gangplank. "General Arrex—you made it back!"

Arrex gave her a tired smile. "Only a few hours prior, Heiress. I am very glad to see you have all returned. Had we known what transpired—"

"None of that, General," Jan said firmly. "My choices had already placed too many in danger. I would have never wanted your men involved too."

"We heard you were captured by the Aces, your highness," one of the soldiers said, his voice thick with emotion. "Sire—it is very good to see you alive."

"You as well, corporal," Ĵan replied with a slight smile.

Rain began falling softly as the last of the wounded were transported away. Allie drew her cloak around her, so tired she felt she could hardly stand. Two carriages arrived to carry her, Dandio, Ĵan, Rygal, Darion, and Iriam to the castle. She rested her head against the window, watching as the buildings and roads sped by.

Despite her weariness, she felt on edge. Even simple things seemed somehow sinister. A group of soldiers moved through a crowded marketplace, hands on their sword hilts. Three cloaked men slumped in the awning of a towering building. A child was knocked down by his larger companions.

Weeks of being in danger seemed to have ingrained a fear and distrust in her, making it difficult to relax even now that she was home safely.

They reached the castle. There were twice the usual number of guards on the walls; she saw the tension and unease in their stances. What must the last several weeks have been like for the commonwealth of Caer Sia? How many had known the truth of what had happened in Wiverrun, of how close the Ace-Lord had come to victory? Or had these men only heard rumors, and their minds had sculpted them into fears?

She distantly heard Dandio giving orders. Servants took Mel up to the hospital, and she heard Ĵan argue against going for treatment himself. Eventually the king was persuaded; despite his outward recovery, Allie knew he was far wearier than he would admit, and his wounds were still fresh.

"When will Cahadras come?" she asked.

"When she is ordered," Iriam answered.

"What if that's too late?" Allie heard the doubt in her voice, but she couldn't help it. Though the Stars had destroyed the Bruin, it troubled her that they had not come sooner. Even more mortals could have died—many mortals—and they would have simply let it happen.

"She will come, Heiress," Iriam said. His tone held a gentle reprimand. "She has promised to heal Mel, and so she will. But our matters here are insignificant compared to others."

He studied her a moment. Allie didn't feel like questioning him further, but he continued. "There is something else I must discuss with you, Asescia. I will allow the king time to rest and recover, but then we must speak."

Allie nodded, too tired to feel any curiosity. She could guess what Iriam wanted to talk about. He'd had that almost fearful look in his eyes ever since she'd revealed her powers. His uncertainty should concern her more than it did, but she wasn't sure what he was worried about. While the darkness of her powers was disturbing, it had allowed her to save Jan and Mel. Besides, if the Ace-Lord's intent was to create a new Wielder of Isilas, she had no reason to ever touch it again.

Unless, as she had begun to suspect, there was another purpose behind those powers…

Whatever that purpose could be, Allie decided, she didn't want to think about it now. She walked up the stairs to her room. The space had a strange, empty sort of feel to it. She lay down, needing the respite a few hour's sleep would provide. But sleep would not come. Even in the darkness her closed eyes provided, her mind spiraled back into the void, where she stood on the strange arching bridge and felt the blackness close around her.

Vessel...

The voice whispered in her dreams, dying into echoes.

Vessel... Life-Blood... Mortal bound, bound, bound...

Bound by fate, by war, by the Prophecy. Invisible chains surrounded her in the darkness, tightening as though to break her in two.

. . . . . .

When Allie woke, the rain had stopped and a dreary afternoon sunlight shone through the window. Muted sounds had awakened her, and she tensed, reaching involuntarily for her sword, still half asleep and unable to register the sounds. People were talking softly to each other, shuffling past. Dishes clinked somewhere beyond her room. All were completely normal, harmless sounds.

Taking a breath to steady her racing heart, she stood and stretched. She hadn't bothered to change clothes before lying down, and now changed into a clean dress. She ran a comb unsuccessfully through her tangled hair, and washed her face in the basin. The cold water refreshed her, though the grime around her fingernails and scalp would need a more thorough washing.

She headed down the short hall. The servants she passed greeted her with smiles that showed their relief at seeing her alive. The familiar faces, sounds, and smells helped ease her nerves. She was home. Home, and safe for the time being.

Darion met her at the base of the stairs. His injured leg was bound tightly, and he moved with a limp. "How are you feeling?" he asked.

"A little sore," Allie admitted. "How's your leg?"

"Stiff, but the nurse said the sprain will heal," Darion answered. "Iriam wanted to talk to you. He and the Star Queen are waiting."

Allie looked at him sharply. "Cahadras is here?"

"Yes, we're all meeting in the council room. I don't know what it's about, but they asked me to find you," Darion said. He looked more curious than worried, but Allie felt a twinge of unease.

"Who's all here?" she asked, following him down another corridor—he moved slowly.

"The High King and your father, and Rygal," Darion answered her. "Iriam seems more serious than usual, so it must be important."

Mel.

Her stomach dropped. "Darion—did Cahadras treat Mel?"

Darion noticed her pale face and guessed what she feared. "It's not Mel. Cahadras went to treat him earlier. He's still in the hospital wing, but it sounds like he's doing better."

Allie let out a sigh of relief, more curious than afraid now that Darion had assured her of Mel's improvement.

They reached the council hall. Three guards stood outside the doors, but they allowed them inside without question. More soldiers patrolled the hall. The Red Dawn knights, it seemed, were determined not to allow their king to fall into danger again.

Five people waited inside. Jan was seated at the head of the table. Iriam stood to the left, a tall shadow beside Cahadras' shining form. Dandio and Rygal sat beside Jan, their faces showing the same intrigue Allie felt.

A glance at Iriam brought her unease back. The Neutral's face was grave, and his expression showed both concern and sorrow as he studied her.

Iriam spoke as soon as the doors closed behind them. "Sit down, child. Master Blackbird, you may stay as well."

"Is Mel all right?" Allie demanded.

"Sit, Asescia," Iriam said. "Mel is recovering."

Allie sat down; Darion remained standing, looking unsure. "I thought it would be more time before we arranged another attack," he said with a glance at Dandio.

"It is not for matters of war that I asked you here," Iriam answered. "This is a dark matter. I trust the subject will remain among those present, with the exception of Ajaha," he added, looking at Dandio.

Dandio nodded. "She has been delayed in Mata City—war in the north has erupted. The rebel Direns and their forces marched against the allies of Gayrile. Ajaha and Lord Roan are working with Lammar to try to salvage the alliances before the matter gets any further out of hand."

"The rebels attacked?" Allie repeated, stunned. She remembered what Jarus had mentioned before the council in Mata City, about the rebel Direns trying to use the confusion of the Ace-War to win back their lands. But she had no idea they would dare attack their countrymen, not in a time like this, when so much was at stake.

"They've attacked Flameton, according to Lammar's reports," Dandio said. "That was two days ago. Since then, the rebels have fallen back into the Wandering Wood. They might strike against the humans in Bridgeport, but it seems the loyal Brownae tribes are holding them back."

"These matters must be discussed later," Cahadras said firmly. "We must discuss the Ace-Lord, and the Heiress."

Allie's questions about the war in Gayrile evaporated. She looked at Cahadras, confused. "Me?"

The Star's blue eyes seemed to bore into her own, as though Cahadras could see her thoughts. "Tell us, Heiress. During your captivity among the Aces, you were brought before the Ace-Lord, were you not?"

Allie nodded slowly. "Yes. He gave me Drisilas, and spoke some sort of spell—an enchantment. I think that's what made me able to wield the sword, and kill the enchanted soldiers… because he wanted me to be the Wielder of Isilas."

Again, she wondered why that mattered. Isilas was corrupted, but until it was Wielded by someone again, it was not much use to the Ace-Lord.

"Can you recall the words of the spell he spoke?" Cahadras asked.

Allie racked her thoughts, trying to remember. "He held my head… it all went blurry and dark for a minute… I can't remember," she admitted finally, shuddering at the memory.

"I can assume what they were," Iriam said quietly, and spoke, his deep voice sending chills down Allie's spine: "*Aranac, devariss, vey dovannon.*"

The words filled Allie's mind, as they had when the Ace-Lord had spoken them while white fog filled her mind. She'd heard them there, in that tower, while ice spread down her throat and clutched her heart.

"Were these the words, Asescia?" Iriam asked.

She nodded, suddenly unable to speak.

"What does that mean, Iriam?" Jan asked, his brow furrowed. "Is that the spell the Ace-Lord used to give her the powers to wield the Stone?"

"That was only a portion of it," Iriam replied. "The words are in the ancient Netrocrian tongue. It is an old spell, perhaps created by Kahlifis himself. We may not know the truth of its origins. What we do know is that it is very rare, its use only appearing once or twice throughout all of history. It is called the Life-Blood spell."

The chills running down Allie's spine turned to cold hands, wrapping around her. "I—I've heard that before," she said haltingly. "In the Patch. There was a voice speaking—it said 'Life-Blood' and 'vessel' and something about a mortal bound… but I didn't know what that meant."

"I do, now," Iriam said. "I had suspected it when you first came to

Mata City. Your account of your powers, the white fire of Drisilas, and primarily, your ability to kill the enchanted, made it all the clearer. But not until now do I know for certain." He took a breath. "The words of the spell, if spoken in the Coonsian tongue, would mean this: *Death bound, vessel of strength, life bound to life.*"

Bound, Allie's mind echoed, and felt the icy chains drawing close.

"Bound?" Dandio repeated, an edge in his voice. "What does this mean?"

"It means," Iriam said quietly, "that the Ace-Lord has chosen her as his vessel for the Life-Blood spell. A portion of his power fills Asescia, giving her the ability to kill the enchanted and to warp the Star-Stone. As long as the Heiress lives, so will the Ace-Lord's power grow. His hand has bound you, and his hand alone may release you, and thus is the snare of the Life-Blood spell. Whoever casts it is the only one who may release it, and only by death may the vessel be freed. And if the caster is killed, then the one they bound must follow them to death."

Allie's mouth was dry, but she managed the words. "So I have to die, if we're going to win."

"No. If you died, the Ace-Lord would lose the power vested in you, which would certainly weaken him, but he would not share your death. Though the spell would be broken, the Ace-Lord would live on, having gained nothing besides breaking the resolve of those who care about you," Iriam said gravely. "It is a two-fold curse. The Ace-Lord ensures his invulnerability as long as you live, for if, by some magic he is killed, so will you die. He also ensures that you remain alive long enough to do as he wishes, and every one of your actions will aid his plot of corruption."

"But he no longer has the Stones," Jan said, and the desperation in his voice tore at Allie's heart. "Why does he see the need for such a strategy?"

"There are other means by which the Ace-Lord's conquest might succeed," Iriam said. "While the Star-Stones are needed to open the Dark Realm, the Ace-Lord has likely been seeking an alternative ever since Mel first defeated him. He knows we will never willingly give up the Star-Stones. Thus, he will corrupt the mortals, break them down until they accept his rule to end the bloodshed. The process will be slow, but he has more time than we. The Life-Blood Spell is a risk he now sees fit to take."

Cahadras spoke, her voice grave. "The hearts of the mortals are fragile things. Asescia is the Heiress. Her actions, her fear, her anger, will gradually strengthen the Ace-Lord. Others may turn against her, acting wrongly in their own turn out of fear. The darkness gifted to her will showcase the Ace-Lord's strength, causing some to turn to his side."

What Cahadras described was even worse than the spell itself. Allie sought for something, anything to prove them wrong, to deny the truth of the curse. But every memory only proved they were correct. The escape from Castle Droco—she'd been the one they had tried to keep from escaping. The fight on the bridge—one of the guards had slashed at her, and it had been Redeyes who had knocked him into the Patch, protecting his master's vessel. The power to kill the enchanted soldiers—the Ace-Lord's powers thrived on the lust for revenge that lurked in her heart. The power to pass through the voids, the way she was unaffected by the illusions, the way Drisilas had blazed white fire at her touch…

And of course, the reason the Aces had allowed her to free Jan and Mel. By now, the Ace-Lord had realized the only way they would serve his plans was if they were broken down, corrupted… and she would be his vessel to bring that corruption about.

Every one of her actions had been within the Ace-Lord's plan. Now, she was nothing more than his pawn, twisted to serve him.

"Though Mortal be unwilling; A spell has made the binding," Cahadras quoted, and for the first time, Allie detected sympathy in her voice. "The mortal is often unwilling in the transaction of the Life-Blood spell. That is why they are allowed death as a way to escape its clutches. But the mortal's death will not bring about victory. Only the death of the one who casts the spell will do that."

"Surely there's a way to break the spell," Rygal interjected. "Iriam— surely there's some way."

"There is none, son of Maran," Iriam said gently. "Only the Ace-Lord's own magic may remove the spell from Allie."

He so rarely called her that name. Her heart ached at the pain on his face, the same pain reflected in the expressions of the others in the room.

"How do we counter this?" Jan said, standing so abruptly his chair slid backward behind him. "I refuse to accept this as our fate. If the Prophecy tells of this curse, what does it advise us to do?"

"There is nothing that can counter the Life-Blood spell," Iriam said. "However, the Ace-Lord's plan is based largely on what he believes we will do—and the actions of mortals are often unpredictable. He expects far too much to occur. Thus, even in the binding, his own curse will backfire with every right choice Asescia makes."

"There aren't many of my good choices to help much," Allie said, forcing a wry smile.

"Nonetheless, the Prophecy will guide you," Cahadras said. "Its words regarding the bound mortal are now clear. A choice is still before you, as written: *When willing warrior be gone at dawn; Ace-Lord, mortal, together one.*"

Lest the Shadow ever thrive, Allie's mind finished.

"So she's marked for death, then?" Dandio demanded, his voice torn in desperation. "Either by escaping the Life-Blood spell, or at the time that thrice-accursed death lord has appointed for her?"

"The Ace-Lord does not appoint death, contrary to his own belief," Cahadras answered him. "I tell you this for your benefit, not your aggravation, son of Galaruel. The time has come. The heart will betray. Truth is the only constant."

The responsibility settled on Allie like a massive weight. She took a deep breath. "I—I won't use my powers for the Ace-Lord. I'm not going to play his pawn," she said firmly.

A rare smile flickered over Cahadras' serious face. "That resolve will serve you well, child," she said softly. "I pray your integrity will remain, no matter how dark and difficult the future may become."

Allie glanced at the others. The helpless fury had faded from her father's eyes; only sorrow remained as he looked at her. Ĵan's face was rigid with anger. Darion looked stunned. Rygal's brow was furrowed; she could guess he was searching for some strategy that would release her. Something that would break the bond the Ace-Lord had cast upon her.

She knew there was no such release. She knew it by one look at Iriam's expression.

"I will consult the Star rulers," Cahadras said after a pause. "If this curse is even slightly against the words of the Prophecy, know that we will strike. I will return by tomorrow's eve."

"Thank you, Cahadras," Iriam said.

The meeting was over. Nothing else was said, no futile words of comfort or quiet. Allie felt the fire stirring again in her heart, angry, helpless fire. Yet cooling the flames were the icy chains, which she could feel slowly tightening around her, clawing at her every breath.

41

No Words

A gray dawn greeted Allie the next morning, as though the storm of her confused and angry thoughts were a physical thing. Everything before yesterday's fateful meeting with Iriam and Cahadras felt a lifetime away, as though it had been lived by another person. Some of it had, in a way. Who she had been before the Ace-Lord had bound her with his spell, and who she was now, had only her name and body in common.

She had slept very little, and decided to head the library to avoid any conversations. Rain splattered the windows as she sat, a large book in her lap, the way she had weeks ago on the day Darion had first come. The day everything had changed.

As it had happened then, it was Rygal's voice that drew her out of her dark thoughts. "Allie?"

She glanced over. Rygal stood in the doorway, Darion behind him. The concerned looks on their faces sent an unwelcome flare of irritation. There was nothing they could do or say to fix what was done. Why try to pretend otherwise?

She pushed the feeling away. "How's Mel?" she asked shortly.

Cahadras had been confident that Mel would wake soon on his

own after she had left. When Allie had checked on him last night, a little color had returned to his face, and his eyes were closed. Whatever dark coma he'd been in while a captive of the Aces had been replaced by quiet sleep.

"He's still resting," Darion said. "Cahadras might check on him today."

"Is she back?"

"No," Rygal answered. "Did you want to talk to her?"

Not particularly, Allie thought, but she just shrugged slightly.

Thankfully, neither of them asked about the curse, or inquired into the web of her conflicted thoughts. "There will be another meeting in a few hours," Rygal said. "Your mother had sent more agents to the south a few weeks ago, and they've returned today with a report for Jan."

Allie looked at him uneasily. "More news?"

"This news sounds good, at least," Darion said quickly. "Kamon's warriors are blocking the southern end of the Strait, and the Coopers have the northern end protected, so the Aces won't be able to travel by sea. And the Guardians are coming to Caer Sia, right?" he added with a glance at Rygal.

Rygal nodded. "Yes, Lammar's working on a strategy to stop the rebel Direns. We'll strike back soon, I think. And without Castle Droco, the Ace-Lord's lost important ground in that region."

The Ace-Lord had always intended to destroy Castle Droco, Allie thought, since the ruin had served its purpose. But they both looked so desperate to cheer her up that she didn't have the heart to remind them of that.

"Well, that's good," she said, closing the book and rising.

Rygal nodded to the large tome. "What's that?"

Allie let out a breath. "More history. I wanted to look and see if there's any records of the Life-Blood spell in the past, and what it led to." Just talking about the spell made her feel sick. It reminded her of the darkness that hung over her, of the source of the new power within her. She felt corrupted, like poison in a bottle of wine.

"Any luck?" Darion asked.

"Not in this one," Allie admitted, "but this book only covers the last century or so. I think I'll have to look further back than that."

"I have some spell books you can look through also," Rygal offered. "They're Guardian spells, mostly, but there are some old ones they referenced as well."

"I appreciate that," Allie said, glancing away, "but you know those books probably won't have anything about dark magic. The Guardians' spells rely on the High Light, not the Ace-Lord's power."

"It could be worth looking, all the same," Rygal said softly. "Who knows... maybe the Guardians wrote about counter-spells when they wrote about fireforms."

"Fireforms... you'll have to teach me a few of those," Darion said with a slight grin. "Lighting fires to keep the Dal-kerri back is one thing—being able to create your own fire arrows may be even more helpful."

"Fire's tricky," Rygal told him. "All I can make are sparks, and that's after months of practice."

"Well, I've got time," Darion said, shrugging his shoulders. "Redeyes hates fire. I'd like to keep it that way."

Allie smiled slightly. Their lighthearted banter eased a little of the burden in her mind.

A blare of trumpets startled her, and she clutched her sword hilt before recognizing the sound. "That's the herald," she realized. "Someone's here."

"Might be Aryion and the Wildkids," Rygal said hopefully.

They headed out of the library and down the well-lit corridors to the main entrance, following the distant sound of several voices below. Allie strained her ears, trying to make out the words, but they were still too far away. She heard the low creaks of the drawbridge, then the clatter of horse hooves in the courtyard. The voices grew louder, filled with urgency.

They ran down the last flight of stairs, stopping as the doors were opened beyond to admit the newcomers within.

Allie's initial feeling was relief. Five Wildkids entered, the rest of the group waiting in the courtyard beyond. Three people had come with them—a stout man and a slender woman, and a small girl with blonde braids holding tightly to Dusty's hand. Allie recognized her as Mel's little sister Misty, and knew the couple standing beside her must be Mel's parents.

Aryion's mission had succeeded. The Smallbuttons were safe in Sia.

The thought had barely crossed her mind when she realized something was terribly wrong.

Dusty was stumbling to keep her footing, her upper arm bandaged with a dirty rag that was spotted with fresh blood. She leaned heavily on Newuel's shoulder, though her younger brother looked about ready to collapse himself. Allie glimpsed the rest of the Wildkids outside, standing by their exhausted horses. Ten warriors. That was all. She looked at the gateway at the far end of the courtyard, waiting for the rest to appear. But the cobble road was still.

"Are you all right? What's happened?" Rygal asked immediately, pushing past the guards to reach Dusty.

Dusty coughed, gasping for breath. She was shaking—either from exhaustion, pain, or some deeper fear. "Dal-kerri," she breathed.

"Where is Mel?" the woman asked, stepping forward. Her face was blotchy from tears. "Please—where is Mel?"

"He's safe," Allie reassured her. "He's asleep in the hospital wing."

Mrs. Smallbutton gave a sob of relief and buried her face in her hands. Her husband wrapped his arms around her, looking at Allie with teary eyes. "Thank you," he said hoarsely. "Thank you."

"I need to speak to the king," Dusty said. "Can you take them to Mel—they've been very worried for him."

Darion offered to take them up to the hospital wing. Rygal tried to have Dusty to go with them, but she refused adamantly. "No. The king must hear my report. We have to act quickly—I don't even know what can be done now—"

In the same way Allie had not immediately noticed the Wildkids'
ragged state, she had overlooked something else about their
reappearance. Something far worse. "Dusty—where's Aryion?"

Jan appeared at the top of the stairs; seeing the Wildkids, he
welcomed them and ushered them down the hall into the council
room. "Sit down, and catch your breath. Please fetch Dandio quickly,
and bring them some water," he added to a servant, who promptly
headed down the hall to obey.

Dusty remained standing and launched into her report with a
tremulous voice, refusing to wait any longer. "My king. Good. I'm
so glad you're safe. The Aces have a second Patch, opened some ten
miles north of the Appledale township. We were caught by Dal-kerri
on our way back to the coast—Dal-kerri and two Aces. Most of my
squadron is dead or injured. The Hummingbird—"

"Dusty," Jan said, raising his hands to slow her. "You are safe here.
Slow down, and try to breathe."

Dusty exhaled shakily, but did not take the cup he offered. "Jan—
Appledale—they've attacked. The force that attacked us were headed
south. I don't think they knew of our mission; they ran into us by
chance."

"Have they taken the township?" Jan asked, his face serious.

"No—that didn't seem to be their mission either," Dusty stammered.
"There were two Aces, and at least a hundred Dal-kerri hounds.
They just appeared out of the woods—Newuel almost ran into the
void during the retreat," she added, looking at her brother. "We had

no warning, no sign—we didn't even scent them until they were on top of us. They were headed to Appledale. We were outnumbered—I didn't want to stand by while the township was attacked, but we had the Smallbuttons with us, and Aryion… Aryion didn't want to put them in danger…"

Allie saw Jan's eyes glance over to the Wildkids near the door, then turn back to others in the council room, as though he had just realized he'd missed something. "Dusty… where is Aryion?" he asked at last, his voice very quiet.

"Gone," Dusty whispered hoarsely. "He's gone, with at least half my squadron."

The word punched Allie in the chest. Gone. Grief stabbed her heart like a blade. He was gone.

Jan closed his eyes. Allie pressed a hand to her chest, taking deep breaths to steady herself. She didn't expect to feel the grief this deeply. She had hardly known him, not like the others. Yet remembering the ranger, his quiet leadership, their companionship during the brutal journey to Mata City, the way he'd advised and guided her, the way he'd trusted her to navigate the void and free Mel, even when the others had doubted her… she hadn't realized how much she had come to admire and trust him.

And now… now he was dead.

"Dead?" came Dandio's voice. He stood in the doorway, listening silently to the report.

"I don't know." Dusty ran a trembling hand through her hair. "He went back to Appledale, with a group of my warriors. He ordered us to run for Cattrick Fief. The Dal-kerri pursued us, but the Aces went south to Appledale. We fought off the hounds with fire, like we did in the Magno Forest," she added, nodding to Allie. "I turned back as soon as we finished off the hounds, and rode back to Appledale."

She closed her eyes. Allie knew what was coming, and did not want to hear it. "The Aces didn't claim the township," Dusty said finally. "That's… that's something to be grateful for. One of the civilians informed me that the Aces had threatened to return and kill every civilian there, if Appledale again offered shelter to the New Blood or his kin. I don't think the man knew what New Blood meant, but he understood they were talking about Mel."

"And your warriors?" Rygal asked.

Dusty's gaze was distant. "Dead. All of them. Every warrior that went back to try to stop the attack—the Aces killed most of them with their ice, and then the Dal-kerri ripped them apart. I couldn't even identify most of the bodies." She stopped, her eyes hollow with horror.

"But you did not find Aryion," Jan said slowly.

"There were fourteen bodies," Dusty replied quietly. "Fourteen went back, and I found all of them. Even if I couldn't identify them, they were the only ones with weapons. There is a chance one of them was a civilian, but…"

Wordlessly, she laid a longsword on the table. The blade was streaked with Dal-kerri blood, but Allie recognized it without a doubt as Aryion's sword.

"And the void?" Dandio asked.

"Still there. I rode past it on my way out. I rejoined my group just north of Carna—I did manage to convince Carna's town guard to go south and help Appledale, but I think most of them blamed us for the attack. They were suspicious to see Wildkids at all." She shook her head bitterly. "We rode hard through the night and made it to the coast, then sailed here."

Rygal studied Aryion's sword, his expression hollow with horror. "And… you saw no other sign of…?"

Dusty glanced up at him. "Mel's father believes Aryion survived somehow," she said at last. "But if he's alive, then he's in the hands of the Ace-Lord."

A long silence. Allie was not sure which option was more likely. The Aces had very little reason to keep Aryion alive as a prisoner, not unless they wanted to ransom him for Mel. But she could not accept the alternative. Aryion could not be dead, not after everything he'd fought through. And yet she could find so little hope in Dusty's report.

Jan finally spoke, his voice heavy. "Thank you," he told Dusty. "Your mission was not unsuccessful. Had you been a minute later, Mel's family would likely be dead too."

Dusty nodded, her eyes dull with exhaustion and grief.

"What should we do?" Allie asked, suddenly feeling very small.

Dandio glanced at Jan. "I… I can prepare a reconnaissance team to Appledale to aid the townsfolk," he offered. "Unless you think we should not…"

"No, I doubt our involvement will anger the Aces against Appledale any further," Jan said. "They have made their point clear. We must help the civilians."

"I need to talk to Mel," Dusty said quietly. "I don't want… his parents shouldn't have to be the ones to tell him."

No one argued with her, or bothered to tell her Mel was unconscious. Allie led her up to the hospital wing. She passed Darion on the way, and could tell from his grim expression that the Smallbuttons had told him of the events of the mission. "Do… should we…" he began hesitantly.

"There will be a relief force sent to Appledale soon," Allie answered. "We… we might be able to help with that."

Darion nodded slowly. "And… Aryion?"

Allie shook her head, unable to come up with any words. Nothing could express her worried thoughts, nor give a definite answer about the ranger's fate. "We don't know," she said softly, looking at the floor. "I just don't know."

Darion took her hand lightly for a moment. He seemed to want to say more, as if he were seeking for the right words, but instead he let go and headed down the stairs.

A nurse allowed Dusty and Allie to see Mel only on the condition that Dusty would have her injuries treated afterward.

"He is still asleep," the nurse added. "He is showing signs of improvement, but we do not know when he will wake."

Allie nodded, secretly glad to hear this. Let Mel sleep. Let the painful truth be put off for as long as possible.

The Smallbuttons were inside. Mel's mother sat in the chair beside the bed, holding her son's hand, and his father stood on the other side. Misty sat at the foot of the bed, her thin young face drawn with concern. "What's going to happen to us now?" she asked fearfully, looking between Dusty and Allie.

Dusty gave her a small smile. "Nothing for now, Misty. Mel's getting better. You're safe in Caer Sia."

Misty nodded, but Allie could tell she was still afraid.

"You saved him?" Mrs. Smallbutton asked softly, looking at Allie. "It was you who rescued him from the Aces?"

Allie nodded, wishing she could fully appreciate their thanks. She was glad to have been able to save Mel and Jan, of course. But it only reminded her of what bound her, of the truth of the curse she bore. Of what the Ace-Lord had done.

"We were so worried," Mr. Smallbutton said, his voice trembling slightly. "Aryion had told us…" He trailed off abruptly.

"Maybe he made it," Misty said, looking with wide eyes at her father. "Maybe he's alive."

"Let's hope for that," Dusty agreed with a faint smile. "I'll be back in a moment. Let me know when he awakes."

She and Allie had both turned to leave when Mel coughed and stirred. Mrs. Smallbutton drew her hands back, looking down at the pale face, and Misty moved hopefully to her brother's side.

Mel's eyes opened, bloodshot and dazed. He rubbed them, his face confused. "Mom?" His voice was weak and rasping, but he had spoken. Relief shot through Allie. Mel was awake, conscious and aware of his surroundings. He was back.

"I'm here," Mrs. Smallbutton said, while Mel's father squeezed his hand. "We're all here. You're safe."

Mel blinked in the bright light; Allie could see him slowly registering his surroundings. He clearly recognized he was in Caer Sia's hospital wing—he'd awoken here after his last confrontation with the Ace-Lord.

She could almost see him remembering that moment, as he looked between each of his family members, around the room, and out the door to the hall, as though expecting his companions to walk into the room like they'd done before. Waking turned to confusion as he looked around again, then he turned sharply to Dusty, fully registering her weary face and bleeding injuries.

"Aryion?" he asked, voice stronger. "Where's…"

He did not finish. Dusty had only hesitated for a moment, but that was enough for the fear and the reality of the truth to sink its teeth into him.

"Mel… I'm sorry," Dusty said, her voice catching. "He's gone."

Allie could practically see the weight of the news falling upon Mel's shoulders, crushing him. His face crumbled in shock and disbelief. "No!" he choked. "No—he made it out—I saw he was still on the bridge—"

"I'm sorry," Dusty said again, shaking her head miserably. "I'm sorry, Mel. The Aces might—"

She got no further. Mel covered his face with his hands as sobs racked his ragged frame. Allie stepped forward, knowing she could say nothing to ease the pain. Knowing there was no reassurance she could give.

She heard Mel's parents murmuring words of hope as they held their son. Stubborn hope, that was all they had now. She wished she could say something to help him, to suggest that his mentor might yet live, that the war could be won, that everything would be all right.

But in the end, the only voice that filled the room was Mel's wordless cries of grief. And there were no words to stop it. No words that would make it right.

42

§ § § § § § § § § §

An Oath and a Sign

Mel did not know how long he sat there.

Once the questions and uncertain answers lapsed into silence, his parents left the room, promising to return in the morning. He felt Misty's little hand pat his shoulder before she left too. He heard the soft sounds of movement throughout the hospital wing as night fell.

And still he sat on the bed, knees drawn to his chest, tears dried on his face, as night came at last. He knew he should feel tired, but the long unconsciousness seemed to have given him enough sleep for a long time.

Once he managed to form questions past the tears, he'd learned that days had passed. Nearly two weeks since he'd fallen from the bridge. It had felt longer being a prisoner of the Ace-Lord, and there was no way to know how much time had passed. He remembered nothing of that time, just scattered, shadowy memories of fear and pain. His mind seemed to have blocked most of them out. Or maybe the Aces had wiped them from memory.

They had regained the Blue Stone, Allie had reassured him. It was stored safely in the throne room—not that he cared much about that now. Isilas, it seemed, had been corrupted and removed from

Drisilas' hilt. The curse rested not on Jan, but on Allie. The cold manner with which she spoke of the Life-Blood Spell that bound her to the Ace-Lord concerned Mel, but he seemed to be able to only process one terrible thing at a time.

How long he sat there, while dark thoughts ran through his mind, he had no idea. The moon rose in a cloudy sky out the window. At last, knowing sleep would not come, he got up and walked stiffly from the room. His muscles ached from long inactivity. A few nurses monitered the patients, but he avoided them easily, making his way down the stairs and into a corridor.

He had no idea where he was going. He'd grown so used to following Aryion's lead, Aryion's orders, Aryion's voice wherever it called him.

And now Aryion was gone.

Captured, perhaps. Dusty had admitted it was a possibility, though unlikely. Perhaps the Ace-Lord had kept Aryion alive for ransom, forcing Mel to surrender and use the Blue Stone to unlock the Dark Realm. The Ace-Lord had learned he could not torture Mel into compliance. His weakness lay in his loyalty to others.

Without thinking about where he was going, he found himself in the moonlit throne room. The Blue Stone sat on a small table next to Isilas, which shone as hollow as his heart felt. He placed a hand over the blue orb, feeling the familiar smooth sides, the faint warmth from its core. Isilas felt cold in comparison.

Next to the table with the Star-Stones were two packs, which he recognized immediately as his own and Aryion's. His mentor's battered sword lay beside them. The Wildkids must have brought them here. How often he'd hauled those packs around, checking supplies, refilling water flasks, sharpening tools. He lifted them both and held them close, and stabbing pain radiated through his heart.

In a flash, he knew what to do.

"I'm coming," he whispered against the leather pack, challenging the shadows in the room. "I'm going to go—go find him—and free him—and not look back."

He set the Stone on the table, turning away. Golden light lit the room behind him as he did, and he spun around, stumbling back against the table.

"I am glad to see you have recovered, New Blood," Cahadras said, her quiet voice holding a rare note of gentleness. "Why have you come here?"

Mel dropped the bag. "I—I have to leave," he said. "I'm sorry. I can't keep carrying the Stone. I have to help him."

Cahadras did not ask who he meant. She glanced at the Stone on the table, then back at Mel. "Tell me, child, did you not choose to guard the Stone? To protect it with your life?"

"I did. I do," Mel stammared, shaking his head. "But—Aryion's out there—he might be dead, and if he's not, he's in the hands of the Aces—"

His voice gave out, and he swallowed hard to keep back the tears. He had no plan. He could hear the futility, the hopelessness in his own voice. Even if Aryion was, by some miracle, alive, there was no chance that Mel could help him, not alone.

"I promised to the join the Shards, and I did," he said. "I've played the part of the New Blood. My role in the Prophecy is over."

Cahadras looked at him carefully, shaking her head very slowly. "As I told you in Kamon, child," she said, "the High Light is writing your part, and this is not the end of it. Nor is it the end of the story for others for whom you now fear."

Mel looked up, a glimmer of hope entering his heart. Cahadras continued. "As for the Blue Stone and your task to guard it, the choice must be yours, as it has been from the start. Should you lay that task down, I cannot stop you. But a great many others may suffer should you do so. The burden is heavy. The Lord of Death will seek to break your resolve if you continue. But know, also, that should you succeed, you will undoubtedly save the ones you love."

Mel looked at the Blue Stone, sensing the choice Cahadras lay before him. The cost of carrying the Stone. The risk of casting it aside and pursuing his own goals.

As though sensing his thoughts, Cahadras spoke quietly. "Should you choose to continue guarding the Stone, you must promise to protect it. As the last Wielder, your choices and survival are imperative for the success of the mortals. You must lay aside your personal desires and be willing to lay your life down."

Mel stared into the blue light reflecting from the silver table. Light that terrified the dark. Light that the Ace-Lord could not overcome. Light that had once brought breath back to Aryion's lungs.

Slowly, he took the Stone in his hand, feeling a new resolve fill his broken heart. "I'll protect it. I promise."

"This is no simple promise," Cahadras warned. "The Star Council trusts you with this important task, as the High Light wills it. But you have risked the Stone before. The time has long passed for such recklessness."

Mel closed his hand around the Stone and let out a breath. "I know. Then… I can offer a better promise."

Aryion's sword lay next to the packs, the blade now cleansed of Dal-kerri blood. Mel unsheathed the blade, watching the blue and golden light reflecting off opposite sides. He took a deep breath. The words filled his head, as though Aryion were whispering them to him.

"*Warrior here this Oath I swear. May no dark night or mortal fear. May nothing cause this Oath to break. This vow I swear.*" He paused, nicking the palm of his hand with his mentor's blade, and watched his blood join the blue light reflecting off the steel as he finished the vow. "*This Oath I make.*"

Blood ran down his hand, sealing the promise. The words of the Blood Oath faded into the shadows of Caer Sia.

He glanced up at Cahadras and thought he saw something like approval in her proud features. The Star Queen only nodded. "You redeem the Blood Oath. So let this redeem the hour. Be wise, New Blood. Be strong in your resolve, and know that the High Light yet guides you."

Fire played across her brow in a crown of flames, before she vanished in a streak of gold against the moonlit sky.

Mel closed his bloodstained hand over the Stone. A few tears had sprung to his eyes as he'd spoken the words.

The Oath bound him. He would no longer join the armies of Sia, battling against the Ace-Lord's warriors. No, his would be a quieter war, the war of the New Blood. He would abandon his personal hopes and desires in favor of protecting the Stone. He would embrace this new role set before him. This he'd promised, so that the Stone would remain secure.

"Wise choice, child," came Iriam's deep voice behind him. The Neutral stepped forward, placing a gentle hand on Mel's shoulder. "Your mentor would approve of your decision."

Mel nodded, but did not speak, only looked out at the moonlight. He had no idea what would happen next. No idea what the future held. But he knew, at least, that his next steps were guided by the Light.

. . . . . .

Despite his fatigue, Mel insisted on joining the meeting the following morning. So much had happened since he'd been gone, and now he felt an urgent need to help with the planning and learn what their next strategy would be.

It was a quiet group that met in the council room. Jan sat at the head of the table, his face grim. He gave Mel a slight smile as Mel sat with Allie and Rygal. Though tired, they both looked glad to see him up and improving. Darion was here too, seated at Allie's other side, as were Dusty and Joesp. Dandio sat with Glentree, Admiral Dessian, and two other generals. Iriam stood behind Ĵan.

Ĵan spoke once everyone was seated. "We cannot discuss the details of our plans today," he said. "There are many items to discuss, many strategies to be made. However, I can at least share our immediate course of action, and what I ask of each of you."

He turned to Dandio, who laid a map of Coonsia on the table. "The Elven warriors of Elimar have joined the Red Dawn, which means we can better protect the northern border. I intend to send a group to Appledale to aid the civilians as well," he added with a glance at Mel. "The Patch there must be found and secured. We must not allow the Aces to send their forces that way again, for the safety of Appledale."

Ĵan nodded. "We have also received word from our reconnaissance teams in the south. We know the Ace-Lord's position is in Ar-Salem, and which species and tribes of the area have allied with him at his fortress there. It seems the Aces have left the Magno Forest for now."

"Are the rebel Direns joined with the Ace-Lord?" Allie asked.

"Not as far as Lammar can tell," Rygal told her. "They're fighting against both sides, despite their small numbers. The Brownae tribes are holding them back, but they need our help." He looked at Dandio. "I think Lammar made you aware of the Guardians' mission back to Gayrile?"

Dandio nodded. "Yes, his message arrived yesterday. The Red

Dawn will aid the Guardians, that much I can promise, but we need better information first. If we aren't careful, we might walk right into the midst of both rebels and Aces."

"Gayrile will be protected," Jan said. "Our actions, however, must be cautious. Lammar requested that you join him, Rygal, and aid his efforts to spy out the rebels' position in the Wandering Wood."

Rygal nodded, looking eager to return to his homeland.

"As for the Wildkids," Jan said, glancing at Dusty, "I would like to know your intentions."

Dusty looked up. "The warriors I have lost are a testament to the Ace-Lord's strength. I don't know if it will be enough to convince my father to send more warriors here, but he cannot overlook the threat. My forces will leave to Kasabren, and, I hope, return with the strength of the Clans."

"The journey over land will take you the better part of the year," Rygal said slowly.

"We have no way around that," Dusty said wearily. "Our boats aren't made to weather the sea. You'll just have to hold out until we come back."

"It is a long journey either way," Dandio agreed, "but I think we can help shorten it." He turned to Admiral Dessian. "You know the southern waters better than anyone else in Sia. I assign you to this mission. By sea, the *Blue Moon* can transport the Wildkids in a more timely manner."

"Of course, sir," Dessian said with a nod. His eyes were alight with the prospect of the journey.

Dusty looked grateful. "Thank you. We'll be back as soon as the Clans are rallied."

"We will look forward to your return," Ĵan told her. He paused before continuing. "Now… as for Aryion. If he is captured, it is likely he is in Ar-Salem, but we have no sure way of knowing if he survived. Not only that," he said, looking at Mel, "the Blue Stone must be protected. I do not wish to command you to stay here, but that may be the wisest choice. I do not think Aryion would have you throw your life away recklessly."

Mel felt all eyes turn to him. Just as he had last night, he sensed the choices laid before him. Yet the fresh wound on his palm reminded him of what choice had been made.

"I'm not giving up hope that Aryion's alive," he said finally. "But… I've also made a promise. One that I can't go back on."

He laid the Stone on the table before him and turned his palm up for them to see. The blue light shone on the clean cut on his hand; he saw the surprise on everyone's faces.

"A Blood Oath?" Rygal said softly, shocked. "Mel…"

Mel took a deep breath. "A Blood Oath, to protect the Stone. Cahadras spoke to me last night—she said the same thing you did," he said, nodding to Ĵan. "And she said that my role in the Prophecy isn't over—that none of our stories are finished. I don't know what it means yet, but I do know this—this fight's only just begun. We need to act as the High Light guides, not just by what we want."

He glanced away, a little surprised by his own speech. But Iriam nodded slightly in approval.

"Your choice, and your sacrifice, is commendable," the Neutral told him. "Know that it is not overlooked. Other allies will come, allies long forgotten. The time has come to seek the Druids."

Mel glanced at him, wondering what this could mean.

"Our spies and informants will do all they can to gather news," Jan said. "The rest of you, I urge you to seek peace in the Prophecy."

There was a pause. Mel could sense the fear, the grief, the uncertainty in every mind present. Yet hope, too. Hope, and a fierce determination.

The fight would continue. The only course of action was to go on, into the darkness, into the icy uncertainty, pressing toward the Light at the other side.

Jan dismissed the council. Mel saw Dusty and Joesp talking with Admiral Dessian and the generals, likely planning their mission to Kasabren. He heard Rygal and Dandio discussing a strategy for Gayrile and the battle that awaited there.

Only he and Allie remained sitting in the council room as the others left. The New Blood and the Mortal. One bound by oath, the other by curse.

What would come of the bonds that clutched them? Where would it all end?

Those questions were not his to answer.

"Do you think he's still alive?" he asked her quietly.

Allie thought for a moment; he could see the uncertainty on her face. "I'm not sure," she said finally. "We've seen what the Aces are capable of. But… I think if they've taken him, they'll try to use him to get to you. To make you give up, or use the Stone for them." She let out a breath.

Mel had been thinking the very same thing, and worried again if he'd done the right thing. What good was it to fight for the world, if the person he was fighting for was lost?

And yet…

There had been hope in Cahadras' words last night. Hope that reassured him that he'd made the right choice. Hope that told him he was acting as he was meant to. Hope that the New Blood still had a role to play in this wide world.

"I'm going to help him," he told Allie. "Even if I can't go myself, I'm going to do everything I can to get him out. I promise."

"You could talk to Admiral Dessian before he leaves," Allie suggested. "I know we have some ships specifically for rescue missions—small frigates that can move very fast in and out of places. If Aryion's in Ar-Salem, maybe he could be rescued from the Strait."

A small frigate.

The spark of an idea entered Mel's mind at her suggestion, and for the first time in several painful days, he felt a small smile cross his face. "Yeah. I like that idea."

He reached into the pack at his feet and dug in the top pocket.

"The only challenge would be finding men to carry out that mission," Allie said, her brow furrowed in thought. She looked a lot like Dandio when she was thinking hard, Mel thought. "Perhaps you could ask Lammar, once's he's back."

Mel found what he was looking for, drew it out. The Blue Stone's light glinted off the small red pin in his hand as he held it up. The red bear insignia of the Dricaster Brethren snarled at him from its carved place.

Words, lighthearted words spoken months and months ago on the shores of Esile, entered his thoughts anew.

"If ever you have need of me, show that pin to any pirate in the north. They'll find me."

An armored warship wouldn't be able to attempt a rescue mission. A small frigate—like the *Burman Marie*—just might.

Mel closed his fingers over the pin, felt it press against the cut on his palm, and looked at Allie. "Thanks, but that's all right. I think I'll figure something out."

Epilogue

"Forgive me, my lord," the Deputy whispered, his voice edged in fear as he knelt before his master.

The Ace-Lord did not look at him, only placed a hand on the elegant arched doorway in the lower level of Ar-Salem, staring into the swirling shadows. A doorway to wherever he chose. A gateway from one place to another.

How very well the mortals had played the parts he had written for them. How well they had acted. The matter of the Stars' involvement was a concerning one, of course. Should another instance of that nature occur, his plan would need adjusting. But the Stars could not interfere. Their Prophecy demanded it.

But it troubled the Deputy all the same.

The Ace-Lord turned to face him, the shadows sweeping about him, the faint light of evening beyond catching a glint of his silver armor. One day, he would no longer need illusions to disguise his ruined frame. One day, the Dark Realm would engulf them all, and the mortals would bow in servitude, as some already did. One day all illusions would become his deathly reality.

"Stand," he ordered in a soft voice.

The Deputy straightened. The Ace-Lord saw the fear in his eyes. Such a satisfying thing, fear. Such a useful tool. How easy it was to create fear, even when the hearts of mortals were so stubbornly turned against him.

"Forgive my actions," the Deputy said, clearly fighting to keep his voice calm. "I thought to test the limits of the Prophecy. I thought the Bruin might be the final stroke to bring about your mighty empire."

"A flattering thought, but not a logical one, my Deputy," the Ace-Lord informed him. "You know this conquest is not one that will be won by brute strength or skills of war. This is a game, Deputy. A methodical, intricate, glorious game. It is a game that will endure as long as the words of the Prophecy are in play. It is one that the mortals must play their parts in, as foretold. But know also—it is a game that I will win."

The Deputy looked at him with interest. The Ace-Lord continued. "The Life-Blood spell ensures the heart of the Liznee child. She is my vessel, my beautiful pawn. Yet she must learn her role. Redeyes will make certain she plays her part well, and her power will grow with my own."

"And if she does not?" the Deputy ventured hesitantly.

The Ace-Lord laid both hands on the sides of the silver archway. White ice ran along the structure, slipping between the fine cracks, then with chilling strength the ice snapped it into pieces as though it were made of clay. The archway shattered. The shadows of the void swept into the castle in a mighty rush, clouding the sky like smoke.

"So shall I break any that resist," the Ace-Lord answered. "Once their purpose has been completed, they will be destroyed, as I have destroyed Castle Droco."

The Deputy stared at the broken archway. The door was closed. The only doorway remaining was the Ace-Lord's, in the high tower of this castle wraught from darkness. So, too, would the only choice for the mortals lie in his master's plan. He nodded, clearly impressed. "What task do you require of me now, my lord?" he asked.

The Ace-Lord glanced back. "The matter of Castle Droco is concluded, Deputy. Now, the task before you concerns the New Blood... and the prisoner we have recently acquired."

The Deputy smiled. "What information do you wish from him?"

"No information," the Ace-Lord answered. "A far greater purpose awaits this mortal, a purpose that will bring the New Blood into my hands forever. He too is my pawn now. He must serve."

The Deputy inclined his head in a bow. An eager light shone in his wicked eyes. "It will be as you say, my lord. He will comply, or he will be shattered."

With a bow, he left the black marble hall.

The Ace-Lord stood beside the closed doorway, watching the red sun sink through the stained glass window, and whispered the words of the Prophecy to himself, though they seemed to burn his lips.

When willing warrior be gone at dawn,
Ace-Lord, mortal, together one,
When the Shadow has arisen.

"There lies their doom," he said aloud, his quiet voice whispering over the stones of the mighty fortress. "No mortal will ever willingly choose the fate the words speak of."

And no words argued otherwise, no thoughts proved him wrong, and no voice spoke as he stood before the broken archway and the shadows of night fell upon the Flats.

The Aces will return…

Glossary/Pronunciation Guide

Aces....................race of Netrocrians who grow stronger through fear

Ajaha Ki (ah-ZHA-ha KEE).....................Dandio's wife; a skilled courier and politician

Alfona (al-FO-nah)...............tribe of native Cantrians in the Magno Forest

Arrex (AIR-rex)............................. Hyenin general in the Red Dawn

Aryion Paya (AR-ree-on PY-ah)...........................ranger known as the Hummingbird

Asescia Ki (ah-SESS-see-ah KEE) ....the daughter of Dandio and Ajaha, hieress to the crown of Caer Sia. Also known as Allie.

Caer Droco (care DROH-koh)...........................ancient kingdom of Kahlifis

Caer Sia (care SEE-uh).......................................the capital of Coonsia

Cahadras (cah-HAD-drass) .... queen of the Stars

Cantrians (CAN-tree-ins).......................most common type of Essense-filled being; includes humans and elves

Coonsia (COON-see-uh) ....country on the Mainland of Orlell

Daffodalion (DAFF-oh-DAHL-lee-in) ....Coonsia's neighbor, the largest country on the Mainland

Dal-kerri (dahl-KARE-ee)........................... wolf-like beasts in the Ace-army

Dandio Ki (dan-DYE-oh KEE) ....commander of Caer Sian army. Brother of the king.

Darion (DARE-ee-in)........................newly made young ranger of Wiverrun

Dessian (DESS-ee-in)................................. Liznee admiral of the Red Dawn

Dusty..fiery and skilled Wildkid warrior

Fargrin (FAR-grin)................................. enchanted captain in the Ace-army

Fyrocrians (FY-roh-CREE-ins)......Essence-filled individual whose power manifests as fire and light

Glentree...giant, loyal warrior; Dandio's deputy

Graysil (GRAY-sill)...Dusty's youngest sister, gray fur

Iriam (EER-ree-ahm)............................. Neutral, advisor to the High King

Jan Ki (ZHAN KEE)................................... High King of the Liznees

Joesp (JO-esp)......................... Wildkid warrior, Dusty's brother. Black fur

Kadryion (KAD-ree-on)..chieftain of the Alfona

Kahlifis (KAHL-eh-fis)..........................rebel Netrocrian king; now known as the Ace-Lord

Lammar (la-MARR)..........................Siren, interim leader of the Guardians of Gayrile

Liznee (LIZ-nee) .... a race of silver-skinned Fyrocrians native to Coonsia

Mel Smallbutton... young ranger apprentice

Nellioh (NELL-ee-oh)................Wildkid warrior, Dusty's brother. Red fur

Newuel (NEW-wull)................ Wildkid warrior, Dusty's brother. Gray fur

Netrocrians (net-tro-CREE-ins)..............Essence-filled individual whose power manifests as ice and darkness

Neutral...race of Netrocrians who remained loyal in the Dividing War. Thought all but extinct now

Redeyes.. black tiger-like beast serving the Ace-Lord

Rygal (RYE-gull) ....young warrior and member of the Guardians of Gayrile

Wiverrun (WIV-err-un)................................tiny village in the Magno Forest

Wolfsbane..a captain of the Alfona

Acknowledgements

Thank you to my mom, for your early editing. Thanks for catching the "typos, spelling errors, and heresy," as we fondly put it.

Thanks to the writer's group of Calvary Chapel McMinnville, who revised and edited several of the first chapters of *The Prophecy of Three*, as well as gave feedback for the Prophecy itself. Special thanks to Shelli Owen, whose advice helped particularly in the grammatical realm of the story.

Special thanks to Rebekah Smith, who edited draft #2. It's amazing to see a writing student become a fellow author and editor, and I'm so grateful to you.

All love to my husband Levi. Most of chapter 22 was his idea.

And to the Orlellios... thanks for making it all worth it.